I0573058

Dancing on the Ashes

Dancing on the Ashes

BOOK TWO

HALCIE DAWN

Copyright (C) 2025 Halcie Dawn

No part of this book may be used or reproduced in any form or by any means, electronic or mechanical, including photocopying, recording, or by any information storage and retrieval system without prior written consent of the author except where permitted by law.

The characters and events depicted in this book are fictitious. Any similarity to real persons, living or dead, is coincidental and not intended by the author.

Published by Halcie Dawn
Edited by Elaine York/Allusion Publishing, www.allusionpublishing.com
Cover Design by Stacey Blake/Champagne Book Design, www.champagnebookdesign.com
Formatting by Elaine York/Allusion Publishing, www.allusionpublishing.com

CARE ANNOUNCEMENT

Halcie Dawn's novels contain serious and complex content.

For a full list of Trigger Warnings and/or Content Warnings,
please visit https://www.halciedawn.com/my-books

For Pops and Mimi

*Thank you for raising an amazing son and daughter.
For gifting me with a loving, supportive, funny,
sexy, and honorable husband. He's my miracle.
And for blessing me with the kindest and
most loving sister-in-law.
We miss you, and we love you.*

And

For everyone who needs their numbers

*It's okay to need them. It's okay to say them.
And just so you know... My number is five, too.
Said backward. At a very fast pace.*

Author's Note

Dancing on the Ashes is Book Two in *The Flames Duet*.
This is <u>not</u> a standalone novel and
should not be read until after you devour...
Counting the Flames: The Flames Duet Book One

The Hill Family Universe

The Flames Duet is a standalone duet in a larger, interconnected parent series of duets and novels—*The Hill Family Universe*. While *The Flames Duet* can be enjoyed by itself, the reader will experience a more immersive and pleasurable reading journey if *The Reality Duet* (*Escaping Our Reality* & *Finding Our Reality*) and *The Skeptic's Duet* (*The Skeptic's Playbook* & *The Believer's Game*) are read first. *The Flames Duet* <u>will</u> contain spoilers about your favorite Hill Family characters and events from *The Reality Duet* and *The Skeptic's Duet*.

Halcie Dawn Novels

The Hill Family Universe

The Hill Family Universe is a large, interconnected parent series of duets and novels. While each duet—or singular novel, when applicable—can be enjoyed by itself, the reader will experience a more immersive and pleasurable reading journey if the suggested reading order is followed. Reading the duets out of order <u>will</u> result in spoilers about your favorite Hill Family characters and their defining life events.

Suggested Reading Order
The Reality Duet

Escaping Our Reality: The Reality Duet Book One
Finding Our Reality: The Reality Duet Book Two

The Skeptic's Duet

The Skeptic's Playbook: The Skeptic's Duet Book One
The Believer's Game: The Skeptic's Duet Book Two

The Flames Duet

Counting the Flames: The Flames Duet Book One
Dancing on the Ashes: The Flames Duet Book Two

Hey, Y'all!

Dancing on the Ashes: The Flames Duet Book Two

For my spice lovers...
I told you to hang in there with me. Well, it's about to happen.
And, oh, hot damn...it happens.

For my love-triangle haters...

You should know by now that Ridge is our honorable hero.
Needless to say, there is no Trigger/Content Warning
listed on the website for the MMC cheating.
You should know him better than that. Wink wink.

Chapter 1

Ridge

"I can't believe you're getting married."

My brother's voice echoes through the speakers of my truck. There's an underlying shock to his tone that reminds me of when we were kids.

I can't believe you got the last piece of cake.

I can't believe you won at checkers.

I can't believe you got a date with her.

Chuckling, I make a left turn, heading toward one place I never thought I'd go. "Don't act so surprised, dipshit."

Cullen snorts in the phone, and I can hear the telltale sound of him stacking cases of beer in the cooler at the bar. "You know that's not what I mean. I'm just saying I never thought you'd..." He sheepishly trails off.

But that doesn't matter. I know exactly what he wants to say.

I never thought you'd marry someone like her.

Like Kimber.

And if I'm being completely honest, neither did I. If you'd asked me ten years ago to describe the woman I wanted to spend the rest of my life with, she definitely wouldn't sound anything like Kimber-Shay Willis. But times change. And, so did I.

Especially after everything that happened within just the last two-and-a-half years. Our family has been through Hell. Multiple

1

times over. But we emerged. Stronger, healthier, happier. The monster who hurt Carrie is rotting behind bars. Holt, Merit, and Daire are all happy and healthy. And, more importantly, together. Right where they should be.

Cullen clears his throat, trying to backtrack. "I just mean, I never thought it would happen this quick."

He's right. In the big scheme of things, it did happen quickly. Kimber and I only started dating over the summer. I think everyone was shocked when I proposed on New Year's Eve. Well, everyone except for Kimber. She basically set the stage for it. I wanted it to be a private moment, something between just the two of us. She wanted it to be at the stroke of midnight in front of half the town at the annual New Year's Eve party thrown at her family's flagship luxury car dealership.

So, I know it's quick. I'm not stupid.

But I want a family. I'm not getting any younger, and I want a life with someone.

I wanna grow old with someone.

Make babies with someone.

"I know it seems rushed. But it just feels right, you know?" My reply is strong and firm, giving no indication of the small little tendril of fear that slowly creeps up on me from time to time, making me question whether or not I'm doing the right thing. And with the right person.

It's just nerves. Everybody goes through that. Don't they?

Marriage is a big deal. A really big deal. The biggest.

And not every couple out there can have the unwavering and epic kind of love that I've grown accustomed to seeing. My parents? Holt and Merit? Crutch and Ella?

Well, I do realize that they're the exception and not the norm.

And I'm fine just being in the norm. Give me boring conversations, squabbles about who's doing which chores, and weekly family trips to Costco. I'm cool with that. Because I've already had epic once before. And it didn't end the way I wanted it to. It *couldn't* end the way I wanted it to. Why? Because it wasn't the right thing to do.

Hell, I bet ninety percent of the marriages in the world are filled with perfectly normal, non-epic love.

Fine. By. Me.

Cullen sighs, "As long as you're happy. That's all that matters." Shuffling the phone, he puts me on hold while he signs for a liquor delivery. "Sorry about that. So, what are you up to?"

I work my neck back and forth, stretching my muscles. The movement has my bandage snagging against my shirt. I peek down at my chest, making sure there's no breakthrough blood soaking through the fabric. "Headed to meet the wedding planner."

"That's right." His laugh vibrates in my ears. "Kimber was very proud of the fact that she got an appointment with Wexler Events on such short notice. She wouldn't stop talking about it."

Tell me about it. Wexler Events is one of the top five premiere event planning companies in the Southeast, and Kimber refuses to meet with anyone else. Of course, I'm hoping they'll cut us a little break on the pricing because of Dad and Cullen. I mean, c'mon, people from all over the state fight to get *The Elegant Taste* as a caterer. Dad's cooking has only gotten better with time, basically meaning it's gone from 'awesome' to 'holy shit my mouth is having a foodgasm with every single bite'. And Cullen is the visionary. That kid is a powerhouse, breathing new life and dreams into both the catering business as well as his and Will's bar—*The Last Call*.

In fact, C could have planned the whole wedding for us, but Kimber wants the status that comes with being a client of Wexler Events. Fucking status. Like I'm gonna get some kind of red-carpet treatment if I flash a wedding program with Margo's portrait on it. Nope. Cost of the power bill will still be the same. Wait at the doctor's office will still be the same. Fight during rush hour traffic will still be the same.

"Well, I doubt you're meeting with Margo Wexler herself. Last I heard, she's working an event in Atlanta for a movie studio. Are you meeting with one of the other planners?" he asks.

"Yeah, Amy. Amy Smith."

"Oh, shit. I heard she was back. I haven't seen her yet, though."

"Back? Back from where?"

"She left town a few years ago. Something about taking care of sick family. But she's really good. The best, actually. She only worked for Wexler for about a year and a half before she left. I was kind of surprised to hear that Margo hired her back. You know that woman's bat-shit crazy and holds a grudge like a kid with a stolen pony."

He's right. Margo is crazy. Both he and Dad hate working with her. Fortunately, most of the time, she only works personally on the bigger jobs out of town and uses the planners on her staff for the local events. "You worked with her before? This Amy girl?"

"Yeah, several times. She started as an assistant but was quickly promoted to a planner. She was the lead on several big parties and weddings that we catered. Before she left town, that is."

"Well, let's hope she's ready for Kimber," I deadpan.

Trust me, I know that sounds bad. But Kimber likes things...a certain way. She can be a little hard to take in the beginning. She's a completely different person once you get to know her, though. Well, not *completely*, but she will be once she adjusts to the love that I can give her. And the love that my family can give her. She just didn't have the kind of family life that I did growing up. I mean, shit, she even calls her dad by his first name. She just needs love and support. And as my wife, she'll never receive anything less.

Because I only plan on doing this once.

Marriage means forever in my book. Come hell or high water.

Cullen hums through a long moan. "Mmm, I don't know about that."

"Don't know about what?"

"If Amy can handle Kimber. Amy, well, she...she's different," he answers slowly, concentrating on his words.

"What's that mean?" I pull into a parking spot in front of Wexler Events. Looking around for Kimber's Mercedes, I'm not surprised when I don't see it. She's late for everything.

"I don't know. It's hard to describe." He smacks his lips. "But hey, I haven't seen her in years. She's probably different from how she used to be. Who isn't, right?" He pauses for just a split second before he changes his tone. I can literally hear him smiling through the phone. "But there is one thing I hope hasn't changed…"

I know where this is going. It probably has something to do with big boobs or a tight ass. "Oh, yeah?" I draw out my syllables, playing naïve to my baby brother's teenage-like hormones.

"Her looks. She's fucking hot. Like, steaming hot."

I can't help but laugh. Cullen may sound like a pig, but he's a really good guy. Sweet and charming and goofy and protective. And he may fool a lot of people, but he can't fool me. He can't fool anyone in our family. He wants to settle down just as badly as I do. But just like me, he's spent years searching for something that only existed in the past. Something like what he had with *her*. With Langley. And just like me, one day he'll face reality. He'll come to grips with the cold, hard truth…

Some of us aren't meant to live our destinies.

It's just not in the cards for us. Our love, luck, and tenacity travel at different speeds. Never matching. Never syncing. Never aligning.

And I'll be the good big brother. I'll show him that he can have a happy life. Without destiny.

I'll go first. I'll lead by example. I'll marry Kimber, love her, and be her other half. Her missing piece. I'll give her the family that she's always craved, the normalcy that she doesn't know she wants.

And then, one day, he'll realize he needs to move on too. Because living in the past isn't good for anyone. One day you'll wake up and discover the regrets of your old life—your old self, your old happiness—have gobbled away the hours, days, weeks, and years. And you're left with nothing but crumbs on your plate.

I plan to make the most of the small specks of food left on my platter.

"Well, that's good to know." I lean my head back on the headrest and close my eyes, allowing the mid-January sun to soak into my skin and heat me from the inside out. Playing into his hand, I drawl with a hearty dose of sarcasm. "Too bad for Amy this stud is already taken."

Chapter 2

Ridge

She's here.

How do I know? The screech of her tires and the rev of her engine as she whips her fancy, black sports car from the road and into the parking lot in front of Wexler Events. I slant open an eye and look at the clock on the dashboard.

Seven minutes late.

Kimber is always late. Always.

Work. Meetings. Dates. Family dinners. Funerals.

She's gonna be late. I've grown to accept it. It's part of who she is. There's no point in getting mad about something as silly as that.

I turn off the engine and climb out of my truck, watching in amusement as she shimmies out of the tiny car and scuttles across the asphalt. She wiggles her arm, trying to get her handbag into the crook of her elbow so she can balance her coffee cup and her cell phone in her hands. I'm already crossing the distance between us when a gust of wind blows her blondish hair in her face. It clings to her painted red lips. Looking like a sexier version of Cousin Itt, she stops walking and sputters, trying to spit the offending strands back into their hair-sprayed position.

With a gentle hand, I pull the hair away from her mouth, careful not to spread her lipstick. As soon as she's untangled, I quirk a brow. "Better?"

She gifts me with a brilliant smile. "Much better." Teetering forward on her high-as-shit stilettos, she air-kisses my cheek. Personally, I'd like a little contact, but again, that would mess up her expertly applied lip liner. Her eyes dart behind me, and she frowns. "Babe," she fusses, lacing her perkiness with an exaggerated whine, "why didn't you go in already? I don't want them to think we're late."

I snort on a laugh. "Kimber, we *are* late. And why the hell would I go in without you? I have no clue what all ideas you have going on in your head. The only thing I know about weddings is that I've gotta wear a white shirt and black pants when I'm carrying around a tray of meats and cheeses for Dad."

It's true. I'm more than happy to help Dad and Cullen when needed; but I couldn't tell you the first thing about how someone goes from a ring on the finger to ballrooms with chandeliers. And cascading flower arrangements. And drunk uncle conga lines. So far, no one in our family has had a big wedding. Raylee and her husband Will eloped, doing a wedding/honeymoon combination in Tahiti. Obviously, for cost reasons, it was just the two of them. Ella and Crutch married at the courthouse. Same thing with Holt and Merit. Well, technically, I guess they married at the hospital. But you know what I mean...simple...

Don't get me wrong, I've been to my fair share of fun weddings. And I'm excited for ours. I just hope Kimber doesn't go over the top.

All of a sudden, I'm hit with flashbacks of Kip and Brianna's wedding in Atlanta. All those years ago. The visions whip across my brain like mental lightning strikes, flickering bright and scorching my gray matter.

That girl.

Who did I go to the hotel with?

What was her name? Kendall? Kara? Karen?

Damn. I nearly slept with the vile woman, why can't I remember her name...

Kate.

That's it. Her name was Kate.

Of course, thinking about Kate makes me think about the other girl. The girl who was my *only* girl. At least back then.

And in response, my chest throbs. Every part of me pulses in time to my heartbeat—my muscles, my tendons, my nerve-endings. Drum. Drum. Drum. The pounding rhythm makes my sensitive skin sizzle, pulling me back to the pain of a month ago. The ink. The burn. The scars.

And the lies I told Kimber.

It's mostly healed. There's just one teensy-tiny area with a stubborn scab that keeps spotting blood here and there. And considering Kimber's still pissed about the whole thing, I wear the bandage to keep the pin-dots of blood from seeping through on my shirts. No need to make her angrier.

Give it a couple more days, and I should be good as new.

With my body *full*, my mind will be *empty*.

Clear. Blank. Void.

Free from obsessive thoughts. Free from painful memories. Free from the chains that were keeping me locked away, keeping me shackled in a cage.

I unleashed myself.

I unburdened myself.

I liberated myself.

And now, I can start my life with Kimber with a heart fully committed to no one but her.

Kimber shoves against my stomach with the hand that's fisted around her phone. I can feel the scrape of her engagement ring through the fabric of my old Belly's T-shirt. "Well, you're gonna have to learn a lot more than that, Ridge. This is our wedding. And not only that, it'll be the social event of the year. I've got clients to impress." She bops her head in the air. "Now, go."

I spin on my heels and guide her toward the door with an invisible hand on her back. She doesn't actually like for me to touch the small of her back, so I have to leave an air barrier, if you will.

Like I'm a freakin' mime.

"Do you need me to carry your coffee?" I ask.

"No, I've got it." She gives me the side eye, skimming her eyes up and down my body. "You couldn't have put on something a little nicer?"

I chuckle. It's not like I'm wearing ash-covered turnout gear. I'm in jeans, an old T-shirt, and a jacket. We're going through a little bit of a cold snap right now. Otherwise, I'd be quite content sporting my cargo shorts. After all, Alabama winters have no dress code.

The sun sinks low in the horizon, casting the late afternoon in the early shades of shadows and twilight. I shift my gait, hurrying ahead and putting two steps between us so I can cross the sidewalk and hold open the door. Her body grazes against mine when she walks inside. I use the opportunity to tease her with a playful little wink. "I seem to remember you saying you liked the way my ass looked in jeans. I do believe it was the topic of conversation on our first date."

She flicks her tongue against her teeth, tsking me. "That's back when I thought you had money. Maybe I was just trying to sell a car." Her laugh is low and sultry, and she winks back at me, trying to ease the sting of her semi-truthful jab.

Still...shit like that hurts.

I may not have a bank account like Holt's, but I'm not exactly sitting around fretting about how to put food on the table. Not like my parents when they were young and starting out, freshly married without a pot to pee in.

My displeasure must be evident. Because she leans into me, nuzzles against my neck, and then nibbles on my earlobe, carefully using only her teeth and not her lips. Her hot whisper eases some of the sudden tension knotting in my shoulders. "Babe, you know I'm just kidding. I'm sorry. I know I said I would do better about that." Pulling away, she blinks at me with sincerity in her brown eyes and a frown on her pretty face. "You know the crude jokes and sassy remarks I have to crack at work to keep up with the men." Another blink. Her eyelashes fan across her face. She got them too long this time. I have no idea how she can see through them. "Please forgive me. It was a reflex."

I kiss the top of her head. "It's already forgiven."

"Hello, I'm Celeste. How may I help you?" A petite blonde, with short hair and dangly earrings, greets us.

Kimber turns, immediately shedding her vulnerability and replacing it with her never-wavering confidence. "Yes. Kimber-Shay Willis. I have an appointment." She proudly lifts her chin in the air and cocks a hip in my direction. "We're getting married."

The blonde lifts her eyebrows and tosses her hands in the air in congratulations. "Wonderful! We're so honored that you've chosen Wexler Events for your special day." She shushes herself, acting through her theatrically planned sales pitch, pretending to share her epic trade secrets. "A once-in-a-lifetime event. We'll turn all those dreams into a reality."

I have to bite the inside of my cheek to keep from retorting with my own snide remark, à la Kimber-style.

Yeah. For just the right price those fantasies can morph into existence.

I hope Chip has his pocketbook ready.

My future father-in-law told his only child that she can have whatever she wants. That offer may very well come back to haunt him.

"I'll let Amy know you're here." Celeste makes her way through the showroom and disappears through a side door.

The storefront is more elaborate and overwhelming than I could've anticipated. There's a sitting area up front with plush couches and chairs, and there's another sitting area at the back centered around a gas fireplace. It's occupied by four people. They're each thumbing through portfolio books and chatting excitedly. Various displays of wedding and other event paraphernalia are scattered throughout—tables, bookshelves, and curio cabinets. There's an opulent lighting fixture hanging from the middle of the ceiling. It looks like a gold crown that a king would wear, with all these little twinkle lights woven around it. The free sections of the walls are decorated with massive black-and-white photographs of the fancy events—weddings and parties. Each photograph is outlined in a sleek gold frame. Over in the far corner, there's a man in a three-piece suit standing in front of a table stacked with glass tumblers. He's just staring at them. Like he's waiting on whiskey to rain down from the heavens and fill the liquor glasses with shots of distilled happiness. About halfway down on the left side is a series of doors, including the one Celeste disappeared into. I'm guessing that's where the offices are.

Setting her purse down on the armrest of the fluffy white couch, Kimber dives headfirst into her phone, refusing to miss one email, text, or social media alert. Stuffing my hands in my pockets, I meander around to a tall display cabinet of linen napkins.

Damn. It's gotta be twelve-feet tall.

How can there be this many linen napkin options in the world?

They're hanging from loops with little pull chains on them, decorating the shelf like clown scarves. I grab a blue one and pull it closer to me. When I do, the chain causes the cabinet façade to inch forward.

What the hell?

Holy crap. It's a multi-panel display. You know, like how a store would display movie or music posters, in a flipping contraption. I swing open the first 'door' of the cabinet, and I'm met with a whole new display of...that's right, more linen napkins.

I step closer, furrowing my brow at two off-white swatches of fabric. These colors look identical. But obviously, they're not. Because one is called *Autumn Cotton* and the other is called *Coconut Milk.*

And then...it happens.

My whole fucking life changes.

In. One. Single. Second.

And it's all because I hear *her* voice.

For the majority of my adult life, I've been half-functioning. I've been trudging through my days at only fifty percent capacity. My veins have carried dead blood into my heart. Deoxygenated. Lifeless. Void of the one essential element that my body needs to survive.

And my heart was supposed to replenish what was missing. It's the sole function of the organ.

But it never did.

This whole time my body has been acting under the marionette of my soul. And apparently, my spirit had a death wish. Because it terminated the job. Sabotaged the role.

But then...BAM.

I hear *her*.

And my heart springs into action.

Doing what it's meant to do. Doing what it's failed to do for almost nine-and-a-half years.

It pumps life into me.

Electricity and vitality and bliss shoot through my arteries, bringing air to the parts of my body that have spent close to the past decade rotting a slow and painful death. My organs, my cells, my DNA...have all been suffocating. Without my consent.

And she heals me. She resuscitates me.

Just like she did back then. Just like she did in that supply room.

Her voice burrows into the depths of my very being.

And she saves me.

"Ms. Willis, it's a pleasure to meet you. I'm Amy Smith."

My entire body trembles. Despite my state of dress, I can feel the chill bumps as they break across my arms. My vision pinholes, growing fuzzy around the edges, making me feel drunk and delirious. With unsure footing, I take a step back, edging my body around the open display door.

I say a thousand prayers, begging the universe for it to be true.

And then I say a thousand orisons, begging the universe for it to be anything *but* true.

I close my eyes. And when I open them, there she is.

She's older. And even more gorgeous than I remember. More beautiful than when she comes to me in my dreams, lithe and airy, forcing me to wake with my body drenched in sweat and twisted in the sheets.

She's staring down at a leather portfolio, so her storm-cloud eyes are hidden from view. Her raven hair is pulled back in a low ponytail, with waves cascading past her shoulders. Black, long-sleeve shirt. Black ankle pants. Simple black loafers. The neckline of her shirt is scooped into a circle, giving me a perfect view of the delicate lines of her collarbone. And nestled right underneath is her necklace.

My necklace.

Our necklace.

The black diamonds catch the light, throwing a glittered prism into the air between us.

She flips through the pages of her folder. "Congratulations on your engagement, Ms. Willis. I've been going through the profile you completed for us. I see you're looking at a November wedding, ten months from now." Even with her head bent, I can see the furrow of her brow and the worry line decorating her forehead. She picks up some more pages and thumbs through them. "Please forgive me, but I don't see the name of your fiancé in our paperwork."

I take a step forward. Her nickname falls from my lips, filling me with a torrent of ache and agony, comfort and solace. "Bird."

Chapter 3

Orah

Of course, she'd be late.

Why wouldn't she be.

Why do all the entitled bitches choose the last appointment of the day? I know why...because they know they can show up late and then keep you late, knowing you'll never turn them away, never tell them no.

Because this is a commission business.

And I need the commission.

Never mind the fact that I told Momma I was gonna bake a white chocolate truffle cheesecake tonight. She even went to the fancy person's grocery store to get me some of the melting wafers that melt without scorching...and taste like a chocolate paradise on your tongue.

I know women like Kimber-Shay Willis. I've planned weddings for them. I've planned birthday parties for them. Engagement parties. Anniversary parties. Children's birthday parties. I once even planned a vaginal rejuvenation party.

Well, I guess a more accurate description would be...I planned the celebration to commemorate the fact that a woman received a vaginal rejuvenation after her divorce.

Now, don't get me wrong, I'm not knocking toot toot maintenance. Hell, if I ever get over my debilitating fear of sex and have intercourse more than a handful of times, the day may come when I need to revitalize my own below-the-belt atmosphere.

But does it have to be applauded with a party? With a catered lunch served by shirtless men and cocktails named after the honoree's body parts? If I never hear the words 'Put-Your-Piña-in-Lola's Colada' again, I'll be a happy woman.

Of course, I never share any of these unfiltered feelings with anyone but my family, mainly Tabby, to be precise.

To my co-workers and my clients, to everyone outside my circle of trust, I'm the ultimate professional. Stoic and concentrated. Polished, gracious, and hardworking. And I'm more than happy to plan any event, as per the details of my employment.

And yes, in case you didn't realize, Tab is the official author of the 'toot toot maintenance' terminology. Much to the chagrin of my brother, I might add. Apparently, after gifting me with the turn of phrase, she started calling Boaz her *'mechanic'*. And started requesting frequent toot toot maintenance. So, I don't think anyone was surprised when the daycare teacher reported that Eden was calling all of her classmates *toot toots*. In her cute-as-a-button, blossoming toddler babble.

I guess the real reason things like that—or women like that, women like this Kimber-Shay Willis—chafe my ass is that it reminds me that I was a hair's breadth away from becoming one of them. If things hadn't gone the way they had. If I hadn't forced us to go to the movie theater that night. If instead, we went to eat with Emmett and Laurie and Dylan. And then spent the evening searching for hermit crabs on the shores of the white sandy beaches.

I shuffle the papers on my desk, opening the portfolio once again and skimming the details. It's easy to see that Kimber-Shay is going to be high-maintenance. Even if I weren't able to deduce that from this initial online questionnaire, the warnings Celeste gave me would be enough.

Apparently, Celeste's older sister went to school with the twenty-six-year-old luxury car dealership heiress. At the most expensive private school in the state, which just so happens to be in this town. Celeste's family doesn't come from astronomical sums of money; apparently, her sister was awarded a scholarship to go there. From what Celeste said, a girl—an alumni of North and Camden Academy—went missing several years ago, and her parents used to offer a select number of scholarships in memoriam.

Anyway, according to Celeste, there may not be enough commission in the world to make me happy about working with Kimber-Shay.

I glance up the second I hear footsteps walking down the hallway. As always, my desk is facing the door. I need to be aware of what is coming toward me. At me. For me.

Celeste peeks in. Her silver teardrop earrings swing back and forth against her neck. "Knock. Knock." She wiggles her eyebrows. "Showtime."

I take a deep breath and give her a small smile. "I'll be right out."

I take a quick moment to gather my faculties, to center myself.

I close my eyes and rub my fingers across the rows of small diamonds on my necklace.

One. Two. Three. Four. Five.

And just like always, the skin underneath the band of my smartwatch burns, smoldering with the connections that I've forced myself to imagine never existed in the first place.

Gripping the leather folder in my hands, I make my way out of the office and into the showroom. My eyes immediately land on her. I dart my gaze up and down, doing my best not to openly stare. Although, technically, I could gawk at her all I want; her face is buried in her phone.

Her hair is a mix of light brown and blonde. She's wearing a low-cut, cream-colored blouse. The pale shade highlights the tanned skin of her plump cleavage. She's wearing skintight, red leather pants. And by skintight, I mean I have no idea how she pulled them over her feet, let alone her knees, thighs, and butt. And her five-inch heels perfectly match her shirt. Her purse is perched on the edge of the couch, and I can't help but notice that it matches perfectly with her pants.

Does she do this every single day?

Does she coordinate her outfits in such a meticulous manner?

Is she always so put together? So pristine? So...untainted?

I discreetly wipe my hand against my waist, ridding myself of the nervous sweat that appears when I meet strangers. "Ms. Willis, it's a pleasure to meet you. I'm Amy Smith."

Kimber-Shay glances up and flashes an award-winning smile. "The pleasure is all mine." She eyes my extended hand and lifts her own, showing that she's bogged down by her coffee and her cell phone and unable to accept my offer of a handshake.

She makes me anxious. Nerves flame in my stomach, making me fidgety and self-conscious. There's something in the air, an unease floating through the nooks and crannies of the store. It covers the displays in a hazy fog. It smothers the inventory in a heavy, murky mist—the invitations and floral arrangements and crystal platters. Even the linen napkins. A breathy chuckle falls from my mouth in little spurts.

I open the portfolio and start flipping through the pages, trying to calm my worry. There's no reason for me to be feeling the way I'm feeling. And I can only pray I'm not on the brink of a panic attack. I haven't had one of those in years. The last thing I want is to experience something like that at work. Where no one knows my past, knows the horrors I experienced.

And I definitely don't wanna have one in front of Kimber-Shay Willis, the luxury car princess of the Southeast.

"Congratulations on your engagement, Ms. Willis. I've been going through the profile you completed for us. I see you're looking at a November wedding, ten months from now." I look at the data, hunting for the groom's name for the hundredth time. "Please forgive me, but I don't see the name of your fiancé in our paperwork."

"Bird."

And then...it happens.

My whole fucking life changes.

Time stops.

Everything stops.

My breath. My heart. My life.

My body trembles, instantly responding to the voice that's plagued my dreams and nightmares for almost ten years.

Years of misery *without him.*

Years of gratitude for having *once known him.*

The man who gave me my life. And then stole it from me when he decided to walk away.

I feel dizzy and faint, almost too woozy to even lift my head to discover the truth, to confirm with my eyes what I already feel in my soul.

I close my eyes and slowly raise my chin, inch by inch.

And then I count. I count for my destiny or my demise. Which will the fates give me this time?

Because I've had both.

And I often wonder if I can ever have one without the other.

One. Two. Three. Four. Five.

Chapter 4

Ridge

Ifollow along with her counting, watching in fascinated awe as her pink lips mouth the numbers, murmuring them to no one but herself.

And then, her eyelids pop open.

The folder slides from her fingertips, and before it can even clatter to the floor, she's launching herself at me. I dip down and rush toward her, wanting to make the most of our embrace, not wanting to miss one single second of having her in my arms. She crashes into me with all of her might, all of her force, all of her strength.

Our bodies instinctively fall into a long-abandoned, but never-forgotten position. Her arms fold around my neck, securing me in place by the bend of her elbows. My hands circle her back, with my forearms settling against the low curve of her spine. It's like the arc was made just for me, molded into place, patiently awaiting my return.

I straighten, lengthening my body to its full height and lifting her in the air. Her right leg hitches, circling around my thigh. The dangling tiptoe of her left foot taps against my shin as I gently sway back and forth.

I'm overwhelmed. I'm overcome. I'm overjoyed.

There's too many emotions vying for top position in my brain. The swirling confusion leaves me muddled and baffled. Like a tornado in a bottle, I'm swirling around and around, being pulled under by the centrifuge.

The scent of her coconut hair.

The sound of her heaving sobs.

The touch of her hot breath as it skims across my earlobes.

The taste of her salty tears drenching the air.

But what really gets me is the almost imperceptible way her chin shifts back and forth across the sensitive skin at the crook of my neck, where the muscles of my left shoulder marry with the edge of my collarbone.

If I didn't have this jacket on, would she find *it*? Would she nuzzle her way into the collar of my T-shirt, find the long-healed scar, and gently kiss the now almost-flat wound of our past? The faded blemish spawned by twenty-five stitches and three small half-moon cuts.

Cuts caused by her.

Created by her.

By her fingernails.

During the first, last, and only time we kissed.

My whisper is laced with all the things that should be said. And all the things that *shouldn't* be said. "Zipporah..."

She squeezes me tighter.

And then, a new feeling is added to the wretched storm wrecking my mind.

Guilt.

Wait. Should I be doing this? Why does something so right feel so wrong?

And then, little knives poke against the shell of our cocoon. The world we're secreted into fades. Reality cracks the exterior, and piece by piece our shell falls to the ground and disintegrates.

I open my eyes—which I didn't even realize were closed—and concentrate on the scene slowly coming into focus. Celeste is on my left, frantically bouncing from one foot to the other. Her hands hover in the air as she debates the best way to pull Orah and me apart. "Amy! Amy, what's wrong? What happened?"

The group of people that were gathered around the back-wall fireplace are staring, with two of them standing up to get a better look. Two others have emerged from the side doors, sneaking away from their offices so they can check on the commotion. Even the dude praying for whiskey has an eye cocked in our direction.

And then there's Kimber.

My fiancée.

The woman I'm going to marry.

The only woman I should be hugging in such an intimate way.

Her face is contorted in a grimace. Her cheeks are red with anger. It's pretty clear to see she's been yelling my name, trying to get my attention, and I've been ignoring her.

I blink. Willing myself to fully regain consciousness. So I can do what's right. Do what's expected of me. Do what I need to do.

But before I can make those smart choices, she flings her coffee cup on the ground. The lid pops off, and toffee-colored liquid splatters everywhere. Including the white furniture. She pounces on me, shoving against my right bicep with her hands. Well, really, it's just one hand. Because she refuses to drop the cell phone from her other. Normally, I wouldn't stumble, but I'm caught off guard by the whole situation. My footing falters, and I take a baby-step away from Kimber, before righting myself. I loosen my grip, preparing to separate from Orah. I have to be gentle, though. I don't want her to fall.

And when I'm plumb in the middle of trying to untangle our bodies, Kimber hauls back and slaps me across the temple. The unexpected pressure to my temporal artery sends a bolt of pain flashing through me before it quickly dissolves. The telltale burn of a cut pierces the skin above my ear.

She cut me with her ring.

The engagement ring I slid onto her finger twenty days ago.

The engagement ring I overheard her telling Mamie that she wants to upgrade before the wedding because the diamond isn't big enough.

"What the hell, Ridge!" Her screech dwarfs the rest of the chaos happening throughout the room. "Who is this! Are you fucking this girl! Are you cheating on me!"

Her questions aren't even questions. They're immediate accusations.

Orah lifts her head, accidentally grazing her tear-soaked lips across my cheek in the process. Gasping, she scrambles from my hold. The second I set her on the ground, she stumbles away from me, side-shuffling to put a respectable distance between us.

"Are you sleeping with the wedding planner!" Kimber screams.

Orah's red-rimmed eyes ping from person to person, flitting about in a constant state of bewilderment. She holds her breath, trying to stave her gasps and sniffles.

I'm fucking astonished.

Astonished that she's here. In front of me. Within arm's reach. Back in my life.

But that astonishment rapidly fades, and it's replaced by anger. Plain old fury. Vile and disgusting and soul-crushing.

I. Fucking. Hate. Destiny.

And because I'm terrified of doing the wrong thing, of being the bad person, of being the villain in Orah's path to recovery...

I make the second hardest decision of my life.

I turn away from her and take a step toward Kimber.

"Kimber, please."

She walks backward, jabbing the air with her manicured fingernail. "Don't you dare...you fucking cheater."

I hold up my hands in surrender. "I would never cheat on you. Ever. That's not who I am. I made a commitment to you." I turn my head, nearly coming unglued at Orah's disheveled and honest appearance. Because didn't I once make a commitment to her? To My Brave Girl.

To always come when she called.

To always be there for her.

To heal her.

To save her.

I lied. I took advantage of her, didn't I?

Shame eats away at my insides like acid.

"This is Orah. She's an old friend." I rake my hand down my face and tap my chin, searching for the right description. "One of my dearest friends, actually. We...we haven't seen each other in nearly ten years."

Well, nine years and four months to be exact.

Kimber crinkles her brow. "Your friend?" Her tone hitches in disbelief.

"Yes."

She plants a hand on her hip and snaps her gaze back and forth between the two of us. "Oprah?"

I can't help but growl, low and under my breath. She knows what name I said, she's pronouncing it wrong on purpose, trying to assert her power over the situation. "Orah," I answer, confirming my *friend's* identity.

Celeste interrupts, shaking her head back and forth. "No, no, no. This," she says with a hand flap to Orah's torso, "is Amy. Amy Smith." She looks at Orah and shrugs her shoulders. "Do you know an Orah?"

Orah's eyes widen, and I can feel the desperation as it soaks through her pores, covering her in a sheen of sweat. She doesn't want her co-workers to know her past. She doesn't wanna detail the horrors she went through. She doesn't wanna be treated differently, eyed like a commodity. Framed as the posterchild for tragic events.

I nod to Celeste. "You're right. Orah's just an old nickname. Her name is Amy."

Kimber folds her arms across her chest and frowns at me. "I don't buy it, Ridge. Why didn't you tell me you knew her? I told you we were meeting with *Amy Smith*." She presses her lips together before popping them apart. "You somehow failed to mention this would be a little reunion."

"Why don't we go into the conference room? We can speak in private." Orah slices through the tension, her tender vocals acting as the sharpest knife. She discreetly wipes her face with her fingertips, trying to clean the mess of tears and mascara.

Kimber stomps a heel against the tile, finally conceding when Orah offers a soft smile and steps backward, giving Kimber a wide berth to take the lead. When she barges past, Orah gives her a polite direction. "Last door on the left, Ms. Willis."

I glance at the mess of spilled coffee. "I can—"

"We'll handle it."

I drag a staggered breath through my lungs, forcing an inhale so deep it stings my breastbone. Putting one boot in front of the other, I make way to follow Kimber. Orah's hand reaches out and snags the sleeve of my jacket. My heart lodges in my throat. "Ridge." She pauses before looking up at me. And the storm clouds shifting and churning in the depths of her eyes make me weak in the knees. "You're bleeding."

Tilting my head, I wipe my brow and temple, scowling when I feel miniscule drops of blood dotting a small line. It's probably no bigger than a paper cut, but still...

And then my thumb grazes my cheekbone.

What the hell?

Lifting both hands, I scrub my face with my palms, rearing back in shock when the action sends even more liquid racing down my cheeks. The moisture weaves through the paths of my five o'clock shadow.

What the hell? I've been crying.

I *am* crying.

I clear my throat, "It...it's more than blood."

Her assertion is simple. And probably the most honest thing that's ever been shared between the two of us.

"Isn't it always."

Chapter 5

Orah

I'm a zombie.

I don't even know how I'm functioning.

After calming Celeste's fears that Ridge wasn't some kind of psycho kidnapper, I gathered my discarded folder and papers and fished my ink pen out from underneath a chair. I asked her to clean up the spilled coffee and told her that if the stains didn't come out with our handheld upholstery cleaning machine, that I would order and pay for a professional cleaning.

And I politely requested that the drama of the past few minutes stay within the confines of the store. Meaning, there's no need for her to call Margo. And seeing as how she's the only person I'm semi-close with at work, I asked her to smooth things over with the other planners and employees. Everybody likes Celeste so, fingers crossed, they listen to her and keep Margo out of the mix.

Holding my head high, I walk across the showroom. I'd love nothing more than to take a quick bathroom break. Take a moment to gather my thoughts and fix my appearance. Well, in all honesty, what I'd really like to do is run away.

Run away from this building.

Run away from this town.

Run away from the woman who is obviously set to marry the man I'm still madly in love with.

The man who was my everything.

The man who I thought would wait for me. Who instead told me to heal on my own. Because what we had was wrong. What we had was wicked. What we had was a figment of my imagination, driven only by our traumatic connection.

But he was wrong.

What we had might've been *created* by a traumatic connection, but it wasn't driven by it. What we had was powered by love and lust and friendship. What we had was supposed to last forever.

He didn't turn his back on me when I told him the truth—the truth of that night and the choices I made.

He stayed by me. He held my hand. He walked with me through the consequences of the decisions made by the old Orah, the girl of my past, the teenager I didn't wanna be anymore.

Through it all, he stayed. And he quietly loved me.

I might've been young. But I knew what we had was authentic, genuine, and pure.

And he knew it too. He just refused to acknowledge it. Because his warped sense of integrity and honor were more important than me.

More important than his Brave Girl. His Little Bird.

I should've listened to my own thoughts from back then. I knew being in love with him would cause me nothing but pain. Because I knew he would never be able to admit the truth to himself. To me. To the world.

And sure enough, here it is, nine years and four months after the only meaningful kiss I've ever had, and he's still causing me pain.

I'm still causing me pain.

Because didn't it all start with me? Wasn't I the catalyst igniting the fuse of our catastrophes?

The blinds of the conference room door are slanted open. And through them, I see Kimber-Shay sitting at the oval table, with lines of hatred etched into her face, as she vigorously taps on her cell phone, her fingers flying over the keyboard with the speed of a court reporter. Ridge is behind her, pacing back and forth, talking, and animatedly waving his hands in the air.

I can't believe this is happening.

Where the hell has he been for the past near-decade?

And what the hell is he doing here? In my town? Of all places?

And more importantly, what the hell is he doing marrying a woman like Kimber-Shay Willis?

Ignoring the lingering stares from the party at the back of the store—including Anniah, an event planner who really doesn't like the fact that Margo hired me back—I give a soft knock on the door before opening it and making my presence known. Kimber-Shay glances up from her typing assault, and Ridge freezes. I turn and slowly shut the door behind me, using the stall tactic to my advantage to count my favorite numbers.

When I spin back around, I'm at a loss. What am I supposed to do?

Kimber's already sitting down, and she's on the side of the oval that's facing the door. My choices are to either sit down next to her, which would look a little weird, or sit with my back facing the door.

If I sit with my back facing the door, I won't be able to see anything that may happen. I won't be able to see if someone runs through the showroom, intent on harming those of us trapped in here.

My already erratic and frayed heart starts to pitter-patter even faster, strumming against my ribcage like hummingbird wings. Stress and agitation choke me, making it hard to swallow.

She slaps her phone on the table and wiggles her head in my direction. "Well?" Her snarl is saturated in snarky disapproval.

My eyes lock onto his.

Oh. Holy. Shit.

That hurts.

Tiger Eyes. Eyes that can heal or kill. With one simple glance.

Dark brown and outlined in a light brown-yellow color.

Tiger's Eye—SiO_2 + FeOOH + (Al, Mg, Na).

My knees weaken, and my hand flies to the wall, searching for something to stabilize me, something to hold me up. In tandem, Ridge lurches forward, wrapping his hands around the back of a rolling chair.

I can feel what you feel.

He looks from me to the door and back again. "Kimber, let's move to the other side of the table."

His suggestion takes me by surprise, stealing the oxygen from my exhausted lungs.

"What? Why? I'm already sitting down," she snips.

He skips a hand down his face and taps his chin. One. Two. "It's...uh...it's company policy. Employees need to be able to see the storeroom."

Her face scrunches. "What? Are you serious? How would you know that?"

"There...there's a sign." He stutters on his lie. "Somewhere out front. I saw it."

She pushes her phone and purse across the table. "Ugh! Fine. Whatever." He holds her chair out for her, making it easy for her to move, but she doesn't even acknowledge him. I skirt around the opposite side, like we're playing a game of musical chairs or duck-duck-goose. While she's looking down, I catch his attention and mouth a silent 'thank you'. Once we're all tucked in place, she scoffs her passive-aggressive complaint. "Happy?"

I'm not sure if she's asking Ridge or me. So, I play it safe and stay quiet.

"Now, does someone care to explain to me what's going on," she barks.

He licks his lips, drawing my attention to his almost-clean-shaven face. Gone is his short and tidy beard. In its place is a simple scruff, no more than a day or two's growth. "Amy and I met back when I worked in Florida. Back in White Sky."

Hearing the name 'Amy' roll from his tongue makes me feel feverish and sick. It feels wrong. It feels like we're disrespecting the past. More than we already have.

"Then why didn't you say you knew her?" she asks again.

We can't keep this part hidden. Not from the woman he's supposed to marry, not from his wife. He can't start his marriage with a lie. A lie to protect me. All because I'm still fighting the demons of the girl I was before that night.

"It's fine. Tell her the truth." I sound stronger than I imagined I would.

He pauses, not exactly sure how far I'm willing to go, what truths I'm willing to expose.

I grab my ink pen and hold it between my hands. Spinning it around, in circle after circle, I silently count the rotations as I talk. "He didn't tell you he knew me because he didn't know it was *me.*" I clear my throat. "I wasn't Amy back then. My name was Orah. I changed my name after..." I break off when he shifts in his seat.

"After?" Kimber-Shay prods.

"After we lost touch."

"Ooookayyy. And why did you change your name?"

My stomach flip flops with discomfort and unease. I haven't talked about this in years. When I set foot in Alaska, I introduced myself to everyone I met as 'Amy'. The only person, outside of Boaz, who knew my legal name was Zipporah was Naja, my boss. Well, her and a handful of the guys who used to follow me on social media before the attack. But, Boaz did what big brothers are supposed to do, and he threatened them within an inch of their lives to keep their snide comments and the name Orah to themselves. So, when I legally changed my name to Amy a few months later, no one even knew the difference.

But what makes my insides somersault even more, what tosses my psyche into a wild and turbulent summer storm, is the fact that the name 'Orah' means nothing to her. There's no recognition. No awareness. No *'Aha! So, it's you he was stuck in a room with. It's you he held hands with during a hostage situation while your best friend was bleeding to death on the floor next to you. It's you he comforted, you he put fuzzy slippers on, you he was prepared to die for'.*

There's nothing.

Kimber-Shay Willis is blank. This is a bedtime story she's never been read. Like a scolded child, she's been put to sleep with no fables of boogeymen. Of damsels in distress. And of the princes who save them.

I stop spinning my pen and focus on Ridge. "How much does she know? How much have you told her?" For some reason, I'm unable to stop the bitterness from soaking into my words. Hostility leaks from my tongue and coats the syllables, drenching them in pain and disbelief.

Did *I* mean so little to him that he can't even bring himself to tell her what happened? What we shared? What we went through?

Or...does *she* mean so little to him that he can't even bring himself to tell her what happened? What we shared? What we went through?

And if *she* means so little to him, why the fuck is he marrying her?

He clenches his teeth, and his jaw tics. His fingers splay across the table, and he digs his fingertips into the glazed top, turning his knuckles white. "What do you think I told her?" His barking allegation is filled with indignation, creating a palpable strain between the two of us, reminding me that I'm no longer sitting in front of a young twenty-two-year-old boy, but a near thirty-two-year-old man.

And for a moment, I'm taken aback. I'm actually shocked speechless.

Is he angry with me?

For thinking and asking that question, is he seriously upset with me?

My mind springs to life with a ticker tape of memories—of question games and meals shared over a hospital bed. Of panic attacks and hot baths. Of cupcakes and necklaces. Of hugs and shoulder kisses. Of secrets whispered in the dark, between two beating hearts. Hearts that were just minutes away from stopping, from ceasing to exist, all because of two rotten and evil guys.

And out of all those times, all of those events and defining moments, I don't ever remember My Hero being mad at me.

Not. Ever.

I've seen him mad, yes. Furious and ferocious. Explosive and intense.

But never at me.

I open my mouth and gulp air into my body, hissing at the phantom pain under my right breast.

Kimber-Shay hammers her nails against the table. "Helloooo? Tell me what?"

"I changed my name because I was weary and fearful of the trauma I endured." I swallow. "Ridge and I know each other because I was his patient. And he was my paramedic."

She leans forward, intrigued by my commentary. "You were his patient?"

I fold my right hand around my left wrist and squeeze the black silicone band of my smartwatch into my skin. I let the lie travel through my body, like a frigid sleet on a Deadhorse, Alaskan day, and I allow the cold and frozen falsehood to quench the burn of my skin. "Yes, I was only his patient."

Chapter 6

Ridge

Bull-fucking-shit.

That's two hateful comments in a row.

First, she laces her voice with jaded condemnation, acting like I didn't tell Kimber about everything that happened in that room—and everything that happened *after* that room—because I'm ashamed of her. Because she's some dirty little secret that needs to stay hidden in the shadows, away from the breaking sunrise.

Yes, it's true that I tried to downplay our relationship back then. But that's just the way it had to be. It was the only way to protect us. From the general public. From the reporters. From the lawyers. From the government officials. From the people who wanted to steal my job away. From the onlookers who would have twisted the facts, who would have said that my genuine and legitimate feelings for her were nothing more than the perverted lust of an older man preying on a younger, innocent girl.

It was the only way to protect us from ourselves.

It was the only way to give her the freedom to heal, unencumbered and detached from me. Me...the walking reminder of the night she nearly died.

And when my regret eats me alive, when it consumes me, leaving nothing but shards of bone and chewy sinew in its wake, I remind myself that we had no other choice.

I had no other choice.

Because despite what happened, I still hold firm to the belief that loving her the way I wanted to back then was wrong.

But I didn't keep all of this from Kimber because I'm embarrassed or disgusted by Orah.

Nothing about Orah is dirty. Nothing about her is broken. She was, and apparently still is, the epitome of everything that's perfect and unblemished in this messed-up world.

And yes, a small part of me still wonders if Orah's feelings for me were amplified and skewed, simply because I'm the one who fled into that room. And not someone else. But does the 'how' or 'why' even matter anymore? The result was the same...she wanted me to love her, to wait on her, to be with her.

And now, here she is calling herself nothing more than a patient.

We're older. Wiser. Smarter.

And we both know, that no matter what I told myself, no matter what I told her, Zipporah Smith was never just my patient.

She knows it. I know it.

Damn.

If only things had been different. If only we'd met at the beach and not in a janitor's closet hiding from gunfire and explosions. If only she'd been older and not a high school junior. If only the movie theater attack had never happened...

It could be us planning our wedding right now.

Us planning our lives together.

My hand flies to my mouth, physically stopping the cynical chuckle from bursting out. Who the hell am I kidding?

Planning our wedding *right now*?

More like getting ready to celebrate our eighth wedding anniversary *right now.*

Because if we'd met just one year later, on the sandy beaches of White Sky, during her Senior Spring Break trip, I would've been begging John for his daughter's hand in marriage the night of her high school graduation. We'd be happily married. With me picking up the kids from school so we could visit Little Bird at her bakery shop. We'd ply the children with cookies and brownies and sneak off to the back where I'd capture her in my arms and lick the sugar from her body. And I'd never stop telling her how much I loved her.

But that's not *my* life.

That's not *her* life.

That's not *our* life.

I'm getting married to Kimber. I love Kimber. I'm going to have a life and family with Kimber. In my mind, the marriage commitment started the second I pulled the ring box from my pocket.

I force myself to repeat the mantra again.

You know, just for good measure.

I. Love. Kimber.

But the possessiveness in my soul—the greed for Orah that shouldn't be there—won't allow me to stay quiet. "She was more than just my patient."

My fiancée turns to me, her face etched with question and distrust. "You dated her? The two of you were a couple?"

I slide my hand over Kimber's, doing my best to give her my undivided attention. "No, we didn't date. But she was my best friend. For several months." I can feel Orah's stare. It's tactile and tangible, piercing my jugular like a knife. I may not tell Kimber everything that happened between me and Orah, but I refuse to start my marriage on a lie. I've done enough of that, and I can only imagine how much worse it will be if Kimber finds out the truth months from now instead of right here at this conference table in the middle of Wexler Events. "We helped each other navigate a very dark period in our lives. Something stressful and filled with tragedy." I clear my throat, fighting the urge to drag my hand down my face because Kimber hates it when I tap my chin. "She was my very best friend. We knew each other for five months, and when we parted ways, we did share a kiss."

Orah gasps.

Kimber yanks her hand away from mine. "What? You kissed?"

"Yes, sweetheart."

I could be imagining things, but I swear I hear a sniffle from Orah's side of the table when the term of endearment rolls off my tongue.

Kimber immediately jumps to the conclusion that a kiss means more than just a kiss. "So, I was right. You screwed her?"

Rage swells in my heart, making the tortured organ feel like it's about to explode and leave me with a gaping chest wound.

Right here.

Right in the middle of this inquiry.

Caught between the woman of all my forevers and nevers, and the woman who is supposed to be my always.

"What the hell, Kimber? I already told you that we didn't sleep together."

"He's telling the truth," Orah chimes in. "We...we were best friends. And when I moved away, we kissed each other goodbye. That's it. We haven't had any contact in the past, almost nine-and-a-half years."

Nine years and four months. If anyone is actually counting.

If *Orah* spent time counting.

Kimber purses her lips into a thin line and darts her eyes between the two of us. It reminds me of one of those cat clocks where the tail swings back and forth, timing itself with the cat's shifting eyes. Left. Right. Left. Right. "Huh. Okay." She smacks her lips, rubbing her lipstick together. "So, what was this '*dark period*'? What was this supposed tragedy?"

She asks the question with a heavy dose of skepticism, like she doesn't truly believe that anything *that* bad could've happened to us. To me. Kimber has a hard time fully comprehending what I go through as a firefighter and paramedic. From where she's sitting, I come home at the end of every shift, unscathed and whole. So, how hard can my line of work be...

Even when I tell her stories of what I've been through—what I've seen—it's like it goes in one ear and right out the other. In her mind, it's only the firefighters in movies dealing with life-threatening situations. Those of us who wear turnout gear in real life are doing nothing but alarm drills at the elementary school and tossing the extinguisher on toaster oven fires.

The only time I've ever seen her really excited over my line of work was after we started dating when she googled my name and saw that I had been recognized on the national stage for one of the wildfires in the Smokies and, of course, the movie theater attack. She called me a hero and spent the next two weeks gushing over my actions to all of her fancy, high-dollar friends and clients.

I'm about to reply when Orah beats me to the punch.

"I'm assuming you know about the movie theater attack? That happened in White Sky? The ten-year anniversary will be this April."

Kimber stills.

"I was at the movie theater when it happened. Ridge saved me." Her eyes float in my direction, never quite pausing long enough to gauge my reaction.

Kimber bounces in her seat. Her open blouse bounces with her, dropping and revealing the lace edge of her push-up bra. I make a move to adjust her top, but her flailing hands cut me off. "No shit! Oh my gosh, he saved you?!" She whips in my direction and starts fawning all over me, rubbing her hands down my jacketed arm. Her fingers drop to my thigh, and she gives my upper leg a squeeze. "Babe! You saved her! I knew you were a hero, but this..." She trails off and nods in Orah's direction. "Meeting someone you actually saved? This is just epic. You're an icon."

"Kimber, it's—"

She cuts me off and spins back toward Orah. "What happened? Were you shot? Did one of the explosions get you?"

Orah's face pales, and she reaches for the comfort of her necklace, her fingers twittering over the bird charm.

I slide my hand across Kimber's shoulder, using the opportunity to fix her shirt so her bra isn't exposed anymore. "Kimber, it's not exactly something a person likes to talk about with a stranger."

"But I'm not a stranger. Y'all are friends, and now she's my friend too. This is amazing." She balances her elbows on the table and powers her rapid-fire ideas with her jazz hands. "*Our* wedding planner is the woman *you* saved from a terrorist attack." She giggles uncontrollably. "Oh my gosh, this is the best thing to ever happen to us. I was worried no one in the Southeast would want to cover our nuptials. But now? Oh babe, every magazine in the entire country is going to be fighting over the story rights. Think how good this will be for the dealership. For Margo."

What. The. Fuck.

My body immediately breaks out into a cold sweat, making the T-shirt stick to my back. The slight hum in my ears rises exponentially. It's loud and obnoxious, like a jet engine is trying to land in my ear canal. I tap my boot up and down on the floor, pounding my foot like a jack hammer.

I dare not even look at Orah. My heart won't be able to handle it. I'm not strong enough.

Because I can already feel the panic tugging at her, threatening to pull her under the surface.

"No." The simple syllable vibrates in my throat.

Kimber ignores me. "And we need to do something to celebrate the ten-year anniversary. An engagement party or shower? Maybe even a sale at the dealership." She picks up her phone and starts pecking away. "An anniversary sale could really be the boost we need for the new stores down south. The Mobile market is close to White Sky. And just think about the new Tamp—"

Unable to control myself, I bang my fist against the table. Orah's ink pen jumps, and the framed pictures on the wall bump. "No!"

Her cell phone clatters to the table, and in exaggerated form, Kimber slowly turns. "What the hell, Ridge?"

"Kimber, we aren't selling our wedding to magazines or newspapers or tabloids. We aren't celebrating the ten-year anniversary of the attack with a party. And we're definitely not capitalizing on it and turning it into a marketing event for douchebags to get ten percent off on their midlife-crisis vehicles." I lean forward and stare my fiancée in the eyes, marking my dominance, which I've rarely done in the course of our quick courtship. "And under no circumstance, whatsoever, will you tell anyone who Orah is. That's her story to tell. Not yours. Not mine. You will refer to her as Amy and nothing else. Understand?"

After a beat, her stiff shoulders slump, and her head lobs forward. And then, she lunges from her chair and into my lap. Despite my fury, my reflexes respond accordingly. I push back from the table so she doesn't trip and bust her face. And then, I spread my legs, making room for her. With her legs between mine, she sits on my thigh and buries her face into the crook of my neck. Her arms encircle around me, and for some reason the heat of her body feels strange. It doesn't feel like it did yesterday, or even this morning. Despite the warmness leaking from her, I'm still very much cold and numb.

"I'm sorry, babe," Kimber mumbles. "You're absolutely right. I have no idea where that came from. Please forgive me."

There's a noise that draws my attention, and I find Orah looking down, busying herself with the folder in front of her.

I rub my hand across Kimber's back. "It's fine." And when she winces from my touch, I try not to let that hurt my feelings. "Why don't you sit back down," I suggest.

It doesn't take a rocket scientist to see that this public display of affection is making Orah uncomfortable.

Shit. It's making *me* uncomfortable.

Once Kimber makes it back into her own seat—you know, like the grown-ass woman that she actually is—Orah eases back into the conversation, fumbling with her thoughts in a scratchy timbre. "If, umm, if media coverage of your wedding is important, and you wanna share your personal moments with...with others, I can set you up with one of our other event planners. I may not be the best fit for your needs."

Fear races through me, fast and violent.

No...

Kimber reaches across the table and snatches Orah's hand in hers. "No, Amy, that was totally on me. I was being inconsiderate and foolish." Lifting her free hand, she laughs and twirls her fingers around the top of her head. "You know me, I had my saleswoman crown on. Instead of my wedding tiara." She laughs, deep and hearty. "I'm glad this happened. Us meeting like this? It's...destiny. I'm glad you and Ridge have a chance to reconnect." She glances back at me and gifts me with a genuine smile, not the fake one she uses to sell cars. "All I want is for Ridge to be happy. And if he's happy with you planning our wedding, then I'm all for it." Sighing, she untangles her hand from Orah's and sits back. "After all, happy husband, happy wife. That's what they say, isn't it?"

Husband... that's me.

Kimber's husband.

Wait, isn't the adage actually 'happy wife, happy life'?

And for the first time since I met Kimber this past summer, a horrid thought rips through my mind, frying my brain like an egg in a frying pan.

Can I really make Kimber happy?

"Kim—"

I'm not exactly sure what I'm gonna say, but it's a moot point. Because my sentence is sheared and shaved by the blaring ring of her cell phone. Ignoring us, she answers the call and prattles away. And it doesn't take but two seconds for me to realize that she's bailing.

Are you fucking kidding me right now.

She hangs up and spins in her rolling chair, playfully slapping me on the knees. "Babe, I gotta run. There's an emergency." She nods her chin between me and Orah. "But you got this, right?"

"I've got this?" The sarcasm dripping from me could fill a ten-gal-lon bucket. "Kimber, we're not done talking. Don't you wanna know more about..." I verbally fade away and instead wiggle my finger back and forth between Orah and myself, indicating the general, yet complex, relationship between me and the girl from my past.

Kimber furrows her brow and scoffs, like I'm making a big deal out of nothing. I suppose she's developed selective amnesia to the fact that just twenty minutes ago, she accused me of being a lying cheat. And I suppose she's also developed temporary blindness. Because she's not even acknowledged the small line of dried blood decorating my temple.

"You said she's your friend, what more is there to know." She delivers her blasé statement with a shrug. "Chip needs his best closer. I've gotta go do a wine and dine. Three custom orders are riding on this, Ridge."

Orah takes a deep breath and rises from the table, steeling herself into a brave, no-nonsense formation. "Ms. Willis, we can't very well plan a wedding without the bride. And if you wish to marry in November, we need to get started forthwith, without delay." She taps the paperwork in front of her. "Your wish list is quite extensive."

"Don't worry, Amy. Everything will work out just fine." She tucks her purse in the crook of her arm. "I'll call you tomorrow to schedule something."

I'm completely stunned, and quite frankly appalled, by Kimber's behavior. So, needless to say, it takes me by complete surprise when she bends down and plants a kiss on my lips. And I'm even more stunned when she lingers, suckling my bottom lip between her own. It's overtly sexual and sensual. And, to be honest, that's not really something Kimber is. Behind closed doors, she's not much on kissing. Or foreplay. Or...experimentation.

Out in the parking lot, she wouldn't even kiss my cheek because there was a chance her makeup would smudge. And now, she's sucking my face like I'm a candy cane. She's obviously marking her territory. Like a dog peeing on a mailbox. She bops the end of my nose with her red-painted fingernail. "Don't wait up."

And with a flourish, the woman wearing my diamond ring flees the room.

Leaving me alone with the woman wearing my diamond necklace.

Chapter 7

Orah

He stands from the table, watching her as she saunters out of the conference room, leaving us with nothing but a sashay of her hips and the smell of her floral perfume.

For a few beats, we're both completely silent, trying to comprehend what has happened to us over the past twenty minutes of our lives.

Reunions.

Accusations.

Slaps.

Name changes.

Wedding plans.

Kisses. Love. Hate. Shock. Fear. Joy.

My mind and body are battered and bruised. Battle-worn and picked-apart, I feel like a scarecrow with no stuffing.

He turns and faces me. And for the first time, and without *her* judging stare cataloging my every move, I soak him in.

How can someone look so different, yet still the same?

Cocking his hands on his waist, his Tiger Eyes peruse my body, devouring me alive. His dark brown hair is styled short, thick with a slight wave to it. Back then, there was still a somewhat-boyish curve to his face—a little roundness to his cheeks, a mild softness to the set of his square jaw. Well, there's nothing boyish about the man standing in front of me now. He's masculine and virile. All hard lines and brutish strength. His shoulders are broader, his chest wider, his thighs bigger.

His lips fuller.

And when I blink, it's me I see pressed against them.

Not her.

My eyes crawl over him. One second and one appendage at a time.

One. Two. Three. Four. Five.

We won't talk about what appendage number five was. Let's just say my sister-in-law and best friend would be proud of me.

Wetness pools between my thighs, sending a decade-old ache deep into the cavern of my belly. Desire flutters through my chest like a curtain billowing in the wind. A feathery breath escapes—from the both of us—filling the space between us with the passion of lovers who were never actually lovers.

And with slow and exact precision, his mouth inches into a smile. Bright and brilliant. Filled with unadulterated happiness. And then, he starts laughing. Loud and boisterous. Overcome, he lurches forward, balancing his hands on the table and hanging his head between his shoulders, as his entire body shakes with laughter.

The sound is sweet music to my ears. And after a split second, I join in. Allowing the giggles to take control of my emotions and fill my haggard body with good-mood endorphins.

He bolts upright and stabs his hands through his hair, fastening his fingers together on top of his head. Through a low and husky chuckle, he guffaws, "What the hell are you doing here?"

"Me?!" I cough, making room for my shrieked blubbering through my laughter. "What are *you* doing here?"

We both know we're not talking about this conference room inside of the fancy-schmancy Wexler Events, where he is the groom of a wedding. That's a conversation for another time. Another day. Hell, another century.

For right now, we're obviously using the word 'here' in the broader sense. Meaning this state, this town.

His hands fall to his side. "What are you talking about? I live here. This is my hometown."

My head jiggles like I'm a bobble-head doll. "Since when?"

"Since always."

"No," I correct him, like I'm the author of his life story. "No, you're from Florida. Your hometown is White Sky."

He gives me a sly, wicked grin. "No, Little Bird. It's not." Leaving that denial hanging in the air, he takes off his gray jacket and tosses it across the chair that Kimber previously occupied.

Oh, fuck me.

His forearms.

I slink into my chair like melting Jell-O and try to force the only two brain cells I have left in my skull to work. "What are you talking about?"

"I was living in White Sky when we met, when we knew each other. But that isn't my hometown. That's not where I'm from, where my family lived, where I grew up."

My attention is immediately drawn to his T-shirt, and I use that as my physical evidence. "There!" I holler, with a finger point. "Belly's. You worked at Belly's. You're still wearing their T-shirt."

He cackles again and wipes a tear from the corner of his eye. A tear that's now falling for a completely different reason than it was just a while ago. "That doesn't prove that White Sky is my hometown, Orah. That just proves that I'm a cheap bastard who doesn't like to buy new shirts."

I draw my hands to my face and cradle my chin. "I'm so confused. You talked about your parents visiting your apartment. Like…a lot. And your best friend and cousin were at the University of Florida." I flip through my mental card catalog, pulling out memories of us, of our conversations, of our previous life together. "You told stories about everyone in White Sky, like you'd known them your whole life—Belly, Dottie." I sit up straighter. "And the hurricane?! The hurricane from when you were in high school that destroyed your neighborhood and made you wanna be a firefighter and paramedic."

He takes a deep breath and spends a second just smiling at me before he rebuts. "That wasn't a hurricane. It was a tornado. An Alabama tornado." He pushes a finger into the tabletop. "Right here. In this town. Where my childhood home survived the damage."

"I...but..." I stutter, not even sure how to proceed. "But you'd already been with the department for two years when we met."

He flops down in the chair. "I moved from Alabama to White Sky as soon as I graduated from Fire College."

"When did you move back here?"

He leans forward, inching closer. "Nope." His eyes spark with a sexy little tease. "My turn."

My hands automatically shift closer to his, barring any power of my own. His magnetic pull is still present, even after all this time, after all this distance. "Okay, Ridge, your turn," I concede.

"How in the hell are you sitting in front of me?" His eyes dance across my face, refusing to settle in one single place. It's like he's afraid that I'm an optical illusion, like I'm about to disappear, melt into the atmosphere, never to be seen again. "How in the world did you go from Alaska to Alabama?" His brow crinkles, making him look younger. "Wait, did you even go to Alaska?"

And before I can even confirm my logistical history, his mouth drops open, and his pink tongue darts out, excitedly licking over his bottom lip. "Holy shit. You spent those years working with Cullen and Dad." He squirms in his seat. His hands and arms shake in nervous energy. He's so frenzied and frantic, I wouldn't be surprised if he hopped up on the table and started breakdancing. "Why didn't you tell them it was you?"

"What are you talking about? Working with your dad?"

Ridge is making absolutely zero sense. I've been in South Carolina. I only moved back to Alabama a couple of months ago. And I only know one person named Cullen.

Oh my god...Cullen *Conway*.

Conway. Conway. Conway.

Is he talking about Cullen Conway?

Fielding my unspoken question, his jabbering flies through my ears and into my noggin, clinking and clattering through my mind like a marble in a Mason jar.

"Jeff Conway. Cullen Conway. My dad and brother own *The Elegant Taste*." He tosses a hand to the side, and I can only assume he's gesturing toward the parking lot. "I just talked to my brother on the drive here. He said he worked with you several times in the past. That you were here and then moved away and now you're back again."

This is too much. I can't process the information being tossed at me. It's all jumbled together like the confetti in Times Square on New Year's Eve.

I take a deep breath. My fingers lift to my necklace, and I count, giving myself time to think. Time to remember. Time to grow skeptical.

"Jeff Conway is your father?"

"Yes."

"Cullen Conway is your brother?"

"Yes."

"Then, you lied to me."

He rears back like I'm the one who slapped him in the face and not his fiancée. "What?"

"You told me your brother's name was Sea. You told me stories about him. About the dares he used to accept and how he looked for you in the lunchroom on the first day of high school. You told me he went to college in Georgia."

"All those things are true, Bird. I didn't lie to you."

I heave a frustrated grunt. "You told me his name was Sea."

He stills for a moment and scrubs his hand down his face, giving himself time to marinate on my claim. And once again, he laughs. Except this time, it's a cross between a gravelly moan and a taunting snicker. It turns my blood into heated molasses. Thick and sticky and hot. "C—the letter 'C'. Which is short for Cullen. It's his nick-name. We all call him that. My family, my friends, everyone."

"I...I thought you were saying 'Sea'. S–E–A. Like the ocean."

"Why would my brother's name be Sea?"

I shoot him a look of displeasure. "Gee, I don't know, *Ridge*." I place a heavy emphasis on his geographic name, conveying my message with a Tabby-sized dose of snark.

He puts his hands up in surrender. "Point taken, Zipporah Smith."

"But Cullen told me he went to college here, in this town."

"He did. After he graduated from community college in Georgia, he came back home and completed his junior and senior years. He graduated with his bachelor's."

"But Cullen told me that he only had one brother and that he worked for the National Park Service."

"Yeah, for a time I did."

Are you kidding me? "What? You did? You stopped being a fire-fighter?" I can't believe he would give up something so vital, so im-portant. Something that was essentially a part of him, body and soul.

Well, he gave up *me*, didn't he...

"No, I was still a firefighter." His thumb finds the edge of my leather portfolio, and he traces the thick seam edge, picking at a loose piece of stitching. "It's a long story."

This whole line of questioning is giving me a headache, which is the last thing I need because I'm already in the middle of a pret-ty heavy *heart*ache. Literally. Seeing him again after all this time is giving me palpitations. I can't even comprehend what's happening.

And since my mind can't really focus on *him* and what this re-union means, I pinpoint another fact, ready to dismantle his asser-tation that I've unknowingly befriended his family. "But you told me that your dad worked in insurance. That's not what Jeff told me. Jeff said that he managed a restaurant. Cullen told me that too."

"That Christmas, after we..." His eyes dip to my lips, leaving me to fill in the blank of what he was going to say. "Well, Dad left his insurance job. He wanted a little more relatable experience before making the catering business his full-time gig. He managed a restaurant for a little over a year."

Leaning on my elbows, I massage my temples, trying to ease the tsunami of details that are pounding against the back of my eyeballs like ten-foot waves. Which, of course, doesn't feel good considering the pressure that was already present from my crying fit.

You know, the crying fit I had in his arms.

Wrapped in the one place I've dreamed of for the past almost nine-and-a-half years.

Except in my fantasies, he didn't have a fucking wild hyena of a fiancée wielding her engagement ring like a weapon.

"My turn," he repeats.

My mouth drops open, and my hands limply fall to the tabletop. "You already had a turn."

"No, you never answered my original question. What happened to Alaska? How are you in Alabama?"

"Well, I—"

Ridge's cell phone shrills to life, intruding on my attempted explanation. He leans to the side, pulling it from the front pocket of his jeans. His old and lovingly worn T-shirt catches against his fingers and lifts, giving me the faintest tease of the side of his abdomen. I avert my gaze, refusing to recognize the desire erupting throughout me. And with bated breath I listen to his one-sided conversation.

"Hey."

--

"Yeah, I'm just finishing up here."

--

A serious frown decorates his handsome face. "No, Chip called her into work."

--

"I know."

--

His smile returns. "I'm on my way."

He hangs up. Pushing from the table, he stands and pockets his phone. The thought of him leaving makes me unstable. I wanna collapse on the floor and throw a temper tantrum, kicking and screaming and begging him to never leave me again.

Instead of doing what I want, I fold my hands in my lap and squeeze my fingernails into my skin, refusing to cave in to the all-consuming urge to count. "Oh, you're leaving? I...I guess you and Kimber will just let me know when we can meet again?" Scooching away from the table, I spin in the rolling chair, turning to the credenza in the corner of the room where we keep some sample books stacked on top, between two bookends. "Did you wanna take home a few sample books to loo—"

A high-pitched squeak bleeps from my mouth when Ridge grabs the back of my chair and spins me around. I'm about to rotate past him when he clamps both of his hands on the armrests, effectively caging me in position. I can smell the faint whisps of his cologne. Different from what it used to be, but no less intoxicating.

And damn, how'd he move that quick? Without me even seeing him?

He gifts me with a cocky smirk before releasing his hold on the chair and straightening his spine.

"Are...are you leaving?" I choke.

"My turn," he says for a third time, actively avoiding my bleak query.

"You keep saying that."

"I can't help it if my turn gets interrupted by life."

Life. Such a simple word.

But is there any other syllable in the human language that contains so much happiness and sorrow? That one word is meant to carry us, to sustain us. From birth to death. From first breath to last breath. From beginning to end. From Alpha to Omega.

Life can be given to us.

And it can be taken from us.

We can live it.

Or it can pass us by.

Pushing the complexity of his statement to the side, I just nod. "So, Alaska to Alabama? Well, I—"

"No, that's not the question this time." His protest echoes low and intimate, like a distant rumble of thunder so far away you wonder if the storm will ever reach you.

"What's the question?"

He holds his hand in front of him, his palm outstretched to me. "Do you trust me, Little Bird?"

And I don't even have to answer with my words. Because my body does it for me. My *life* turns into *living*.

I wrap my fingers around his. And follow him out the door.

Chapter 8

Ridge

I catch her reflection in the darkened passenger-side window.

And I nearly drive off the road.

I can't believe she's here. Sitting right beside me.

I am beyond flabbergasted. I'm beyond shocked. I'm...well, I'm not exactly sure what the hell I am.

I have a myriad of emotions floating through my body. Like ashes rising from the flames and dancing in the wind, I'm wild and scattered. Untamed and uncontrolled.

But I do know one thing...

I. Am. Happy.

I'm filled with a calm I haven't experienced since the moment she left me kneeling in the sand.

Reeling from the taste of her lips and wishing I could be the boy she wanted me to be...

Instead of the man I had to be.

She presses her finger against the window, testing the coldness as it tries to invade the heated sanctuary of the vehicle. She wipes the foggy condensation back and forth, leaving a small little fingerprint.

My Brave Girl has morphed into a full-fledged woman.

She's so gorgeous that it hurts to even look at her. Her beauty physically handicaps me. My muscles twitch, my heart skips, and my blood runs hot. Even my bones feel like they're teetering on the edge, about to shatter into a million pieces.

But it's fine. Because I can be a *man* and a *gentleman* all at the same time.

I can embrace the lust and longing, conceding that it's just the natural and biologic reaction of my body to hers.

Just because the attraction is there, doesn't mean I'm gonna do anything about it. I would never cheat on Kimber. That's not who I am.

But what harm can come from looking...

Despite being fully covered by her modest, black top, it's plain to see that her breasts are larger. The part of my body fueled by nothing but basic, animalistic desires is drawn to her, filled with an urge to eagerly map the seductive slope of her feminine skin. Her breasts, her nipples, her surgery scar. It's a carnal hunger, making me wanna lick all the way from her collarbone to the circle of her belly button. Her hips are wider, her ass tight and round in her work pants. She's all luscious curves and long lines. And her raven hair is longer than it used to be, cascading from her ponytail in soft waves. I can't help but wonder if she curled it or if it somehow turned wavy, all on its own.

And then there's her eyes.

Her bright gray eyes are filled with stories—loaded with the love and pain of a woman who's fought wars. Struggle after struggle. And emerged from the battlefield stronger, more capable, more resilient.

I can't wait to learn everything about her.

And then a horn honks behind me, pulling me from my trance. Reminding me that I have boundaries. Big-ass boundaries. A pad-locked fence. Covered in barbed wire. With volts of electricity running through it.

Pressing my foot on the gas, I give a little wave in the rearview mirror to the person behind me, apologizing for holding up the green light. Of course, it's dark outside now so my effort to be polite is moot.

Orah turns in her seat. Her lips quiver with indecision. Oh...to make fun of me, or to give me grace. Which will it be?

The devil on her shoulder wins, and she cocks an eyebrow. "Distracted?"

I switch positions, taking control of the wheel with my right hand. "Of course, I'm distracted," I confess, unable to stop my own smile from swallowing my face. "I'm still in shock." I drum my fingers on the steering wheel. "In fact, I don't think I've ever been this shocked." I tsk my tongue between my teeth. "And that includes the time I caught my grandparents doing you-know-what on the back porch."

She gives a half-gasp, half-gag. "No!"

"Yes. And it goes without saying, I paid C my twenty-dollar allowance to pressure wash all the patio furniture after that."

She giggles and tugs on her seatbelt, giving herself room to angle more toward me. "Well, I'm still surprised too." She mimics the noise I made via a click of her own tongue. "Even more surprised than when I walked in on Tabby, three years ago, doing you-know-what."

"No!" I scream so loudly the people driving in the car next to us actually look in my direction.

Okay, first of all, I'm gonna have to bleach my brain. Because I refuse to have images floating around in there of my sweet, spunky redhead doing the unspeakable act of fornication. Nope. Nope. Nope. Not Tab. She's too innocent and goofy. In my heart, she's forever a ball-buster getting shushed by Laurie for her inappropriate and outlandish comments. She's not some grown woman having sex.

And second of all, how on earth could I have gone this long without asking about said high-spirited redhead?

"Okay, I think you just gave me a heart attack." I shake out my arm, giving the air a little punch, trying to whip the picture from my mind and out my fist. "So, we'll just pretend you never said that." I side-glance at her and wait for her to nod in agreement. "Now tell me, how the hell is she? Is she good? Does she live here too?" I lean my elbow on the doorframe and shuffle my hand through my hair. "If she's here in town with you, I may *literally* have a heart attack. A fucking real one."

"No, she still lives in South Carolina." Her hand clutches the console. Her black-painted fingernails fiddle with the closing latch, flicking it back and forth.

Her giddiness is evident. And infectious.

"Okay, Zipporah. What's going on? What aren't you telling me?"

She yanks her hand away and shoves it under her thigh, trapping her antsy movements. A content—and completely breathtaking smile—finds its home on her face. "She lives in South Carolina. In our hometown. With her husband. And their daughter."

I can barely concentrate on the twists and turns, leading the way to Holt's house. "Are you serious?! She's married? With a family?"

"Yeah."

"That's amazing. I'm so happy for her."

"Me too." And then My Brave Girl falls into serious theatrics, pulling out all the stops, acting like she's in the middle of a Shakesperean drama. She frowns and furrows her brow. Pulling her fingers to her face, she strokes her chin like she's waxing a goatee. "In fact, I think you may know her husband."

"Me? I know Tabby's husband?"

She sighs. "Huh. Yeah, I think maybe you do."

"No, I don't. I have no clue who—" I interrupt myself with another scream when I finally figure it out. "What?! Not Boaz. Are you kidding me right now? Tabby married your brother?"

"Yep." She grins, obviously proud of her self-produced spectacle.

"How in the world did that happen?"

She settles back in the passenger seat and absentmindedly plays with her necklace. "Things changed after that day at the inquiry. When all the people, you know...when he had to carry her?" She phrases her statement as if it's a question, as if I could actually forget something so violating and traumatic. "Tabby always had a little bit of a crush on Boaz, ever since we were little. But she never made a big deal out of it. I mean, she didn't sit there and pine after him, crying over her unrequited love. They were always friendly with one another and talked and teased. But something changed after that day. It's like Boaz started seeing her as her own person and not his little sister's best friend. After we left for Alaska, they stayed in touch. Web calls. Emails. They even wrote letters to one another." She fixes her gaze on the window, and the glow of my dashboard highlights her reflection, flashing it back to me in a haunted eeriness. She's turned away from me, determined to hide the melancholy that mars her angelic face. Because Boaz and Tabby did all the things that she wanted us to do. Me and her.

And just like me, I think she's mourning the possibilities that never were.

After a moment, she forces a smile and returns to me. "Anyway, things got really interesting during Christmas break of Tabby's senior year of college. Boaz and I were both home for the holidays. We had two weeks off."

"Yeah?"

"Well, by then, their," she wiggles her fingers in an air quote, "whatever-you-wanna-call-it had been going on for over four years." She pins me with a stare, "But during this whole time, they never officially became a couple. I mean, they hung out whenever we were in the same town, but they never dated exclusively. And according to Tabby, they had only kissed two times." She gives a little shrug. "Anyway, we were home for Christmas break, and Boaz asked her to do something. Go on some night hike or star gazing or something like that. She turned him down."

"Because she was mad? Because she wanted commitment?"

Orah giggles. "No, because she had a date with someone else."

"Uh-oh. And I'm assuming something about *that* date on *that* night didn't set well with Boaz?" I have a feeling that Boaz and I are very similar souls when it comes to the green-eyed monster.

"You are correct. He drove straight to Tabby's house and spent the whole night waiting on her to get back. He was just sitting on the front porch like some kind of crazed stalker."

"Okay..."

"And when they pulled up, Boaz chased the guy off with a baseball bat."

"No shit?"

"He told her that she couldn't date anyone else. That he was madly in love with her and he refused to live another second of his life without her. And then..." She pauses and leans closer, gifting me with the scent of her shampoo. "He told her that they were gonna get married the second she graduated college. So, if she wanted more than cold beer, gas station pizza, and recycled flowers from the funeral parlor in town, she better get with me to start planning a wedding."

"Really?"

She gives a little shrug. "When he finally made it home that night, he immediately started applying for new jobs. He got a high-paying position with a civil engineering firm and moved back home that February."

"So, the two of them decided to get married...when they never even technically dated?"

She nods.

I chuckle and flick my blinker, taking a left-hand turn. "What did John have to say about that?"

"He asked what took him so long."

Chapter 9

Ridge

What took him so long…

I'm wondering if Orah's father should've been a philosopher. Or perhaps a professional matchmaker. The guy sure seems to have a lot of insight into the love lives, or lack thereof, of his two children.

I adjust the temperature of the truck, turning the heat down a notch. "So, your dad knew something was going on between the two of them? For all those years?"

She scrunches her nose. "We're talking about Boaz and Tabby. They weren't exactly being stealth about it."

"And Emmett?"

"Tabby's family has always loved Boaz." She makes a chirpy little sound, like a happy bird. *My* Happy Bird. "We all saw what happened that day. The way he cared for her, protected her. They fell in love right before our eyes. I don't think any of us were surprised."

I snake a hand across the back of my neck, massaging the tight skin. "Man, and now they have a kid together."

"Eden. She'll be two in May."

"That's so…" My voice fades into the background, swallowed by the hum of the truck as I navigate the neighborhood. "Hold up. You said you walked in on Tabby." An empathetic wave of bile swooshes around in the pit of my stomach. "You saw your brother having sex?"

It's one thing for two brothers to accidentally catch one another in the act. Hell, I've even walked in on Holt before. But for a baby sister to catch her big brother? Yeah, no thanks. I don't even have a sister, and it gives me the cringe.

Of course, despite the ick, that shit's still hilarious.

From a strictly objective point of view, of course.

Because again, in my head, Tabby Morrison has never—nor will ever—have sex.

"No." She shakes her head slowly, moaning across the word, with her mouth shaped in a circle like a singing porcelain doll.

"No? If she wasn't with Boaz, who the hell was she with?"

Orah clutches the base of her throat. Like she's trying to physically strangle the picture from her body. "Boaz was out of town on a business trip." Her hand slides up her face, and she covers her eyes. "Tabby was sprawled across the bed, with a...a...toy...down there. They were on a video call, watching each other." I try my best to hold my laugh inside, but it's not going according to plan. Instead, I snort. She slices her fingers apart, peeps at me, and then slams them shut again. "Oh my god, Ridge, the noises my brother was making on the other side of that phone. I ran out of the room and started dry heaving."

By now, I'm cackling so hard, I can barely catch my breath.

She flings an arm and playfully, yet gently, slaps me on the bicep. "It's not funny. I was mortified!"

"Oh, Bird, I know. But it's still funny as hell." I point a finger in her direction. "I would've paid money to see your face." I lick my lips. "Fucking priceless."

"Nothing about it was funny." She folds her arms across her chest and pouts.

"Of course, it is. Or you wouldn't have even brought it up. You think it's funny. Admit it."

I lift an eyebrow, waiting on her to agree.

Eventually, she gives me a dramatic eye roll and caves, "Okay. It might've been a little bit funny." Despite the darkened interior, I can see the flush as it colors her cheeks.

Our raucous commotion quiets, and we spend the next several minutes driving in silence. Which I don't mind. Silences between the two of us were never strained. And hardly ever uncomfortable. There's something to be said for that. Sometimes, the most beautiful gifts of life come in the ease, in the quiet. They creep through the stillness, unaware and unassuming. And like sunbeams bursting through a gray sky, they fill you with peace and contentment.

I take the turn onto Holt and Merit's street, and with every passing tree and mailbox, my excitement grows.

"That was nice." Her serene declaration blankets me in warmth.

"What was?"

"Laughing. Joking." Her eyes chart a path of discovery across my face, from the top of my forehead to the bottom of my chin. She's learning me. Studying me. Exploring the lines and freckles that I forced her to abandon so long ago. "So much of our time back then was spent being serious, spent wallowing in grief." She gnaws on the corner of her mouth. "It feels good to laugh. With you. I nearly forgot what you sounded like."

Not me.

I remember everything.

The texture of her blood on my hands. The feel of her heartbeat strumming underneath my fingertips. The wetness of her tears soaking my skin. The heat of her breath on my shoulder.

The curve of her hip under my grip.

The flavor of her tongue in my mouth.

I fucking remember it all.

And most days, I wish I didn't. Because those memories are the sweetest form of torture known to exist.

Breaking our trance, she looks past me to the giant house that sits just beyond the security gate. "Holy shit. Ridge, is this your house? Do you live here?" Her face drops, transforming the awe into indifference. "Wait, is this Kimber's house?"

She's right to think that. And yes, Kimber does live in a huge mansion—with her father, I might add—but this house makes Kimber's look like a pauper's cottage. "No, this is where Holt lives." I lower the window and punch the security code to open the gate. "Remember? My best friend who played football?"

"Are you serious? He's back here too? In y'all's hometown?" She sits forward, trying to get a better look at the façade of the house. "Sweet mercy, he must've been one heck of a ball player."

Based on her reaction, I can only assume that My Brave Girl still hides from the news, albeit TV, Internet, and print. Otherwise, she would know exactly who I'm talking about. Because my best friend is just now getting his life back, after being plastered all over the media for nearly a full year. Heck, back this time last year, I even remember seeing an interview where a reporter asked one of the astronauts on the International Space Station to give their opinions on Holt's supposed crimes.

She slides her hand across the console, breaching no-man's land, and inching her way toward my side of the vehicle. "What are we doing here? Why'd you bring me here?"

I pull down the driveway and park outside of the garage of the Big House. I ignore her most recent question, and instead respond to the first. "So, this house actually belonged to Ella before Holt bought it. Ella grew up here." I point to the garage. "There's actually two sections to the house. The main living quarters is what we've always called the Big House." I point to the privacy fence, indicating what's on the other side, past the opulent swimming pool, hot tub, and waterfall. "And on the other side of the backyard is what we call the Children's Wing. It's basically a two-bedroom apartment. There's a breezeway that connects the two." I switch off the ignition. "Holt moved back home three years ago this month, after he retired from the NFL. He ended up buying the house from Ella."

Through the glow of the light filtering in from the open garage, I watch as she reaches for the comfort of her necklace and silently mouths her numbers.

Why is she having a moment?

What's wrong?

What about this is upsetting her?

Is she nervous because I've brought her to an unfamiliar location?

"Ella." Her tone is flat and void as she repeats the somewhat familiar name. "You told me she was your cousin." Her head whips in my direction, and her brow furrows. "But Cullen told me he didn't have any first cousins. He said both of his parents are only children." Her throat gurgles when she swallows. "Did you lie to me? Were you dating her? Back then? I remember one time she was in your apartment in the middle of the night. Were the two of you...together?"

"What? No, absolutely not. Ella's like a sister to me. We grew up together. She and Holt are *actually* cousins. His father and her father were brothers." I shake my head, trying to convey the innocence of the situation. "C's right; we don't have any first cousins related to us by blood. But Ella's been a part of my family for as long as I can remember. It's just easier sometimes to call her my cousin. Calling her a friend seems...inadequate." And even though I shouldn't, I reach out and wind my hand around hers. My thumb finds the band of her watch. And when my finger slips underneath, gliding across the sensitive area of her pulse point, she gasps, hissing air between her teeth. "My family tree doesn't grow in the ground, Orah. It grows in my heart." With my free hand, I tap my chest, instantly connecting with the bandage and the nearly healed skin.

She nods. "Okay."

I release her hand, and she immediately fiddles with her watch, creeping her fingers across the places I just touched. "I'm sorry, Ridge." Her whisper is soft and almost too low to even be heard.

"For what?"

She debates lying. I can see the indecision as it plays across her features.

"And tell me the truth, Orah."

"I'm sorry for even asking that question. It shouldn't matter to me who you dated back then. It's not like we..." She scratches her forehead, connecting with the area that was cut, but never scarred. "Our relationship wasn't like that."

Another lie.

Apparently, the lies we've told ourselves have only gotten stronger and more persistent over these past several years.

And I guess, she's just like me.

Depending on the day—the hour, the minute, the second—our recall of the past varies. Memories are what you make them. And sometimes, I remember our love. Like it's the only thing that was ever real. Our connection, our passion, our kiss. And for those moments, no one can convince me of anything else. There's no alternative. Orah was, and always will be, my soulmate.

And other times, I remember our friendship. And only that. I think our love wasn't real. That everything was make-believe. That Chief Latner and Dr. Evans were correct. That I was nothing more than a grown man in a position of authority, taking advantage of Orah and her youthful crush. I remember that I did what was right, because loving her was wrong.

People say that hindsight is 20/20.

Well, that's a steaming crock of shit.

Because my ability to agree or disagree with the decisions of my past changes just as much now as it did back then.

My hindsight isn't 20/20. It's 20/fuck-if-I-know.

When I don't comment, she forges forward, switching her vulnerability for amusement. "My turn." She nods at the house. "Now, answer me. What are we doing here? And why are there five-thousand other cars here?"

I pop the buckle on her seatbelt, quickly catching it so it doesn't fly up and hit her in the face or chest. "Ever had my dad's lasagna?"

Chapter 10

Orah

Before I even know what's happening, he jumps out and races around to my side. By the time he opens the door, I've untangled myself from the seatbelt. The moment he offers his hand, I take it, not even bothering with the stupid should I, shouldn't I game. I hop down, and when he leans past me to slam the truck door, I hold my breath. He tugs me through the maze of vehicles and into the garage.

"Huh?" My body instantly reacts to the frigid, outdoor temperature, and the confused word fogs around us like smoke.

"My dad's lasagna? Have you had it before? At any joint events you've done?"

"Uhh...there was lasagna at a Christmas party once. But I was too busy to eat any of it."

"Well, you missed out. Now's your chance to make up for that."

"We've come here to eat lasagna?"

He opens a door and guides me across the threshold and into the house with a gentle hand on the small of my back. Voices trickle down the hall in a wild mix of laughter and chatter. "Yeah. It's family dinner night."

I do a little frog hop, overcome with anxiety and nerves, and grip his left bicep in both of my hands. "Family dinner? What are you talking about? Who all is here?"

"Everybody."

I tilt my head to the side, casting him a look of annoyance.

Well, I think it's a look of annoyance.

But My Hero seems more amused than annoyed.

"Who's everybody?"

Taking advantage of my clutched position around his arm, he starts walking, moving my body forward. "Everybody. Ummm… about twenty people, I reckon."

"Twenty people?!"

He pauses in the middle of the hallway. The marble floor is shiny and spotless. I can only imagine how cold and smooth it would feel on my bare toes. He points to an open door on our left. "That's the gym."

Unable to stop my curiosity, I peek over. There are rows of expensive equipment. Some I'm familiar with and some I'm not. I know what a treadmill looks like. And an elliptical machine. But some of the things in here look like spaceships. There's a huge TV hanging on one wall, and the other wall is mirrored, with weight machines and other free weights in front of it.

Okay.

So, how good of a football player was this dude?

Based on this room alone, I'm guessing *damn good*.

Ridge puts one foot in front of the other, dragging us closer to the noises. And the smells. Which unfortunately for me, already have my mouth watering and my stomach growling. We pass a bathroom and an office. And then, it's clear to see that the kitchen is the next room. We stop again in the hallway, right where the precipice of light shining from the kitchen ends. We're standing in the shadows, hidden away from everyone in the room. But if I move my foot, just one single inch forward, I'll be in the light.

Unhidden. And known.

Unprepared. And surrounded by strangers in an unfamiliar place.

It's different when I'm attending the events I've planned. I've had months to prepare myself. Months to walk the venue and devise escape routes. Months to familiarize myself with all of the hiding spaces. Months to hype myself up to be surrounded by hundreds of strangers.

But this?

Why on earth did Ridge think bringing me to a family dinner was the smart move?

My vision grows blurry, and my heart roars in my chest, reverberating against my breastbone like a sonic boom.

Folding his free arm around himself, he pries my fingers from his upper arm. I didn't even realize I was holding him as tightly as I was. Before his T-shirt falls back into place around the firm muscle, I catch a glimpse of the half-moon indentions from my fingernails. His thumb presses into the life line of my hand, gently massaging the pressure point as he forces my hand lower.

Down. Down. Down.

He lets go.

But not for long.

As soon as my arm is back in position, nestled against the curve of my hip, he grabs ahold of me. His fingers intertwine with mine, clutching me tightly, burning every hard callous from his skin into my own.

He's strong and sweet.

An unmovable mountain. A dollop of honey.

When he speaks, his voice is more than a command. It's an unwavering belief.

In me.

"I want you to meet my family, Orah. No one here will ever hurt you. You don't need to be scared. You don't need to panic. You don't need to run. I can be your safe space. If you'll let me." He takes a deep breath. So deep, the oxygen spurts into his chest in staggered rungs. I make a move to grab my necklace, but I stop when he squeezes our clasped hands. He crushes my palm, riding the thin boundary between comfort and pain.

And then...he counts.

He takes my numbers and makes them his own.

Relieving me of the festering need that oppresses me dozens of times a day.

"One. Two. Three. Four. Five."

As soon as the last number is muttered into existence, he crosses into the kitchen, pulling me tightly, making sure I'm beside him.

And not behind him.

That's his way of nonverbally consoling me, telling me there's nothing to be afraid of with these people. There's no one here that he needs to protect me from. No one here who wishes me harm.

The flurry of activity doesn't immediately stop with his appearance. Despite my anxiety, I'm able to focus on small, little bits of the scene playing in front of me—the expensive appliances, the fancy granite, the gorgeous light fixtures. This kitchen is a baker's dream. Think of all the desserts I could make with all of this counterspace. And I could be wrong, but I think there's a soda fountain machine and custom ice maker tucked in the corner of the massive pantry. There's a bounty of food spread across the island, and nearly every available amount of space is occupied by someone.

"Everybody, this is Orah," Ridge announces in a booming delivery, determined to be heard above the chaos.

The way he says my name tells me that the people here know *me*. At some point, throughout the years, they have been privy to some—or maybe all—of our story.

Do they know about our late-night conversations? About our hugs? Our tears? Our secrets?

Do they know I asked him to be with me, to love me, to wait on me?

As if on cue, every single person in the room stops what they're doing and turns to face us. All chitchat ceases. Everyone takes a beat, bouncing their attention from our faces, down to our clasped hands, and then back up. There's a bevy of wide eyes and slack jaws.

Well, I take that back. There's a bevy...minus one.

At the far end of the island, there's a beautiful brunette with a baby snuggled against her chest, firmly held in place by the crook of her right arm. Her hair is piled high into a messy bun, and she's wearing a pink sweatshirt. She's holding the infant with one hand and trying to scoop lasagna onto her plate with the other hand. "Who's Orah?" Her question resonates loudly in the muted room, startling her. She glances up, and a blob of food drops from the serving spoon onto the countertop.

An extremely attractive guy, donning a backward baseball cap, wraps his right arm around her from behind. His left arm must be injured; it's in a sling. He angles his body just enough so that he can rub his front against her backside, without fear of harm to his wound. His hand slides over hers, where together they cradle the sleeping baby. Blond hair peeks out from underneath his hat. It curls around his neck, giving him a boyish charm. He whispers in her ear. As she digests whatever information he relays, her eyes nearly bug out of her head. She drops the spoon back into the large pan, blushing bright red when the metal clanks together. "Sorry," she murmurs.

Ridge chuckles.

And the guy plants a kiss, that's definitely more than a peck, on the curve of the woman's neck.

I'm scared to look around, but too nervous not to. Afraid of gawking like a weirdo, my gaze flits from one person to the next, every single time I blink. My eyes shutter the images back to my brain in a series of still photographs.

And I can tell you one thing after studying this collage...something is in the water. Because all of these people are breathtakingly gorgeous.

I guess that shouldn't come as a surprise. I mean, I knew Cullen was sexy, in addition to being nice, which is why I agreed to go on the date with him. In perfect timing, my blinking internal camera lands on him.

I really should've noticed. I should've put two-and-two together.

They resemble one another. Not exact but similar. They both have dark brown hair; although, the shades vary. They're both the same height. They have the same coloring. The same small spattering of freckles across the bridge of the nose and apples of the cheeks. But My Hero has Tiger Eyes. And Cullen's eyes look like grass on a spring day.

And yes, there's the name thing.

But I don't ever remember Ridge calling his brother by any name other than 'C'. Not only that, but Ridge had a habit of calling him 'brother' and using that same term when talking about his best friend and his fellow firefighters.

So, can I really be faulted for not seeing it?

And for thinking that his brother's name was '*Sea*'.

Besides, there is somewhere between sixty thousand and one-hundred-thousand people with the last name Conway in the United States. Approximately.

I should know. I researched it when looking at my name change.

Why would I think that the small-town Alabama Conways have any relation at all to the small-town Florida Conways?

I don't know…

Maybe, deep down, some part of me knew that I was befriending more than just a work colleague. Maybe a part of me knew that he was connected to Ridge. That he shared a history with him. Shared a life and a home. Memories and experiences. Blood and DNA.

Because I marked myself with Ridge. I walked away from that beach with his blood under my nails and his saliva on my tongue.

So, maybe my heart knew what the rest of me didn't.

Ridge squeezes my hand tighter.

Cullen is the first one to speak. Well, intentionally speak with aforethought, I mean. He outstretches a tentative hand in front of him and takes a step forward. His movements are slow, his pattern of speech cautionary and deliberate. He's treating Ridge like he's a frightened animal, ready to scurry off and hide at the first whiff of danger. "Brother. That's Amy." He nods his head at me. "Amy's the wedding planner. That's not Orah."

"Yeah. It is."

Cullen tosses a concerning look back at Jeff, and then he drops a caring hand on his brother's shoulder. "Ridge. It's not. That's Amy."

Ridge bursts out laughing, instantly filling the tense room with levity and happiness. He knocks Cullen's hand away. "I'm not senile, C." He untwines his fingers from mine, and instead drapes an arm around my back, settling his firm muscles into the curve of my spine. A shivering tingle shoots down my pelvis and into my legs. "This *is* Orah." He clears his throat, still talking around his lingering snicker. "Amy is Orah. Orah is Amy."

Cullen sucks in a breath and takes a step back. "Huh?"

"I...I changed my name," I explain with a stutter. "I changed my name from Orah to Amy. After what happened. After the movie theater."

My mention of the movie theater doesn't add any new shock or confusion to Cullen's already-stunned face; so, I suppose, it's safe to assume that they all know I was one of the girls trapped in the supply room with Ridge.

Cullen bends down, sinking closer to my eye level. "You're serious?"

"Uh-huh."

"You're Orah?"

"Yes."

"Seriously?"

"Yes."

He straightens back up, his brow furrowing in thought. "Did you know it was me? What about Dad?" He tosses a hand in Jeff's direction. "Did you know it was us? Why didn't you say anything?"

I can feel the pink tinge of embarrassment as it races down my cheeks and into my neck. My left eye starts to twitch. "Well, it's kind of a complicated story, but no...I had no clue you were related to Ridge." I look over Cullen's shoulder and catch Jeff's eye. "Either of you. I promise." My lip quivers, but I hold my head high, doing my best to snuff the fire of my emotions before it even ignites. "And no one at work knows about my past. They only know me as Amy."

He stares at me.

He pinches the bridge of his nose like he has a headache, and then props his fingers on his hips. "Okay, let me get this straight. You are Orah Smith. From the movie theater. You changed your name to Amy. Somehow found yourself in Alabama. Worked with me and Dad on several events. Never knew that we were related to Ridge. Moved away from Alabama. And now, you're back in Alabama." His mouth falls open, his finger jerks into the air like he's had a major lightbulb moment, and then he blows a raspberry, spraying spittle in my direction. "And now you're the wedding planner for Ridge and Kimber's wedding."

Shit. I almost forgot about Kimber.

Almost.

Afraid that I may start crying, I just nod. "Yep."

His face breaks into a smile, and he snorts, pulling me into a hug. Which I don't mind; we've hugged before. "That's some crazy-ass coincidence."

Jeff steps forward and squeezes Cullen's shoulder, nonverbally telling him to step aside. "Or some would call it destiny." He folds me into a gentle embrace, patting my upper back with a sweet, fatherly affection. I've always liked Jeff. He's charming, funny, kind, and more importantly, cool under pressure with a thick skin. Which definitely comes in handy when working with Margo. "It's such a pleasure to see you again. We were so excited when we heard that you moved back into town. We just had an event with Wexler last month. I had hoped to work with you, but they stuck us with Anniah."

Cullen rolls his eyes. "Talk about high maintenance."

Jeff playfully bops Cullen in the stomach. "Son, hush. Pick and choose your audience."

"Oh, it's okay," I interject. "She can be that way. She's still upset that Margo hired me back."

"And why wouldn't she hire you back? You were the best she had. You were gone for what? Three, four years? I can tell you right now that we weren't the only ones upset by your departure. Everyone I know preferred to work with you. You were a highly sought after commodity, my dear."

Ridge, who quickly replaced his hold on me after I hugged his brother and father, grazes his thumb back and forth across the ripple of my spine.

Jeff turns and holds out his hand, welcoming Dana into the conversation. "Do you remember Dana? I think you two met a couple of years ago at an event."

We did. A server called in sick so she came to help Cullen and Jeff with the service and clean-up. I remember bragging to her about how good everything looked. When I was getting in my car that night—overly exhausted and mentally drained—she caught me and gifted me with a bag filled to the brim with leftovers. I can still remember how good the prime rib sliders were. "Absolutely. How are you, ma'am?"

"Oh!" She blinks rapidly, trying to keep her unshed tears from spilling over. She sniffles, and then a nervous little giggle erupts from her. The force of it breaks the dam, and the tears start rushing down her cheeks. She swipes at them with her fingertips. "Oh, my goodness. I'm so sorry. I just…" She chokes on a swallow. "I thought I may never get a chance to meet you, to know you. And to know that I *did* meet you. That we shared some time together without even knowing it…" She reaches out and encases her hands around mine. Her skin is soft, and she smells like cherries. "It's such a beautiful and surprising turn of events." Lifting her left hand, she tenderly pats my cheek. "My sweet girl, thank you for being there for my boy that night."

An elephant crawls onto my chest, using my body as his own personal nap mat. The heaviness is suffocating. Crushing. Oppressing. Making it hard to focus on anything but the intensity of the connection I share with these people in front of me. These basic strangers. I glance around, focusing on the kind smiles and tender gazes of those patiently waiting to meet me. And it makes no sense...the kinship, the inherent bond that I feel.

Because they weren't there. They weren't in the movie theater. They weren't sheltering in place from the bullets and shrapnel.

They weren't hiding away from the series of poor choices that led them to that storage room. The room with no clock on the wall and a floor filled with blood.

They weren't there, but that doesn't stop the connection.

I'm tethered to them. Simply because *he* is.

"No, Mrs. Conway, he was the one who was there for me. He's the only reason I survived."

Chapter 11

Orah

He's the only reason I survived.

And the truth of that statement hits harder than she knows. It punches me in the gut with a vicious and unforgiving strength. Because despite the beat of my heart and the breath in my lungs, I don't feel like I've actually lived the past nine-and-a-half years.

I feel like... like I've only *existed*.

All because I've been without him.

His mom drops her hand and snuggles against her husband. "Please call me Dana."

"And what about you?" Cullen asks. "Do we call you Orah or Amy?"

That's a good question.

What do they call me? What do I wanna be called?

I'd be lying if I said it didn't feel good to hear my 'real' name being used again. To hear it spoken in love and friendship, by someone other than my parents, Boaz, or Tabby. Even Eden doesn't call me Orah. For her, I'm Aunt WahWah.

"Oh...ummm..."

Ridge shuffles a smidge closer to me. "How about Orah in private and Amy in public?"

They all nod in agreement.

"And maybe call her Amy when Kimber's around. I don't wanna confuse Kimber." Above the thin line of his facial hair, I can see the redness of his cheeks. "I sorta made a big deal about making sure Kimber keeps Orah's identity to herself." He gives a little shrug. "Our reunion was a little chaotic for her. For Kimber, I mean."

"Chaotic?" Jeff laments with a heavy dose of skepticism. "Is chaos why you have dried blood and a bruise on your head?"

Ridge's jaw tics. "It's fine. It's nothing."

Jeff grunts, and Cullen mumbles something unintelligible under his breath.

Taking the opportunity to slink away, Ridge introduces me to everyone else. The injured, hot blond is his best friend, Holt Hill. Former NFL quarterback and current high school football coach. Merit is his wife, and their son—Ridge's godson—is named Daire. He's four months old. Ridge is completely taken with the baby and promptly steals him from Merit, peppering him with forehead and nose kisses until he slants open his tired eyes and gives Ridge a gummy, little smile. Of course, Holt teases Ridge that it's just gas. Merit is friendly and personable. There's a thin pink scar that runs down the side of her right temple, ending just above her ear in her hair line. You can't even see it when she looks straight at you; it's only barely visible when she turns her head. And it does nothing to detract from her beauty. Merit is self-employed, and she's a few days away from opening not just one store, but two. *Run and Jump and Twirl* is a children's shoe and clothing store, and *The Letterhead* is a stationery and printing store, offering graphic design on all levels. But what impresses me more than their accolades, and their obvious money, is the way that the injured man dotes on his wife, constantly touching her and kissing her and checking to see if she needs anything. I even catch him winking at her. To which she giggles and snorts, "Not now, *sir*. Eat your lasagna instead." Which must be some kind of inside joke because he just tosses his head back and laughs, completely enamored with her.

I meet Holt's sister, Raylee, and her husband Will. Not only does Cullen partially own and work with his father at *The Elegant*

Taste, but he partially owns and works with Will at a downtown bar, *The Last Call*. Over the years, I've heard several people talk about how great it is, but I've never actually been there.

He introduces me to Holt's parents, Ray and Teresa. And some longtime family friends, Patrick Marcum, who exclusively goes by the sentimental last-name nickname 'Marcum', and his wife Nancy.

At last, we make it to the far corner of the opulent kitchen, where a man and woman are huddled in intimate conversation, focused solely and wholly on one another. Their intensity and sexuality are tangible, making a heat rise to my cheeks and a flutter of lust creep through my belly. The man is an absolute beast, taller than everyone else here. True, he only bests Ridge by a couple of inches, but still. He's got light brown hair and haunted, pale green eyes. And the woman looks like a model. She's way taller than me with honey-colored wavy hair and eyes that remind me of the fired-top of the last crème brûlée I made. She also has really good posture.

The guy offers his hand. "I'm Ryland Crutchfield. Please call me Crutch. Everyone does." He turns, looking at the woman like she alone has the power to destroy cities and then singlehandedly rebuild them, brick by brick. "And this is my wife, Ella."

"Ella!" The name rumbles from me in an exclamation, as I fight both excitement and nerves.

"It's a pleasure to meet you." She gives me a tight, but welcoming smile. "I feel like I know you. Like you've been a part of our family for a decade without even knowing it. What the two of you went through..." Her gaze bounces between Ridge and myself. "Sometimes that kind of intensity doesn't seem real. Especially to the rest of the world." She sneaks a look at her husband, and he responds by sliding a hand around the back of her neck, and massaging her, rubbing back and forth across her skin with his thumb. It reminds me of what Ridge was doing to my spine just moments ago. "I'm glad your reality has brought you here, Orah."

Emotion clogs my throat, and I'm not exactly sure how to respond.

So, I don't.

Instead, I clutch my necklace, and I count. Except this time, my numbers are muted. They're far away in the distance, hanging in the horizon like a rainbow, never quite allowing me to see where it begins and where it ends. It's a satisfying reprieve. Because, normally, they slam in front of me like a thunderclap.

Through my hushed compulsion, I find out that Crutch is a Sergeant Detective with the sheriff's department, and Ella owns a forensic consulting firm, which basically means she's a detective too.

The end of our conversation is derailed by the pitter-patter of feet and a high-pitched squeal. A young girl, about eight or nine, comes skipping into the kitchen, followed closely by a pre-school-aged boy. He's attempting to skip as well, but he can't quite master the rhythm and instead ends up jogging on his tiptoes with a sporadic hop here and there.

The little girl squeezes between people and climbs onto a barstool. "I'm starvin'! I thought that movie was never gonna end."

The little boy stomps over to the fridge and pulls out a juice box.

"Here, I already made y'all a plate." Raylee sits a paper plate of food in front of her, and then she sets a smaller-portioned plate right beside her in front of an empty barstool. She nods to the boy. "Ty, come eat."

Catching my eye from across the room, she introduces the kids. "Orah, these two ragamuffins belong to me and Will. Anna is eight, and Tyson is three." Anna tries to talk, but she's already stuffed a piece of garlic bread in her mouth. So, instead she settles for a wave.

And then, another round of children come around the bend. This time, there's no running because a little girl with light brown hair and glasses is holding hands with a toddler boy as he does the toddler high-step beside her. And trailing behind them, pecking away on his cell phone, is a teenage boy. As soon as the toddler hears Crutch, he starts screeching. "Da-da. Da-da. Da-da!"

Crutch weaves around us and squats down, holding his arms wide open. The little boy pulls away from the girl and does a very wobbly and wiggly run into his father's arms. When he stands, Crutch tosses him in the air and dramatically catches him, making a whooshing sound through his teeth. "Oh, my goodness, you're so heavy," he exclaims.

Uhh, I beg to differ. Much like the other men in this room, including Ridge, Crutch could probably lift the baby with nothing more than a pinky finger.

Ella sighs in perfect contentment. "That's our son, Harlan. He goes by Hardy."

"He's so precious. How old is he?"

"Fifteen months."

"Congratulations."

"Thank you. And this young man here..." She curls a come-hither finger at the teenager. He puts the phone in his pocket and stands beside her, giving me his undivided attention. "Is Marcum and Nancy's grandson, Nate. He's fifteen."

"Nice to meet you," we say at the exact same time.

"And, last but not least..." Instead of finishing, Ella simply nods to the little girl.

The child stares up at me, with a disconcerting half-frown molded onto her beautiful face. She pushes her glasses up on her nose, and I notice that her eyes are the same fetching color as Crutch's. After a beat, she extends her hand, "Hello, ma'am. My name is Laura Margaret Crutchfield. It's a pleasure to meet you. I'm the niece to Ryland and Ella Crutchfield. My momma's name is Brooke. I'm nine years old. I'll be ten at the very beginning of September. I'm usually the oldest in my class. I love to read. I plan on asking for a puppy for next Christmas. I'm gonna name it Peeve. Get it? My *Pet Peeve*. But it'll have to live with my aunt and uncle because our apartment doesn't allow pets. And my favorite color is pink."

Nate scrunches his nose and knocks his forearm against her shoulder. "I told you last time that you're talking for too long. Your normal, shorter one is better. People are gonna think you're strange if you tell them all that stuff within the first five seconds of meeting them.”

With her hand still dangling mid-air, she cocks her head and pins him to the floor with a menacing glare. “And you know that introductions should have a hook, context, and backlink.”

“Background,” he corrects her. He tosses me an apologetic look. “I’m sorry. I was having to do homework about the proper way to write an essay, and she got ahold of it.”

I give a little shrug. “I don’t mind.” To be frank, this might be the easiest and most simplistic conversation I’ve ever had. I wipe my palm against my black pants before shaking her hand. “I, well, I have different names. My name growing up was Zipporah Smith. Everyone called me Orah. And then, I changed my name several years ago to Amy.”

“Why?” she asks.

“Laura,” Ella softly warns.

There’s something different about Laura. You can sense her intelligence, her eagerness to understand the world around her. And quite frankly, her impatience for bullshit. And because of that, I’m totally honest with her. And in my verity, I both relish and detest the heat from Ridge’s Tiger Eyes as he stares, watching my every move, absorbing my every word. “Because there are approximately one-million ‘Amys’ in the United States. And approximately three-million people with the last name ‘Smith’. Everything I researched said that there are about twenty- to thirty-thousand people with the first- and last-name combination of Amy Smith. I changed my name to be invisible.”

“But why would you want to be invisible? The best feeling in the world is being noticed by the people who love you.”

She’s right. It is. “I didn’t become invisible to them, and they still call me Orah. I wanted to be invisible to everyone else. There were some people who were mean to me. And there were people I was afraid of. Strangers who kept wanting to ask me questions and talk about the bad things that had happened to me. I was tired of talking about bad things.”

She squints her eyes and looks around the kitchen. "Who are you here with? Uncle C? Uncle C is strong and nice. He'll protect you from the bad people and the bad things. And if he protects you, then no one will need to call you 'Amy' anymore."

Ridge clears his throat and lovingly slides a strand of her hair through his fingertips. "She's here with me, Laura."

Laura straightens like a board, elongating her spine and rolling back her shoulders. "But you already have a girlfriend. Uncle C doesn't." She takes advantage of our shock and forges forward, pummeling us with her thoughts, hard and fast, like she's a gold-medal prizefighter. "Unless you changed your mind. Is she your girlfriend now?" She points a dainty finger in my direction.

What. The. Hell.

The blood rushes down my body and pools in my toes, planting me to the ground like I'm a statue. Immovable and inanimate. One single topple, and I'll break into a pile of stone rocks and pebbles.

Ridge fumbles, strangling on his speech. "No...it's not...I mean, we're not..." He takes a deep breath, fortifying his resolve to explain our not-so-explainable situation. "We're just friends. We haven't seen each other in a really long time, and I wanted to introduce her to everyone because I was so happy to see her again. But, Kimber's still my girlfriend. We're getting married, remember?"

"But you can change who you wanna marry." She flaps her hands in the air and slaps them against her thighs.

Crutch shifts Hardy in his arms, quickly reacting to the situation unfolding. "That's enough, Little Girl. It's time to eat." He reaches for the closest paper plate and waves it at her. "C'mon, fix your plate."

Laura ignores him. "It's easy. I mean, I was gonna marry you," she yammers, with an eyebrow wiggle at Ridge. "And now, I'm gonna marry him." She hooks her thumb in Nate's side, poking the teenager in the ribcage. "You just need to change who you're gonna marry, and then you can help her and save her and keep her safe. You save people all the time. So you know how to do it. And then she won't be scared anymore. And she can be Orah all the time." She dips her chin, and her glasses slide down her nose. "I hate being scared too. When I have nightmares, Uncle Ry has to come in and save me."

My whisper is drugged and sluggish, slinking from my lips in a sloppy, sloth-like fashion. "Ridge already saved me. A long time ago."

Before weaving around us, she grabs the paper plate from Crutch's hand and snorts. "Sometimes, saving someone takes more than once."

Chapter 12

Ridge

"Have you recovered?" Holt's tilted drawl rattles through the speaker of my cell phone.

"Recovered? From what?" I turn on the kitchen faucet and wash my hands, rinsing the poultry seasoning from them.

"Uhhh. Gee, I don't know, dumbass. How about randomly seeing the woman you love but who you thought was gone forever. After what? Nearly ten years. And finding out she's supposed to help plan your wedding to a completely different woman."

Yeah.

How about that.

I dry my hands on a towel and lean against the kitchen counter. "You mean the woman I *used* to love."

My best friend pauses. For a second too long. And despite his best efforts, there's a giddiness hiding in the depths of his tone. "Kimber?"

And that hopefulness breaks my heart. More than a little. I know my family isn't jumping for joy at the prospect of me marrying Kimber. But I had hoped that they would be warming up by now, to both the idea of our pending nuptials and to Kimber herself.

True, the majority of my family knows about my real feelings for Orah. They know about the how and why of our departure. After our goodbye, it became too cumbersome to carry the loneliness by myself. The regret was tortuous and heavy, and it left me faltering, trudging through my days on unstable quicksand. And what made my recovery from the drug known as Zipporah Smith even more difficult was the fact that an equal part of me was completely remorseless. Because I knew I was making the right decision by supporting her move to Alaska and giving her a clean break from me.

But let's be real. Basically, I chose my job and my reputation. I didn't want the world to pin me as the bad guy, the immoral man, the slimy predator. And so, part of me was actually *proud* of what happened, proud of the trajectories that we chose. I falsely labeled myself as a martyr.

The whole thing was a vicious circle.

Penitence and impenitence.

Round and round and round, I went.

I was running on a hamster wheel. For a fucking decade.

I was exhausted and dizzy.

And that's one of the reasons I decided to jump off the wheel. Stop the rotation. Fall in love with someone else. Marry someone else. Live my life with someone else.

Because I was beyond exhausted.

I wanted happiness. Not chronic weariness.

And now, look at me.

Not only did the wheel run me over, smushing me to the pavement like roadkill; but it pulverized me into mushy bits and smoked me as jerky in a matter of minutes.

I rake my hand down my face and tap my chin. "No. I'm talking about Orah. Orah's the woman I *used* to love. Kimber's the woman I love *now*."

"You sure about that, brother?"

"What's that supposed to mean?"

"It means that Friday night was the happiest I've seen you in years. And you think no one noticed that you couldn't keep your hands off her?"

My hackles are immediately raised, and I push away from the counter and pick up my cell phone. "Hey, I didn't do anything inappropriate. I...I was just being gentlemanly. That was a lot for Orah, being surrounded by a houseful of strangers in an unfamiliar place. And you know I broke away and called Kimber. I told her I was with Orah and begged her to leave work and come to the dinner."

"I know you did, and I'm not saying you crossed a line. I worded it wrong. I'm just saying the small things—the innocent things—made you happy. Holding her hand, touching the small of her back, pulling out her chair."

"But are those things '*innocent*' if they made me happy?" Shit. I don't even know where that question came from or why I asked it. Especially out loud.

Holt jumps in, not missing a beat. "I think you're the only one who can answer that."

I set the grilled chicken on the table, still reeling from my earlier conversation with Holt.

I might tell myself that my interaction with Orah was innocent and filled with nothing but pure intentions. But let's be real. It wasn't.

Because those same thoughts that plagued me in the truck on the way to Holt's house have consumed me for the past forty-five hours. Ever since I dropped her off at her vehicle in the parking lot of Wexler Events at nine p.m. on Friday night after family dinner. Visions of my tongue sweeping down her body, from head to toe. Images of my fingers, finding her—all of her—for the very first time ever. Fantasies of her, sliding on top of me, freeing her mind of her demons and insecurities, with every thrust of her hips.

And all of that is wrong.

I can only assume it's how emotional infidelity starts.

Naturally, it's making me feel like fucking shit.

And what's even worse, is despite how horrendous I feel, I still wanna talk to her.

To My Brave Girl.

To My Little Bird.

I want to ask her about her day. I wanna know if she's still baking. I wanna know how she made it from Alaska to Alabama. I wanna learn why she left this town and then came back. I wanna find out how John and Ann have been doing all these years. Did they ever remodel their kitchen like they wanted to? Did Ann get the promotion she deserved?

Can I have a friendship with Orah and nothing more?

Am I strong enough to do that?

Am I *capable* of doing that?

Because I refuse to cheat. I've seen what it can do. I had a front row seat to it, and it nearly tore my baby brother apart. I can't do that to Kimber. I can't allow myself to get caught in the web of deceit, to drown in the waterfall of temptation.

With a frustrated sigh, I walk away from the plethora of food—food which is now getting cold—and flop onto the couch. I glance at the clock on the wall, begrudging the fact that Kimber is already fifteen minutes late.

And it's not like she's in the middle of a sale. She went to Sunday brunch at the country club with her mother and her two ex-stepmothers. Ex-stepmothers? Former stepmothers? I'm not sure of the exact terminology. Anyway, they had brunch and then went to the spa for massages and facials.

I haven't seen her since she walked out of the Wexler conference room. That's not unusual, though; she usually only stays at my place a couple of nights a week. I reported for shift at seven on Saturday morning, finishing my twenty-four-hour tour this morning. I came home, cleaned house, went downstairs to the gym, and then cooked us a nice dinner.

Bored and restless, I turn on the television and flip to a news channel, just giving myself some background noise. I never reinstalled my social media apps, even after Holt was drafted; so instead, I mindlessly thumb through the contacts on my phone, pausing when I get to Orah's name.

She told me she still has the same cell number.

She never changed it. All this time, she's been one small click away. One little green telephone icon is the only thing that's separated us.

In the background, the muffled voice of the news reporter drums on. "And speculation still swirls regarding the health of the Vice President. There's been no official statement from the White House yet regarding the rumored visit to a local D.C. hospital last night. Political pundits from both the left and right—"

"Hey, babe!" Kimber pushes through the heavy wooden and steel door of my penthouse apartment loft.

I turn off the TV and scramble to help her with her bags. "Did you go shopping?"

What I really mean is...is this why you are now twenty-five minutes late? Am I really gonna have to eat cold chicken because you needed another blouse?

Of course, I'd never actually say that. Because I don't wanna be an asshole to my girl.

I set everything down on the side chair, and she wraps her arms around me, hugging my backside. "Well, we felt so energized after the massages, we had to do something."

I turn around, glad to see she's only wearing clear lip gloss and not actual lipstick. When I lean in for a kiss, she returns it instead of pulling away. She tastes like dark roast coffee, and she smells earthy and spicy. I'm guessing from the oils rubbed onto her face and body during her day of pampering.

"Well, c'mon, I'm starving."

"You could've eaten without me. I'm sorry you had to wait." She circles her hand around my bicep and kisses my shoulder as she follows me to the table. "Oh, babe, it looks so good. Thank you."

I like her when she's like this. Calm. Affectionate. Appreciative.

I mean, I love her when she's like this.

I settle her at the table, leaving her to fix her plate while I grab some drinks—a beer for me and a glass of red wine for her. As we eat, she fills me in on the latest gossip regarding her mother, her former stepmothers, and all of the pretentious society members who run in their clique, and who will most likely be invited to our wedding. Like a good fiancé, I smile and nod. I ask questions where appropriate. I follow her cues, laughing and gasping when needed.

Of course, in reality, I couldn't give two tiny leprechaun shits about who is facing bankruptcy with his financial advising company, who drove their luxury golf cart through the wet concrete of the new pickleball court, and who is carrying around a fake Hermès bag. Hell, for the first two months we dated, I thought she was saying 'air mess'. I thought she was talking about some kind of free barf bag the airline companies were giving out to first-class passengers.

After we're done, she heads over to the couch, relaxing while I clear the table and load the dishwasher. With the open floorplan and modern warehouse-vibe of my place, I have a perfect line of sight to her. "So, did you call Amy yesterday to schedule another appointment time?" I carefully drop a handwashed knife in the silverware drawer, pretending my thoughts about the wedding planner haven't been consuming my mind.

She flops a hand in my direction while staring down at her phone. "I told her you would give her a call tomorrow to set something up. It's been so busy, I need y'all to start planning without me. Plus, I'll probably need to make some trips over to the Georgia and South Alabama dealerships in the next couple of weeks. Maybe even the one in Tampa. We're still working the kinks out with that purchase. So I can just come in once y'all narrow down some of the choices. I told her to give me three choices of each thing, and I'll pick from that. But don't worry, I sent her some more ideas so she has plenty of inspiration to know what I like. I emailed her some really awesome pictures from the Aberdeen wedding in Memphis."

"Really? You want us to basically plan the whole wedding without you?"

She cocks her head, looking at me like I'm a spoiled child. "That's not what I said, and you know it."

"I have work, Kimber. And I don't know anything about this fancy stuff."

"I have work too, Ridge. You know that each of our dealerships is the fastest growing in its market. The demand for luxury is there. It's what people want. We have to catch all that we can while the fish are biting. Besides, you have Amy and your dad and your brother. Y'all are more than capable of narrowing the field down to three options for me to choose from." She sucks her lip between her teeth. "Opulent options."

I drag my hand down my face and tap my chin, earning me a scowl from my future wife. I decide to switch the subject to avoid a fight. "Who are the Aberdeens?"

She plops her phone down in her lap and arches an eyebrow. "Only the First Family of Ribs."

"But you don't even like ribs." She hates eating with her fingers. She thinks it's uncouth.

She rolls her eyes. "I didn't send her pictures of ribs. I sent her pictures of the venue, of the flowers, of the table settings. And they had the cutest wedding favors. They were custom-designed Swarovski Crystal ballpoint pens with the wedding couple's monogram on them. They had pink ones and black ones. So cute."

"Are you serious? They did that for the entire wedding party?"

She laughs. "Babe, don't be ridiculous. The ink pens were for all the guests. That's what a wedding favor is. They gave better gifts to the wedding party. Waterford carafes to the bridesmaids and Ping Drivers to the groomsmen."

I break out in a cold sweat and grip the edge of the kitchen island, begging myself not to lose it. Just because Chip has enough money to wipe his ass with twenty-dollar bills doesn't mean I want him buying expensive presents for every Tom, Dick, and Harry who will be coming to our nuptials.

And I can tell you right now that if I present Cullen, Holt, Crutch, and Will with a golf club that costs as much as a car payment as a 'thank you' for being my friend, they will laugh in my face. I'll never hear the end of it.

"You know I'm fine with a small wedding? All I need is you."

She folds her arms across the back of the couch and smiles at me. It's soft and genuine, flooding me with daydreams, making me see the possibilities that could exist for our future. "And all I need is you." She blushes and giggles. "But…"

"But you need the big wedding because of the business. Because of your clients." I can't stop the stoic cynicism that laces with my statement, braiding it together in a disgusting bond.

Why can't our wedding be about us? Why does it have to be about selling cars?

"It's not just that, Ridge. I *want* the big wedding. It's a celebration of our love, of our lifelong commitment. I want it to be the most magical day of our lives."

I shut the dishwasher and put the last bowl of leftovers in the fridge. "You're right, Kimber. I want you to have whatever makes you happy."

I'm nearly to the couch when she shrugs and picks her phone back up. "Besides, what does it matter? You're not the one who's paying for it."

I stop dead in my tracks. I'm frozen to the spot in livid anger. I hate it when she brings that up. When she hangs her money—Chip's money—over my head. Both Holt and Ella are millionaires. Several times over. And well, quite frankly, a hundred times over in Holt's case. And neither one of them have ever made me feel like a lesser person simply because my bank account doesn't have as many zeroes.

Instead of curling up next to her and channel surfing while she plays on her phone, I head into the bathroom, telling her I'm taking a shower. Despite the fact that I had one this morning before leaving the station and another one after my workout. And later that night, when she finally crawls into bed next to me and asks me if I want to have sex, I fake a yawn and tell her I'm exhausted.

I don't really see the point in pushing my disappointment to the side just so I can get a piece of action. Besides, it's not like some new itch is gonna be scratched by getting frisky with Kimber tonight.

Because every time is the exact same.

And by exact, I mean...exact.

She never wants to make out. She alleges not to care about foreplay. Calls it a waste of time and just a means to an end. No toys, no seduction, no variation.

No aching anticipation.

No...*if I don't have his hands on me right this second, I'm gonna die.*

No...*if I don't have her mouth wrapped around my cock right this second, I'm gonna explode.*

And our position? Yeah, that's always the same too. Her bent over the side of the bed with me taking her from behind.

Always the side of the bed.

Always me taking her from behind.

Always.

She doesn't want us to look at one another. In her opinion, facial expressions are never appealing in the middle of intimacy. Scrunched noses. Crinkled foreheads. Double chins. All the things she fights on a daily basis with creams and moisturizers. And I don't even know how often she goes for her facial injections and fillers. I once heard her badmouthing her esthetician—yes, I learned that term—because she wouldn't break protocol and allow Kimber to come back for more work before the recommended time had passed.

I stare at the ceiling, lost in thought, watching the moonlight as it plays across the ceiling fan blades. It doesn't take long for the truth of my life to slice through me like a scythe, filleting me right down the middle, from sternum to pelvis. I'm a near thirty-two-year-old man, and all I've ever done is *have sex.*

Now, don't get me wrong, I've had a lot of it.

Beaucoups of perfectly fine, wet-your-whistle sex.

But I've never *fucked* someone. Yes, I know most people think the two are one and the same, and they use the words interchangeably. But I don't think they're the same. Like, at all. To me, *fucking* is a word filled with indescribable passion and lust. It's more than just sex. It's a clothes-ripping, rabid-drooling, nerve-quaking, cum-soaking, fire-inducing, heart-panting, scream-making event of carnal hunger. It's so primal and animalistic that the only word that can properly characterize it is the one that you were forbidden to say throughout your entire childhood, lest your grandmother wash your mouth out with soap.

And if I'm being completely honest, I've never *made love* to someone either. I've never had that level of intimacy. That soul-crushing and mind-altering action of turning two bodies into one. That God-given gift of staring into the eyes of the person you love more than life itself and knowing that your devotion will traverse this world and carry into the next. Knowing that stars will burn and die, but your longing to be held in the arms of your lover will never fade. Never flicker. Never dim.

So.

How do you like that.

What does that say about my upcoming marriage? Can a union last through thick and thin, better and worse, good and bad, if all we do in the bedroom is have sex? Like we're ticking some chore off of a to-do list.

I suppose if I'm fine with ordinary love, I need to be fine with ordinary sex.

In nonverbal response, my fiancée turns, draping her hand across my chest. In her sweet, sleep-fueled cuddle, she unknowingly grazes the phrase, numbers, and picture that blaze for someone else.

And I fall into a fitful slumber, wondering if honor and integrity kill everyone's destinies.

Or just mine.

Chapter 13

Orah

"You know, I can send Boaz down there to rough him up, okay? Just because he's a hero doesn't mean that he's above an ass-whoopin'. Plus, my husband has really been working out lately. Talk about buff."

"Seriously? I just threw up a little bit in my mouth."

Tabby shushes me and forges forward. "I can't believe he hasn't called or texted you yet. It's been what? Two-and-a-half days?" She sucks in a sharp breath and basically repeats the timeframe with an eardrum-bursting scream. "Two-and-a-half days!"

"Kimber-Shay said he would call today to set something up."

"Oh, don't even get me started on that hussy."

"Tab, it's not nice to call other women hussies." Trust me, I know. I was on the receiving end of that commentary for many years.

She growls. "Listen, I understand that, but…"

I lean back in my office chair and double-check the time. I only have about ten more minutes before I have to leave. "But what?"

"But he's supposed to be marrying you. Not her."

I simulate a lighthearted laugh. And even that takes a Herculean amount of strength. Because I've been thinking all the same things that Tabby's talking about. In fact, I've not only been thinking them, but obsessing over them. My scattered and sporadic sleeping habits have been even more troublesome over the past three nights. In fact, I don't think my eyes even closed on Friday night. Thankfully, I didn't have any events on Saturday, so I didn't have to worry about frightening strangers or damaging Margo's reputation with my bloodshot eyes and my sleep-deprived, bloated face. But I don't really think that comes as a surprise to anyone. When Momma found me in the kitchen at four a.m. making chocolate banana bread, she didn't seem stunned.

Obviously, I take too long to respond.

"You female dog," she fumes, using the 'bitch' alternative so my little niece doesn't get into even more trouble at preschool. "Don't you fake laugh with me."

"I'm not fake laughing," I protest. "We haven't even talked to each other in years, let alone seen one another. How in the world are we supposed to...be together." I can't bring myself to say 'get married'. That's a vivid alternative that hurts too much to consider. "You can't very well jump into a relationship commitment when you've only kissed the person once."

"Care to tell that to your brother? I'd like to remind you that we had only made out twice before he barged off my porch and told me we were getting married."

I close my laptop and reach underneath my desk and grab my purse. "Maybe you're a better kisser than me," I joke.

"Well, of course, I am. But from what you told me, you literally made the man fall to his knees. Where he proceeded to wallow around in the sand like a hatching sea turtle."

"That's not exactly what happened, Tab." I stretch my back, refusing to give in to the temptation to go back to that afternoon, to go back to that kiss. To the way his tongue tangled with mine, the way his body pressed against me—firm and taut—the way his hand slipped under the hem of my shirt and grazed my bare skin—if only for the briefest of moments. Once again, I deny myself the satisfaction of reliving those memories. Why? Because they always result in an oppressing and overwhelming thirst that can only be satiated with my hand down my panties. "Anyway, he's engaged to marry someone else. He loves her. He's not just going to walk away from that. I accepted it. You need to as well."

She cackles through the phone. "Nope. I refuse to accept that."

Eden chirps from her car seat. "Nope. Nope. Nope." Her precious chatter is like the sweetest dessert. Rich and fulfilling.

"Hi, Eden, my sweet baby girl. Aunt WahWah has to go to work now."

"A fancy luncheon for accountants. Why in the world would Margo accept a job like that?" Tabby huffs.

"Because they are *rich* accountants. Need I say more?"

"Alright. Well, this conversation isn't over. Call me as soon as you hear from him."

We hang up, and I'm nearly to my car in the parking lot when my phone rings again. Tabby is notorious for calling back with 'oh, one more thing'. She insists it's a casualty of Mommy Brain. So I fully expect to see her picture on my home screen.

But it's not Tabby.

In fact, there's no picture.

Only a name.

My Hero.

My heart thrashes in my chest, and a thousand butterflies swarm through my stomach. I lean against my car, making sure I have a watchful eye on the people milling around the expensive SUV to my right. I don't remember seeing them in the showroom, and there should be no reason for them to be loitering.

One. Two. Three. Four. Five.

My hand is shaking so fierce it takes two times before my finger swipe works, accepting the phone call from the man who is the ultimate definition of *complicated past.* "Hello?"

His sigh is deep and rough. Textured and meaningful. Heartwarming and heartbreaking. "Damn, Orah."

"Wh–what?"

"I haven't heard your voice on the other side of the phone line in so long. I forgot how good it sounds."

"Ridge…" Tears spring to my eyes. I'd like to blame my reaction on the winter's sun as it shines down on me, but we all know, that's not the cause.

"I'm sorry," he apologizes. "I just didn't realize how nostalgic this would make me." Even though he quiets, I can feel that his thought isn't done. "Do you ever think back on it? On all of our late nights, all of our phone calls?"

Only every single day. "Yes."

"Yeah. Me too."

There's a melancholy in his tone that traps me and holds me hostage. I want nothing more than to break free of the chains and comfort him. Show him how strong I can be. Run to him, slide my arms around his neck, and hide him away from whatever sadness is trying to steal his joy.

But that's a job for the woman he's marrying. Not me.

He picks back up, lacing the conversation with a chipper disposition. "So, when can you meet up again? Kimber said she wants us to narrow down some of the wedding stuff before she makes her choices."

Yeah, she does.

I have a feeling this is going to be the worst wedding-planning experience of my life. And that educated opinion is completely unrelated to the fact that I'm in love with the groom.

"Well, I'll need to look at my calendar. I know next week is—"

"How about today?"

I stand up straighter, bouncing my backside off the door handle of my car. "Today?"

"Yeah. I…I wanna see you."

"You wanna…" My words hide from the daylight, afraid that if I repeat them, I'll attract attention to the feelings I'm not supposed to be feeling. Afraid that I'll show my cards, draw awareness to the hopefulness that lives deep in my soul.

"Yeah. I wanna."

From my perch, I watch as the people cross the parking lot and head inside. "Well, I'm about to head to an event. I'm directing a luncheon from noon until three. It'll be four by the time I finish and help pack up."

"I'm free tonight."

"Ummm. Well, Momma is having a monthly birthday celebration at work tomorrow, and I said I would do the desserts for it."

"Wait. Hold on." I hear a shuffle on the other side, like he's shifting positions. "Your parents are here too? John and Ann are in town? They live here? And not in South Carolina?"

"Yeah." I roll my eyes, slightly embarrassed to share my lack of solo adulting. "I actually live with them."

"Then, it's settled. I'm coming over. I'll help you bake."

"Are you serious?"

"Yeah, why wouldn't I be? You can just text me your address. Is five too early to come over? I can bring dinner if you want. For John and Ann too."

I toss a hand in the direction of the store. "But I won't have any of your paperwork with me. I wasn't planning on stopping back by here after the luncheon. And I'm already outside by my car. I have to head out; there's no time for me to go back inside and get it."

"That's fine. We can just talk about other stuff. There's still so much for us to catch up on. Don't worry, I'll make a normal appointment to talk about the wedding stuff." He clears his throat. "But I wanna be your friend, Little Bird. I want you in my life. Maybe tonight, we can just focus on that."

His friend.

That's what I want too. I swear, I do.

But what I don't understand is...if I want it so badly, how come that particular word hurts so much.

Chapter 14

Ridge

I pull up in front of the house. Turning off the ignition, I sit in silence for a moment, just staring at the gray and white brick home with its black shutters. I watch the home until my automatic headlights fade to black.

Here.

For the past few months, she's been living *here*. In this beautiful, well-kept home. No more than fifteen minutes away from my loft.

She's been *here*.

Right under my nose.

Baking cakes while I was having a part of her scorched into my body. Watching the New Year's Countdown with John while I was proposing to Kimber. Working at Wexler while I was running into burning buildings. Grocery shopping with Ann while I was doing my fiancée from behind.

The front door flings open, and the front porch light flicks on. Even from here, I can see the brilliant smile on her face as she scurries down the sidewalk, half-skipping, half-running, eager to see me.

She's wearing black leggings and a ginormous black sweatshirt. It falls off her shoulder, gifting me with a glimpse of her black bra strap. Her raven hair is gathered in a messy top knot, and it bounces with every move. The cold snap hasn't let up, and it's even chillier now that the sun has disappeared from the sky. Her cheeks flush in the freezing temperature, and she shivers, drawing my attention to her bare feet.

No wonder she's cold.

But the chill doesn't stop her. She's not slowing down, not giving up. She's coming for me.

Fuck. Me.

Is this what it could be like? What it *should* be like?

Coming home to someone who's actually happy to see you...

I open the door and climb out of the truck, ready to snag her in my grasp. "Orah!" Like the pathetic pussy that I am, there's no disguising my giddiness. On instinct, my arms open wide.

She responds accordingly, mimicking me, ready to launch herself into my waiting embrace. But things change. In the blink of an eye. She pounces to a landing, smack dab in front of me, wobbling as she abruptly stops her momentum. Her face falls, and I can instantly read her.

Instantly feel her.

Should we be hugging?

Is that crossing a line from friendship into something forbidden?

Hell, with us, isn't everything forbidden...

The thought of not feeling her against me is unbearable. So I coax her into the decision. You know, the decision that's so right, it's wrong. "It's just a hug, Orah. We hugged Friday night. It's fine. Friends hug."

She cocks her head to the side and studies me, marinating on my claim. She shifts from one set of tiptoes to the other, fighting a losing battle with the cold concrete.

I laugh. "Your toes are gonna fall off."

Her lip quivers against a fresh smile.

And in perfect synchrony, we fall into one another. I lift her in my arms, determined to keep her black-painted toenails free of frostbite. I twist her back and forth, enjoying the way her feet slap against my shins. "It's good to see you. I missed you."

She curls her arms around my neck tighter and lays her cheek on my shoulder. Her whisper sends a flume of heat cascading down the length of my spine. "I missed you too."

With her still in my arms, I open the back driver-side door and grab the large bag of takeout from the floorboard. She wiggles, pushing to be set down. "Here, let me help you."

I strengthen my grip, refusing to give her even a millimeter. "You can help me by getting inside. Why on earth did you come outside without any socks or shoes on?" I hip bump the door closed and then take long, wide strides.

Her reply is plain and simple. And quite frankly, it may be the kindest thing I've ever heard. "Because you were here, Hero."

As soon as I cross the threshold into her house, Ann catapults into us, not even giving me time to set Orah down. I dramatically overexaggerate a whoosh of air, allowing my body to bend a little with the extra weight of another person. The last thing I need is for Ann to bounce off of us, fall backward, and smack her head on the hardwood floor. She traps us in her hug, laughing and crying. In fact, I'm pretty sure she's rubbing snot on the back of Orah's sweatshirt.

John comes up beside me. Grinning ear to ear, he takes the bag from my hand. "Ann, you're gonna break the poor boy's back. Give him some space, will you?"

"Oh! Oh my! You're right." She disengages her spider monkey setting, climbing off and giving me room to plant Orah on the ground. As soon as My Brave Girl takes a step back, Ann replaces her. Once again, crushing me in her motherly hold. "It's so good to see you. Oh, Ridge. We've missed you like crazy."

I do my best to keep my composure, but it's a hard thing to do. Tears well in my eyes, making everything wavy and distorted. "I've missed y'all too, Ann. I can't believe you're here."

After a couple of moments, Ann clears the way, making room for John. I quickly wipe my eyes and shuffle my palms across the front of my jeans, ridding myself of the evidence of my tears, of my tender emotions. John doesn't even bother with a handshake; instead, he drapes an arm around my shoulder, patting my back like a proud father. "Ridge. About damn time, my boy."

"Sir, it's so good to see you."

Both of them look basically the same as the last time I saw them, in the parking deck after the congressional inquiry. True, they both have a little more gray hair, a little more girth around the midsection, and a few more wrinkles lining their faces; but it's clear to see that they are both still madly in love with each other. And clear to see that they both still love and admire their daughter, just the way I do.

Well, maybe not *just the way I do*. But you know what I mean.

In a flurry of chitchat, we head into the kitchen, where the table has already been set. Orah takes the bag from her father and opens up the overflowing containers of takeout food. I figured something family-style was the easiest so I stopped by Holt and Merit's favorite Japanese steakhouse and got chicken and steak-fried rice with all the fixings.

Before sitting, John opens the fridge, grabs a bottle of beer, and dangles it from his fingertips. "Ridge?"

Oh, hells yes. Anything to calm the clusterfuck happening in my stomach. It's a jumble of excitement, anxiety, happiness, and trepidation. Which only intensifies when Orah, who's next to me, leans closer and asks me for a fresh napkin.

After we fix our plates, we fall into a somewhat more nuanced pace of conversation. "So, I hear congratulations are in order," I tease.

Ann quirks a brow, and John mumbles around a mouthful. "Huh?"

"A granddaughter?"

They both beam brighter than a midday sun. "Oh, Ridge. She's gorgeous. And so smart."

"And a fiery, little sprite," John adds. "You know she got that from Tabby." He chuckles. "Boaz is gonna have his work cut out for him when that girl gets into high school."

I shake my head in good-humored disbelief. "I couldn't believe it when Orah told me. Boaz and Tabby. Married. Parents."

"Them two kids were meant for each other. They all like to say things changed after the inquiry. But I saw the writing on the wall years before that. I knew if they would just trust in their destinies, their lives would be filled with unimaginable happiness."

Ann reaches over and pats John's forearm. "And that *unimaginable happiness* was crying crocodile tears earlier because she got in trouble for not eating her grilled chicken, potatoes, and carrots." Ann bites back a smile. "She thought if she threw all of her food on the floor, it would have to go into the trash can. Meaning, she could then have her chocolate pudding dessert as a main course."

"It must be hard to be away from her, away from your only grandchild. Didn't you wanna stay there with her?" I ask.

They share a fleeting and discreet look. The same kind of look that married people often share, when they know more than they are letting on. It fills me with a momentary wave of unease. John scoops another helping of rice onto his plate. "No, moving was the right choice. When Orah decided to come back here, I checked into job postings, just out of curiosity. When the auto factory had an opening, basically doing everything I was doing in South Carolina, but at a higher salary..." He breaks off and gives a little shrug. "We knew it was the best decision."

Orah nearly chokes on her water. "Me? I had no plans to come back here. Y'all were the ones telling me how good I had it at Margo's and that I needed to see if I could get my old position back."

There they go. Sharing that same look.

Huh. I wonder if Kimber and I will ever have the married-couple-has-a-secret look.

I tap my elbow against Orah's. "You never did answer that question, by the way. How did you get from Alaska to Alabama?"

She points her fork in my direction, giving me a playful smile. "I believe you withdrew that question in favor of a different question."

"Well, I'm reinstating it as of right now." I retaliate with my own fork and steal a piece of steak from her plate. "And for the love of all that's holy, eat while you talk, or we'll be sitting here until the summer honeysuckle blooms."

She rolls her eyes, rolling her neck in the process. Once again, her sweatshirt slips down her shoulder, exposing the strap of her bra. It's plain and simple. No lace. No frills.

Kimber wears black undergarments because she thinks they are sexy.

But I know that Orah wears black undergarments because she doesn't want to see the crimson stains of blood if something bad were to happen to her again.

The curve of Orah's neck is so alluring, so perfect. Like a moth to a flame, I'm drawn to it. My stare maneuvers across her skin, memorizing everything—the small freckle underneath her earlobe, the line of her muscles, the beauty of her necklace as it nestles against her flesh. It takes me longer than it should to realize that I'm looking at her right shoulder. Leaning forward, I hook my finger in the collar of her sweatshirt, tugging it down just a tiny smidge. And there, underneath the light of the kitchen chandelier, I see the small scar from my decompression needle, lining the area of her second intercostal space. I trace my forefinger across it, bringing to fruition my wish from all those years ago—to check my work, to check the scarring, to see if there's anything that I should've done differently.

With my touch, she sucks in a sharp breath.

But she doesn't shy away. In fact, she leans in.

Her eyes latch onto mine. With a blink, she gives me dominion, gives me the power to decide what comes next. She's the prey, accepting her fate. She's the exotic animal dancing across my Tiger Eyes, tempting me with the hunt.

Clearing my throat, I adjust her top, hiding both her tiny scar and her bra strap. And in the process, the bird charm on her necklace slips underneath the fabric as well, playing a game of hide and seek from the scrutiny of the world.

I turn forward, doing my best to pretend that nothing happened. Which is hard to do based off the way John and Ann are staring at us. Hating myself, feeling the burn of shame as it creeps across my cheeks, I do what any honorable betrothed man should do.

I scoot my chair a little farther away and ask for someone to pass the salt.

Chapter 15

Orah

He scrapes his palm down his face. Landing on his chin, he completes his signature tap. One. Two. "May I have the salt, please?"

My skin sizzles, and my blood boils to the surface, singeing me from the inside out. His touch has the power to lift me up *and* tear me down. All at the same time. All in the same moment.

In one tick of the clock's second hand, he can make me feel everything.

And now, he wants to add salt to his already-perfectly seasoned food. Like his fingers weren't just on me, tracing the tiny scar carved by his hand the night he saved my life.

"So, Alaska to Alabama?" he prompts, once again drawing the line in the sand between our friendship and what I know we both secretly want. Because deep down, how can he not want the exact same thing as me?

Wouldn't I know? Wouldn't I feel his platonic distance?

But when I'm next to him, I don't feel the invisible lines of camaraderie loosely tying us together. I feel the barbed-wire rope of passion tightly knotting us into one. The binding is sharp and punishing and authentic.

Of course, none of that matters.

Because Kimber wears his ring.

And the Ridge I know would never walk away from commitment.

He may love me, but he obviously loves her more.

Grabbing my fork, I push my food around on my plate, fighting the nausea that's suddenly swishing in my belly. "Alaska was…a gift."

Staring down at the table, he smiles. "I'm glad."

"Life on the Slope is beautiful and rewarding. Desolate and hard. I learned so much from Naja, my boss. Not just about baking and business, but about life. She didn't hover over me or smother me. She taught me the basics, and set me free to do my own thing. She wanted me to experience both success and failure. Because the two walk hand in hand and are never far apart. She said Alaska is like that—it's the land where opposites are two halves that make the whole." I lean back in my chair, trying to recall Naja's words of wisdom. "Midnight Sun and Polar Night. Green fields and white snow. Crystal clear water and frozen ice roads. In the North Slope, you can't have one without the other."

Unable to avoid me any further, he sets his fork down and turns to look at me. "Sounds like she was a bit of a philosopher."

"She was."

Dad rises from the kitchen table and grabs another beer for him and Ridge. "Don't listen to Orah. Naja might've wanted to teach her that failure is a part of life, but my baby girl did no such thing." He sits back down, and Ridge thanks him for the beer. "She covered spike rooms in both Deadhorse and Prudhoe Ops. Everybody liked that she didn't do frou-frou desserts. She made things that you actually wanted to eat, things that your momma and grandmomma made."

Ridge takes a swig, and I watch as the muscles in his throat work with his swallow. "That's amazing, Bird. I had no doubt you could do it."

Reaching for my napkin, I notice that my watch has shifted, and the edge of my marking is peeking from underneath the band. I move my hands to my lap, and tuck everything back into place, hiding the evidence. "Thank you."

"And the event planning?" he questions.

"That part of Naja's business really took off. She passed a lot of the planning and coordinating responsibilities on to me. It felt good to be needed and valued."

His jaw tics, and he twists his head to the side, trying to erase the building tension bunching in his shoulders. He thinks that last comment was a dig at him, an insult. A bitter allegation of blame all because *he* didn't need me, *he* didn't value me. But that's not the case. That statement was innocuous. I had no intention of making him feel bad.

At least, I don't think that was my intention.

Hell, then again, maybe it was.

"And how did that event planning lead to the job with Margo?"

"There was an executive from a sea freight shipping line, from a big company down in Mobile, who was working a six-month stretch out of the Prudhoe Bay Operations Center."

"Mobile, Alabama?"

"Uh-huh, yeah." In nervous habit, I reach up and fondle my necklace. "He was wanting to plan a surprise party for his wife. Two weeks after coming home from Alaska was going to be his thirtieth wedding anniversary. He hired Wexler Events. But he also hired Naja—and subsequently, by default, *me*—to work on his behalf from Alaska." I shrug, "Margo liked my work ethic, my ideas. We worked together from October until March. Boaz had left in February, so when she offered me a job at the beginning of April, I accepted."

He furrows his brow, and I know he's thinking back to our conversation about Boaz and Tabby, trying to place the timing. "So you moved here when you were what? Twenty-two, about to be twenty-three?"

"Yeah, that's right."

He shakes his head back and forth, a smile returning to his face. "I can't believe you moved to my hometown. Out of all the places in the world."

Yeah. And where were you?

Of course, I don't say that out loud.

By now, we've all finished eating. Mom stands. "Y'all keep talking. Let me clear the table."

"I can get it, Momma."

She whips a hand at me, shushing me. "No, y'all visit. I can get it."

I ignore her and grab my plate. "No, I'll get it. I need to start working on the desserts. It'll be easier for me to put everything away, especially the leftovers; I have ingredients stuffed all in the fridge."

She stacks Dad's plate on top of her own. "What you mean is… you don't want us in here messing up your domain."

I bite my bottom lip, trying not to give her the satisfaction. It's true; everything has its rightful place in my kitchen. I don't want things out of order or in the wrong area. It screws me up. And I swear it makes my finished product taste different, not as good.

Everything needs to go right where I want it.

"I'll help her," Ridge adds. "That's what I promised to do. I'm gonna bake."

Dad rocks back in his chair. "You're gonna bake?"

I swear Ridge puffs out his chest like a little boy declaring he's about to embark on a dangerous and manly mission. "Yep. I'll be the best sous-chef she's ever had."

Dad frowns. "I don't think she's ever allowed a sous-chef to be in her kitchen. Taste testers? Yes. But helpers? No."

"Hey! Tabby used to help me all the time."

Mom jumps in. "You said Tabby turned everything into triple the work and kept licking everything, even when she had a runny nose and sore throat."

Dad sits up straighter and points a finger in the air. "I still blame her for giving me the flu and making me miss the Black Friday sale at Home Depot that one time."

I walk over to the sink and start rinsing my dish. "Again, with the Black Friday sale. Dad, they put those wet/dry vacs on sale every single year."

He harrumphs and folds his arms across his chest. "That's completely beside the point. It was fifty percent off that year, sweetie. Fifty!"

Ridge joins me at the sink, handing me both his plate and the ones he confiscated from my mother. His laugh is hearty and comfortable, warming me better than a hot oven with the door open. "I mean, he's not wrong. A man can never have too many wet/dry vacuums."

I wet my fingers and fling water into his handsome face. "Don't you encourage him."

Mom tugs on Dad's arm, pulling him from the table. "C'mon, John. Let's give the kids time to themselves. We can go finish our show. Last night's episode ended at the good part."

Kids...

I don't really think we can be classified as that anymore.

Not at thirty-one and twenty-seven.

When they leave the room, we work to clear the table. Not doing much talking except for Ridge to ask where things go. Once the dishwasher is loaded and the leftovers are stored, Ridge leans against the kitchen island and gives me a wicked smile.

A smile that takes me back. And takes me forward.

"Alright, Little Bird. Take control. Tell me what to do. I'll be a good boy...I'll listen."

Chapter 16

Orah

He does the heavy lifting for me, holding the bowl over the greased 9x13 baking dish, so I can scoop and smooth the chocolate Rice Krispies into their rightful place. Once I garnish them with even more chocolate chips and cut them into squares, they can officially update their name, adding the word 'Treat' to the end.

He wiggles the bowl in my face, using my occupied hands to his advantage, and pretends to rub melted chocolate all over my chin. "Dishwasher or handwash?"

"That can go in the dishwasher, but the saucepan where I melted the stuff together needs to be handwashed."

"Gotcha." He makes his way over to the sink and sets to work while I put the finishing touches on the Rice Krispies.

The past four hours have flown by, and true to his vow, Ridge has been very helpful. We've made several batches of brownies—cheesecake swirl, butterscotch, red velvet, and chocolate truffle. We've done cookies—white chocolate snickerdoodle, peanut butter, and birthday cake. And now, Rice Krispie Treats—both original and chocolate.

Clearly, Momma will once again be the belle of the ball for the monthly birthday celebration. I always offer to make a cake, but everyone seems to love the smorgasbord of treats that remind them of their childhood.

We've laughed and giggled, teased and taunted. We've kept everything light and whimsical, even our conversations. We've talked about books and music and food. And he's even told me some stories about his family and friends.

I push the finished product to the center of the kitchen island, next to the others. "They need to cool a little more before I cut them." I take my place beside him as he rinses the last dish and stacks it in the drying rack. I soap my hands and wash them, carefully scratching away the last bits of sticky marshmallow.

He once again leans against the kitchen island, with his hips cocked against the top of the counter and one leg casually crossed over the other. His old Belly's T-shirt is streaked and stained with all sorts of ingredients, from melted butter to gooey peanut butter. His hair is disheveled, and there's a small streak of flour on his cheekbone.

All in all, I think it's safe to say which image I'll have playing on repeat in my warped mind when my hand slides between my legs tonight.

I suppose I should think about Tristan. Or at least, attempt to. But all I ever think about is *him*.

My Hero.

Thoughts of him are the only thing that calm my overactive brain when it comes to sex. Touching myself doesn't even feel good unless I'm dreaming about him. Our kiss has been the movie of the week for nine years and four months. And no matter how many times the film runs, it never falters. It doesn't skip or freeze. The picture never loses its clarity. It's still as bright and vivid today as it was back then.

I've done my best to explore my sexuality.

But that's been hard to do. After what I went through.

Sex was used as a weapon against me. True, I'm the one who picked up the sword and marched into battle, but it wasn't long before I was disarmed. Levi knew better. He knew what he was doing was wrong. He took what didn't belong to him and ran away from the battlefield, relishing in his victory over the weak. And then, those boys—those vile men—they taunted me over my defeat.

For years, I doubted my decision. I regretted the choice I made, thinking that things could have been different for Tabby if I had just given them what they wanted. That she could've walked out of that theater with her body intact.

But we all know that's a lie.

They stood in the movie theater corridor and offered me a Queen's Gambit. An upfront sacrifice to gain the advantage in the end. But it was a false move. Because they had the upper hand from the start.

And my previous boyfriends have wondered why it's so difficult for me to let go. For me to hug and kiss and touch. For me to give my body to them. Freely. Confidently. And without reservation.

Most of them just think I'm a prude.

In fact, to avoid it, I've told some of them that I'm waiting for marriage. That definitely weeded the garden a few times, plucking out those who were simply too impatient to see the color of my panties.

I'm a grown woman who is afraid of physical intimacy. I've been with two men. Well, not counting Levi, of course. The most meaningful relationship I had was with Breck. He was one of the oil and gas workers on the Slope. The budding romance started when I was twenty.

Ten dates before I let him kiss me.

Five months before I let him touch me.

And eight months before I finally had sex with him. Considering I had a full-blown panic attack right in the middle of intercourse, during our first time together, I fully expected him to walk away and never look back. But he didn't. He stayed with me. He put up with my counting. He tolerated all of my coping mechanisms. He even endured my sleepless nights and thrashing nightmares. Only asking one singular time who Ridge was and why I screamed for him in my slumber. Breck was kind and caring and attentive. In another time, in another universe, I could've loved him.

But how could I?

When my heart belonged to someone else.

We broke up after a year, when I still wouldn't let him remove my shirt and bra. He said he wanted to explore *all* of me, love *all* of me. I suppose a part of him was tired of always making love to a woman wearing a black tank top. He knew I had a scar and wasn't comfortable showing that. But in the end, he said the problem didn't lie with my scarred torso, but with my scarred heart. We ended the relationship as friendly as two people could under circumstances such as that. I wished him happiness and love. And he wished me peace.

So, the million-dollar question is... if I'm terrified of sex, why do I think about it all the time.

Like ALL the time.

Correction: The actual question should be...why do I think about sex with *Ridge* all the time.

True, our kiss may have been the movie of the week for the past nine-plus years. But there's been a whole damn TV series playing too.

And trust me, it's gotten some good reviews.

The episodes are delicious, and the reruns spectacular.

Episode 101: He stands in the shadows of the room pumping his mammoth of a cock. He's been banned to the corner, like the bad boy that he is. His Tiger Eyes absorb me, watching my every move as I slowly undress. And then he crawls to me. He traces his tongue from my ankle and up to the thin pink line above my pubic bone. Up. Up. Up. And finally landing on my thick stapled scar, where he licks the wound he first discovered in the parking lot of a movie theater. He lovingly whispers, "No one is ever taking you from me again."

Episode 310: I'm standing at the kitchen island, mixing cupcake batter. And for once, I'm not dressed in black. I'm wearing a pink skirt with red and orange flowers all over it. I feel pretty and feminine and carefree. He strides into the room with intense purpose. In one fell swoop, he wraps an arm around me from behind, reaches under my skirt, shoves my panties to the side, and pushes his fingers into my core so deep it brings me to my tiptoes. I moan in pleasure and cry out in ecstasy. He circles his free hand around my neck and forces my face to turn sideways. My lips graze his cheek. His bruising erection presses into the small of my back—the contoured curve that he loves so much. And then he growls, "Doesn't Little Bird remember the rules? You look into my eyes when you scream. That's the only way for me to capture your demons."

Episode 619: We're in the middle of the playroom, cleaning up the massive pile of Hot Wheels and Barbie dolls while the kids nap. He's played hard with them all morning long, and I know without a doubt, they're down for the count. Which is a good thing. Not only is this room a disaster, but I have to get started on the order of two-hundred custom cookie sandwiches for the bake shop. I'm bent over, picking up a doll with a mass of tangled hair when he swoops me off my feet. The air rushes through me on a giggle. He tosses me on the couch and drops to his knees. Before I even have time to react, he's dragging me to the edge, dangling my ass off of the cushions. And in less time than it takes for a match to ignite, he has my leggings and panties in a crumpled mess on the floor. He buries his face between my legs, making me tremble and squirm. He devours my pussy like a starved lunatic, biting my clit and tonguing my tunnel. He trimmed his beard just yesterday, and the sharp edges burn the insides of my thighs. And it makes me even wetter knowing that my body will bear his 'stache rash for the next several days. I moan and mewl, letting him know that I'm close. He pulls away, covered from nose to chin in my glistening juices. And then he seethes, "If you think I'm letting that gorgeous pussy come on anything but my cock, you've got another thing coming, Zipporah Smith." He tears off his clothes and climbs onto me. Holding the back of the couch, trying to distribute his weight so I'm not crushed by the heaviness of his muscles, he slams into me. Over and over and over. One of my hands tangles in his hair, and the other slides across his left shoulder. With a punishing grip, I dig my fingernails into the memento left behind from the twenty-five stitches that looked like little black flies. "Who did you say? Zipporah who?" I press my nails farther. If he thinks I'm scared to shed his blood, he's wrong. His laugh is low and gravelly. His heated breath fans across my face and smells like spearmint. "Zipporah Conway. My wife. My everything."

"Why are you staring?"

His voice draws me from my reverie. And that's a real shame too. Because Episode 805 is a real doozie.

I dry my hands and drape the used towel across the sink divider. Obviously, I can't tell him that I'm mind-scrumping him, so instead, I ask a question that's been nagging me. "What happened to your beard? It's," I tug on my black apron, straightening it, "so short, barely there."

He scrubs his palm across his chin. His facial hair is a smidge longer than when I first saw him on Friday, but it's still not a beard. It's still not what decorated his face back in the day. "I shave a couple of times a week. Kimber doesn't like beards. She prefers me to be clean-shaven." He balances his hands behind him, gripping the edge of the countertop. "I would lose my mind if I had to shave every single day, so we compromised."

"So, when are you supposed to shave again?"

He licks his lips and then glances away, studying something on the far side of the kitchen. "It was supposed to be this morning."

He defied her. Defied her edict. Defied her preference. But what does that mean?

"Why are you here, Ridge?"

He turns back to face me, frowning in boyish charm. "What do you mean? I came to help you."

"It's ten o'clock on a Monday night. Why aren't you at home with Kimber? Surely, she's missing you." I hate the way her name tastes on my tongue.

"She's at her house. She worked late and didn't get home until nine." He tosses a look at the red velvet brownies. "It was when we were taking those out of the top oven."

"Y'all don't live together?"

His face is solemn, not really giving me much. "Not technically. She may stay over a night or two a week, but she lives with her father, Chip, in his mansion. Next to the mayor's house."

"And where do you live?" When he names the swanky, remodeled commercial building that's downtown, I'm shocked. "Wow. Really?"

This time his face does give me something...a little twitch of his lip as it fights against a smile. "Why'd you say it like that?"

I traverse the galley between us, walking from the kitchen-sink side of the countertop to the kitchen island. I spin one of the pans—the one with the oldest batch of cereal treats—and touch a corner of it with the underside of a spoon, testing the tackiness. Satisfied with how they're setting up, I grab my knife from the butcher block and start cutting them into squares. "I've been in those condos before. We had a client who lived there. We did his birthday party on the rooftop terrace. He was in the penthouse. Malcom something," I murmur, not quite remembering his last name.

"Yeah. Malcom Garcia. He's my landlord. I'm renting from him."

I freeze in position, taking care not to chop off a finger before looking up at him. "You're in the penthouse loft?"

"Yeah. I moved in at the beginning of November. It was Kimber's idea. It's what she wanted. Before that, I was renting a small apartment on the outskirts of town."

"Oh, okay."

With a laugh, he pushes off from his leaned position and turns around. He mimics me. Grabbing a spoon, he flaps it against the edge of a pan. "What's going through that head of yours, Orah?"

"What?" I squawk, chirping the objection, layering it with innocence and disbelief. "Nothing."

He lifts an amused eyebrow. "Seriously?"

With a grumble, I lower my head and go back to cutting and plating the desserts. "It's just...that's a very elaborate building. Very modern, very sleek, very minimalist." I shift the pan from his hands to mine and start to work on that batch. "And very..."

"Fucking expensive," he adds, filling in my blank.

I chuckle and use my forearm to rub at an itch on my nose. "Well, yeah."

"And that's not the kind of place you pictured me living in?"

"No."

"And where did you picture me?"

I shrug, trying to ignore his question with mere indifference.

"No, c'mon, tell me. I wanna know."

"I don't know. For some reason, I always pictured you in a little country house. Small and cozy, yet beautiful. Something you remodeled yourself. With acreage and a barn that you…" I slow, despising the heated blush that scalds my skin. It instantly makes me hot and churns a gallon of acid in my stomach.

"That I what?"

"Remodeled into this crazy fireman-training thing. Like with equipment for those drills and stuff you like doing."

He falls quiet. And if I didn't feel his presence beside me, if I didn't see the shadow of his body as it lumbers over me, I wouldn't even know he was there. I put the last Rice Krispie on the serving platter and shift my position so I can face him. I cock my left hip against the counter and fold my arms across my chest. He fixates on me, watching my every move with a sincere intensity.

I switch the subject, deciding to protect the fragility of my heart with the reality of our situation. "We need to start touring some of the possible wedding venues. I'll start calling them tomorrow and find out which ones are still available. Some of the places Kimber picked book up five years in advance, so y'all are definitely going to be limited on choices."

He blinks, trying to drag himself back to the appropriate topic. "Five years?" He wrinkles his forehead. "Which venues in town book up that far in advance?"

"In town?" My mouth falls open, and I debate not even telling him the truth. Because, I mean, is it really my place? But then I say fuck it. After all, I'm the wedding planner. Disclosing such information is completely within the purview of my job description. "Ridge, none of the venues are in town. Don't you know that? Kimber wants a destination wedding."

His spine straightens, and his shoulders jerk backward, pulling him into a prim and proper state. A perfect little toy soldier. "A destination? What destination? Where?"

I run through the ticker tape of possibilities. "Charleston, Knoxville, Nashville, Savannah, Palm Beach, and Jupiter Island."

He sucks in a deep breath and then rushes through his sentence, refusing to release his exhale. "Please tell me you're kidding."

Disappointment shrouds me like a curtain, covering me from top to bottom. "She didn't tell you? Y'all didn't discuss it?"

The air heaves from him in an exaggerated fashion. "No. She failed to mention that important detail." He pauses, taking a moment to kickstart his thoughts with his comforting chin tap. "How does she expect Dad to do the food when he won't have access to a kitchen?"

"I can narrow the search to facilities that have on-site commercial kitchens. Destination weddings and events have skyrocketed over the past several years. So, on-site kitchens are more prevalent than you think."

He pins me with a stare. "And you like making your desserts in a strange kitchen? Without the pots and pans and ovens and spatulas that you're used to?"

I must give a look that conveys my true feelings because he just gives a one-huff chuckle. "Yeah, my dad feels the same way." He spreads his hands across the countertop, propping himself up like he's suddenly become too exhausted to function. He drops his head, hanging it low. The movement is slow and non-intentionally sexy, making the muscles pop and flex under the thin fabric of his worn T-shirt. Despite the defeat coursing through his massive frame, he's tight and tense.

And because I'm a glutton for punishment, because I'm unable to keep myself tucked in the reality of my situation, I reach out and place my hand on his back. I nestle my palm in the valley between his shoulder blades. My fingertips trail gently back and forth, across the beads of his spine. Each caress acts as a conduit, sending bolts of electricity from his body to mine, numbing my skin in a sweet, biting pain.

And when he undulates underneath my touch, moved by the power I know that he feels, I nearly collapse on the floor.

"I...I should go," he croaks. "It's getting late."

I can't trust myself to move my hand; so instead, I take a step backward, forcing myself to create distance. As a result, his body is now too far away for me to reach.

I've given him the appropriate space to retreat, to flee.

But he doesn't.

He's locked in the same position, frozen in place at the kitchen island, staring at the swirls in the granite like it holds the answers to all of our quandaries. "When can I see you again?"

"I have available appointments tomorrow afternoon? I should be able to have a list of venue availabilities by then."

He pushes off from the counter and spins to face me. "I report for shift tomorrow morning."

"Your tour is Tuesday morning to Wednesday morning?"

"Yeah, and then I'm going to the technical school to present in some of the health science classes."

"Really?" My moment of awe morphs into a smile. "That's amazing."

"How about Thursday?"

"Thursday?" I squint, trying to mentally picture my calendar. I know I have something, but my mind is filled with *him*, making it hard to focus. Grabbing my phone, I flip through my schedule. "I have a final walk-through and some meetings on Thursday morning. I won't be free until about three."

"Perfect. There's some place I wanna take you. And that timing will work out just great."

"You wanna take me somewhere? But, Ridge, we have to work on wedding stuff."

He tosses his hand in the air. "And we can. Nobody says we can't do both—work stuff and fun stuff."

Nobody says it, huh?

And does that '*nobody*' include the pretentious-as-hell, secret-holding fiancée who wears his engagement ring?

Chapter 17

Orah

"**A** bar?"

Flipping the ignition, he turns and stretches his torso. With a casual confidence, he drapes one wrist over the steering wheel and then balances his other forearm on the console. "Not just any bar." He twiddles his perched fingertips in the direction of the wooden sign. "Will and Cullen's bar."

"*The Last Call*," I read the name out loud.

It's nestled in the middle of a trendy, yet classic downtown block. Red brick. With a large sidewalk that is decorated with a spattering of outdoor tables. There's street parking and then a smaller parking lot around on the right side.

"Yeah. I'm assuming you haven't been here before?"

I shake my head. I'm sure it doesn't take a great deal of intuition for him to know that voluntarily placing myself in a bar is something I do my best to avoid. Noisy. Crowded. And filled with inebriated men. No, thank you.

I'm not like a 'regular girl'; I can't just go out for a Saturday night on the town. I'm not loose and carefree. Those characteristics died with the seventeen-year-old me.

I mean, the amount of planning and mental preparation that it takes for me to effectively navigate the events that I plan, and subsequently have to attend, is embarrassingly mindboggling. I don't really tell anyone about it because I'm scared of what their response may be.

Just get over it. It happened ten years ago.

Why are you still this way? Forget about it, will ya?

Stop playing the woe-is-me card.

"Perfect. I was kinda hoping that was the case." He lifts the ballcap from his head and settles it back down, trying to tame a thick wave that must be aggravating him.

"Why were you hoping that was the case?" I tap the strap of the work bag that's tucked around my feet. "I'm sure Cullen and Will have an amazing bar, but I don't really think it's the appropriate place to conduct business. I mean, we might not even be able to hear each other."

He snorts on a quick, one-grunt chuckle. "It's three-thirty in the afternoon, Bird. Trust me, it's not that wild." He teases me with a wink. "Yet."

He hops out of the truck, and by the time he trots around to my side, I'm already sliding out of the seat. He takes me by the elbow, making sure I don't trip or stumble when my black flats hit the ground. He reaches past me and grabs my work bag. "Purse?" he asks, tossing me a look over his shoulder.

"Yeah. I need my ID, don't I? And I need my card in case I get something to drink."

Instead of grabbing my purse, he slams the door. "You don't need your ID. C knows how old you are." His bare arm grazes against me. "And drinks are on me. Always."

I could protest.

I could object and tell him that he just paid for dinner for me and my parents the other night. I could easily criticize his blanket statement, because there, in fact, may come a time when his future wife doesn't appreciate him buying drinks for another woman.

But why fight it? I know Ridge. Plus, it's not like he has to actually buy me anything pricey; I don't drink alcohol.

The mild winter of the South is back in full force, draping us in the last rays of sunshine before the moon becomes king for the night. I like the way my black shirt absorbs the warmth. Not just from the blazing fireball in the sky, but from the scorch of his fingertips as he guides me toward the front of the bar. I try to pretend the heat is a comforting elixir. A healing tonic. A soothing syrup. One big gulp, one deep swallow, and it will calm the sickly nerves eating away at my stomach lining.

There's a sign hanging next to the door that gives the bar hours, with an asterisk underneath confirming times may vary during football season. As with any tried-and-true bar in Alabama, an eleven a.m. college game warrants an early opening, I'm sure. But what really catches my attention is the white sheet of paper taped right at eye level with a handwritten note on it.

Closed today for inventory from 3 p.m. until 7 p.m. See ya at 7!

I point to the bulletin and do my best to hide my jubilation. "They're closed."

"I know. They're closed for us."

"What?"

He shrugs a shoulder. "Well, not just us, but the whole family."

I open my mouth. A sad little squeak comes out before I chomp it closed.

He wants his entire family to be involved with the planning of his wedding? And we're all meeting at a bar to discuss it?

"They're not really doing inventory. They do that kind of stuff in the mornings. This," he knuckle-taps the paper, "is a second-generation, family drink-talk-laugh-bitch session."

"A what?"

"It's something new that Will has planned. Every few months they'll shut the bar down for a few hours, and all of us can come in and just hang out. Our parents will take turns watching the little ones, and we'll just sit around and laugh and talk and have a good time." He glances at his watch. "Holt just left school, and he's picking up Merit. Raylee, Crutch, and Ella should be here soon. They're finishing up at work."

"And Kimber?"

His plump lips fall into a thin line. "Hopefully, she'll come. I called and left her a voicemail to remind her."

Interesting.

I don't think I'd ever need someone to remind me to spend time with Ridge. Spending time with him is *all* I wanna do. Twenty-four hours a day. For-fucking-ever.

And that, of course, is where the problem lies.

"I figured this could be good for you."

I stab my breastbone with my finger. "Good for me?"

"Yeah." He shifts my bag, giving himself the freedom to drag a palm down his face and tap his chin. One. Two. "I spend a fair amount of time here. Sometimes, I even work the bar when they are short-staffed." He swallows in a loud, almost-comical way. It covers My Hero in a boyish vulnerability. "And they have awesome bands."

"Okaaayyyy…"

"I want you to be comfortable here, Orah. Completely at ease. I want you to feel protected and empowered and safe. I wanna be able to invite you to listen to a band on a Saturday night and know that you won't be sick with worry."

Oh my god…

"I figured I could show you everything. Walk it with you. Show you the layout. All of the exits. Even the hiding places, if you want. And we can turn the radio up really loud so you can feel the vibrations and the echoes. You know, get the sense of what it's really like when it's super crowded with a band playing. Sometimes, the speakers can make the bathroom walls shake and vibrate. I wouldn't want that to scare you. And the bar top is like a giant rectangle, with short sides. It's on the left side of the wall. Because of the counter hatch, there's only two barstools on the short, right-side of the rectangle. If I sit you at either of those, you'll be able to see the front door and watch who's coming and going."

My knees start shaking, riding a tandem wave with my heart. Without even thinking, my left hand flies to my necklace, searching for my black diamonds and Tiger's Eye stone. The precious jewels designed by the even more precious man in front of me. But my fingers can barely move, can barely count my pattern. Because the skin of my wrist—the skin hidden by my watch band—is stinging so badly, so fiercely, it makes my hand shake.

So instead of counting, I clutch the little bird in my fist. I squeeze and squeeze and squeeze, leaning into the ache of my fingers, wondering if I could ever apply enough pressure to actually splinter my bones.

Am I strong enough to do that? Powerful enough? Mighty enough to damage the basic design of the human body? A body that's built to withstand the things our soul can't. A body that's meant to walk and run and bend and twist. All without breaking.

I know that Ridge is. He's strong enough. He's powerful enough. How do I know?

Because he's damaged me...

His featherlight touch has crushed me in its grip.

I'm beyond repair.

Apparently, I only *thought* I was decimated when he chose to let me go. I only *thought* there was nothing left of me to break. Because his tenderness is so gentle, so caring, so compassionate...it's actually violent. Destructive. Savage. His love is a vicious and brutal attack.

"You...you would do that for me?" I stutter.

"I would do anything for you."

For a moment, we stare at one another, absorbing the intensity of that simple sentence. Six words causing an infinity of heartache.

My body starts to buckle. I wobble from side to side. He edges closer. So close I can feel the tips of his shoes as they scuff against mine. His chest presses into my still-fisted left hand. He lowers his head, scattering his whisper across the shell of my ear and down my spine.

"Stand straight. Stand tall. I'm here, Orah. I'm gonna do what I should've done back then. What I promised to do." I close my eyes.

And when he licks his lips, I hold my breath, just so I can hear him better. "I failed you. And I won't let that happen again. I'm fucking furious that those bastards are still taking pieces of your life from you. Ten years later. I won't let them. You hear me? I *refuse* to let them. If I have to walk you through every single building on this side of the Mason-Dixon just so you have calm instead of chaos, that's what I'll do."

"And what happens when I want more than an escort, Ridge? More than a man with a servant heart? More than a trauma partner? What happens when I want more than you can possibly give?"

His voice is low and cracked, shattered like glass. "Then, I'll somehow give more."

"Brother?"

It takes a second for us both to process Holt's presence. And when we do? We separate ourselves by the respectable distance. By the distance that we should've been maintaining, but weren't.

I drop my hand to my waist and plaster a smile on my face, giving a polite greeting to both Holt and Merit.

Merit rushes forward and envelops me in a kind and genuine hug. "Orah! It's so good to see you again." She's wearing purple cropped leggings, multi-colored tennis shoes, and a bright green sweatshirt. The material looks soft and luxurious, and I can't help but notice that both of her store names are printed on the front. She catches me reading it and fans her hand down her breasts and stomach. "Do you like it? We printed some with both store names on it. Kyra, she's my best friend and business partner, designed it. We have all colors. I'd be honored to give you one. My treat. Would that be okay?"

"Oh, you don't have to do that."

Her hair is down today, and when she shakes her head, it dances around her shoulders like a cascading waterfall. "Seriously, it would be my pleasure." She whips to the side and playfully bumps her shoulder against mine. "It's my ploy for free advertising," she quips with a wink.

I can't help but laugh. "Then, yes, I would love to be your walking billboard. Do you have it in black?"

She nods. "Absolutely."

Holt's cautious eye is still darting between Ridge and myself. But he seems to snap out of his unspoken judgment when Ridge loudly clears his throat. Taking that as his cue to engage, Holt leans forward and kisses the apple of my cheek. "Orah, I'd like to formally welcome you to the first inaugural," he curls his fingers into air quotes, "bar inventory." I'm pleased to see the cast and sling are gone from his left arm, and even more pleased that he doesn't seem to be in any pain when moving.

Merit tucks herself against Holt and slides a wandering hand underneath his untucked shirt. "What are we waiting for? Let's go in."

Holt winks at his wife. "Is my baby excited?"

She purses her lips. "Listen here, Holt Hill. You know the stores open on Saturday. Sa—tur—day. As in, the day that's two days away from today. You know I'll be so busy between those and Daire, I'll barely have time to pee. Let alone grab a beer with everybody." She tugs her hand from his shirt and pokes his rib. "I pumped breastmilk for two days to get a surplus so I can have a few beers this evening and not worry about our son growing hungry."

"Or getting buzzed from your boob," he adds.

Giggling, she playfully pushes against him, even though he doesn't budge at all. "Yes, that's right, *sir*."

The way she says 'sir' nearly has *me* wetting my panties.

Ridge rolls his eyes. "Fucking hell, guys. Can't you give it a break for two seconds?"

"Us!?" Holt laughs through his exclamation as he waves a hand between the two of us. "Y'all were the ones..." He fades, and a thick silence engulfs the four of us. Oppressing us. Chaining us to the concrete sidewalk.

I guess the lack of distance between me and Ridge looked even more scandalous than it felt.

All of a sudden, the bar door opens, and Will pokes his head out. "I thought I heard people talking. Are y'all waiting on an engraved invitation or what?"

"Maybe we are," Holt banters back. "And I just so happen to know a great little store where you can order custom-made invitations for just such a thing." He beams a wide smile at his wife.

Will spins on his heels, popping the door in a wide berth so we can follow behind him. "Trust me, I'll be giving my sister-in-law plenty of work. Kyra already said she can design our band posters. Which is good because Cullen sucks at it. He tries to add these humorous and wise proverbs to the ads." He blows a raspberry, basically indicating that Cullen's additions are crap. "And the only person who finds them humorous or wise is C."

As I cross the threshold, my nerves bubble to the surface, making me fidgety and jumpy. Sensing my unease, Ridge reaches for me. The second our fingertips brush, he pulls me into his grasp, melding our palms together by the quick and nimble work of his rough-hewn hands. His hard-earned callouses feel like sandpaper against my delicate flesh.

He sets my work bag down on a table and does a visual sweep of the area. "Speaking of, where is C?"

Will bobs his head. "He's in the back room."

"Sounds good. Y'all start without us. I'm gonna give Orah the tour."

With our hands still firmly clasped, Ridge does exactly as promised. He shows me everything. Literally. No detail is too small. No barstool is overlooked. He even opens the bathroom storage closets to show me the toilet paper.

I can definitely see the appeal of the business and why everyone likes to spend so much of their free time here. The main room is filled with tables and the bar itself. To the right is a large and airy room with a stage for the live music. The bottom half of the main room houses the pool tables with a few secluded booths and the restrooms beyond that. There's an emergency door tucked between the men's and women's bathrooms. Ridge carefully points out that it is locked, preventing anyone from entering via the back alley, and he confirms that an alarm sounds every time it opens from the inside. On the left of the main room is a swinging door that opens to the office and inventory storage.

As soon as he pushes through the door, he presses his tongue against his teeth and lets out a shrill whistle. It actually gives me a fright, and I end up squeezing his hand even tighter. I don't have time to recover before an equally loud whistle comes from underneath one of the cluttered desks.

"What the hell are you doing underneath there?" Ridge asks.

Cullen's reply is muffled and mumbled. It's clear to my eardrums that navigating the small confines of the desk-coffin is not conducive to his size or frame. "An invoice I need is stuck at the back of this desk drawer. I'm having to pull it from the backside." His hand emerges from the abyss, and he works to crawl out. And then he misjudges the distance and knocks his head on the open desk drawer. "Ow! Motherfucker." He finally pounces to his feet. With a scowl on his face, he massages the crown of his head. "I told Will that buying these mammoth desks from the bank foreclosure auction would come back to bite us."

"So, you're blaming your messiness on foreclosure karma?" Ridge spouts a good-humored tease.

"No, I'm blaming it on my big brother. I seem to remember him once betting me that I couldn't sleep all night long on the confetti from the paper shredder." Cullen cocks his head and deadpans, "You really messed with my psyche." He taps the mess of paperwork scattered around. "This is the result."

Ridge's laugh is loud and infectious. "It was more than worth the money." He waggles his eyebrows into his hairline. "He got a papercut on his dick."

I'm in the middle of a snorting giggle when Cullen snarls, "I *had* to sleep naked. Nudity was double the money."

They spend the next few seconds jarring back and forth about the voracity of the bet, and I take time to look around the room. There's shelves and boxes filled with liquor on the right, and on the left is a massive, walk-in, refrigerated room with beer and kegs. There's a desk next to Cullen's, and that one is equally disheveled. I can only assume it belongs to Will. So, unless Ridge paid money for Will to strip down naked and wallow in hamster cage clippings, I think messy is just the name of the game for both of the business owners.

"Okay, enough of this foolishness. Let's head out." Cullen skirts the desk and walks out past us.

"We'll be there in a minute." As soon as we're back alone, Ridge points to the see-through fridge doors. "The sides of the fridge that you can't see are galvanized steel. It'll definitely provide some level of protection if something were to happen. And there's enough kegs and beer cases in there for a person to hide easily." He peeks around me and points to the bottom liquor shelf. "Extra jackets and sweatshirts are there," he says matter-of-factly, like pointing out hiding places and planning escape routes is a normal activity for couples.

Except we're not normal.

And we're not a couple.

Despite the weirdness of this tour, it's given me a level of comfort that's usually not present the first time I visit an unfamiliar public place. After all this time, Ridge is still giving, supplying me with unspoken love. Time and distance have not diminished the generosity of his heart. In all honesty, his selflessness has done nothing but grow. It's multiplied. It's expanded. Exponentially.

Unable to stop myself, I take a step closer and fold our joined hands against the crest of my breastbone. His knuckles graze my necklace. His forearm nestles in between the mounds of my breasts. Looking down, I watch in fascination as his muscles and tendons flex, jumping with nervous energy.

What I wouldn't give for him to slide his hand across my chest.

One. Small. Inch.

That's all it would take.

One small inch left or right.

And then he could slide his fingertips around my sensitive skin. Tweak my nipples. Caress my flesh. He could make me moan and cry. Make my back arch. Satisfy the ache that's been plaguing my body for nearly a fucking decade.

"Thank you." My whispered gratitude is soft and thick. It's a puffy white cloud filling the horizon.

His Tiger Eyes widen. His pupils dilate, eating away at the stolen gem. And then, with a simple nod, he pulls away, separating our hands, separating our bodies. "Yeah, of course." He tosses a hand in the air. "We should probably head out there."

We make our way from the back room and to the front of the bar, where—just as promised—he offers me a barstool on the right side, giving me an unobstructed view of the front door. Crutch, Ella, and Raylee make their appearance as I'm sitting down. They take the empty seats between us and where Holt and Merit sat down.

Cullen sets a string of fresh, cold beers in front of Holt, Merit, and Crutch. Will's working on some kind of drink for Raylee, filling a cocktail glass with some kind of soda and liquor mix. Ridge nudges my elbow with his own. "What do you wanna drink? Beer? Wine? Mixed drink?"

"Oh, she doesn't drink alcohol," Cullen blurts out, not giving me a chance to answer. And unfortunately, his confident and cavalier manner does nothing but raise suspicion for the quick-assessing firefighter.

Ridge's forehead wrinkles into furrowed rows of confusion. "What? How do you know that?"

Cullen's pouring some kind of thick dark beer from a tap. His attention is solely focused on the glass in front of him as he flicks his wrist ever so slightly, whipping foam from the top of the frothy drink into the drip tray. "From our date."

Oh no.

In less than a nanosecond, Ridge's perplexity morphs into something dangerous and sinister. Two emotions that I've only associated with him a small handful of times. And each of those times were the result of him wanting to bash someone's face into the pavement for hurting me, for taking advantage of me, for using me in ways that he never wanted anyone to use me. His shoulders roll, his back tightens, and his jaw clenches. The shift in his demeanor is so noticeable, so intense, that everyone immediately stops what they're doing and turns to stare at him. The collective of the Hill, Crutchfield, and Conway families are enthralled by the transformation, equally stunned and worried.

Including his own goofy, clueless, and sexy brother.

Ridge's beautiful eyes narrow into slits, with his gaze darting between Cullen and myself. Eventually, he pushes from his barstool. One foot props on the footrest running the length of the bar, and the other stomps against the hardwood floor. The noise bursts through my eardrum like a sonic boom. He leans across the bar top and points a finger at Cullen. "You're fucking dating her?!"

Cullen's cheeks pink. He slowly and cautiously sets the full beer on the counter. "It's not like that. We—"

Ridge interrupts, not giving him a chance to explain our one and only date. "You son of a bitch! How could you? You know what she means to me." His verbal assault slams against Cullen with a ferocious and uncontained momentum. Like a runaway tractor trailer careening down the steep mountainside road, he can't control himself. He can't stop. "She's. Mine."

Ella breaks into the melee, commanding the room with her calm, sophisticated, and honey-coated voice. "But she's not yours, Ridge. Because *you're* not *hers*."

My heart turns to stone and drops low in my stomach. His vibrating body freezes in position as he forces his brain to absorb the truth of Ella's proclamation. And for me, it's the most painful truth to ever exist.

And then, just because destiny is a vindictive bitch, his cell phone starts to ring. My eyes flicker down to where the vile device shines bright with a picture of Kimber's face.

There you have it…

He just decreed that I belong to him. And to celebrate his announcement, his fiancée is calling.

"Excuse me." He mutters in contrition, shrouded in pain and shame. Grabbing his cell, he strides away and disappears through the swinging doors of the back room. His every step is burdened and heavy, bogged down with the weight of the world.

If he loves her so much, why is he suffering? Why is he tortured? If she's his one and only, why is he fighting to keep me?

Is it simple nostalgia and friendship? Or is it something more?

For me, for my heart, there's no question that it's definitely more. It feels like my world is finally spinning on its axis again. After being suspended in a perpetual state of darkness and zero gravity, I'm basking in the light. I'm grounded and stable, walking with a steady foot in the warmth of the sun.

Raylee slurps on her drink. "Soooooo, you two went on a date, huh?"

Cullen heaves a sigh. "It was years ago. Before Orah left town." He leans across the bar and gives my hand a gentle squeeze. "I'm sorry. I wasn't even thinking. I didn't mean to blurt that out." He slides his hand back to his side and takes a hearty gulp of his beer. "I've been meaning to talk to Ridge about it. It's completely my fault. I should've told him before now."

"It's not your fault. You have nothing to apologize for."

Merit taps her fingers against the bar like a crawling spider. "That was pretty intense." She cocks her head in thought. "Are you mad at him? For the way he reacted?"

Instead of immediately commenting—or deflecting—I look around at the sea of faces. I study this close-knit group of family and friends. Their love and fondness and protectiveness for one another is clearly evident. It's etched across their souls like an easy-to-read instruction manual. Plain, straightforward, and without pomp and circumstance.

Step 1. Be Our Friend.

Step 2. Always Show Up.

Step 3. Love Unconditionally.

My desire to be honest and real and raw with them has taken me by surprise. Typically, I do everything I can to avoid new friendships. Because true friendships mean letting your guard down. And it never fails that when I let my guard down, the past comes back to haunt me. The ghosts and devils and demons come out swinging, wanting to make me scream and cower and run in fear.

But none of their faces contain the judgment and disgust that terrify me.

I see nothing but genuine kindness and concern. And that can be the only plausible reason for why I say what I say. "All I've wanted for the past ten years is to be his. So, how can I be mad at him for saying the things that I want to be true?"

I can feel what you feel.

Our axiom, our verity, our motto.

But what I really want from him is...I *feel* what you *feel.*

Because when I take out that one little word—that pesky, miniscule, three letter 'can'—the truth spawns a whole new reality.

And that reality gives me a Hero.

A lover.

A husband.

That reality gives me Ridge.

Chapter 18

Ridge

"That was really fun. I'm sorry that Kimber couldn't make it."

Even if I couldn't see the silhouette of her gorgeous face—and see the sincerity engraved into it—I would hear it.

I'm not stupid. It doesn't take a rocket scientist to know that Orah's not exactly fond of Kimber. And who the hell can blame her? Kimber hasn't exactly been presenting her best and most friendly face as of late.

I feel like I've barely seen her. She's driven by success, obsessed with the challenge of making her family's string of dealerships the very best in every single market. And I don't begrudge her of that. I swear, I don't. I love a woman who wants to work hard and provide for herself. It's one of the reasons I was first attracted to Kimber.

But...it does get frustrating.

In fact, sometimes, I wonder if she even *likes* spending time with me.

She promised she would come hang out with us today. She literally took my hand in hers, looked me in the eyes, and told me she would be there. And when she called to tell me she couldn't make it, that the dealership outside of Atlanta had an 'emergency' and needed her to swoop in to save the day, I knew it was all a lie. Oh, she was in Atlanta all right, but she actually left for Atlanta first thing this morning. She knew she wouldn't even be in the same state as me come four o'clock, let alone sitting beside me on a barstool.

How in the world does she expect my family to fall in love with her when she never spends any time with them?

I flick my blinker, taking a left turn onto the roads that lead back to Wexler Events. "I had a great time too."

"After you calmed down, you did."

There it is.

She's finally calling out my asshole behavior.

When I finally emerged from the back room, after my not-quite-pleasant phone call with Kimber, everyone chose to blissfully ignore my ignorant and fucked-up behavior. We talked and laughed and joked like nothing was wrong. Like I wasn't a complete Neanderthal idiot.

And they weren't the only ones sticking their heads in the sand, selectively disregarding the ten seconds before my phone rang. I buried my head so far deep, I was waiting on the lava of Hell to singe my sideburns.

I. Had. To. Hide.

I. Had. To. Forget.

Because if I didn't? There was a very high probability of me sliding across the top of the bar and pummeling my baby brother's face into a Jackson Pollock design of blood and teeth.

How could he do this to me? I love the kid. More than my own life. And here he is, dating My Brave Girl. My Little Bird.

My...

Well, you know what she is.

I'm not even sure there's a word for how livid I am. Let's just say that after I drop her off, I'm heading to the gym, taping a picture of C to the punching bag, and going at it. And I don't plan on leaving until I have carpal tunnel and bruised knuckles.

Has he held her hand? Kissed her? Touched her?

My grip tightens on the steering wheel. My forearms twitch with the pressure.

"Heroes don't look good without any teeth."

It takes me longer than normal to process her nonsensical observation. "Huh?"

"You're clenching your jaw so tight, you're about two seconds away from your teeth exploding into little white clouds of enamel." She balls her fists together and then balloons them out. "Poof."

I open my mouth and work my jaw back and forth. "Haha."

She stills, waiting for me to add more to my limited response. But what more can I say? I'm irrationally jealous. And rationally envious. Because what man in his right mind wouldn't want to be with Orah. She's the epitome of beauty inside and out. Strong. Resilient. And utterly remarkable.

Unhappy with my silence, she purses her lips and tries a different approach, an approach she knows without a doubt that I won't ignore. "My turn."

I pull my right hand from the steering wheel and shake it out, trying to loosen my body in preparation for the conversation that I don't wanna have. "Your turn, huh?"

"Yep." Her left forearm slides across the console, and I'm inexplicably drawn to the delicate lines of her wrist. When she sees me eyeing her watch, she tugs it down just a smidge, fiddling with it until it's in just the perfect spot. "So, what was that about? Why didn't you give Cullen a chance to explain?"

I focus on the road, pretending that the dark skies, headlights, and stop signs are the only thing of importance. "You know why."

"Do I?" With a sigh, she lets her head fall back against the headrest. "Sometimes, I think I know every single thing about you, Ridge. Your feelings, your thoughts, your hopes, your dreams. It's like we were one big picture that got sawed into tiny little jigsaw pieces and now we've been snapped back in place. And I can finally see the image that didn't make any sense when it was broken."

"And other times?"

"Other times, I feel like I'm looking at a stranger. I'm dealing with a man who thinks and acts completely different from the way he should, from the way I *want* him to."

My tongue is thick in my mouth, making it hard to speak. "And how do you *want* me to act."

"You know how," she retorts, slapping me with a comeback similar to my own.

"Orah…"

"So, I'll ask again. What was that about? Why did you act like that?"

"Because I don't want my brother to date you." It feels like the brim of my ballcap is about to snap through my brain, like a pile of rubber bands belted around a watermelon. I yank the hat from my head and toss it onto the backseat. "Fuck, I don't want anyone to date you."

"You realize how crazy that sounds, right?" Instead of fueling her tone with embittered sarcasm—the way Kimber most certainly would—her voice is soft and sweet, powered by nectar and honey.

"Oh, I'm fully aware."

"You're getting married. And you're upset about the idea of me dating someone?"

"Yes."

"But why?"

"Because for ten years, you've belonged to no one but me. Yes, we parted ways. We said goodbye, we didn't see each other, we didn't talk; but that didn't matter. There's not been a single second of a single minute when you've not walked beside me. You became a part of my soul the very moment that door closed and you said you could help me." My heart rages in my chest, and an unbearable pain races down my ribs and gathers in the pit of my stomach. "You've been helping me, Zipporah Smith. Every single day. You just didn't know it."

She waits, giving me her signature five seconds to think about how demented my feelings are. "You're about to walk down the aisle and commit to spending the rest of your life with Kimber-Shay."

I bite the inside of my cheek. Hard. Forcing myself to focus on the love I have for Kimber. Because I refuse to dwell on that small, nagging sentiment that I rushed into things. That I made the wrong decision. That what I feel, that what drew me to her in the first place, isn't love at all, but just a covetous longing for a wife, for a family, for a companion. "I already committed to her. There's no changing that, no going back."

"Then stop fighting it. Forfeit the tug-of-war. Drop the rope."

My eyes flash to hers, wishing I could see the storm clouds circling within. But alas, it's too dark, and I'm met with nothing but black circles.

Drop the rope.

But it's not that easy.

Not when the rope is wrapped around your heart instead of your hands.

We spend the next few minutes in silence. I make the turn into the Wexler parking lot and pull up next to her car. I turn off the ignition, but neither of us make a move to get out. And despite the heaviness engulfing us, I'm still comforted by the fact that she's sitting beside me. There's something about her presence that calms the part of me that's been rampaging for the past decade. My soul's been screaming, protesting, fighting, and I was too numb to even realize it.

She sighs. "It was only one date. And it was over four-and-a-half years ago."

I offer a weak concession. "You don't have to—"

"Don't I?"

Of course, I'm a shithead and can't even grace that with a response.

"It was the summer after I moved here. Cullen and I had already worked a couple of events together, and he asked me out. We went to dinner and then took a walk down by the river. We spent the night talking. That's how I knew that your dad was a restaurant manager. And that your parents are only children, without brothers and sisters of their own. And that his brother, aka *you*, worked for the National Park Service." She looks out the window, and the streetlamp gives just enough light for me to see the feminine curve of her jaw and the slender lines of her neck. "It didn't take us long to realize that we were meant to be nothing more than friends. Cullen is stunningly handsome, very attractive. But I wasn't attracted *to him*. And he felt the same way. He said there was something about me, that he looked at me more like a little sister."

She turns, pinning me in place with the weight of her darkened features and the sultry timbre of her testimony. "No touching. No kissing. No nothing." The inhale of her breath sends a wave of heat throughout my body.

And my cock responds.

Painfully.

Further cementing the fact that I'm a dickwad of epic proportions.

"N—nothing?" I stutter.

"No, Hero. Nothing happened between me and your brother."

Shit. Why does that relief feel so good.

Of course, that's short-lived. Because she folds her arms across her ample chest and verbally attacks me below the belt, metaphorically slicing my still-erect dick in two. Where it promptly bounces off the floorboard of my truck and shatters into a million pieces. "But I *am* dating someone." The stealthy, little phallus ninja strikes me with her horrid truth. "Tristan Hardwick."

My vision blurs, and it feels like fireworks are exploding inside of my skull. "Excuse me?"

"I'm dating Tristan Hardwick."

"You're dating? Tristan Hardwick? The fucking douche from the furniture store?!"

She frowns. And if I weren't about to spontaneously combust, I'd find it cute. "He's not a douche. He's...nice."

I scratch my hand down my face and tap my chin. One. Two.

Oh hell, I need it again.

I tap that shit another two times for good measure.

"Orah, he's a complete asshole."

She flaps her hands in the air and then slaps them on her thighs. "He's not an asshole. He's...he's a real gentleman."

Oh, that's rich. I drape an arm across the center console, crowding her space. And ignoring the intoxication of her coconut-scented, raven hair when she flips her ponytail behind her shoulder. "No, he's not. I've had to deal with him on more than one occasion. And I'm pretty sure Wikipedia paid for his picture to be included under the definition of anal leakage."

I can feel her rolling her eyes. "Anal leakage isn't in Wikipedia."

"Wanna bet."

"Ridge..." she warns.

"I'm not joking." I tick a finger in the air. "I responded to a call where an elderly man fell down the steps at his store. His handrail was broken, and when the guy went to grab it...boom! The guy broke his freakin' leg. And in the middle of triage, Tristan tried to bribe the poor guy with a thousand dollars and asked him to sign a non-disclosure agreement." I hold up a second finger. "And Kimber invited him to the dealership's New Year's Eve party. He came with Penelope Meyers, and by midnight, he was making out with Neecee Jones."

"Oh, you mean, the New Year's Eve party where you put a ring on Kimber's finger? Is that the one you're talking about?"

Ouch.

I bypass that comment and ask another question. "How long have y'all been dating? Is it serious?"

She fists her hands together in her lap. "We're going out tomorrow night. It'll be our fourth date."

"Just your fourth date?"

"Yeah."

"Good. So, it's not that serious."

"I didn't say that." Her whisper slinks across the interior of the vehicle, piercing the armor that I like to pretend protects me.

"So, what *are* you saying?"

Her hand meanders up her chest and possessively seizes her necklace. She shifts in the seat, and when her face catches the dim rays of light and shows me the tears cascading down her cheeks, I want nothing more than to pull her into my arms. I wanna drag her across the console and settle her on my lap. And hold her until everyone else disappears. Until it's just us. Me and her. And a world of endless possibilities. "I'm saying…I'm tired of screaming out for someone who will never answer."

My throat closes, and my lungs constrict. My body revolts against oxygen, refusing to partake of the one thing needed to keep me alive. "You…you still have nightmares? You still call out for me?"

"I didn't say that," she repeats.

"So, what *are* you saying?" Just like her, I parrot back my earlier words.

Sniffling, she reaches down and grabs her work bag and her purse. Before I can process what's happening, she's pulling on the door handle. "I'm saying that I put us on the schedule to tour the Knoxville venue next Friday evening at three p.m. Your shift will end at seven that morning, and it's a five-hour drive, with a one-hour time change. I can cancel if you want, but she told me that six other couples are scheduled to tour within the next two weeks and all of them are looking to book for November and December events." She hops out of the truck and turns around. "Considering you squashed Palm Beach and Jupiter Island, and considering Nashville and Charleston are not available, we are down to two—Knoxville and Savannah. As your wedding planner, it's my recommendation that both you and your fiancée keep this appointment. After all, we're talking about the most important day of your life." She slams the door and climbs into her own car.

And when she drives away, I'm still sitting like a dumbfounded moron, frozen in position.

The most important day of my life…

Well, that already happened.

Chapter 19

Ridge

I shuffle through the display of cars that cost more than most people's homes. My boots resonate on the marble, contrasting with the noises around me—classical music piped through surround-sound speakers, hushed conversations about horsepower and Nappa leather, and puckered assholes greasing themselves open to shit mountains of hundred-dollar bills all over the floor.

Well, perhaps, I'm being dramatic.

But that's what it feels like.

Biting back my sarcasm, I politely nod to a group of salesmen huddled in the corner of the showroom and round the corner to head into Kimber's office. She's sitting behind her desk. Chip is leaned back in one of the chairs opposite of her. "Ahh, there's my favorite son-in-law." He cackles at what's become his go-to joke. Bending down, I shake his hand. "I hear you're whisking my daughter away."

I tug my T-shirt away from my sweaty skin. The weather matches my mood. Hot, unstable, and indecisive. This Yellowhammer winter day is masquerading as spring, giving us a prime recipe for thunderstorms, and even a tornado or two. I offered to stay in town in case I was needed for an emergency shift, but the latest forecast has the bad weather hitting northwest of us, so the Chief dismissed me. And with the timing of our little voyage to the Volunteer State, we should miss the rain both coming and going. "Well, unless she's wanting to get married here, in town—which would be totally fine with me—she's gotta pick a venue before everything gets snatched up."

Kimber glances up from her laptop and gifts me with a brilliant smile. "Babe, you know how all those places work. They say they're completely booked, but when you flash a little extra green their way," she waves a manicured hand through the air, "suddenly, they become available."

"Well, Amy's done her research, and I think you better play it safe." I lean back against the wall, secretly congratulating myself for continuing to remember to use the name 'Amy' around Kimber. "If you don't like this Knoxville place, we'll have to tour Savannah sometime next week."

"I can't do next week. We're flying to New York City to shop for my wedding dress."

An irritating muscle spasm contracts low in my back, propelling me forward from my lazy position. "You're doing what?"

"Dress shopping. In New York City." Shaking her head, she furrows her brow and returns her attention back to her computer screen. "I told you about it."

"You most certainly did not."

An almost imperceptible pink blush rises to her cheekbones.

And there you have it. She damn well knows she didn't mention dress shopping in New York City.

"Well, I can't very well be expected to find a dress here. Or even in Atlanta. I need something that's gonna blow everyone's minds."

"And you have to travel one-thousand miles to find that dress?"

She shuts the laptop and scoots back in her leather wingback, finally giving me her undivided attention. "Ridge, how can you still be so naïve? People may forget a bad filet mignon, but they won't forget a bad wedding dress. My dress has to be perfect. It has to be the star of the show."

"But it's not a show, Kimber. It's the first day of our marriage."

Chip dramatically pushes up from his chair, moaning and groaning, acting like he left the nursing home this morning instead of the men's spa. Of course, maybe the moaning and groaning isn't an act. I did have the misfortune of overhearing Kimber say he was having laser hair removal done on his scrot, taint, and ass. "Oh, you know how these women are. Just let them do their thing. As long as it keeps them happy and out of our way."

Out of our way?

But I don't want a wife who's *out* of my way. I want a wife who's *all up in* my way.

Kimber grabs her purse and picks up her ever-present cell phone. "I don't know what the big deal is, Ridge? It's just five days. I'll leave on Thursday night and be back on Tuesday night."

"You need five days of shopping to find a dress?"

Rounding her desk, she leans in and scrapes her fingernails up my neck and into my hair. She purrs against the shell of my ear, "You have so much to learn about women." And then, for good measure, she grinds her tits and pelvis against me. Considering we haven't had sex in weeks—not since five days before Orah came back into my life—I guess, that's her way of throwing me a bone.

She spins around to Chip and air-kisses his cheek. "We're driving back tonight. Try not to send the company into bankruptcy before then." Her laugh tinkles through the air on gold fairy dust as she walks out, with me following closely behind her.

The drive across town to pick up Orah is pleasant enough. We chitchat about Kimber's early morning and how proud I am of her for agreeing to leave right after her seven-thirty a.m. sales meeting. Of course, she does get one small dig in...she sweeps her finger across the dashboard of the truck and talks about it needing a wash.

Kimber wanted to 'borrow' a dealer car for the drive. Apparently, she thinks pulling up to the venue in a teeny-tiny sports car will give the right illusion to the venue hosts. I quickly nipped that in the bud. Where did she expect Orah to sit? In the trunk? And there's no way in hell that I would ask Orah to drive five hours by herself on her dime to a place that Kimber will most likely turn down anyway. I know without a doubt that she still has her eyes on Jupiter Island. I might've told Kimber that rats would have to grow twelve-foot dicks and fuck elephants before I would force my family, with all of our little kids, to travel eleven-and-a-half hours to a wedding destination. And during holiday season, no less.

I guess I could've just used the old adage of 'when pigs fly', but I was feeling extra poetic that day.

Orah's standing on the sidewalk in front of Wexler Events when we pull up. I offered to pick her up at home, but she politely declined.

We've talked and texted a handful of times since last Thursday night. She wanted to be mad at me; I know she did. Hell, I deserved to be in the doghouse. My obvious jealousy did nothing but blur the lines of our re-emerging friendship. So, I wasn't necessarily surprised when I texted her Saturday morning after my shift, and she waited five full hours before texting me back.

Five. Full. Hours.

Three-hundred minutes.

Eighteen-thousand seconds.

I even called John, who I was surprised to learn still has the same phone number as well. I pretended that I needed to ask him a question about changing the oil in my truck. Of course, I know the man's not stupid. He knows I know how to change the oil in my truck. And even if I didn't, I have my own father to ask. But, like the humble man that he is, he politely answered my generic, dumbass question, and then didn't bat an eye when I asked if Orah was busy working at an event. He confirmed that she was home. Which made me growl in frustration.

And hey, he's the one who first started talking about what a douche nozzle Tristan is.

Well, I *think* John started talking about it.

I mean, I was still tired from work. I guess there's a small possibility that I brought it up. But that's completely beside the point.

Because the point is...John doesn't like him either.

I jump out of the truck and race around to open the back passenger-side door for her. I'm excited to set my eyes on her after not seeing her for an entire week. I wanted to see her—to get together, to hang out—but she's had a busy week with events and meetings.

I rake my eyes across her body, eagerly adding new memories of her beauty to my mental filing cabinet. She's gone a little wild today because her black blouse has short sleeves, with little ruffles feathering around the tops of her shoulders. But these ruffles have dark gray polka dots on them. I know it's still dark, but I count that as a win. She's wearing black pants that end just above her ankles and black loafers with little tassels on them. Her raven hair is twisted back in one of those clip thingies. But of course, what really looks good is her necklace—*our* necklace—nestled between the delicate lines of her collarbone.

I grab the work bag from her shoulder and lean across the backseat, setting it on the floorboard. Then, I offer my hand. And when she slides her fingers against mine, she lifts her chin in the air, giving me a refreshing dose of her bravery. She opens her mouth to speak, and then...

Kimber's cell phone shrills to life. The noise is so jarring and unwelcome, that even the winter bird perched on the end of the Wexler Events sign squawks and flies away. Without hesitation, she answers and starts prattling in conversation.

My jaw clenches, clamping my teeth together in a tight grip. I can feel the jump of my muscles underneath my skin. Twitch, twitch, twitch. It's like ants are marching in a parade up and down the side of my face.

Orah cocks her head, studying me, absorbing me with the same intensity that I just used on her. With her free hand she reaches up and traces her black-painted fingernails across my much-longer-than-normal facial hair. Her touch relaxes my tightened jaw, and a heated shiver races across my chin and down the back of my throat. "You still haven't shaved. A few more days, and it'll look just like it did back then."

When her wandering fingers drop, I chuckle, pretending her comment is light and carefree. When it's anything but. Because we both know that my fiancée doesn't like it. Yet, that hasn't stopped me from growing it. I reach my own free hand up and scrub my cheek. "I guess I always liked the feel of a beard."

"I liked it too."

Clearing my throat, I ignore the visions conjured by that one simple statement. Visions of the one singular kiss that both invades me and evades me. "We better get on the road."

With a soft smile, she settles into the truck, and we start the drive to Knoxville.

As I pull onto the interstate, I realize that somewhere along the way, I've become the punchline of my own joke.

A hero, a little bird, and a princess walk into a bar...

And who the fuck walks out?

Chapter 20

Orah

"So, why'd you move away?"

Torture.

I'm four-and-a-half hours into a torture session that even the most well-trained operatives couldn't survive.

Let's just say I've had to count my numbers so many times, that I've started doing them in different languages.

Uno. Dos. Tres. Cuatro. Cinco.

Un. Deux. Trois. Quatre. Cinq.

Ein. Zwei. Drei. Vier. Fünf.

The loud and obnoxious phone conversations. Where she dishes out distasteful and hateful comments like she's serving mac and cheese at an all-you-can-eat buffet.

The more-than-blatant, and obviously meant-for-my-eyes, possessive touches. She's grabbed Ridge's bicep and squeezed his thigh so many times, I'm surprised he doesn't have a heat rash.

And then, there's the decisions about some of the wedding stuff.

Now that she's trapped in a car with me, I've been able to show her some more precise options, based on availability and assuming she chooses this Tennessee venue for her nuptials. As with most large venues, the hosts won't allow just anybody onto the premises; the vendors have to be vetted, with an impeccable reputation. And trust me, trying to convince them that *The Elegant Taste*, an out-of-state company, is more than capable of catering the event and providing all of the necessary liability insurance came as no easy task.

In every category, I have options that I know, without a doubt, that Ridge would like. Items that are simple, yet meaningful. And each and every time, she's disregarding those almost immediately and flocking to the things that are elaborate and ornate. And super expensive.

I honestly have no idea how the two of them are in a relationship. Half the time I don't even think Kimber likes Ridge, let alone loves him. You know the adage 'two halves make a whole'? Well, in this case, it's more like two halves make a clusterfuck.

"Amy?" Kimber's screech irritates my tender eardrums.

"Pardon?"

"You worked for Wexler for a while, moved away, and then came back. What made you move away? I can't imagine it was job related. Margo is just phenomenal. The way she's been able to mold her company into something that even the big cities don't have? It's just amazing. I can't believe anyone would willingly leave her. She's just a peach."

I don't think anyone who actually knows Margo would describe her as a sweetly, ripened piece of fruit. Margo only wants one thing out of life—to win.

"I moved back to my hometown in South Carolina to help care for a sick family member."

Ridge glances at me through the rearview mirror. His Tiger Eyes are layered with concern. "I totally forgot about that. Cullen mentioned something about a family illness. Who was sick?" Even as he's asking the question, his brow furrows together, replaying our conversations over the past two weeks of who I *have* and *haven't* talked about. Being the smart man that he is, he instantly figures it out. His face falls into a frown, and his whisper is heavy. "Your grandmother."

"Yeah." Emotion clogs my throat, making it hard to swallow. I reach underneath my necklace and massage the area. I press my fingertips deep into my skin, wincing when I feel the rungs of my trachea.

"What happened, Lit—" He cuts himself off. Tossing a look at Kimber, he replaces my cherished nickname with the name that still means nothing to me. "What happened, Amy?"

My wandering hand meanders lower, dipping into the neckline of my shirt. I find the small scar from the decompression needle that he used to save my life. I take a deep breath, focusing on how the air fills my healed lungs. And when I exhale, I remove my hand and fold it in my lap. "Metastatic metaplastic breast cancer. She was diagnosed when I was twenty-four, right after Thanksgiving. I moved in with her that January."

"Into her house?"

"Yeah. Mom and Dad were both working. Boaz and Tabby were newlyweds, building their life together and working their jobs. I was the only one without any ties. I moved in with her. Took her to treatments. Spent time with her. Kept the house in order."

Kimber, who's pecking around on her phone, decides that the world can't keep rotating around the sun unless she pipes in with her two cents. "Oh my gosh, that's so tragic. I can't believe you had to give up your career like that. I hope those people appreciated it."

Ridge's jaw drops open. Literally.

And me? I'm instantly filled with anger and disgust. And I'm about one second away from ripping her thousand-dollar extensions from the high-lighted and low-lighted perfection known as her hair.

He pops his neck and tightens his grip on the steering wheel. "Kimber, that's fuc—"

I interrupt him, wanting to stand up for myself, wanting to be the brave girl that he sees when he looks at me. "*Those people* are my family. There's nothing I wouldn't do for them. And I didn't give up anything. Not one single thing." My fingers twitch, eagerly reaching for a light brown, impeccably coiffed beach wave. I shove my palms underneath my thighs, forcing myself to temper my wrath. "I got to spend time with my granny, soaking in her love and life lessons. Not only that, but I ran a small, neighborhood baking business during those years. For hours and hours, she would sit with me, keeping me company in the kitchen. We talked and laughed and ate more raw cookie dough than humanly possible. There's nothing about that time that I would trade."

Despite the horrors of it all, my declaration is true. I gave my all to her, and I will never, ever regret it. I cried with her, held her hand, cleaned her body when she was too weak to lift a finger. I massaged her muscles when she was achy and sore. And then stopped massaging her muscles when she was in so much pain that even the bedsheet touching her skin was excruciating. I said my goodbyes, I listened to her death rattle, and I kissed her lips after the last earthly breath exhaled from her lungs.

But I also laughed so hard I peed my pants when we dressed like Sonny and Cher for Halloween. And when we walked the elevated trails of the Congaree and I told her that I was terrified my love for Ridge would never stop, she hugged me and told me that some loves were never meant to die. And when I was scared out of my mind to create new life, to give all of myself to something that could never be mine, she comforted me and told me to follow my heart.

So, no, I don't regret my years with her.

But that doesn't mean that I'm happy she got cancer.

I hate that this vile and disgusting disease invaded her body. That it fed off her organs and bones and tissue like the deplorable parasite that it is. Cancer is a thief. It's tricky and cunning, indecisive and indiscriminate. Its patterns are erratic and arbitrary, yet delivered with a pinpoint accuracy, determined to complete its warped mission of destruction, no matter the cost. It's a violence wrought by an invisible perpetrator. There's no offender to arrest, no criminal to prosecute, no felon to punish.

At least my bad guys are dead and in the dirt.

Granny's particular bad guy, however, is still wreaking havoc, decimating innocents at the rate of over six-thousand women worldwide every single day.

Ridge angles his body. Keeping his eyes on the road, he slides his right arm into the backseat and gives my knee a squeeze. "I'm so sorry." His eyes flicker to the rearview again. "When did she..."

"Last February."

Kimber finally looks away from her screen, and when she sees Ridge's arm lingering on my leg, she arches an eyebrow. His fingers curl into a fist, and he quickly releases his hold on me, posting his hands at ten and two. He darts his tongue across his lips. "So, the one-year mark is..."

"Yeah, it's coming up at the end of this month."

Realizing this is the perfect opportunity to assert her dominance, she anchors a hand to Ridge's upper thigh. Her French-tip nails are precariously close to the bulge in his jeans, and he discreetly reaches down and pushes her hand a little farther south, into PG territory. The silent reprimand doesn't seem to faze her. "So, why'd you move back to Alabama?"

"I wasn't planning to, but my parents pushed me to reach back out to Margo. Frankly, I was shocked when she offered me my old job. I wasn't even going to accept it, but my parents encouraged me to give it another try."

She snickers. "What a twisted turn of fate." She lifts her hand in the air and wiggles her fingers back and forth, forcing the sunlight to play against the prisms of her diamond. "Now, you get to be a part of the best wedding ever."

Yeah. Lucky me.

Fortunately, I'm saved from responding because Ridge flicks his blinker, taking the exit offramp. We arrive at the venue with only ten minutes to spare. I'm glad the weather is better up here than it was back at home. The temperature has cooled, even though it's still unseasonally warm for February in Tennessee. The mid-sixties is a welcome change from the high-seventies that I woke to this morning.

More importantly, the wind here isn't carrying the ominous smell of impending rainstorms.

I'm definitely not one for the pomp and circumstance of opulent weddings, but even I have to admit that this facility is astounding. It's just outside of the city limits. Close enough to give attendees their choice of hotel accommodations, but remote enough to cloak everything in an intimate privacy. Covering twenty acres, the property is a photographer's dream.

We all climb out of the truck and are taking in our immediate surroundings when Kimber's cell phone blares to life. Again. "Oh! I've been waiting on this call." She flaps her hand in Ridge's face. "Y'all go on without me. I'll catch up." She walks away from us, placing herself out of earshot.

Ridge sneaks closer to me and grabs my elbow. "Orah, I want you to know that I—"

"Amy?" A short, petite, and very pregnant woman suddenly appears from the shadows and rounds the waist-high cobblestone fence.

"Mary Ann?"

With a bright smile, she nods, and we shake hands. I step back a smidge, giving Ridge room to lean forward for his introduction. "Ridge, this is Mary Ann, the event manager for the property," I say.

In the brief moment of silence between their 'hellos', I hear the scuff of gravel underneath heavy footsteps. My spine stiffens, and my head swivels left and right, searching for the culprit. Sensing my unease, Ridge closes the distance between us and settles his hand on the small of my back. The weight of his palm comforts me. It fills me with a fortifying strength, reminding me that not every unexpected noise is a sign of danger.

A middle-aged man with a jovial grin walks around the back of the truck. He's wearing a flannel shirt and overalls. Whisps of his fluffy white hair stick out from underneath his ballcap. "Holy smokes!" He stops right in front of us and rocks back on his heels. "Aren't you two kids a handsome couple. I bet half the single men and women in the lower forty-eight are gonna be weeping when y'all walk down the aisle."

My hand flies to my somersaulting stomach, Ridge's eyes widen like saucers, and Mary Ann's face pinks in embarrassment. It all happens at the exact same time. Like we've choreographed our reactions to fall together in perfect comedic timing. "Oh!" Mary Ann exclaims. "No, Rick, this isn't the bride and groom. This is the wedding planner and the groom."

His caterpillar eyebrows fall into a line as he studies us. "Huh."

Feeling like a chastised kid, Ridge releases me from his hold. He twists forward, offering a firm handshake to the man. "Sir? Ridge Conway, pleasure to meet you."

Mary Ann jumps in. "Rick is our head maintenance engineer. He'll be able to walk you through any special requests that you may have regarding electrical, plumbing, even landscaping."

"It's a pleasure to meet you, Rick," I add, hoping to diffuse the awkwardness.

"Oh, you too, hon."

Right then, Kimber makes her appearance. Her stiletto heels click and clack and wobble as she trudges back to us. "Sorry about that!" She swoops in front of me and limply dangles her hand in front of Rick. Like she's a princess waiting on someone to kiss her knuckles. "Kimber-Shay Willis, the bride." With her hand still posed in mid-air, she jerks to the parking area behind us. "I run the largest and fastest-growing string of luxury car dealerships in the Southeast. So, obviously, the majority of our guests will be driving high-dollar vehicles. Gravel can be rough on premium autos. What's the likelihood that you can pave this whole area before November?"

And I shit you not, in what I can only describe as one of the most epic moments of my entire life, Rick slaps her hand, like he's giving her a low five and yelps, "Zero percent chance, princess."

I snort, quickly camouflaging my giggle with a cough. If I were to listen closely enough, I'm sure I'd be able to hear Kimber's blood rapidly simmering to a boil.

Mary Ann jumps in, trying to cover for Rick's bluntness. "Let's begin the tour, shall we? We have a lot of ground to cover before it gets dark."

Trying to diffuse the drama, Ridge steps forward and fixes a hand around his fiancée's waist. Kimber shrugs him off with a grunt of disgust. "Uh, stop. Didn't you hear her? We have a lot to see." She pretends to lower her voice, but really, it's just theatrics. "Besides, I think we both know this place will never live up to our standards. Jupiter Island was on the list for a reason."

Chapter 21

Orah

We spend the next hour and a half exploring. By the time we make it to the large outdoor patio of the main building, the sun is setting low in the horizon, casting the world in shadows of pink, orange, and black. The concrete and stone decking expands out over the rolling hills that eventually fold into the peaks of the Smoky Mountains. Leaning against the waist-high deck wall, I take a deep breath, trying to center myself, trying to find my peace in the chaos that is known as Kimber-Shay.

"So, this is actually where most couples decide to have the ceremony," Mary Ann confirms. "As you can see, the views at sunset are breathtaking. And if the temperature dips low, we can always set up portable stand heaters around the perimeter. You'd be surprised at the amount of heat they provide."

"Oh!" From the shelter of the covered-roof area, Kimber squeaks to life. "I've been waiting on this email all day long." She bounds down the four steps that separate the two sections of the massive terrace. "Babe, hand me your keys. I'll wait for you in the truck."

Ridge bounces his gaze between me, Mary Ann, and Rick. Once again, the tension in his body morphs him into someone almost unrecognizable. His shoulders bunch, straining against the thin fabric of his well-worn and well-loved T-shirt. Stuffing his hands in his pockets, he tips forward, whispering in Kimber's ear, no doubt telling her that she's being rude.

"Don't be ridiculous," she scoffs. "They understand." Cocking a hand on her thin waist, she continues, "Besides, selling these cars is what's gonna pay for our wedding. So, if they want the privilege of hosting us, then I'm sure they won't mind me conducting a little business." She waves her cell phone in his face. "This auction lot is massive. And we need to win it." And then, she does the exact same thing she did that afternoon when I first met her. She shoves her tongue down his throat. For a split second, he loses his balance and seesaws back and forth. Thankfully, he recovers, which is a testament to his coordination, especially considering the fact that his hands are still neatly tucked in the pockets of his jeans. As quickly as her assault begins, it ends. She wipes the slobber from the corners of her mouth and then holds out her hand. "Keys?"

With a grimace, his hands finally pop free from their self-imposed prison, and he gives her the key fob.

"Take your time, babe. There's no rush. This will take me a while." And with a phony goodbye and a fake thank you, she trots past Mary Ann and Rick, leaving the three of us emotionally spent and physically drained. And we're not even the ones who are marrying her.

Turning away from me, pretending to admire the view from the left side of the patio, Ridge wipes his hands back and forth across his lips, removing any traces of his betrothed.

"So..." Mary Ann starts again, cautiously repeating her spiel. "This is where most ceremonies take place."

"Hey," Rick's rich and velvety timbre cuts through the discord, "why don't you two kids stand there, and Mary Ann can take your picture. That way, you can get a feel for what the crowd will see when they look at the bride and groom."

I study Ridge's back.

It's plain to see that he's hurting.

And because of that I ache for him. It's a pain that's real and tangible, burning across my torso. A scalding heat leaks from my heart. It scorches through my sternum, down my ribcage, and gathers in the tight, waxy skin of my scars. "I...I don't think that's necessary," I stutter. "He, I mean, we...we get the gist."

He spins around, hiding behind a mask of indifference. "No, let's do it."

"Let's do it?" There's no hiding my surprise.

"Sure. We need to see what it looks like."

"We do?"

Ignoring my question, he stalks over to Mary Ann. "Here. Use my phone." He pulls up the camera app and then hands her the device.

I'm still standing there like a deer caught in the headlights when he grabs my hand and tugs me behind him. He leads us over to the middle of the terrace, where the deck wall is decorated with a wrought iron fleur-de-lis. "Here? Is this the middle?"

Mary Ann works to center us in the picture frame. "Yeah, that's the middle. But you'll need to switch sides. Typically, the groom is on the right, from the audience's point of view."

Gripping my shoulders, Ridge does a half do-si-do, swapping us. "Like this?"

"Yes."

"But you gotta get closer than that," Rick hollers. "Unless you wanna toss the ring on her finger like you're playing a game of horseshoes."

I purse my lips and frown in his direction. "Rick..."

Unlike me, Ridge obeys Rick's directive. He closes the distance between us.

His body brushes against mine, sending a delicious chill from the top of my head to the bottom of my toes. I'm unable to hide it; my shudder is easily visible.

"Are you cold?"

"Maybe." The wishy-washy response gets stuck in my mouth. The sound barely escapes. Instead, it floats through the air like a foggy mist.

"The cold front is starting. That must mean the storms are passing through down south, back at home." His calloused hands fasten around my wrists. When his finger, yet again, accidentally slides underneath my watchband, I nearly collapse. I suck in a harsh gulp of air, and my knees buckle. "Whoa, Little Bird." He presses against me, holding me flush against the broadness of his chest.

My fingers close into a fist. I wish I could grab my necklace, but I can't. Because he's still holding me captive.

The colored beams of twilight fire against his face, setting his Tiger Eyes ablaze and shading his beard in embers of red and burgundy.

Beautiful is too ugly of a word for him.

He's...utter perfection.

"You're unsteady." His whisper is dark and dangerous.

"Because you make me that way."

His hands slowly ease upward, traveling over the chill bumps that now decorate my skin.

Inch. Inch. Inch.

His tongue darts out, and he licks his lips.

Inch. Inch. Inch.

His thumbs press into the soft, tender skin of the insides of my elbows. "Then, hold me, and I'll keep you steady. I'll save you."

He drops his hands, leaving me barren, and oh, so lonely. Without any aforethought whatsoever, I hook my own hands around his elbows and mimic his actions, charting a path across every muscle, every tendon.

Up. Up. Up.

My fingers tremble. My core quakes.

I feel like I'm losing my mind.

And then he gifts me a small dose of sanity as I creep higher to his shoulders.

His mumbled words pierce my soul.

Inch. "One."

Inch. "Two."

Inch. "Three."

Inch. "Four."

Inch. "Fi—"

"Okay, I've got it. Such a stunning picture." Mary Ann's now-happy and chipper announcement cuts through Ridge's utterance of my last number, chopping it in half before it can give me the relief I so desperately need.

Not only that, but the disruption reminds us of who we are and of what we're doing.

And why it's wrong.

We break apart. Searching for space. Searching for oxygen not breathed by the other person.

In a state of dazed confusion, Ridge skips a hand down his face and taps his chin before muttering an apology. "I'm sorry." Turning on his heels, he plucks the phone from Mary Ann's hand. "I...I'll just be a moment. I need to use the restroom before we leave."

Rubbing her round belly, she nods. "Absolutely, feel free to use any of the facilities located on the first floor."

He disappears into the building.

"So," Rick tugs on his overalls and pokes his own belly out, "I'm not really picking up on 'affair vibes', but something is definitely going on between the two of you."

"Rick!" Mary Ann chastises, but it's easy to see that the reprimand is halfhearted. I reckon she's just as eager to hear the gossip as her co-worker is.

Technically, I'm under no obligation to tell these strangers anything at all. But I also don't want them thinking I'm some kind of trollop, a floozie just trying to knock the bride off the top of the cake tier.

Mary Ann props her hands on her hips and tries to stretch her back. She's been on her feet for way too long; she's probably miserable. I nod to some outdoor furniture set along on the perimeter. "Mary Ann, you should sit down. You need to rest."

She cocks a hopeful eyebrow. "You don't mind?"

"No, of course not."

Once we're comfortable, I begrudgingly reply to Rick. "No, we're not having an affair. I can only imagine how that looked." I flip a hand toward where we were standing, pretending to be man and wife. "But Ridge would never cheat on Kimber. That's...well, it's just not who he is."

"But you're clearly more than just a wedding planner and her client," he challenges.

"About ten years ago, we were in somewhat of a relationship. We lost contact until two weeks ago." I snag my necklace, twirling the charm between my fingers. "When he walked into my place of business with his fiancée, and I found out I was the planner assigned to their wedding."

Mary Ann slaps the patio table between us. "You. Are. Kidding."

All I can do is shake my head.

"That is...wow. Just wow." She chokes on a giggle and immediately starts to hiccup.

"Uh-oh. There's them hiccups again." Rick pushes from his chair and heads into the house. "I'll get you some water."

"Thank you, Rick," Mary Ann calls behind him.

For some strange reason, their familiarity makes me happy. "You and Rick seem to really get along. That's nice."

She smiles brightly and protectively hugs her baby bump. "Well, that's because..." Hiccup. "He's my father-in-law." Hiccup.

"Your father-in-law? Really?"

She nods up and down, trying to hold her breath. It's a losing battle, and the air whooshes from her in an exhausted exhale. "He's actually the one who got me this job. He's been here for over fifteen years now."

"That's wonderful. It must be so exciting for him to get to see you every single day, for him to see how his grandchild is growing."

"Oh, he loves it. And it really gives Josh, that's my husband, some peace of mind. His mom, Rick's wife, died seven years ago. Her death was just devastating for Rick. Well, for all of us, really. It was right after Josh and I got married. Rick kind of disappeared into his own world. So, we weren't able to bond or build a relationship. Not like I wanted. Then, when this job opened up five years ago, and Rick vouched for me, everything changed." She smiles, happy and content, "This will be his first grandchild...a little boy. Needless to say, he's over the moon." She hiccups again and pats her chest, trying to ease the muscle spasm. "In fact, for the past month I've been craving these sandwiches that a little café down the road does—egg and cheese on homemade sourdough." She gives a little food-porn moan. "He brings me one every morning."

"That does sound good. My craving was always cereal. I swear, I could eat an entire family-sized box of Cinnamon Toast Crunch or Golden Grahams in one sitting."

"Oh! You have a child? Boy or girl?"

The growl from behind me is feral and wild. "You have a kid?"

Chapter 22

Ridge

"You have a kid?"

The words are foreign on my tongue. In all honesty, I'm not even sure that they came from me. I'm completely disjointed and lopsided, so I have no idea if I'm even stable enough to open my mouth and produce noise.

The sun has disappeared behind the trees and rolling hills. The elaborate patio is now glittering with the soft glow from perfectly timed, outdoor lamps. And they're the fancy ones too; the kind that flicker like the flames of a fire.

Slowly, she spins in her chair, turning to look at me. Despite the complete shock and utter astonishment frying my brain like an overcooked slab of bacon, I'm still able to process her beauty. Her strength. Her kindness. Her triumph in the face of adversity. I'm still weak in the knees and unstable, just like she was...mere moments ago. When we were wrapped in each other's arms, pretending to be something we aren't. Playing make-believe as bride and groom, wife and husband, lover and partner.

"Ridge...I..."

"You have a kid?" I repeat.

Rick appears beside me, holding a bottle of water. "Uh, Mary Ann. Why don't we give them a few moments." He holds out his hand and helps her up.

Her gaze latches onto Orah's. "Take your time. I have a few invoices to send out before I can head home for the day. Just come see me in the office before you leave."

Neither of us says anything, even after the strangers—who apparently know more about Orah than I do—have slipped inside. Eventually, she shifts in her chair, making a move to stand. "It's getting late, we should get on the road. Kimber's waiting."

In one second flat, I cross the ten feet separating us and fling myself in front of her. Bending on a knee, I press my palms against her shoulders, forcing her to sit back down. "We're not going anywhere until you tell me what the hell is going on." My eyes land on her stomach. I stare at it, like I have X-ray vision and can see past her clothing and to what's underneath.

Did My Brave Girl grow a baby?

Does My Little Bird have her own Little Bird somewhere out there?

And if she does, why haven't I met her? Or him?

Why hasn't Orah talked about having a child?

A slithering snake of jealousy worms its way into my heart, pumping me full of venom. Because if this is true, if she has a son or daughter, then some guy has lived the life that I wanted to live. He made a family with her, a life with her.

Is there some motherfucker out there dressing as Santa Claus and leaving flour footprints around the fireplace? All to impress a raven-haired little girl? Is there some asshole teaching a little boy with storm-cloud eyes how to ride a bike?

Well, it's obviously not Tristan. I mean, she's only been on four dates with the guy. So, who is this stranger, this man who took what I wanted?

Her hands curl around her stomach. Her black-painted fingernails clutch against the fabric of her shirt.

She's hiding from me.

Why?

The thought of her shying away and closing the door breaks my heart. Because something tells me this door has a deadbolt on it. And if she turns the lock, I may never be able to get her out.

"Bird…" My voice breaks, filled with the fright of losing her. "What's going on? Do you have a baby?"

A tear spills from her eye, but she's quick to catch it. "No. I…I don't have a baby." She takes a staggered breath. "But Tabby does."

"What?" I don't understand what she's trying to tell me.

"Ridge, you were there. You witnessed her injuries. You know what happened."

Memories flash before me, appearing and disappearing faster than my eyes can blink. "Her hysterectomy."

She wipes another tear and then sniffles. "Yeah, her hysterectomy."

I try to put the puzzle pieces together, but my brain feels sluggish and drugged. If someone were to ask me right now to add two and two, I'm not even sure I could pass the test. "You were her surrogate? For her and Boaz, you carried their daughter?"

I wait for her to respond, but nothing comes.

For five seconds.

"There was more to it than that."

More to it? What does that mean?

I reminisce, thinking back on the past decade. And I'm instantly drawn to the vision of a freckled and spunky little redhead, sprawled out in a hospital bed. Complaining about bad breath and crappy food.

There was damage to basically all of her reproductive organs.

The truth crashes into me like a tidal wave, crushing my lungs in a whirlpool of pressure. "It was your egg." My hands slide across her knees, and I hold her thighs, bruising her with my grip, selfishly using her body as my life raft. "They took Tabby's ovaries. The surgery was an emergency; it was all about saving her life. There's no way they could've harvested eggs." My swallow is loud, and it hurts my throat. "It was your egg."

She leans forward, searching for me. And when her own hands land on my shoulders, she spares no time in digging her fingernails into the collar of my T-shirt. When her fingertips find the jagged scar, she sighs. Like she can finally breathe, finally function, finally live. "Yes, it was my egg."

I shake my head, knowing things are way more complex than even just that. "But Boaz…"

"It wasn't his sperm, of course. From the minute they got engaged, Boaz was adamant about that…that if Tabby didn't have eggs to use, then he wouldn't use his sperm." Her fingers work their way back and forth over my skin, leaving tingles in their wake. "They talked about adoption, and that's still something that they wanna do, but they also wanted this."

"I can't believe you would do that."

"It's the least I could do. I'm the reason she was injured in the first place. And when she married Boaz, the consequences of my actions doubled. I was now the reason that my best friend *and* my brother couldn't have a biological child."

"Zipporah, you are not the reason. You know that. What those guys did…it's all on them."

"You've said it a thousand times, but it doesn't change the way I feel. It never will. No, I couldn't have stopped them, but Tabby was there and in harm's way because of me."

Unwilling to start an argument, I just squeeze her tighter.

"Dylan was too young, obviously," she continues. "The other donor was Tabby's cousin, Hayden. He's a few years older than us. Smart and funny. He and Tabby have always been close. Plus, he looks like Tab. Red hair, freckles, all that."

Shit. This is intense. "In vitro?"

She shakes her head. "That's so expensive. And insurance wouldn't pay for it. None of us had the money for that." She nibbles on her lip. "We opted for intrauterine insemination. The OB started me on Clomid, and we only had to do two rounds of insemination. I got pregnant after the second try."

When she says it like that; it makes it so very fucking real.

"I had a C-section. The doctor didn't want to put my pleural cavity and diaphragm through the stress of a vaginal birth. And I was on a strict diet. She didn't want me gaining too much weight. All tests and imaging have shown that my connective tissue is strong and stable, but she didn't want rapid weight gain to tear or herniate any weak spots that couldn't be seen."

All of these years later, and she's still dealing with the damage those monsters inflicted on her body. "But you were okay? There were no complications?"

"No, I was perfect. And she was perfect."

"So, Eden is…"

The tears are streaming down her face now in a steady flow. She needs to wipe her nose, but she refuses to release her hands from my shoulders. And I don't want her to. I need her touch more than I need my own heartbeat.

So instead, I do it for her.

I lift my hand and drag my fingers across her skin, wiping her clean. Not giving two shits what I may look like, I scrub my hand across my shirt, leaving a streak of shiny snot and wet tears on the tattered and hard-to-read Belly's logo.

"Eden is my niece," she answers. Simply. Firmly. And with unwavering conviction.

"The baby that you made? The baby that grew in your body? The baby that you birthed?"

"Yes."

"She's your niece?"

"Yes."

"Bird, wasn't that hard? To know that she was a part of you? To hold her in your arms and then give her to someone else?"

Her confession is strangled and filled with sorrow. It's an anguish so deep that one could dig for a thousand years and never reach the bottom. "It's the hardest thing I've ever done. The hardest thing I *will ever* do. I was a mother who never got the gift of being a mom."

"And you did all this while caring for your sick grandmother?"

"Ye–yes."

God, she's amazing. I knew she was strong, but this? This is otherworldly.

There's not one weak or selfish bone in her body. My Brave Girl has more than earned her name. She's powerful and mighty. She's the fortified lighthouse shining for the sailors lost at sea.

She's the epitome of a matriarch. She had the gift of bringing one girl *into* this world, and she had the honor of ushering another one *from* this world.

She's the Hero in our story.

Not me.

And if I had just been completely honest with her, then maybe we wouldn't have been navigating this life all alone.

If I had just been half as brave as she was...

If I had just trusted her half as much as she trusted me...

It could have been the two of us. Loving, comforting, and living. Through all of the ups and downs. Through all of the hellos and goodbyes.

And through it all, she would have been mine.

Chapter 23

Ridge

"I don't understand why you can't just drive through it," Kimber whines. "Are you really that scared of a thunderstorm?"

I press my fingers into my temple, massaging away the headache that's been raging for the past fifty-five minutes, ever since Orah and I finally joined Kimber in the truck and I had to relay the unexpected change of plans.

I was on the verge of peppering Orah with a million other questions when my dad called. The storms did pass through all right, and they made their impact known. For our town, it was just a normal thunderstorm, but for North Alabama there were tornadoes and flooding. Naturally, it wasn't safe for us to navigate the roads home tonight. So, I made the decision that the best thing was for us to stay in the area until the morning. And with the cabin being only an hour away in the Smokies, we have the perfect accommodations. It's not like I'm asking her to sleep in a fleabag motel. It's a gorgeous three-bedroom chalet nestled in a private, gated community in the middle of the mountains. You can even see part of the Little Pigeon River from the balcony. The fridge is stocked with water, the freezer is filled with frozen pizza, and there are fresh sheets on the beds. What could be better?

"Kimber, I-59 is blocked with downed trees. Traffic on the interstate is backed up for miles and miles. It'll take hours for it to clear."

"So take the backroads." She wiggles her ever-present cell phone. The motion triggers her home screen, and an illuminated image of her bounces around the truck. "That's what GPS is for."

I point to her phone. "That computer doesn't know which roads are flooded and which ones aren't. We're talking about rural areas, Kimber." I suck my bottom lip between my teeth. "You should be glad the worst of it went through the woods, and not towns and cities and neighborhoods." Last I heard, there were no injuries, and that's the best thing that one can hope for in situations like this.

She rolls her head in an exaggerated circle. "Of course, I'm glad about that. Don't make me out to be ogre." Her heel taps on the floormat. "It's just that Chip was expecting me back. Some special buyers are coming in tomorrow afternoon, and he'll probably need me to do a wine and dine."

"I told you, we'll leave first thing in the morning."

"Fine. Fine."

Five minutes later, I'm punching the security code into the main gate and navigating the mountain roads up to the cabin that I called home for a few years. When I turn into the driveway and my headlights illuminate the rustic-charm house, Orah gasps. "Ridge, this is gorgeous."

"I've gotta pee." Not waiting on me to turn off the ignition, Kimber jumps out of the truck and rushes up the porch steps. She's only been here once before, I highly doubt she remembers the code for the keyless entry. By the time I crack open my driver-side door, she's yelling. "It's not working. What's the stupid code?"

I guess I could race up the steps and help her, but damn, if I don't need a little bit of a break. "0315."

From my perch, leaned against the hood of my truck, I watch as she punches in the code, opens the door, and then slams it. Orah joins me, and together we count the lights as they transform the darkened windows. Kimber's obviously going through the entire cabin, flipping every single light switch.

Why? I have no clue.

"You said this was your grandparents' place?"

"Yeah. They bought it and moved up here after they retired." I shift, hooking my thumbs in my pockets. "Gran passed away that December, after you and I last saw each other."

"Oh, Ridge, I'm sorry." Her empathy is authentic and sincere.

"Pop was devastated. I moved up here that following May, after I completed my four-year requirement with White Sky."

"I'm surprised you left. You really seemed to love it there. With your brothers, your Chief. The beach and Belly's."

The weight of the secrets that I've kept hidden from her pins me to the ground. My feet feel like lead. "It just wasn't the same. After everything that happened, I needed a change of scenery."

"And that's where the National Park Service comes in?"

"Yeah. They were in the middle of a hiring initiative for the Wildland Fire Program."

She turns, cocking her hip against the front grill. There's just enough moonlight and glare from the house to gift me with the glory of her eyes. And I'm relieved to see that the red streaks of her sadness have cleared, leaving me with storm clouds and cotton. "Wait, you're telling me that you know how to fight wildfires."

I pound my boot against the driveway, hoping to shatter the burdens keeping me frozen in place. "Yes, ma'am. I've got my Red Card."

"Red Card?"

"It's an inter-agency certificate that verifies I'm certified to report on incident for wildland fires." Turning toward her, I mimic her stance. "I still go once a year for a refresher course and take my Arduous Pack Test."

"Arduous Pack Test?"

"Three-mile hike with a forty-five-pound pack in less than forty-five minutes."

"So, you're...what do they call it? A hot..."

My laugh slices through the stillness of the winter's night, where the only sounds are coming from us and the bubbling river in the distance. "A hotshot? No, I never applied for an IHC credential. I didn't wanna deploy or work long-post travel assignments. My goal was to be here for Pop."

"You worked here until you moved back home?"

"I was here for a little over four years. Pop died the summer after I turned twenty-seven. It hurt to be here alone, especially after spending so much time with him. I was gonna move home, but a guy I knew was promoted to Chief down in Gulf Shores. They were revamping their paramedic service, and he asked me to join. I went down there for about a year and a half before moving home."

"Life's taken you on some interesting journeys." She folds her arms across her chest and shoves her fists underneath her armpits, trying to get warm. It's a good fifteen degrees colder up here than it was in Knoxville, and the thick, black sweater she put on isn't working the way it should.

"We should head inside. It's getting cold."

Softly smiling, she says okay and walks around to the back passenger-side door. She grabs her purse and hovers her hand over her work bag. "Should I bring this inside? Do you think Kimber wants to talk about the wedding some more?"

I snort, "No, I think she's probably done with that for the day."

Hell, at this point, I'll be surprised if she even talks to *me*.

I give Orah the lay of the land. The cabin is two stories with one ensuite guest room on the first floor, along with the kitchen, family room, and a half-bath. The top floor has the second ensuite guest room and a massive master suite with its own balcony. After a supper of pepperoni pizza and a very tense bout of channel surfing, we decide it's best to call it a night. Kimber's already-frustrated mood worsened when I refused to let her watch a car chase movie. I mean, seriously? What does she expect? The entire cast basically dies.

And Orah was sitting right there.

I set Orah up in the downstairs guest room. I show her where the extra toiletries are and how the shower works. I even grab some of my T-shirts from the upstairs closet and lay them on her bed. After all, I can't imagine she wants to sleep in her work clothes.

Hours later, I'm still awake.

Kimber is curled into a ball on her side of the bed, dressed in just her bra and panties. Of course, I had to listen to a twenty-minute spiel about how she doesn't have her creams and washes and all the shit she apparently needs to slumber. So I guess I can't be blamed for the wired energy pulsing through my brain. My thoughts are jittery and jumpy, firing from one random idea to the other.

Heaving a frustrated growl, I crawl out of bed and slide on a pair of sweatpants over my boxer briefs. On bare feet, I tiptoe down the stairs and grab a bottle of water from the fridge. There's a small lamp on in the far corner of the kitchen, giving me just enough light that I can maneuver through the open floorplan without stubbing a toe. I sit on the couch—never in the recliner—and stare out the floor-to-ceiling windows and sliding door. The nighttime sky is clear and bright. The moonlight bounces off the blackness of the river, shooting streams of shadows across the peaks and valleys of the mountain range. And it's even more beautiful when the fireplace is lit, casting the dancing reflection of flames against the glass wall, firing the mountains in colors of red and orange.

How did I get here?

What the hell am I doing with my life?

Is this honestly what I want?

I guess the better question is...is Kimber *who* I really want?

Am I'm still so determined to stay on-course with my commitments that I'm willing to sacrifice anything I could have with Orah?

Because let's be honest. If I'm going to marry Kimber, I can't keep seeing Orah. Not even as a friend.

Because she's so much more than that.

She always was, and she always will be.

I think about her constantly. I dream about her. Fantasize about her. And when we're together, I can't keep my fucking hands off of her.

I'm walking the world's skinniest and highest tightrope, and I'm about to tumble to the ground. There's no safety net. No parachute. I'm one misstep away from shattering every bone in my body. One tiny blunder, and I'll ruin so many lives. Kimber's. Orah's. Mine.

Once again, doing the right thing seems wrong.

I'm no hero. Far from it. I'm the genesis of broken promises. The catalyst of pain. I'm the boy in the storage room who doesn't know what he's doing. The scared twenty-two-year-old kid who believed the raven-haired girl when she said they could save each other.

Because here it is. Almost ten years later.

And I'm not sure I'll ever be saved.

Chapter 24

Ridge

I scrub my hand down my face and tap my chin. And when I find no comfort in that, I count her numbers. Over and over and over. Until my eyes grow blurry and I'm toeing the line between awake and asleep.

So, when I see her hovering in front of me, I should be shocked. But I'm not. Because she's a beautiful dream. A vision I can only pray I've conjured into reality.

She's standing in front of the window, absorbing the black and gray beauty of the night. And when I realize she's wearing my clothes, my cock springs to life. It was hard for me to find dark-colored T-shirts, but I did. The navy-blue fabric falls down the curve of her ass, shielding her panties from view. The lines of her legs are soft and feminine, hard and muscular.

Utterly mouth-watering.

She's swapped her ponytail for a messy and wild top-bun. What I wouldn't give to see her with her hair down. To rake my fingers through it. To have her crawl on top of me. To feel her hot and perfect little pussy warm my dick while her coconut-scent floods me.

"Orah."

Yelping, she spins around. She knows it's me, but it still takes her a couple of seconds to process the scene.

And I do my own processing too.

I process the slope and heaviness of her breasts, the buds of her nipples as they pebble to a point, the sway of her hips as she wavers on her feet. If I were a different man—if I allowed myself to be the man I truly *want* to be—I'd tear that fucking shirt from her body. With my teeth. And map every delicious inch of her with my tongue.

Just thinking about the taste of her has pre-cum soaking my briefs.

And fuck, if that doesn't feel good.

Despite the prison I've forced myself into, I feel free.

"You scared me." She cocks her head, trying to see me better. "Why are you down here, sitting in the dark? You couldn't sleep?"

Wordlessly, I stand from my reclined position on the couch, and I take a step forward. Her eyes dart down to the massive bulge in my thin, crotch-hugging pants. Her gasp is overpowered by her moan. The impassioned noise catches in the back of her throat, speeding the rise and fall of her shoulders as they shudder in time with her breaths.

And then she sees it.

She. Sees. It.

Her eyes widen. Her lips part. Her body trembles.

"Wh—what is that?"

My muscles twitch, undulating under her gaze. "What's what?"

She slides a foot along the hardwood floor, daring herself to creep closer. Her fingertips dangle in the air, tracing the lines of the design. From three feet away. "That."

The brand on my skin flames to life, scorching and throbbing. Sizzling and scalding. Except this time, I don't smell my burning flesh. In fact, if I were to erase the distance between us, there's a very good chance that I could smell her desire, leaking from her core, dripping into the silk of her underwear.

I follow the dips and turns of her fingers. I don't even have to look down to know what she's drawing.

My body is forever engraved with her.

I never thought I would see her again. And there's no way I could live my life with another woman and not honor the never-ending love I have for Orah.

So, I carved her into me. Forever.

On my left pectoral is the strike branding.

A little bird.

And below that is the regular tattoo. In a small, neat script.

Exodus 2:21

When I don't answer, she continues. "I...I know what that is. I know that verse. And...and the bird?" She squints. "Is that a burn? Did you burn yourself?"

"Fire for the fireman." My tongue flicks out, wetting my dry and aching lips. "A tattoo wasn't enough. I needed more. I needed permanent. Forever."

She worries the hem of her shirt—of my shirt—and for the first time she remembers her state of undress. She tugs on it, trying to cover the lusciousness of her thighs. "Why? Why would you do that?"

"You know why."

"Does Kimber know what it means?"

I just shake my head. She knows it's from the Bible, but she's never gone through the trouble of looking it up. Even if a white dove dropped the original papyrus scroll on top of her head, I doubt she would open it to read the verse. I told her it had to do with camaraderie and that I did it to honor the brotherhood I have with my fellow firefighters. She was just pissed that my 'perfect' chest was marred.

"When?"

I clench my fists, knowing she can feel what I feel. Knowing she can sense the guilt of my actions. My decision to make her a part of my marriage—via my body—may be covered in shame, but never regret.

She straightens her spine and rolls her shoulders. Her jaw tenses, and her storm-cloud eyes darken. "How dare you?! How dare you put me on your body when you're asking another woman to marry you, to be with you forever, to give you children."

My body buzzes with a fierce electricity. My dick vibrates with a punishing pleasure. "Bird…"

She holds up her left hand, with her palm facing toward me. "Stop," she orders.

And then I see it.

I. See. It.

I'm not the only one inscribed.

The skin of her wrist is marked. In that sweet and tender area that stays hidden by the thick band of her smartwatch.

I shoot across the floor and grab her hand, pulling her wrist closer to my face and forcing what's been concealed to be revealed.

Except it's not a word at all.

$SiO_2 + FeOOH + (Al, Mg, Na)$

"Orah, what is this?" She halfheartedly tries to pull away, but I don't let her. "Zipporah?"

"It's the chemical formula for Tiger's Eye." Her plump, beautiful lips quiver. "Silica. Iron oxide hydroxide. Aluminum. Magnesium. Sodium."

Holy. Hell.

"Why would you do that?"

"You know why." With her whimpered reply, she gives me more passion, more affection, more love than I've ever had.

"When?"

"In Alaska."

"Years. You've worn me on your body for years?"

"Yes." She pushes into me. Her forearm grazes my chest, and her hip skims across my erection.

"How many men have seen it? How many men have touched you, kissed you, tasted you? All the while you've been marked as mine." My growl is savage and untamed. "Has Tristan seen it?"

"Of course not. And he never will."

"Why?"

"Because I told him that we were through."

My smile is more of a snarl.

"Does that make you happy, Hero? To know that there won't be a fifth date?"

"Fuck, yeah, it does."

The seeds of anger float around her, like dandelion fuzz on a spring day. "And what if I told you that I'm scared of being touched? Scared of being with someone?" Her eyes flash with malice, transforming her spring day into a summer storm. "Scared of making love, scared of fucking. Does that make you happy too? What if I told you there was a boy who loved me? But he had to leave me. Because he got tired of competing with a ghost. He fought for me, day after day, night after night. He comforted me, even when I woke from my sleep, crying for another. But I could never give my heart to him. Because the only man I ever wanted was the one who didn't want me." Her condemnation is panted and heavy, fueled with stinging rain and howling winds. "Does. That. Make. You. Happy?"

Does it?

Does it make me happy?

To know that I'm the ghost haunting her dreams. And causing her nightmares.

"I did want you." The confession slips from my mouth without my permission.

She blinks. Her body loosens, sagging against my grip. "What?"

Her face is flushed, tinted the most gorgeous shade of pink. The air between us swells, contracting and expanding. It's a living, breathing organism. A vile parasite taunting me once again with the *things* that I want to do. Because it would be so simple. In less time than it takes my heart to beat, I could lower my lips to hers. I could wrap her in my embrace. I could show her that it's not touch she fears...because how can you be frightened of your own hand. And every single part of me belongs to her. My hands. My heart. My soul.

But I know I can't do those things. Because once I cross that line, there's no going back. There's no reverse, no redo, no rewind. And I refuse to be the man whose lips are on one woman while his ring is on another. I could never forgive myself. And I would never want *her* to forgive me.

Orah deserves better than that.

Kimber deserves better than that.

Hell, I deserve better than that.

I swear on all that's holy, whatever I decide to do, I'll do the right way. I claim to be a man of honor and integrity...well, it's time to step up to the fucking plate.

I drop my hold on her and step back. Skirting around her, I walk toward the windows. I prop my hand above my head, relishing in the cold as it seeps through the glass and penetrates my skin. Fortunately, my crotch absorbs my somber mood, and my body relaxes from its heightened state of sexuality. My sudden departure leaves her stunned and addled. She slowly turns around, and in the reflection, I see her standing behind me. She winds her arms around herself, fighting for the solace that I'm unable to give her. "What?" she repeats.

"You know I loved you. You know I wanted you."

She shakes her head back and forth. "No." Her feet shuffle forward. And when the movement snags the T-shirt higher around her thighs, I have to close my eyes. Because her body makes me want to smash every vow I just made to myself.

"I felt your love for me," she explains. "I did. I know that part was real, despite what I tell myself most days. But you refused to say it. You refused to fight for me. You refused to wait for me. You didn't want me. If you did, we'd have a life together." She sniffles, drawing my eyes back open. "We'd have a home, a family. We'd have cupcakes and game nights. Sexy dresses and dinner dates. There wouldn't be an invisible ghost lying next to me. It'd be you. With your breath in my ear and your heartbeat under my fingertips, it'd be you."

God, help me. How did I make such a mess of our lives. "They were gonna take my job."

"What? Who was?"

"Chief Latner. The mayor. Dr. Evans." Growing a set of balls, I push off from the window and face her. "All of them. If I didn't stop all communication with you, they were going to fire me for violating the Code of Conduct and Ethics, regarding relationships between incident first responders and patients. And, they'd put the details in my HR jacket. I'd be lucky to even have a department accept me as a volunteer after that."

"What? Why? They can't dictate who can be in a relationship and who can't."

"They can. Companies do it all the time."

"But I wanted you. I needed you."

"Orah, you were still in high school."

She reaches for me, dangling her arm in the air, unsure of what to do. I catch a glimpse of my mark on her wrist, and it paralyzes me. "But I was eighteen. You know that. I turned eighteen before I even left the hospital."

"But you weren't eighteen when I fell in love with you."

Her hand flies to her throat, searching for the relief of her necklace, only to find that it's not there. It's not in its usual and perfect place. I'm guessing she took it off to sleep. "When you fell in love with me?"

"The minute I shut that storage room door, our lives changed in more ways than one."

Her eyes are frantic, jumping from the floor to the ceiling, from my face to my branded chest. "You let me walk away because they were gonna fire you, because they were gonna take your career from you?"

It sounds even worse when she says it out loud. "Our destruction happened for a thousand different reasons. And that was just one." I drag my hand down my face and tap my chin. The action feels different now than it did two weeks ago, before she came back into my life. "I'm debilitated by the regret of telling you 'no'. But…"

"But what?" she snaps back.

"A part of me, and I think it's the biggest part of me, knows that I made the right decision. I meant what I said. We were both drowning."

A tear slides down the sweet roundness of her cheek, and she quickly swipes at it. I have no idea how My Brave Girl has any tears left after what we dealt with earlier tonight. After the secrets and sorrow and courage of her selfless, intimate act came out. She gave her body and soul to her family, desperate to make amends for something that didn't even need amending. She gave her flesh and blood to her flesh and blood.

"We were so young, Orah. And we had all this trauma surrounding us. Death and mayhem. Your hurt was still raw and fresh." I sigh and settle my hands on my hips. "The strangers on social media, Levi, the two shooters. All of these men took advantage of you. The last thing I ever wanted was to be one of those men."

"You're lying to yourself, Ridge. You knew you weren't anything like them. You weren't just some guy who ran into that room and saved me. I didn't fall in love with you because you were the man who happened to show up, the firefighter who happened to survive, the paramedic who happened to save my life. I fell in love with you because of *you*. Your heart, your soul, your spirit. You were the destiny meant only for me."

Destiny.

On that beach, on my knees, I asked her if she believed in it. If she believed that one day our love and luck and tenacity would merge together. And here she is...telling me that destiny was already ours.

And I threw it away. Like it didn't even matter.

Now what the fuck am I supposed to do?

Because for eight months, I've been forcing a destiny with the woman who's currently asleep in my bed upstairs.

Force...

Applying pressure.

Those reflections immediately conjure visions of my paramedic training. Cardiopulmonary resuscitation—CPR. Too little pressure and the heart won't start. Blood and oxygen won't circulate. Organs will die. Death will come, stealthily creeping through the chaos like a venomous snake. But too much pressure? And ribs will break. Sternums will fracture. Organs will bruise and rupture. And death? It'll still come, leaving behind even more damage than if you'd not even tried to begin with.

I've applied too much pressure. I took something that was not survivable, not sustainable, and tried to build a life around it. And all I've done is break. I've splintered an entire world. Shattered myself, Kimber, and the future we can never live.

And to be the man that I want to be, I've got to repair those fractures before I can capture my destiny, my fate, with Orah.

"Ridge?" She calls to me, searching for the man who's standing right in front of her, yet is still lost.

"I…I need some time."

"Some time? What does that mean?"

"I think we need some time apart, some space."

She jumps back like I've slapped her. "Space? It's been almost nine-and-a-half years! That wasn't enough? You need more? After only two weeks, you're ready to hide from me again? Ready to hide from us?"

"I've got to fix things with Kimber. I've got to—"

She jumps in, not giving me a chance to explain my poorly worded explanation. "Of course, you do. The Hero can't withstand anyone questioning his virtue, his morality, his dependability. The Hero would never abandon his fiancée. What kind of man would that make him? What kind of monster?"

"Zipporah, it's not like that."

"Ridge, she slapped you. Accused you of cheating. She drew your blood."

I toss a glance at my stitched shoulder and the thin, fucking sexy-as-hell, fingernail scars left behind by My Brave Girl. "She's not the only one who made me bleed."

"Well, that blood might've been on *your* body, but it came from *my* heart."

And with that, she turns and locks herself in the guest bedroom.

Chapter 25

Ridge

I'm exhausted. Mentally and physically.

The drive back home with a silent Orah and whiny Kimber nearly broke my sanity. At Wexler Events, Orah jumped out of the truck like I was chasing her with a knife. And Kimber? Well, despite my request, and my downright begging that she miss work so we could talk, she skipped into the dealership with a smile on her face and an overpriced coffee in her hand.

I reported for work yesterday morning for my twenty-four-hour shift, and then pulled the lucky card for a double when Clarkson had to call in because his son forgot to tell him about the school play and parent luncheon. I was fully prepared to work his full shift, but graciously Clarkson came in at seven tonight to relieve me.

And for that, I am truly grateful.

I know that science suggests there's no link between full moon cycles and people acting a fool. But I'm here to tell you that full moon madness has been running fucking rampant, especially with the college kids. There wasn't even a chance for me to rest my eyes between calls. Which did consist of a call for a dude with his hand stuck inside of a stuffed beaver. And that's not a euphemism.

When the double fell in my lap, I texted Kimber and told her that I still needed to talk to her. She agreed to meet me at the apartment tomorrow morning at eight. But now that I'm headed home early, I'm going to see if she can come over tonight. I need sleep, but more importantly than that, I need to reset my life. This Band-Aid is only hanging on by one small, dirty strip of glue. It's more than time to rip the fucker off.

Because My Brave Girl is waiting.

And she doesn't know what's happening.

In fact, I even received a voicemail yesterday from Celeste, informing me that she and Anniah would now be our points of contact for the wedding because 'Amy' had some 'unexpected assignments' pop up.

Yeah, we'll see about that.

I'm not looking forward to my conversation with Kimber. I know, without a doubt, that she's going to erupt. She's going to spew hate and vitriol into the stratosphere. Higher than any volcano. I'll be lucky to escape with minor burns. Most likely, my flesh will be charred, and my bone will be exposed.

And the fact of the matter is I have to take it. I have to take every single thing she's gonna dish out. Because this is all on me. One hundred percent. I'm the man who lied to her. I'm the one who deceived her. Even though I didn't know it was a deception.

But I should have known. Because only authentic love is epic. 'Normal' love is a false concept. Because true love is anything but ordinary.

The red lights and stop signs blur around me, fading into the dark night with every blink of my eyes. I'm lost in a daze. So, when my cell phone starts ringing, it really does take me by surprise. The computer dashboard of my truck lights up, showing me a name I haven't seen in a very, very long time.

Well, this should be interesting.

As soon as I answer, her shriek booms through my Bluetooth with enough volume to garner an annoyed look from the guy who's stopped next to me at the light. "You dumbass! Have you lost your mind?!"

"Hey, Tab."

"Oh, no! Don't you 'Hey, Tab' me. That low and sexy voice isn't gonna save you this time." She takes a breath, preparing to yell at me again. "How dare you put that on your chest?! That verse? She told me what it means."

"She did?"

"Yeah... *'in time, he gave his daughter Zipporah to be the man's wife'*. Or something like that."

"Yeah, that's the gist of it."

"So, you admit it. You're a lunatic."

"Pretty much," I say, agreeing with her.

"I can't believe you're toying with her like this. It's not right. You're marrying someone else, Ridge."

"No, I'm not."

There's a moment of silence on the line, and then I hear the muffled familiarity of someone in the background. "I told you it would work out, baby."

"Is that Boaz?"

"Don't you talk to my husband," the fiery redhead spits. "He's too good for the likes of you."

She's right. He is. He's better than me; smarter than me. Because he's been married to the love of his life for years now. And they already have a family together. In my eyes, Boaz is right up there with Einstein.

"Now," she switches her tone, inflecting professionalism like she's in the middle of a PowerPoint presentation. "What did you mean by that? When you said you weren't?"

"I'm calling off my engagement to Kimber. Tonight."

"Calling off your engagement? Or breaking up with her? Those are two very different things, Hero."

"I'm doing both." I turn into the parking lot for my apartment complex, but leave the ignition running because I don't want the phone call to disconnect. "I don't love her, Tabby. I never did. I was wrong. So fucking wrong."

"Aaaaannnndddd," she drawls. "Who do you love?"

I can't help but laugh. "I love your best friend. Your sister-in-law. The woman who helped save your life. I am totally, completely, and madly in love with Zipporah Smith. And I have been ever since that night."

"Well, it took you long enough." She heaves a dramatic sigh. "And you obviously haven't told her this because I just talked to her again a couple of hours ago, before Eden's bedtime, and she said she hadn't heard from you since you dropped her off Saturday afternoon."

"No, I haven't told her. I have to end things with Kimber first, and I've been working a double the last two days." I lean my head back on the headrest and close my eyes. "I've been treading in some very dangerous waters, Tab. I've come very close to doing things that a man with a fiancée shouldn't do." I pop my head up and wave my hand through the air. "Hell, I've *already done* things a man with a fiancée shouldn't do. I've held her hand. I've hugged her, a little too long and a little too strong. I've dreamt about her. Fantasized about her. Wanted her."

Boaz coughs, getting strangled on his own spit. "Dude, chill. That's my sister. I just threw up a little bit in my mouth."

I ignore his teasing. "Kimber deserves to know the truth. I have to be completely honest with her. I can't be the man Orah deserves and not own up to my bad decisions, my bad choices."

"And you're doing that tonight?"

"Yes, ma'am."

I hear movement on the other side of the phone, and imagine Tabby and Boaz lying together in bed, or cuddling on the couch. Talking about their day and laughing about things their daughter said. "You know, she's still affected by it all. You've seen that, right? Most of it hasn't changed, even after all this time. The dark clothes. The flat shoes. The counting. Freaking out over small, little things."

"Yeah, I know."

"But other parts of her are stronger. What she did for her grandmother?" Tabby swallows. "What she did for us?"

"I know. She told me."

"I want her to be loved. Wild and free and unencumbered."

"And I'm gonna give that to her."

"You promise?"

"I swear."

After another minute we end the call, and I climb out of the truck. I was so absorbed in talking to Tabby that I didn't even notice Kimber's car parked to the left of the main entrance.

That's weird.

I guess she decided to spend the night here instead of Chip's house. I glance at my watch. It's seven-thirty. That's also weird. Unless I hound her for time together, Kimber is usually content to stay at work until nine or ten each night.

Nerves build low in my stomach, sending a steady stream of bile and acid swirling up and into my mouth. Well, this is happening. It's now or never.

I take the elevator up to my floor, playing out in my mind the best way to start the conversation. Unfortunately, most of the time, Kimber only responds to raw bluntness. And I don't think there's any way to soften the unfiltered truth of our situation.

Pulling out my keys, I unlock the heavy steel and wooden door and push it open. The TV's on in the living room, blaring a news report through the open spaces of the living, kitchen, and dining areas. Tossing my keys and phone on the kitchen counter, I head over to the couch. I sling my duffle bag down on the leather sofa and grab the TV remote, thumbing the volume down a little bit lower.

The sleek, warehouse condo only has one bathroom, and it's tucked away in the one and only bedroom. I can't imagine she's asleep, so she must be doing that nightly routine with all those creams and oils and concoctions that are supposed to make her look five years younger. My boots shuffle along the hardwood floor, drowning the hushed monologue of the news reporter. "The White House announced the schedule change late this afternoon. The press and media have not yet been given an agenda for tomorrow's news conference, but staff insiders are suggesting it has something to do with the rumored health of the Vice President. Political analysts are saying…"

Why is the bedroom door shut?

And why the fuck are all of my senses suddenly ringing like a five-alarm fire? My sleepy body wakens instantly. The hairs on my arms stand at attention, like someone just showered me in a static charge. My eyes dart to the doorknob, willing it to turn before my hand can even grab it. My ears perk, wondering why the hell I'm hearing noises that I shouldn't be hearing.

And I know.

I just know.

I know exactly what I'm going to see the second this door opens. But that doesn't lessen the pain.

In one fluid motion, I flick the door open and cross into the threshold of my bedroom.

In less time than it takes a 'normal', non-first responder to blink, I've already assessed the situation.

And what a fucking situation it is.

Kimber's naked body is bent over my bed—our bed—in her normal sex position. And standing behind her is a naked man with coiffed, gelled brown hair and tortoise-shell glasses. He's gripping her hips and pumping into her. Hard and fast and unforgiving. His cheeks are bright red with exertion. He's having to lean backward a little bit so his bulbous stomach doesn't get in the way of his actions. And standing off to the side, watching the whole thing is a completely *different* naked man. He's holding his wrinkled-as-hell and old-as-dirt cock in his hands, jerking himself silly. His white hair is a wild mess, and his droopy ass reminds me of the jowls of a basset hound.

Kimber's head whips in my direction, and she screeches. "Ridge!"

The guy with his dick buried in my fiancée glances at me and stalls. He's not even sure what the hell to do. Father Time yells and stumbles backward, landing slap dab in the middle of the chair tucked in the corner of the room.

I sit in that chair every single day to put my shoes on.

Yeah, not anymore.

The muscles in my body contract, physically revolting from the scene in front of me. The pain is hard and brutal. And in a perfect world, I would fold over and regurgitate my lunch all over the floor. But this isn't a perfect world. As can be witnessed. Because the woman whom I don't love—but was gonna marry—is having some kind of threesome with a librarian and his grandfather. On my bed. In my bedroom. In the penthouse apartment that I hate. On the night I was gonna break her heart.

I finally unglue my feet from their frozen position and fly across the room. I shove against the dude, disconnecting his wang from Kimber's...well, you know. "Get the fuck off her," I scream. He yelps in pain. And, in what can only be described as the most disgusting moment of my entire life, the man makes a gobbling sound like a turkey and blows his load all over my area rug.

And then the fucker has the audacity to smile in relief.

"Ridge!" Kimber scrambles to a standing position, pulling the top sheet with her and covering herself. "What are you doing home? You're supposed to be working?"

I drop my mouth open and fling my arms into the abyss. "Oh, I'm sorry! Did I disturb you?!" My voice is a sarcastic sonnet of epic proportions. "I'll just go make a sandwich and watch a movie. Please, take your time." I point to the load-blower. "Sandwich?" I spin around, bringing the other man into the fold. "What about you, Merlin? Lettuce, tomato, and cheese okay with you? Don't worry, I can serve prune pudding on the side."

Kimber bounces up and her nipple peeks out from underneath the sheet. "Ridge, stop! You're being an asshole."

Oh, that's rich.

I clench my fists and grind my teeth. With my growl, I release the destruction and devastation that I want to release with my own body. "Get them the fuck out of my apartment. Now."

I storm from the bedroom, slamming the door so hard that every single picture frame on the wall shivers. I walk to the bay of windows running the length of the living room and drop my forehead against the glass. It's nowhere near as cold as the window was at the cabin Friday night. And beneath me all I see are the bright and blinding lights of our small city's bustling, downtown area. If I look far enough to the right, I'll see *The Last Call*, where my brother and Will are pouring drinks and laughing with patrons. And just across the street and down two blocks, I'll see the sheriff's department, where Crutch is currently working double time on a breaking and entering. And just beyond that, down the hill, is the river that runs through town. And nestled next to the river is the old, abandoned farmer's market. The building that my brother wants to buy and remodel into a huge event center and central kitchen for *The Elegant Taste.*

My family.

The people I love.

The people who love *me.*

They're all around. Surrounding me night and day.

And I nearly lost sight of that.

Chapter 26

Ridge

Nearly lost sight of it?

Hell, I was completely fucking blind.

I nearly tied myself—forever—to a woman who doesn't even like me.

I grab the string and lower the blackout shades, hiding myself away from the activity of the world.

I'm still turned around when I hear them walk out of the bedroom and make their way toward the exit. Grandpa Whistles can't go peacefully, though. "Kate, if you find my dental partial, just give it to Chip. He'll get it back to me."

Oh, for the love of all things holy, if I find that man's teeth in my apartment, I'm breaking my lease and moving.

Once they're gone, Kimber joins me in the living room. But I can tell by her walk that this is gonna be one hell of a conversation. Because she's not even tiptoeing around. She's slapping those bare feet across that hardwood like she's got a point to prove.

"I think Pee-Paw may need to see a physician. He called you by the wrong name."

"No, he didn't. Kate is my first name."

I spin around so fast I nearly give myself whiplash. "What are you talking about?"

"My full name is Kathryn Kimber-Shay Willis. Until I was in middle school, I went by Kate."

"Are you serious? How did I not know this?"

"Why would I tell you that? Kimber-Shay just sounds better. It's more prestigious."

Visions of a drunken wedding and bad decisions with a stranger named Kate flood my mind. And if I remember correctly, I think I said that if I never ran across another Kate, I'd be a happy man.

And here I was, about to marry one.

She tires of my stupor and starts questioning me. "What are you doing here? You're supposed to be at work?"

I slide my hand down my face and tap my chin. One. Two.

Remember, no matter what, she's a woman. She deserves respect.

Remember, no matter what, she's been a part of your life. She deserves kindness.

Remember, no matter what, you told her you loved her. She deserves understanding.

With my mantras embroidered in my mind, on a nice and comfy throw pillow, I grab the TV remote, turn off the quieted cable news, and reply to her with tempered grit. "Turns out, Clarkson didn't need me for a full-double. He came in and relieved me at the half-turn."

"And you couldn't call to let me know?"

"Well, Kimber, I was gonna call you after I got home." I jab a hand though my hair. "You'll have to forgive me for not keeping you abreast of my change of plans. But you see, I wasn't exactly expecting my fiancée to be fucking two strange men in my bedroom."

She's wearing a slinky red nightgown with a matching robe, which strikes me as odd.

"You don't have to be like that. You don't have to say it like that," she snarks.

I can't help the cynical chuckle that rumbles from deep in my throat. "Say it like what?"

"All petty and shit."

"Petty?! We're engaged to be married."

"And *that*," she tosses a hand at the bedroom, flashing the diamond ring I gave her, "has nothing to do with our engagement, with our relationship."

I can't even believe what I'm hearing. If I didn't know better, I'd think she was high. "It doesn't?"

"Of course not. *That* was just business."

"Business? What does that mean? You did that to sell cars?"

She at least has the decency to appear sheepish. Her cheeks pink and she fiddles with her nails, picking at her cuticles.

When she doesn't refute my claim, I press her. "Kimber, I swear, you better not fucking lie to me, did you do that to sell cars? Are you sleeping with men so that they'll buy from the dealership?"

Her eyes narrow, and her jaw tics. "Don't act so naïve, Ridge. I'm a grown woman. It doesn't mean anything. It's just a wine and dine. Plain and simple."

Oh my god. A wine and dine. "So all the times I thought you were just going to fancy dinners, you were actually cheating on me? Trading sex for cars?"

"I'm not a prostitute, you shithead. These are men of affluence. Men with power. Men with money. Sometimes they just need a little something to sweeten the deal. It's the cost of doing business."

"The cost of doing business?! Some guy's jizz is all over my carpet!" I can't even think straight. I feel like my head is going to split open. Right down the middle. Like a hotdog bun. I wander over to the couch and plop down, defeated and weary. "This isn't the first time you've used my apartment for this, is it?"

When she doesn't answer, I *know* the answer.

"How many times? How many men?"

"That's not important."

"It's important to me."

She sits in the side chair. "None of them matter. You're the only person who's important to me."

"That's one hell of a way to show it." I lean forward and massage my temples. And that pressure forces a whole new line of questioning into my brain. My head snaps back up. "He wasn't wearing a condom!"

Kimber's eyes widen, and she feigns innocence. "What?"

"Kimber! He wasn't wearing a condom. Please tell me that was a one-off. Please, please, please tell me you always used protection and that tonight was the exception."

She flips her hair over her shoulder and nibbles her bottom lip. After stalling, the truth blurts from her in a frantic and jumbled race. "I always protected you. That's why I always made you wear a condom. Me and you? We've never had sex without a condom. Never. Not once. You are good."

"What. The. Fuck." Oh, I can't believe this is my life. "You've been having unprotected sex with guys for what? Years? And for the past eight months, all the while I thought we were in a monogamous relationship?"

Her face flares with anger once again. "I told you I protected you. And I get tested every single month for shit." She points to her covered crotch. "This pussy is clean. Fucking pristine."

I tap the hell out of my chin. I'm probably gonna have a bald spot in my beard by the time the night is over. "What the hell were you gonna do if you got pregnant? Pretend it was mine? Remind me that condoms aren't foolproof and let me believe that I fathered a child?"

"That was never gonna happen."

"You were having unprotected sex, Kimber. And from the sounds and looks of it, you were doing it a lot. You were playing Russian roulette in thinking a pregnancy wouldn't happen."

"Oh, for fuck's sake, Ridge. I wasn't gonna get pregnant because I can't have kids."

I'm blown back against the couch cushion, physically assaulted by her proclamation. "Wh–what?"

"I don't want kids. I've never wanted kids. So I had a tubal ligation two years ago."

My vision pinholes and black spots dance across my periphery. "What?"

"I had a tubal," she repeats.

"But you don't have a scar." I have no idea why that's the first thing out of my mouth.

"It's only one incision. Inside my belly button. You can't see it."

"How could you not tell me something like that? You…you know I want children. You know how important having a family is to me." My stuttering whisper is low and pained.

She sits there. Like a statue. Totally mute.

"A tubal can be reversed. Is that why you didn't tell me?" I shake my head back and forth, timing it with my rapid thoughts. "You wanted to adopt, is that it? Foster?"

"No, Ridge. I don't want kids. Like ever. It's true, a tubal can be reversed. But a uterine ablation can't."

"You had an ablation?"

"Yeah. Like I said, two years ago."

I'm totally numb. Frozen and anesthetized. "How could you lie about something like that? About something so fundamental? You know how important the kids are to me. Daire and Hardy. Anna, Ty, Laura, and Nate. You've seen me with them. You know I want that in my life."

"Don't play dumb. You had to know something was up."

"What? What are you talking about?"

She rolls her eyes. "Didn't it strike you as weird that I never had a period?"

I replay the past eight months on a loop. Do I remember her having a period? No. No, I don't. But is that really significant considering that we sometimes went weeks without having sex?

Once again, I scrub my face and tap my chin.

She grunts in frustration. "Can you please stop doing that?" She mimics my actions like she's playing a game of Simon Says. "It's so damn annoying."

And with that, the last little bit of glue comes undone, and the Band-Aid flutters to the ground. "I can't do this, Kimber."

"Fine by me. You're the one who wanted to talk about this. Instead of just being an adult about it. Like I said, it's just work stuff."

"I'm talking about *us*. I can't do *us* anymore."

Her back straightens, and her chin tilts in the air. "What?"

"We're not right for each other. You know that; I know that."

"Ridge, what are you saying?" She contorts her fingers, bending a thumb around the engagement ring that I slid on her finger. The engagement ring that she wanted to replace before the wedding. For something bigger, something grander, something fit for a woman of her stature.

"We can't get married, Kimber."

Her body fills with rage. "You're calling off the wedding? Have you lost your fucking mind?! What will people say? I'll be the laughingstock of the entire state."

I cock an eyebrow. "That's what you're concerned about? You care about what other people will say?"

"Of course, I care! I've worked too hard to build this life, to build this reputation." She closes her eyes and puckers her lips into a circle as she breathes in and out. "Okay. Okay. It's fine. We can just postpone until we work things out. We'll…" Her eyes jump around the room, trying to devise the narrative that fits her storyline. "We'll just tell people that with this being the ten-year anniversary of the shooting-thing that you wanted to really focus on your mental health and healing." She shrugs. "We'll push the wedding to next spring."

"There's not going to be a wedding between the two of us. Ever. We have to break up. We don't belong together."

The bitterness in her heart turns into a malignancy, invading her every cell in a deep-seated hatred. "You. Are. Breaking. Up. With. Me."

Her question isn't even a question. It sounds more like a threat.

"Yes." There's really no need to beat around the bush. "I'm so sorry, Kimber, but I don't love you. The truth is…I never loved you.

I only thought I did. I was just so desperate to find happiness, to build a life, to make a family, that I clung to you. You came into my life during a time when I was weak and scared. The past few years have been so damn hard—with everything that Holt and Merit went through, and Ella and Crutch. You came into my life at a time when I was lost. And I tried to force you to save me."

Her nose crinkles, and her lips curl. "I know what this is," she snarls. "This is all about her, isn't it? Amy. Or Orah. Or whatever the hell she wants to call herself." She stabs the air with a finger. "She did this on purpose. To get to you, to turn you against me. She knew exactly what she was doing. Hell, she probably lied about not knowing you lived in the same town. I guarantee you she knew! And she knew before our meeting that you were the groom, knew that you were my fiancé. This has been her plan. From the very beginning. The little cunt wants to steal my life!"

Her malignancy has now metastasized to my own body, making me feel physically ill. I'm filled with loathing and animosity, overcome with feelings that a man should never feel for a woman. "Don't you dare talk about her like that. Do you hear me?"

Her slow smile is divided in equal halves, part coy and part evil. "I knew it. I knew you were fucking her."

"I. Have. Not. Slept. With. Amy."

"Well, something is going on. Otherwise, you wouldn't be throwing away what we have. So, tell me, Ridge. What happened? You kiss her? Shove your tongue in her pussy? Did she drop to her knees and suck that monster cock of yours?"

"Kimber, I swear…" I bite the inside of my cheek, refusing to lash out in pettiness, in some tit-for-tat battle. The metallic taste of blood mingles with my saliva.

"You swear what?!" She jumps up from her chair and stomps over to me. Leaning down, she pushes her face so close to mine that I have to fling my head back against the couch again, lest our noses bump. "Tell me, Ridge! Tell me what you did."

"We didn't sleep together. We didn't kiss. We didn't do anything that sexual."

She cocks her head, reading between the unwritten lines. "But…"

"But, yes, I've done things I shouldn't have. Things a married man, or even an engaged man, shouldn't do."

"Meaning?"

"I've hugged her. I've touched the small of her back. I've held her hand. I've whispered in her ear. I…I've been thinking about her. Nonstop."

"You've been thinking about her?" Kimber slaps her hands against her thighs. "Can't you see? This is what she planned."

"Kimber," I pause, forcing an injection of empathy into my admission, determined to gift her with compassion. Even though it's hard to do. "I haven't been thinking about her nonstop for two-and-a-half weeks. I've been thinking about her nonstop for ten years."

Her brow furrows as she marinates on my declaration.

"I'm in love with her." I reach out, trying to hold Kimber's hand, but she snatches it away. "I'm sorry. But it's always been her. Always."

She swaps her pain for spite. As easily and effortlessly as she changes her purse to match her outfit. "You are a pathetic loser, Ridge Conway."

Spinning on her heels, she races into the bedroom. There's a flurry of activity as she tosses clothes and toiletries into the expensive luggage that she stored in the closet. For fifteen minutes straight, I sit still, listening to her grunt and groan, bitch and moan. She converses with herself, calling me every curse and slur known to modern language. And before she walks out of my life, she heaves one final insult. "You're gonna regret letting go of me."

Yeah, I don't think so.

I listen as the heavy steel and wooden door eases closed, despite her attempt to slam it, I'm sure. In a coma-like state, I stare at the smoke detector that's above the doorframe to the small entry hallway. Every thirty seconds, the barely visible, little green light blinks, confirming the equipment is in fine working order.

Thirty seconds. Flash.

Thirty seconds. Flash.

Thirty seconds. Flash.

Yep. It's in fine working order. Too bad I'm not.

Standing up, I walk over to the kitchen counter and grab my phone. Holt answers on the first ring. "Hey, brother, what's up?"

"I need your help."

He immediately picks up on my sour mood. "Sure. No problem. What do you need help with?"

"Moving some furniture down to the dumpster."

"Okkkkkaaaayyyy." He makes a clicking noise between his teeth, no doubt getting Merit's attention. "Tonight? Right now?"

"Yep." I walk to the fridge and grab a beer. "And is Dr. Steve Jennings still your team's physician and athletic trainer?"

"Yeah. Why?"

"Think you can pull a favor? Get him to come over too?"

"I'm sure I can. Are you sick?"

"I sure as fuck hope not. Tell him to bring his shit. I need blood work and urinalysis done as quick as humanly possible."

"Blood work? What for?"

"Oh, you know, the usual. Syphilis, hepatitis, the clap."

"Holy shit. Okay."

I twist the beer back and forth in my hand, reading the label, perusing the alcohol content. "And Holt?"

"Yeah, brother?"

"You still got that bottle of Macallan 25?"

He snorts into the phone. "Something tells me I won't after tonight."

Chapter 27

Orah

You'd think I'd be used to the heartbreak.

But I'm not.

The impact of certain emotions never lessens, never eases, never weakens. It hurt then, and it hurts now. Once again, he turned me away. A near decade ago, he turned me away because of his job. Because of my age. Because of our pain. Because of the horrors inflicted upon us.

His. My. Our. Us.

Everything was stacked against us. We were two survivors with the weight of the world on our backs. A burden so heavy that our vertebrae were collapsing and shattering with every step. We were two naïve kids who fell in love, in a room-sized coffin, filled with blood and bullets and fuzzy slippers.

And now? Now, we're adults.

We can make our own decisions, our own choices. We can do what we want. We don't have gunmen and rapists, doctors and therapists, chiefs and mayors telling us what to do. Our strings don't have to be manipulated by anyone. We can move freely, willingly, and of our own accord.

Except he's not doing that.

He's allowing that bitch to engineer his unhappiness. She's defrauding him—defrauding us—of a lifetime of happiness.

She's the disease of my destiny.

Sighing in sadness and frustration, I tuck the salad fork sample back into the display drawer and shut it. These rental companies make a killing. For this one function, I'll be renting fifty place settings from them.

And the rental charge for those fifty place settings? Yeah, it could cover my parents' mortgage payment for six months.

I'm about to head back into my office when the front door chimes. As always, I turn to the sound, ready to look and absorb. Ready to memorize small details in case something happens and I have to give a description of the offender.

Except this is no offender. It's Merit. With Daire snuggled around her chest in a wrap baby carrier.

A frigid and windy cold front has been hanging around, ever since the storms passed through on Friday night. As a result, her cheeks are pink with windburn, and her hair, which is down today, is sticking to her eyelashes and nose. She quickly frees her face from the strands and sneezes, making Daire jump.

"Merit?"

When she sees me, her eyes widen and her face reddens even more, growing bright with excitement. "Ora–I mean, Amy!"

She scuttles across the showroom, giving a side-glance to the people meandering around. Gripping my elbow, she ushers me into the corner.

"Merit, are you okay? Is something wrong?"

She sighs in relief, gifts me with a bright smile, and then wrangles me into a sideways hug, taking care not to smush the baby. "Hey, Orah. It's so good to see you."

Her embrace is warm and sincere, cracking my already-fractured resolve. And on top of that, she smells like sugar cookies. Which makes me wanna burst into tears and spend the entire afternoon in the kitchen. "It's good to see you too." I pull back and scan her from top to bottom. She doesn't look hurt or anything. "What's the matter?"

"You haven't heard from Kimber, have you?"

Heard from Kimber? That would be a hell no.

"No, but there would be no reason for her to contact me." Needing stability to my unstable life, I grab my necklace. "I'm not her wedding planner anymore. I've turned her and Ridge's account over to Celeste and Anniah." I peek over her shoulder, trying to see if either of them is nearby. I'm not sure what kind of wedding calamity has befallen Kimber, but it must be pretty damn cataclysmic if she has Merit running interference for her. They're not exactly Lucy and Ethel, Wilma and Betty, Laverne and Shirley.

"Oh, there's not gonna be a wedding to plan." She delivers the message with a gush of secrets and sarcasm.

My fingers dig into my diamonds. I imagine myself crushing them, being strong enough to pulverize them with just my fist. "They're eloping?"

She frowns. "What? Hell no." Then, she leans closer, holding Daire's sweet little head to keep it from flopping. "There's not going to be a wedding because they broke up."

What did she just say?

My hand falls to my side, and my brain scrambles, unable to land on one coherent thought. "Wh–what?"

"Ridge wanted to tell you himself, but..."

"But what?" Fear circles my heart, squeezing it in an unforgiving vise. It sends a piercing and punishing ache down my chest. My scar responds in kind, pulsing in pain.

Oh my God, he doesn't want me.

After all of this, and even after breaking up with her, he doesn't want me.

My eyes clamp closed, and I do my best to prepare for the news that won't be new.

He. Doesn't. Want. You.

"Well, to be honest," she starts, "he's completely shitfaced."

My eyes fly open. "Huh?"

"He's totally wasted. Like knock-down, drag-out, eat-potato-chips-off-floor intoxicated."

"He's eating potato chips off the floor?"

Her brow furrows. "Of course not. That's just a turn of phrase."

That phrase has never once been turned in my presence. Instead of falling into that rabbit hole, I focus on the moral of the story. "He's drunk?"

"Yep."

I glance at my watch, ignoring the sizzle of my tattoo under the band. "At one in the afternoon?"

"Well, for him, it's not necessarily the afternoon." She pops her tongue against her lips. "Because he hasn't been to bed yet."

"He hasn't slept? Since when?"

"Well, he pulled a tour and a half, during the full moon, mind you. Then, he went straight home, and him and Kimber broke up. That was last night."

"And he was too upset to sleep?"

She giggles and snorts. "Well, you can't really sleep when you don't have a bed. Or a couch."

"Kimber stole the furniture?"

Merit flaps her hands up and down. "I think we're getting off topic. He can give you all the details later. The important thing is he was worried about you, but Crutch and Cullen refuse to let him leave the apartment in his current state." Daire grunts and gives a squeak. "Freakin' great. I think he's about to poop." Merit bends closer to her son, sniffs him, and then gives his nose a little kiss. "Now's not the best of time, son. Just hold it for a few more minutes, and Mommy will love you forever."

I have a fucking headache.

My stomach is drowning in a tsunami of nausea, and everything in me hurts. My brain, my bones, even my teeth. "Merit, I am so completely lost. I have no idea what's happening."

She takes an epic breath, grabs my shoulders, and lasers into my eyes. "Ridge broke up with Kimber last night. He knew he had to do it. He doesn't love her. But in the process of the breakup, he… discovered…some not-so-nice things. I'll let him tell you all about it, but it boils down to him being embarrassed and disgusted with himself for ever thinking they should be a couple. So, he decided to have a drink. Which turned into another drink. And so on and so on. But then, Kimber texted him about an hour ago and said she was going to turn your life into a living hell." She takes another breath, replenishing her oxygen so she can finish her story. "He tried to drive down here. And you know what a stickler he is for drinking and driving. He's going to completely freak out when he realizes he was about to make that dumb decision." She scoffs. "Anyway, Holt and C stayed with him last night, but Holt had to go to school. So, Crutch came over to fill in, and they're keeping him locked in the apartment. That means, me," she hooks a thumb at herself, "and Ella are in charge of checking on you and trying to stop Kimber from doing whatever bat-shit crazy thing is going through her mind."

I regurgitate the highlights. "Ridge broke up with Kimber?"

"Yes."

"And he's drunk?"

"Yes."

"And she wants to ruin my life because? What? She blames me for their engagement ending?"

She smiles triumphantly, proud that I'm finally bringing my A-game to the conversation. "Yes."

And right at that moment, Kimber-Shay Willis struts into Wexler Events, on her five-inch heels, wielding her cell phone and egotistical attitude like a scythe. Her eyes dart to mine, as if on instinct, and she immediately places me in her crosshairs.

In a moment of true and unbridled friendship, Merit steps in front of me, shielding me from Kimber's view.

One. Two. Three. Four. Five.

For once, my five seconds fills me with something more than tranquility; it fills me with freedom. Tired of, yet again, being the prey to someone's predator, I tug on her arm. "No, Merit. It's okay."

"Well, if it isn't the little homewrecker," Kimber chides.

"I'm not a homewrecker."

"My slaughtered relationship would say otherwise."

"If anything was slaughtered, it was killed by your own hand," I protest. "You don't even love him, Kimber."

"Of course, I do."

"You love the idea of him. You love the picture-perfect vision of playing wife to the ruggedly handsome hero. You don't love his heart. You don't love his soul. Everything he likes about himself, you hate."

"You don't know the first thing about him. You think just because you shared some meaningless, little kiss with him a decade ago that you know how to make him happy? Well, you don't. He is mine, you stupid cunt."

"Get the hell away from my family, Kimber." A powerful and domineering voice blazes through the air, melting Kimber's metaphoric scythe in an inferno.

Apparently, we—along with every other person in the store— were too engrossed with the drama at hand to hear the chime of the door. Walking across the showroom, with her head held high, her shoulders pulled back, and her back ramrod straight, is the impeccable Ella Crutchfield.

"Stay out of this, Ella," Kimber barks.

"I most certainly will not." She slides up next to Kimber and stares down at her. Kimber's stilettos are no match for Ella's natural height. "You're accosting my family, including an infant, in the middle of a busy store. In what galaxy is that appropriate behavior?"

Kimber flicks her hair over her shoulder. "The whole town is right about you, you know? You really are a snobby bitch."

Ella's lips curl into a sly smile. "So I've been told."

Kimber rolls her eyes. "This has nothing to do with you. This is between me and this weirdo." She spins, pinning me with her stare.

"Weirdo?" Merit peeps.

"Uhhh, yeah." Kimber scrunches her nose in disgust. "The stupid black clothes. The dumb shoes. You're twitchy and glitchy and jumpy. You even fucking talk to yourself. And don't get me started on that ridiculous necklace." She takes a step closer to me, suffocating me, crowding my personal space. "You're a fucking freak. And he could never love someone like you."

I. Lose. It.

Literally.

My blood congeals into rage. My heart pumps it through the nooks and crannies of my body, filling me with a delirious outrage.

And instead of fighting it, I embrace it. I embrace the fury.

Because I am exhausted. Totally and completely and unequivocally exhausted.

I'm exhausted of being ashamed. Of being objectified. Of being raped. Of being forced to choose between my best friend and my dignity.

I'm exhausted of being shot. Of being traumatized. Of being broken.

And most importantly, I'm exhausted of constantly thinking I don't deserve a future.

I'm tired of being exhausted.

"If you curse one more time in front of my baby cousin," I growl, "I'm gonna pull your hair extensions out, one by one, and give them to Pet Peeve as a chew toy."

Well, that didn't go exactly as planned. Considering Christmas is still ten months away, I highly doubt Laura has received her dog. But you know, for a first attempt, it wasn't too bad. I think Tabby would be proud.

Merit bursts out laughing, and when I spy Ella hiding a giggle behind her hand, I feel like a world champion.

Even Kimber's recent fifteen-hundred-dollar facial can't hide the wrinkles formed by her confusion. Yeah, Ridge might've complained about that ostentatious expense. "Baby cousin?" Her eyes flicker to Daire. Who is now beet red and most definitely pushing out a crap. "That kid is not related to you."

Ella folds her hands in front of her, the epitome of perfect control. "In our family, labels are more than simple semantics." She shrugs. "Too bad you'll never know that."

"Leave, Kimber." I take a step forward, forcing her to take a step back. "Before I call the police. Like Ella said, this is a place of business. I won't allow you to disrupt it any more than you already have."

An evil grin overtakes her face, thinning her lips across her white, straight teeth. "Oh, you have no idea," she snarls. Turning, she walks away, click-clacking her heels and swishing her hips. As she pushes open the door, my cell phone blares to life, jarring the thick tension of the room. With a laugh, she lofts her parting words into the air, lobbing them high and deep, right into my gut. "I'd get that if I were you, Amy. I have a feeling it's important."

Chapter 28

Orah

Fired.

I am fired.

Unemployed. Jobless. Out of work.

As you would expect, Margo didn't appreciate one of her associates 'stealing' the groom. Apparently, that's bad for business when your business is built around planning weddings. She refused to listen to reason, refused to consider any other narrative except for the one that came from Kimber.

After all, Kimber is part of the upper echelon. The high priestess of the highborn. The flaky rim of the upper-crust. Why would a woman, of such sophistication and charm, lie?

Well, she lied because she's a liar.

What more is there to say.

The loss of my job is a tough pill to swallow. Not because I'm gonna miss working for Margo, but because it's left me feeling lost and untethered. My parents upended their lives, and left their only grandchild behind, to move back here with me. While I didn't ask them to do any of that, I think they knew it was the only way to convince me to come back to this Alabama town. I never truly thought Margo would offer me my old job. But once she did? And once my parents said, 'Well, what the hell are you waiting for? We'll just move with you'... there was nothing I could do to finagle my way out of it. I had been teetering on the idea of giving my dessert-making business a real chance, giving it my all to see if I could make it work. In some-ways, it felt like they made this decision without me, that I was just a bystander watching at a distance.

But that decision, it led me back to Ridge.

And now, I'm wondering if the destinies are finally aligning for us. If we can finally be together the way I've always wanted. Although, in my fantasies, I was never navigating the unemployment line.

I've got money saved up, but most of that money I don't consider mine. It's set aside for my parents. While I was taking care of Granny and pregnant with Eden, it's not like my side job of baking birthday cakes had me rolling in the dough.

Get it?

Pun intended.

My parents helped to support me. And since moving here, they haven't charged me any rent or utilities. That's why, after calculating the average rent and utility cost for a moderate apartment in town, I've set aside an equal amount of money for them each month in a separate account.

And one day, I'll give it to them.

Assuming I don't have to break into it. Margo did threaten to make my reputation known throughout town. So, who the hell knows how hard it's going to be to find something new.

I guess I should be crying, fighting waves of snot and hiccups and uncontrollable sobs. But when I started to get emotional in the middle of Wexler Events, Ella told me that I had to be brave. That I needed to hold my head high and not shed one single tear for as-sholes who cared more about the dollar signs in a person's bank account than they do about honor and integrity, love and laughter, family and friendship. And then, she, Merit, and Celeste helped me pack my office and load my meager work belongings into the trunk of my car.

And that's where I sit. In my car. Parked next to Ridge's truck. In the parking lot of his very-modern, very-expensive, not-at-all-him apartment complex.

I take the elevator up to the penthouse floor, and I've barely grazed my knuckles across the door when it jerks open. Standing on the other side is the mammoth of a man with a heart of gold.

"Thanks so much for coming." Crutch brushes a kiss across the apple of my cheek and ushers me across the threshold and down the small entry hallway, where he huddles with me against the wall. "We told him that he's in no condition for some big heart-to-heart, but he refuses to even go to bed until he sees you."

"He's that drunk?"

"He's a little better now. He stopped drinking a while ago, and we've been pumping him with water and electrolytes. He's not much of a hard liquor drinker. He pretty much sticks to beer. So, it hit him. Like a damn freight train."

"You've been here all day?"

He huffs out a half-chuckle, half-scoff. "Yeah, I had to change from active-duty to on-call. Fortunately, there's been no major incidents today." I glance down and see all of his police stuff on his belt, minus the gun, of course. "But Holt couldn't miss school. He was having a coach's meeting. And Will's at the bar; someone had to open for deliveries." He shrugs. "But it's fine. Cullen and I didn't want the girls, or even their dads, to move in the new furniture. The last thing we need, on top of this, is for Jeff or Ray to strain their backs."

Why does everyone keep talking about his home furnishings? "New furniture? Kimber owned the furniture in Ridge's apartment?"

Crutch leans back and peeks down the hallway, spying on whoever may be in the other room. I would assume it's just Ridge and Cullen, but all I can hear is the muffled noise of the TV. "Okay, knowing Ridge, he's gonna try to explain all of this to you as soon as he lays eyes on you. But it'll most likely come out in a jumbled mess. So, I'll give you the short and sweet version until he can explain better."

"Yeah. Okay." I mirror his low voice with my own.

"He got pulled into a double shift. He arranged for Kimber to come over this morning, as soon as he was scheduled to get off." Crutch lifts a brow. "He was done. It was over. He was gonna end things with her. All of it. The wedding, the engagement, the relationship. He finally opened his dumbass eyes and saw her for the horrible person that she is."

"Oh."

He gives me a small, soft smile. The turn of his lips makes his translucent green eyes sparkle. The color reminds me of a pastel frosting I used for someone's cupcakes last year. "He doesn't love her. He never did."

Heat rises to my cheeks. I tame my optimism, refusing to bow to the visions of a future with the man I love. Because I've been burned by that unbridled hope one too many times in the past. "Oh. Okay."

"But things didn't go as planned." He clicks his tongue against his teeth. "He ended up not working a full double. The guy he was covering for came in last night to relieve him. And Kimber was here when Ridge got home."

Typically, one wouldn't be concerned by such a notion—a fiancée waiting in the house of their partner. But Kimber's not your typical fiancée.

"And she wasn't alone," he continues.

"She wasn't?"

He shakes his head. "She was in the middle of a threesome with some guy and his, well, I'm not sure if it was his father, his grandfather, his boss, or just some other random dude. But she was there. Having sex. Cheating on Ridge. On his bed. In his bedroom."

What. The. Hell.

She was cheating?

Running around on him?

On Ridge.

On My Hero.

That evil, wicked bitch.

"Orah?" Crutch commands my name, demanding that my crazed and unfocused eyes land on him. "It wasn't the first time. She's been doing it all along. Basically trading sex for car sales."

My stomach churns in disgust. I slink against the wall, searching for traction because I'm dizzy and wobbly, a fumble of arms and legs that don't want to comply with the orders firing from my brain.

"She…" My hand tugs on my necklace, my thumb tracing the single Tiger's Eye stone. "She's been cheating on him. This entire time? Their whole relationship?"

"Yeah."

"Oh my god." All of a sudden, one small aspect of his horrible commentary finds its way into my mind. "Wait, in his bed? Is that why he has new furniture."

"Yep. He tossed out anything and everything that he thought naked people may have rolled around on—the mattress, the bedding, two chairs, a rug, and a couch. Jeff and Dana went out this morning and bought him all new furniture. We just finished moving it in about an hour ago."

A deep sigh rushes from my lungs, spewing out of my mouth in a wind of anguish and sorrow, fatigue and frailness, relief and alleviation. "Holy shit, Crutch. How could she do that to him?"

"It doesn't matter anymore."

His declaration catches me by surprise.

"Huh?"

"It doesn't matter anymore," he repeats. "Because now, his life can finally begin. He didn't even realize death was stalking him." He squeezes my shoulder. "You saved a dying man, Orah."

He turns, emerging from the shadows of the hall, and bursts into the living room. With shaky footing, I follow him. Ridge is sitting in a chair with a price tag still attached to the back of it, staring out a mass of windows that run the length of the room. Cullen's perched at the kitchen bar so he notices me first. The relief etched across his face is almost comical.

The apartment is neat and tidy. So the overwhelming smell of beer and alcohol permeating the air seems out of place. The scent is spicy and strong.

Whiskey, maybe?

A heaviness settles among the three of us as we wait for Ridge to feel my presence. And, as always, it doesn't take long. There's an invisible chain linking the two of us together. Always and forever. He spins in his chair, crying out my nickname as soon as my appearance validates the tug of the rope, tethering his heart to my own.

Tug. Tug. Tug.

Like a fish on a line.

Well, more like a whale on the line.

"Little Bird!" He launches himself out of the chair, but considering he's sideways, he stumbles and trips over the edge of the couch. "Ooof!" Quickly righting himself, he rushes to me, scooping me into a crushing hug.

Underneath the smell of sweat and spirits, his soap still lingers, making me happy despite the complete shitshow of the afternoon. He nuzzles his wet lips against my cheek and squeezes my ribs a little too hard. But I'd never tell him that.

He sets me back down on my feet and pulls away, just slightly, giving me a full view of his current state of appearance. Messy hair. Bloodshot eyes. Lazy and goofy smile.

Fuck me.

Even inebriated, he's the most gorgeous creature I've ever seen.

His calloused fingertips settle on my waist, making me feel bubbly and tingly. My fingers tangle in the wild hair, curling around the base of his neck.

He leans closer.

Oh, so close.

And then he whispers.

"I don't have gonorrhea."

Uhhh...what?

Cullen jumps up from his reclined position at the bar and clamps his hands around his big brother's shoulders. "Okay, brother! I think that's enough for today." He shoves Ridge away from me, severing our connection. "You've seen her now. Remember, you promised to go to sleep after seeing her." He's talking to him slow and precise, like a parent negotiating with a child.

"C, My Brave Girl is here," he slurs.

"I know. I know."

"I can feel her." He hiccups. "And fuck, if she don't feel good."

With an apologetic shrug, Cullen ushers Ridge into the bedroom.

Don't she feel good....

Let's just hope he feels the same way once he sobers up.

Chapter 29

Ridge

Holy shit, I'm hung over.

I don't think I've ever been that drunk.

And although I'm more than relieved that my rapid tests came back clean for any and all sexually transmitted illnesses, I'm fairly certain there was a better way to deliver the news to Orah than the way I did. My memories are fuzzy, but I'm pretty sure I announced my clean bill of health like a little kid bragging about an 'A' on a report card.

At least this new mattress is super comfortable. Hopefully, I'll be able to say the same thing about the couch and the chairs. I *know* I sat in them, but hell if I remember what they feel like. Or even look like. By the time, C and Crutch moved the new furniture in, I was already lost in a fog of worry over Orah.

Rolling over, I make a mental note to get the total from Mom so I can move money from my bank account to hers. The last thing I want is for my parents to have to pay—literally—over something *I* did as a result of something *Kimber* did. I also can't help but wonder if any passersby have confiscated the furnishings that we couldn't fit inside of the dumpster. I did leave a note so they would know what they were getting themselves into. At the time, I found it quite humorous.

Rest in Peace, old friend. Died a tragic death on the Ol' Jism Trail.

I fumble for the clock on the nightstand and drag it in front of my blurry eyes, cursing when the cord gets hung up.

One in the morning.

Grunting, I crawl out of bed, wincing when my muscles contract in pain. Despite the water C tried to pump down me earlier, my foray into the world of binge drinking has left me dehydrated and achy. I pad across the floor and into the connected bathroom. When I flip on the light, my brain nearly explodes. It takes a second for my eyes to adjust, but when they do, I spy two bottles of Gatorade and a container of over-the-counter pain relievers on the countertop. And when I find the drinks are still cold, I silently thank my brother and vow to return the favor, if and when, he has an emotional breakdown. I chug a bottle of electrolytes and follow it with three pills. Then I settle into the shower for the world's hottest and longest cleansing. Not only do I wash every inch of my body, but I scrub my dick like I'm debriding it of a flesh-eating bacteria. Once my body is a raw and scalded piece of meat, I flip the faucet to cold and force myself to stay under the spray until my teeth are chattering. Thankfully, the freezing temperature washes away the majority of my brain fog and upset stomach.

I'm damn lucky that I don't have to report for my shift at seven this morning. Clarkson is returning the favor and paying me back for the half-shift I covered. I still have to go in today, but not until seven tonight.

Hopping out, I guzzle the other bottle of Gatorade and then brush my teeth until my gums bleed and my bristles are flattened like a pancake. I slip into a pair of boxer briefs and trudge out into the darkened living room to search for my cell phone.

Because I need to call Orah.

Fucking ASAP.

I think we all agree that there's a very real possibility I'll be banging on John and Ann's door before the sun even comes up.

The living room is draped in a soft glow, highlighted only by the moon and the sleepy reflection of a handful of streetlights far below my penthouse level. And even those are fogged, blurred by the gauzy shades that are pulled down three-quarters of the way. My eyes laser on the kitchen counter, searching for my phone. The second I grab it, I nearly shit my underwear because the lamp on the side table clicks to life.

And then the room is illuminated, giving me the one gift I'll never be worthy of. The one gift I'll never stop fighting for. The one gift I'll never take for granted.

Ever. Again.

"You're here." My relief is a simple idiom, filled with a thousand different meanings.

"I told Cullen I would stay. I didn't want you to be alone."

She's standing barefoot, dressed in the same T-shirt from the mountains. *My T-shirt.* I guess that means she took it when we left the cabin. And unless she packed an overnight bag before coming over here late yesterday afternoon, it means she's been carrying it around with her.

Damn. That's hot.

And sweet.

Just like her.

She's strawberries dipped in sriracha. And I wanna eat every fucking last drop until my tongue catches fire.

My eyes travel the length of her, soaking in every last delicious curve and line. And just like it always does when I look at her, my cock swells, fighting against the fabric that's keeping it constrained.

I toss a nod toward my bedroom door. "The Gatorade? The pills? That was you?"

Her hands fold in front of her, and she worries her fingers. "Yeah. I wasn't sure when you were gonna wake up." She quirks one eyebrow into a cute little arch. "You went to bed kinda early."

I shrug, trying to make a joke. "Or late, depending on how you look at it."

She sighs and cocks her head. "I'm so sorry, Ridge."

"I assume they told you? About what I walked in on? What she was doing?" I pause, content with the fact that I'm able to muster the words now without debilitating repulsion. "She's been cheating on me."

"I can't imagine what you're going through."

"I'm relieved."

"Relieved?"

"I'm done with her. It's over." I pull my bottom lip between my teeth. "I'm angry at myself for letting things go on for as long as they did. I should've never even gone on a second date with her, let alone had a relationship with her."

"But what she did was horrible. Completely indefensible. How can you be so forgiving?"

"Oh, I haven't forgiven her. But...I did my own fair share of indefensible things."

She purses her lips and folds her arms across her chest, plumping her breasts in the air. Breasts that are most definitely not corralled by a bra. "I highly doubt that."

"Really? She might've slept with a thousand different men." I take a small step in her direction. "But I'm the one who's slept a thousand different ways with *one* woman. And that one woman wasn't her."

She gasps, reading between the lines of what's not been spoken.

My cock jumps again, begging to be closer to her.

Orah's gaze meanders down my torso, wandering from my chest, down to my stomach. When she lands on my crotch, she does a little jump on her tiptoes and blurts out. "She got me fired."

What. The. Actual. Fuck.

"What?" Surely, I didn't hear her right.

"She got me fired. She called Margo and told her that I stole you, that I seduced you. I was immediately terminated."

My entire body sags in defeat.

In my drunken stupor, I was worried something like this would happen. Kimber's text was ominous and filled with bitterness and vengeance. I'm beyond disgusted that I shared my bed with someone like her. "Shit, Orah. I'm so very sorry. I can call Margo and tell her the truth, try to get your job back."

She unwinds her arms, and instead begins to fiddle with the hem of the shirt, worrying it between her thumb and forefinger. "No, don't." Something tells me that if she were wearing her necklace, her fingers would be around her throat and not down at her hips. "I...I don't think I want to work there anymore."

"You don't?"

She shakes her head.

"Are you sure?"

Her forehead wrinkles, and she gives herself a moment to really think about her professional aspirations. "Yeah. I'm sure. That's not what I want anymore."

"And what do you want?" My inquiry is thick and heavy, weighted by hunger and hope, craving and credence.

"What I've always wanted."

Sweet shit.

If I don't cross this room and take her in my arms, I'm gonna die.

Life's a funny thing. I've spent years pretending that my world was complete without Orah. I mean, damn, I was set to marry another woman. Ready to walk down the aisle, make a life, and hopefully, start a family with a woman who was actually nothing more than a figment of my imagination. And I can't even blame the whole thing on Kimber. I'm just as much to blame as she is. Well, maybe that's not true. I wasn't cheating on her and selling my body for cars, but you know what I mean.

I started the charade.

I blinded my eyes, shrouded my ears, and muted my lips. All by my own choice. I refused to see and hear and speak and think.

I made everything complicated. When, in all honesty, the truth is so far from complex.

The facts are simple. My world isn't complete without Orah. *There is no world without Orah.*

The facts are simple. This love isn't my damnation. *This love is my fucking salvation.*

The facts are simple. She's my redemption. *She's counted the flames. And now, I want her to dance on the ashes.*

With me.

Ten steps. It takes me ten steps to stalk across the room.

I'm within arm's distance when she holds up her left hand. "Stop."

My ears are ringing, and my heart thunders against my ribs, crushing my lungs in a vise. My eyes flicker down, roaming to her wrist where *our* tattoo shines brighter than the Northern Star. It's my homing beacon. It's the compass I've been searching for after a decade of being lost at sea.

When a tear spills onto her cheek, agony rips through my chest, tearing it wide open like a rabid animal is attacking me. She blinks, focusing her glittering, storm-cloud irises on *our* brand. Our brand that marks my body, that seals my heart for only her. For all eternity.

"Orah." My whisper is quiet, raw, and real. It's a plea. A plea for her to realize that I can't take another breath without her.

Her intense stare drifts up to my face. Meeting me, matching my desperation.

The facts are simple. This is it. *This is the moment my life begins.*

"Don't touch me." Her directive is strained, barely audible. Her hand falls limply to her side. "Don't touch me unless you mean it, Ridge. Once you touch me, you'll ruin me. I'll never want anyone else for as long as I live. Your body will wreck me. Your kiss will condemn me." She once again swallows, drawing my attention to the delicate dip of her skin nestled between her collarbones. The hollow where the black diamond bird with the Tiger's Eye stone normally rests. "I've been in a prison for ten years, waiting on you to rescue me with your heart, with your love. So, if this is just some revenge to get back at Kimber, I need you to walk away. If this is just some balm to soothe the anger that's crushing your spirit, I need you to leave. If this is just some fantasy you're chasing, longing to feel the rush of our youth, I need you to turn and not look back." Her lips are chapped, dry with emotion. "Because one touch from you, and I'm yours. Forever."

The facts are simple. She was mine the second I stumbled into that supply room—battered, broken, and scared.

SHE'S MINE.

I take the last step, closing the distance that's separated us for ten long years. Separated us by thousands of miles. Separated us by millions of painful memories.

And I erase all that distance with one small shuffle of my feet.

I grab her waist, forcing her body to align with mine. I slide my free hand around her neck, relishing the heat of her skin against my fingers. She arches her back and tilts her face, fluttering her lust-filled eyes and forcing them to stay open, refusing to miss one single second of this moment. This lightning flash of time that's gonna change the course of our lives for-fucking-ever.

My pledge fans across her, like a hot summer breeze, making her sigh. "I'm gonna ruin you, Orah." Her gasp makes my painful erection even harder. "I'm gonna touch you and taste you and make you come. I'm gonna ruin you for any other man. But that doesn't matter. Because the only man you will ever belong to is me. For the rest of our lives." Leaning into her, I trail kisses down her jaw. My lips chart a purposeful, yet unhurried course. The slow restraint I'm showing leaves me shaking. "Tonight, I'm gonna make love to you. I'm gonna worship every inch of your body, make up for all the long years we've been apart. And then tomorrow? Tomorrow, I'm gonna fuck you."

The second she hears me say *'fuck'*, her body bucks against mine, and she moans.

It's the pinnacle of eroticism.

"That's right, Little Bird, I'm gonna fuck you. Hard and wild. Until your cum soaks every inch of me, and you can barely walk."

My tongue darts out, and I flick it against the side of her mouth, teasing myself with a taste. One tiny, little morsel. Her lips are parted, and her breaths are pumping in a staggered, erratic rhythm. "And you don't have to be scared. Together, we're gonna carve our path. We're gonna find each other in the darkness." I pepper her face with another round of kisses and devotion. "I know sex has always scared you—ever since that night. But there's nothing to be afraid of. Not now. I'm here. I will never let anything happen to you. When you're making love to me, your monsters will cease to exist. They'll suffocate in the strength of our love. And when I'm fucking you? When I'm pounding into you, making you scream my name..." I pause and glide my lips up and down the thin column of her neck, making her shiver. "When I'm grabbing your ass and pinching your clit and biting your tits, those demons will be quiet. Silent. Still. Because nothing in the world will matter but our pleasure."

I pull back, looking into her face, marking her to memory, absorbing every single detail of the woman I love. "You never have to worry about your devils again, Zipporah. It's my job to fight them now, not yours." I pull her even closer, mesmerized by the idea that I'm about to combine our two bodies into one. "So, fuck yeah, I'm gonna ruin you. Because you already ruined me."

Her eyes close. And when another tear escapes, rolling down the pink apple of her cheek, I can't help myself; I lick her face clean with my tongue.

Her concerned whimper is raspy and low. Sultry and sexy. "What if it's too much, too overwhelming? Do we need a safe word?"

The thought that feelings like this, worries like this, crossed her mind whenever she tried to have sex in the past, infuriates me. I wanna strangle the life from any man who ever made her feel unsafe. "Stop." Her eyes snap open, stabbing me in the heart with compassion and tenderness. "That's the only word you'll ever need with me, Bird. We don't need a safe word because you *are safe*. Safe and loved and protected. And if you ever wanna stop—*need* to stop—all you have to do is say the word. I'll fucking listen."

And for five seconds, five heartbreakingly beautiful seconds, My Brave Girl stares into my soul, freely and willingly giving every part of herself to me. One second at a time.

Her apprehension.

Her insecurities.

Her trust.

Her loyalty.

Her love.

One. Two. Three. Four. Five.

I can feel what you feel.

I ~~can~~ feel what you feel.

Fuck me. Those words have a life of their own now. They're growing and multiplying, thriving and surviving. Nothing has ever been more authentic, more true, more real.

There is no '*can*'. Not anymore. Because from here until the end of time, we're gonna be in sync. Our love, luck, and tenacity have finally caught up with one another.

Today, before the rest of the world arises, our destinies will spark. Our bodies will ignite the fire that has been smoldering for nearly ten full years.

And we'll guide each other through the flames. Just like we did back then.

Because Zipporah Smith thinks she's still broken. Little does she know, she never was.

And now, I finally get to prove it to her.

Chapter 30

Orah

The word 'can' has been eradicated from our world.

My Hero erased it with one single blink.

His Tiger Eyes bore into mine. They feed off my soul, like a hungry and carnivorous wild animal. But instead of playing dead, instead of curling into a ball and praying for the attack to end, I fight back.

For once in my life, I give as good as I get.

My hands settle around his waist, instantly falling into a perfect position. It's as if the indentions of his muscles were carved just for me. With my fingerprints chiseled into every dip and curve. His boxer briefs sit low on his hips, so I connect with nothing but his hot, fiery skin. The fever of passion is boiling in his blood, and together with him, I simmer. With a featherlight touch, he holds me, yanking me closer, grinding the steel length of his erection into my belly.

I answer the questions his body is asking of me. And my response is gloriously painful.

My breasts swell. My pussy throbs. And my need for him soaks my panties.

Everything on us is touching.

Our foreheads. Our noses. Our parted lips. Our chins.

His breath smells like toothpaste, and his beard smells like soap.

His own fingers knead the back of my neck, massaging the tender skin at the base of my scalp. Strands of hair loosen from my bun and fall out. With a pained grunt, he takes a step back, untangling himself from me. The action is sudden and severe. It leaves me flustered, confused, and oh, so alone.

"Ri—"

"Take your hair down."

For some reason, of all the things that he could've said, I find this the most unexpected. "What?"

"It's just us. There's no one here to hurt you. No one here to make you bleed. Take your hair down for me." He rolls his massive shoulders, making the little bird on his pectoral jump. "My Little Bird with the raven hair...I need you to show me you're not afraid."

My heart thunders against my ribs, pounding with a brutal force, making it feel like all of my internal organs are bruising. But that doesn't stop me. I pull the scrunchie from my bun and toss it on the table, next to the lamp. My hair cascades around me in a flowy wave. Leaning forward, I swish my head back and forth, letting gravity do its part. He's right. There's no putrid copper smell flooding my nostrils. Only the smell of my shampoo. And there's no sticky mess, no sections congealed together in large clumps. Only the silkiness that's been there ever since I left the hospital and was able to properly shower.

When I lift my head, he moans. Low and slow and loud.

The erotic noise has me pressing my thighs together.

His tongue wets his pink lips. "I can see your nipples. You aren't wearing a bra, are you?"

"N—no."

"Take off your shirt—*my shirt*. And then slide out of your panties. I need to see you."

My stomach flutters, trying to find peace between the battling wings of nerves and excitement.

What's happening?

Why is he doing this?

Granted, I'm not very versed, but sex has never been like this before.

Not to mention, if I take my shirt off, he's finally going to see the ending results of what happened to me after I left his care that night, after they pushed me through the hospital doors and rolled me away from him. He's going to see the lasting damage from the boys who ruined so many lives.

But he'll also see the damage that I volunteered for, the damage I inflicted on myself by trying to make amends to my best friend for what I did. I just wish that destruction was only as deep as the thin scar it left behind. Because that wound has healed. The one in my heart, not so much.

"Wh—why?" I stutter.

"Because I'm about to say the words that I've wanted to say for nearly a decade. And when I say them, I want you to know that I'm talking about all of you. The inside and the outside. All of the scars. All of the wounds still healing. All of the gorgeous parts that make you fucking mine, Zipporah."

My knees shake, making it hard to stand up. To balance myself, I shift my stance, spreading my legs a little farther apart. I grip the hem and lift the shirt over my head. I toss it to the side, and it lands on the brand new couch, covering the tag that's still attached to the corner of the arm.

My heavy breasts swing with my every move. They're sore and achy. And when his fist flies to his crotch and he starts dragging a cupped hand up and down the massive length of his still-clothed cock, my greedy nipples peak even harder. They are so needy for his touch that they're actually going numb.

His chest heaves up and down in short, shallow spurts. "Your panties," he demands.

My fingernails hook in my black panties, and I push them from my hips. They fall to the floor, and because of the spread angle of my legs, the fabric stays in an upright position, tight around my ankles.

We're both drawn to the streaks of white desire that drench the cotton gusset.

That's what he does to me.

He makes me wet.

And now, he knows it.

I step out of my drenched underwear and kick them away. Straightening my spine, lifting my chin, I display myself for him. Fully and openly. Trying to be strong, trying to be the woman he deserves. I resist the urge to cover the tattered skin from my surgery. To shield my scars and stretch marks and imperfections.

He growls. He actually growls. The sexy and seductive roar may come from the back of his throat, but it originates from his heart.

I know it does.

Because I feel what he feels.

Once again, he covers the distance between us, erasing my loneliness with just a few steps. I fully expect him to take my face in his hands, to immediately whisper his adoration. But he doesn't.

Instead, he sinks to his knees and buries his face into my stomach. His hands circle around me, and he spreads his palms across my backside, squeezing and clutching my ass cheeks. It takes only a second for me to feel his tongue as it circles a pattern across my midsection. My fingers tangle in his thick, brown hair. With a string of licks and kisses and bites, he relives the story of my past. He wedges his tongue underneath the base of my right breast and starts with the gunshot that he couldn't see. The wound that nearly *ended my life*. The wound that merges with the scar that ultimately *saved my life*. The surgical line was too wide to heal into colors of white or pink. It doesn't match or blend with my olive complexion. Oh no, this line is a deep purple, scored on either side with little dots from the staples. Not perfectly flat, but not entirely raised, my skin is a cartography of mountains and hills, plains and valleys.

And below that is the stitched stab wound from the surgical drain port. He places a soft, open mouth-kiss on the area, before shifting lower.

Lower.

Lower.

Lower.

He sits back on his haunches, giving himself the freedom to maneuver down my abdomen. I tug on his still-damp hair. Violently. Impatiently.

He kneads my butt in his massive hands, and the motion spreads apart my innermost areas. My core tightens, and beads of moisture leak from me, covering my pussy lips in my molten desire. His beard grazes across my pelvis, and when some of the prickly hairs scrape against my engorged clit, I buck forward, pressing my crotch against his mouth. He groans, covering me in the ticklish heat of his breath. And then, he licks the small line from my C-section. Left to right, end to end, he swallows the joy and pain. The joy of giving my family a child, the pain of losing my own baby.

As quickly as he collapsed before me, he stands. One arm settles in the snug curve of the small of my back, the bend in my body that feels like it was made only for him. And his other hand cradles my jaw, teasing the sensitive connection between my throat and my face. My fingers latch onto his hip bones.

"Open your eyes, Little Bird."

I didn't even realize they were closed. I obey, cursing myself for nearly missing the moment. Because his eyes alone tell me everything I will ever need to know about the Hero in front of me.

"I love you, Zipporah Smith."

My body tips forward, ready to kiss him, ready to declare him as mine. But he teases his head to the side, and tsks me with his tongue between his teeth. "I'm in love with you. Fucking madly. Deeply. Intensely. I've been in love with you since the moment I heard your voice that night. You were the Angel sent to save me from Hell."

His one hand leaves the small of my back and traces the beads of my spine. "I love you," he repeats, making me drunk with happiness. "I need you to know what that means, Bird. Because I'm tired of wasting time. I'm tired of pretending that I can live a happy and fulfilled life without you. Because I can't. You *are* my life. You are my everything." He dips his head and plants a kiss at the base of my neck, where my necklace normally sits. "You fucking own me. My body, my soul, my heart. You're branded into my eternity. Here. Now. Forever. And into the afterlife. I will never let you go. You're gonna be my best friend, my lover, my wife, and the mother to my children. You're gonna be my sunrise and my sunset." His open mouth hovers over mine, stealing the oxygen from my lungs and mingling it with his own. "Tell me you're mine. Tell me I'll never have to spend another day without you. Tell me I can be yours."

My hands slide across the rippled muscles of his shoulders. Instinctively, my fingernails know just the right place. They follow the path determined by the destinies so many years ago. Without warning I dig into his skin, determined to pierce the flesh of his left shoulder. A hiss of pain and pleasure rolls from his body and echoes into my own. "My best friend. My lover. My husband. The father to my children." Lifting to my tiptoes, I suckle his earlobe. "My man. My Hero." He shakes underneath my touch, literally vibrating with the urgency to claim me. "You. Belong. To. Me."

His mouth finds mine.

And nearly nine-and-a-half years after our first kiss, we have our second kiss.

Chapter 31

Orah

Oh god, I was worried that being with him would be too much.

But it's not nearly enough.

Because I want it all.

I want the love and the lust. The sweet and the dirty. The tender and the rough.

With just this one kiss, he has me wanting it all. Because I'm not the slightest bit scared. Not with him.

I'm exhilarated.

I'm intrigued.

And I'm fucking horny.

His tongue tangles with mine, loving and cherishing me, teasing and taunting me. He kisses, licks, and bites. He sucks my bottom lip between his own, pulling me closer to him, melding my naked body against his perfect and chiseled torso. I arch my spine, exchanging my panted moans for his own.

Reading my mind, his calloused hands wander from their new position—around the lush roundness of my hips—back around to the globes of my ass. Chill bumps break across my arms and legs. He fondles me, and with every caress, my pussy cries, begging for his attention. Eventually, a finger glides in between my cheeks, slides across my puckered backside, and dips into the pool of wetness soaking my core. His touch ghosts across the entrance to my vagina, making me cry out.

But he doesn't let me scream into the night alone. He bellows a moan, and then swallows my wail with his eager mouth. And when I try to jerk away to catch my breath, he swirls his drenched finger around my asshole, applying just the right amount of pressure to the sensitive skin, stroking my body in a way that's never been done before.

Ever.

My knees buckle, and I nearly fall. But of course, I don't, because Ridge would never let that happen to me.

"Oh shit, Orah," he growls. "Bird, you can't scream like that."

"Why?" Is he worried about someone hearing us?

"Because I'm on edge. I'm about to come." Dipping his head below my neck, he kisses the small scar from his decompression needle. I pop my chest forward, wishing he would bend farther down and take my nipple in his mouth. Lifting, he brushes my hair from my face. "And I can't come yet. Because I'm gonna worship you until the sun comes up. And when I finally come, it's gonna be with my cock buried so deep inside of you that the world won't even know where I end and you begin."

A delicious shudder races through me.

I want that too.

But I'm also starved for him. And sometimes, the very best dinners come with an appetizer.

"I need you to give me everything. I want it all. Tonight. I don't wanna wait for one single thing." I watch as his eyes dilate, drowning his brown in black. "I want your fingers in me. I want your tongue in me. I want your dick in me." I lick his scarred shoulder, sucking at the small freckles of blood that show underneath his waxy skin. I didn't actually cut him tonight, but the signs of my handiwork are still present. "I want to take you in my mouth."

Raising my head, I skim my fingers down his nose and to his chin. Tap. Tap. One. Two. "Are you telling me that if I sink to my knees and drain your cock dry—right this very second—that you won't be able to make love to me in an hour? That you won't be hard and greedy, ready to fill me with your passion?" Grinning, I shake my head back and forth. "That doesn't sound like the Hero I know."

His chuckle is deep and forbidden. The hypnotic rattle makes my toes curl. I stand there, digging them into the hardwood floor. "Oh, Brave Girl," he grabs ahold of my wrist and directs my palm to his crotch. The front of his boxer briefs is flooded with his pre-cum. I cup his erection, gasping when I realize just how much of a man I'm dealing with.

Just how much of a man I'll be dealing with until my dying day.

"This is what you do to me." He guides my fingers down to his balls. "And I'll always be ready for you. Always and forever."

My mouth waters, and my clit pulses. I start to lower to my knees when Ridge catches me under my armpits. "Wait." He looks around the room. A wrinkle creases his forehead, and I realize, that this may be the first time he's really noticing the new furniture that's decorating his apartment. He leans to the side, snatches a throw pillow from the chair, rips the tag from it, and drops it to the floor in front of me. "I'm sorry. I wouldn't be able to stand it if you bruised your knees." And then he kisses me. Slowly and softly. Pouring years of love into my soul, regulating my out-of-control heartbeat with his steadfast devotion. "Are you sure? I don't mind waiting. I wanted tonight to be all about you. I'm gonna give you everything you've ever wanted. And I'm gonna give you things you didn't even *know* you wanted. It doesn't have to be about me. I can wait."

"This isn't about you." I trace my black-painted fingernail around the outline of *our* brand, over the tattooed letters and numbers of the Bible verse claiming me as his wife. "This isn't about me." I chart the muscles of his abdomen, relishing in the knowledge that all of him belongs to all of me. And me alone. For the rest of forever. "This is about *us*, Ridge. Let me taste *us*."

He pushes his boxer briefs to the ground and kicks them away. I drop to my knees and come face to face with epic perfection. Granted, my sexual experiences are limited. Very, very limited. But even I know enough to know that Ridge's dick is the sexual fantasy of every warm-blooded woman this side of the Milky Way. It's massive. Utterly, totally, and completely ginormous. Long and thick, with a mushroomed head that's engorged, absolutely filled to the brim with his blood and his seed. He's flushed with heat, with tones of purple and pink and red overpowering the gorgeous tan of his skin. The vein that runs the length of his cock pulsates, filling me with an aphrodisiac of kinetic energy.

I clench and unclench my pussy, doing my best to Kegel my way through the all-consuming, all-encompassing hunger that's literally ravaging my body. My desire to be with him—my longing to physically slay the villains still trapping me in that movie theater—is an obsession that's feasting on me, leaving me nothing but a shell of hollow bones and thready sinew.

I have no idea how he's going to fit inside of me.

It seems like a physical impossibility.

But I suppose that's a glorious problem that I'll worry about later.

My hand reaches out and wraps around the base of his cock. Holy shit, my fingers don't even touch. He spasms, and his balls constrict, tightening even farther.

I've only given three blow jobs, and all three of those were with Breck. And in all honesty, I don't remember much about them. Because I rushed through them, wanting to be done with my supposed-girlfriend obligations as quickly as possible. So, all that to say, I'm not entirely sure what to do.

I take a calming breath, and then...I just do what I want to do. I do the things I've dreamed about. The things I've fantasized about. I do the things that make me happy. Because, although I'm the one on my knees, something tells me that I have all of the power.

All of it.

Every last bit.

And that makes me blissfully ecstatic.

I swing low and lick the pad of my tongue across his nut sac. Over and over. And then I suckle one ball into my mouth, moaning around the forbidden sensation. I wasn't sure how it was done, but when I opened my mouth and applied pressure, his body knew exactly what I wanted, and gave it to me. For some strange reason, I'm actually shocked that I can feel the roundness of it with my mouth, that I can feel the organ underneath the taut, thin skin.

He jerks against me and weaves his hands through my hair, massaging my scalp with his fingers. His pre-cum leaks against my cheekbone. "Oh, fuck me."

When I release him, my mouth makes a popping noise, like I'm sucking on a lollipop. I shift upward, eagerly watching as my hand begins to pump up and down his shaft. And with each pass, I squeeze the base of his dick and then twist my fingers around the tip, spreading the moisture that's oozing from his slit across the head of his cock. Tipping forward, my tongue lashes out and tastes him.

One little lick.

He groans.

I can't wait another second

I anchor my free hand around the back of his muscular thigh, and I take him in my mouth.

Let me rephrase. I take as much of him in my mouth as I can.

Which is not a lot, considering his girth.

I dive down, dipping my head over him until I can feel the corners of my mouth crack, and then I bob upward, not fully releasing him, but giving myself enough room to pull some air into my lungs. I repeat the motion, again and again. Never stopping with my mouth. Never stopping with my hand. Because I don't want any part of him to be neglected, to be forgotten.

My motions are quick and precise, slow and lazy. And once I know I have enough balance that I can keep moving without toppling over, I shift my free hand from the back of his thigh to the front of his pelvis. I push my hands through his pubic hair, noting the coarseness and the texture. It's what mine feels like. If I were to let it actually grow, I mean.

Sliding upward, I fondle every single inch of his sweat-covered six-pack. He shakes beneath me. His thighs grate against my forearms, showering me in his perspiration.

"Lo—look up at me." He issues a stuttering command.

I drop my roaming hand and glance up at him. His cock is fed into my mouth, and at this angle, my eyes water and it's hard to breathe.

"Touch yourself, Zipporah. I wanna come unglued with your mouth on my dick and your fingers playing with the pussy that I'm about to devour."

I obey.

My fingers land on my clit, easily slipping back and forth across the wet nub. I press into my vagina, but it gives me no satisfaction. Because I don't want *me*. I want *him*. His fingers. His tongue. His cock.

Assuming it'll fit, of course.

I hurry my momentum, bobbing up and down on his shaft. Pumping him hard. Sucking him hard. Hollowing my cheeks. Lashing my tongue across the thick rim of his head.

I move my finger back to my clit, flicking the bud with the same frenzied tempo, matching the rhythm stroke for stroke.

His fingers tug at my hair. He pumps his hips into my face, overcome with the intensity of the moment. Oh god, I'm wet.

I'm about to...

I'm about to...

I'm about to...

But the second I hear him, I drop my fingers, abandoning myself and the orgasm that was about to find me.

Because I want all of my focus to be on him.

"Oh, fuuuuuuucccckkkkk." His body stiffens, and he thrusts forward. Hot streams of cum shoot down my throat.

Like the good boy he is, he quenches my thirst with his salt and love.

And like his good Little Bird, I eagerly swallow every last drop.

And patiently wait for more.

Chapter 32

Ridge

My body shudders, jerking the last spurts of my powerful orgasm into her perfect little mouth.

Hot damn. She's gorgeous.

And she's right. This release will bide me a little bit of time, but I'm far from done with her.

In fact, I'll never be done with her.

Never.

Pulling away from my still-hard dick, she gives one last purposeful swallow, consuming my desire into her own body. She carefully wipes her lips and then takes a deep breath. Her nipples rise and fall, igniting the smoldering ashes within me, flaming them into an unforgiving and untamed inferno.

It's not prescribed. Not controlled or contained.

It's a wildfire. A Type 1 Incident Command Response. Large and complex. Threatening my very life.

And it must be suppressed.

Hooking my arms under her armpits, I lift her from the floor, making sure she's steady on her feet before I ease my hands down her ribs, settling them on her hips. She giggles, gifting me with a shy smile. Her lips are bee-stung, swollen and puffy.

Her entire body is a mural, painted just for me.

Black hair.

Gray eyes.

Brown nipples.

Bronze skin.

Then there's her scars. Purple, pink, and white. The colors vary, depending on the depth and width of the healed injury.

And below all that, nestled between her lush thighs is her pussy. *My fucking pussy.*

Flushed and heated. Rosy and red. Glistening wet and weeping just for me.

She leans forward, searching for my kiss. But I leave her wanting.

She frowns, unhappy with my decision.

Well, don't worry, Little Bird. You won't be unhappy for long.

"Push your fingers in your pussy. Hard and deep."

Her hand dances across her abdomen. Lower. Lower. Lower. But suddenly, she stops. Her eyes widen, flashing with spunk. "No."

"No?"

She shakes her head. "My turn," she purrs, flirting with me via our ongoing game of questions.

"Your turn, huh?"

"Yes."

"Okay, Bird. What's your question?"

She nibbles on her plump bottom lip, giving pause to her confident and teasing attitude. "What did you think of that? Was I good?" Her mouth drops open, and she heaves a little sigh before continuing. "Did I make you happy?"

I cast a hand around her neck, gently pressing my thumb into the hollow of her throat. I tap a pattern with my calloused fingertip.

One. Two. Three. Four. Five.

Five words for five seconds.

Five words with five-thousand meanings.

"Once. Again. You. Saved. Me."

With my fingers still gripping her neck, she continues her work, following through on my instruction. My eyes chase her, watching her every move.

Past her belly button. Down the mound of her clean-shaven pubic bone.

She dips her shoulder, giving herself better access. I immediately ease my hold. She's bent at an odd angle, and the last thing I would ever want is to hurt her. Her fingers disappear, but based on the heady little moan tumbling into the thin strip of space between us, I know she's done what I asked.

"Now, take them out and show them to me."

Straightening herself, she lifts her fingers in the air.

And my already-drained cock hardens. Past the point of comfort. Reminding me that ten years of fantasies can lead to a shit-ton of sexual tension.

My hand drops from her neck and folds around her wrist, squeezing the skin that's engraved with my mark. I open my mouth and suck her essence from her fingers.

Oh, fuck, yes.

I can tell you right now, this woman's cum is a secret recipe baked only for me.

She shivers. Chill bumps decorate her arms. "Why'd you do that?"

"Because I'm gonna start with your tits. And then I'm gonna finger you. After that, I'll finally get to eat you." I give a little shrug. "So, you see, I needed an appetizer. A little something to tide me over."

"So...you do feel what I feel."

"Always."

I haul her into my arms. Her legs circle my waist. And when I feel her wetness—her sweet and ripe juices—spread across my stomach, I nearly lose my mind. With my hands holding her ass, I trudge through the living room and into the bedroom. She nuzzles against my left shoulder, peppering kisses on her favorite damage. With each and every step, my dick bounces against her underside, faintly giving us a glimpse of what's to come. I lie her down on *our* new mattress and stare at her, absorbing every detail highlighted by the streams of light filtering in from the living room and the bathroom.

Lean muscles. Soft curves.

Flawless and faultless.

Impeccable and immaculate.

Unmatched and unsurpassed.

She's a temptress. An enchantress. A snake charmer.

And I'm the cobra ready to dance to her every directive.

Her eyes land on me. "You're hard."

"I am."

"I felt you rubbing against me. When you walked me in here."

"I felt that too."

Her black-painted fingernail skirts over one of her pointed nipples. "What if I told you that I didn't wanna wait? That I wanted you inside of me right now, right this very second?"

I stab a hand through my hair. A stubborn drop of water, the last remnant of my shower, drips down my spine, mixing with my sweat. "After tonight, I'll never deny you a single thing, Orah. Never. For as long as we both live." I fist my cock in my hand. "But tonight? No, Little Bird, I'm sorry. I can't give you that. Not until I've bathed in your cum. You're gonna soak me. Drench me. Drown me. And just when you think you have nothing left to give...that's when I'm gonna make love to you. And I'm gonna stare into those storm-cloud eyes and watch you fall apart."

Twisting her legs back and forth, she rubs her feet together. She lasers her focus on my crotch, and when my erection grows, even farther, under the scrutiny of her gaze, she gasps. "Hero, there's a good chance you won't even fit inside of me. Don't you think we should find that out now and not an hour from now?"

Letting go of myself, I smirk. "Oh, *it'll fit.*" I crawl up her body, framing her beautiful face with my propped forearms. My right leg slides between hers, opening her wide for me, spreading the smell of her arousal in the air. "The fates have already been too cruel to us. They've beaten us and brutalized us. But that's over and done with. Because nothing can break us, nothing can separate us. We're meant to fit together."

"You don't think catastrophes are attracted to us?"

"Not anymore." I capture her mouth with mine, kissing her until I'm dizzy and weak. And then, I lower myself down the column of her breastbone and across to her right breast. My teeth and tongue tease her nipple, eliciting a series of moans and mewls. I eagerly fondle her left tit with my right hand, reveling in the different textures of her skin. Such a soft and milky breast, adorned with a slightly thicker areola and a peaked velvet nipple.

And, of course, I don't neglect her scars. I shower them with the same lavished attention.

Because they're not just a part of her, they're a part of me. *Of us.*

The story of us is written across both of our bodies. In writing that only we can read.

Her pelvis bucks against me, begging for more. Begging me to be the man who can turn her pain into pleasure.

My hand wanders down the length of her body. And the closer I get to her pussy, the more I start to tremble. My body shivers and shakes, literally jumping in anticipation of what's about to occur.

I pull away from her breast.

Because when I shove my fingers inside her, my mouth is gonna be on hers, swallowing her cries.

I open my mouth and draw my lips across her chin, across her nose.

"I...I...I'm about to come." Her whisper is panicked and urgent.

My hand goes lower.

"I haven't even touched you yet."

"I...I..." Her back arches off the bed. "I know."

Lower.

"Tell me how bad you want it, Orah. Tell me how bad you want me."

She thrashes beneath me, trying to inch her pelvis upward, trying to hurry my movements.

Lower.

She licks her swollen lips, licking mine in the process. "I want you. Oh god, I want you so bad."

Lower.

"Tell me to say it again. Tell me to give you those three little words."

"Tell me you love me." She shouts to be heard over our pants and moans and sighs. "Fucking now, Ridge! Tell me you love me!"

I skip over her clit. I completely bypass it. And I thrust two of my fingers so deep inside of her that she basically levitates off the bed. "I."

Out.

"Love."

In.

"You."

Out.

And then, I shove them in and fuck her insides with a come-hither motion.

So. Fucking. Deep.

She detonates. Her scream flares bright, and then fades away, getting lost in the hazy glow of *our* sex-filled bedroom. Liquid passion leaks from her. It slides down my palm and collects in the bend of my wrist. I temper my actions, easing my momentum and slowing the motion. I nurse her through the entirety of her orgasm. Through the euphoric high, where she squeezes my fingers in a vise. And through the dream-like low, where she moves around me, soft and ethereal, like dandelion fuzz dancing in the wind.

Once she recovers, I kiss the shit out of her and start anew, focusing all of my attention on her greedy, pulsing, throbbing clit. I swirl around and around the sensitive nub. Over and over and over again. And then, I drag my fingers through her slit and coat her asshole in her hot and thick juices.

I go back to her clit.

Back and forth.

Back and forth.

Top and bottom.

Top and bottom.

Front and back.

Front and back.

And then, I drive the same two fingers inside of her and press into her clit with my thumb. I pump into her with a heavy intensity, massaging her G-spot, and never easing the pressure on her ripe little bud.

She jerks her head away from my kisses, choking and strangling on my ravenous lust. "Oh. Oh."

"There's My Brave Girl. Give it to me. Get yourself ready for my tongue. For my teeth. For my beard."

My demand pushes her over the edge, and she comes for me. Again.

And just like before, I take my time, soothing her. Loving her. Adoring her. Once she's settled, and I don't feel the rapid and ferocious pound of her heartbeat, reverberating from her chest into mine, I creep down her body.

Holy. Hell.

Our new sheets are a sopping mess, flooded with streaks of white cum and clear fluid.

I thought I felt it with her first orgasm.

But now, I know for sure.

My Little Bird is a squirter.

And she's all mine.

An electric shot of pleasure ripples through my cock, knowing that I did that to her. On our very first time together. With her very first orgasm.

Talk about feeling like a man.

It should be illegal for an ego to be this big.

Gripping the back of her knees, I bend her legs and cock them to the side, cocooning her around me, like she's the wings of a butterfly. "You're a squirter, Little Bird."

She fumbles around, trying to lift onto to her elbows. "I'm sorry. It only happens every once in a while."

Uh, excuse me?

An entirely unreasonable and completely inexcusable rage crashes through my body. "You've done it before? With another man?"

I refuse to move my hands away from her legs, so instead I blink my numbers, trying to regain my composure.

One. Two.

One. Two.

One. Two.

From her reclined position, with her hair tangled around her flushed and sweaty face, she reaches between her thighs and pets my face. Her fingers find my chin, and she gives me what I crave.

Tap. Tap.

"No, Ridge. Not with another man."

My dick bounces against my stomach. "Your fingers?"

"I have a toy." She teases me with a smile. "And when I screw myself deep and pretend it's you, sometimes that happens." She quirks an eyebrow. "But that toy is the size of one of your fingers." She flicks her eyes to my pelvis, where my dick is mostly hidden by the sheets and my own body. "So, I'm still not exactly sure how you think *that's* gonna fit inside of me."

Ego. Expanded.

"You just lie back, Zipporah Smith, and let me worry about that. I've still got work to do before we get to the main event."

She plops down on the pillow and wiggles her ass back and forth in anticipation. And without hesitation, I bury my face, staving my hunger with the flavors of Orah.

I lick her. I suckle her. I bite her.

I press my tongue into her vagina.

I give her everything she wants, everything she needs. Until she's squeezing my head between her thighs and riding my face through another powerful orgasm.

Languid and satiated, she tugs at my shoulders, scratching my skin with her nails. I crawl back up her body and kiss her, giving her a taste of the sweetest nectar known to mankind. I grind my pelvis into hers, making my already-known intentions dramatically clear. My erection slides across her pussy lips. And when it breaks the barrier, slicing through the heat of her slit, she moans.

I shift, making a move to reach into the nightstand for a condom. The slide of the drawer irritates my senses, aggravating them like nails on a chalkboard. I fish around, quickly finding one. But as soon as the black foil wrapper hits the light reflecting from the bathroom, I pause.

What the hell am I doing?

Am I really about to use the condoms I bought for another woman on My Woman?

Our eyes find one another.

She gives me an almost imperceptible shake of her head. "No." Her whisper can't even be heard; it's just her lips shaping around the silent syllable.

I toss the rubber on the nightstand. Leaning down, I kiss her eyelids. Her nose. Her chin.

Nerves flame in my stomach, mixing with the potency of my obsession, my all-consuming compulsion to feel her. All of her. With no barriers. No inhibitions. The intoxicating blend is more powerful than any drug known to man. It leaves me drunker than the whiskey and beer from yesterday.

"I wanna paint your insides with my love, Zipporah. Will you give me that?"

Her hands tickle my back, drawing across the muscles of my shoulder blades. "Give it? I already surrendered myself to you. Ten years ago. It's finally time for you to claim it."

I'm so overcome I can't even speak.

So, I don't.

Instead, I guide myself into place and press the head of my cock into her.

Her palm flattens against *our* brand, and she pushes back against me. "Stop."

My body obeys her, even before my brain has time to process it.

Frantically, my eyes dart around her face, dipping down to her chest, below her breast.

Damn, have I hurt her?

Is something wrong with her old injuries? Can she breathe okay? Is she too overwhelmed?

She cups my chin, bringing my attention back to her glistening irises. "I love you, Ridge."

I blink.

Tears catch in my eyelashes.

Pulling me on top of her, molding every inch of her body to mine, she tenderly kisses me, and then she rakes her lips across my cheeks, drinking the salt of my tears.

I suppose a greater man would be ashamed of showing such emotion, such vulnerability.

But I'm not a greater man. I'm just Orah's man. And that's all I've ever wanted to be.

Chapter 33

Ridge

I'm sore as shit.

Turns out it takes a lot of abdominal strength not to blow your load prematurely.

I'm achy and exhausted, and I've never been happier.

Tucking the note on the nightstand, I peck another kiss into her wild and tangled hair. She doesn't even stir. She's lost in sleep, treading the fine line between hard breathing and light snoring. Hopefully, she'll stay asleep for the whole time I'm gone.

She needs her rest. Because I have every intention of making my promise come to fruition.

As the first rays of sunlight sliced through the bedroom blinds, I made love to her. It was excruciatingly beautiful. My every thrust was deliberate and controlled. I was her marionette, moving in perfect time to her choreography. Her gasps regulated my depth. Her moans governed my speed. Her screams dictated the tilt of my hips. She alone composed the sonnet of our passion.

And when we came—together and in sync, with whispered vows of love floating between us—I knew that ten years of misery had led to a lifetime of happiness.

So, you see, one half of my declaration has already come true. And this afternoon, once she's slept and recovered, I get to experience the other part.

I'm gonna fuck her raw.

I gently close the bedroom door and then pull my cell phone from the pocket of my jeans. I'd hate for her to miss my note and think I randomly left without saying anything. Just to play it safe, I text the same message that's scrawled across the note I wrote, telling her I've run out for a couple of quick errands—food and such—but that I'll be home soon and that she better stay in my apartment.

I can't imagine her leaving. Hell, she hasn't even showered yet.

My seed is still caked inside of her.

I suppose we should've discussed other modes of birth control before just jumping in. Literally. But does it really matter? One day, she'll be the mother of my children. What does it matter if that day comes sooner rather than later.

The ping from my text pops from the other side of the living room. She's left her things on the table that's sitting beneath the wall-mounted TV. Her purse and work bag are laid beside it on the floor, and on top of it, folded in a neat pile, are the clothes she was wearing yesterday. And perched on top of those, like the cherry on a sundae, are her phone, earrings, watch, and necklace.

I pick up her phone, and the home screen flashes with a series of notifications. Missed phone calls and texts from her mom, Tabby, and Boaz. It mirrors my own. I'm pretty sure every person I've ever talked to since third grade has tried to get in touch with me over the last twelve hours.

Well, I suppose, that's a little dramatic. But it was enough for me to fire off a massive group text to the immediate members of the Conway, Hill, Crutchfield, and Marcum families telling them that I was safe, with Orah, and would reach out to them as soon as I had My Brave Girl captured in my arms forever.

Once I'm in the truck, I press the button for Ann's number. She answers on the first ring. She bypasses the pleasantries and rushes into conversation. "She's still with you, right?"

"Yes, ma'am. She's with me. She's perfectly safe."

Ann sighs. "She told me she was staying at your place last night to keep an eye on you. She was supposed to check-in, but she never did."

And for good reason. "I'm sorry about that, Ann. Once I sobered up, we...had a lot of talking to do."

"Talking?" Her skepticism easily reminds me that she didn't just fall off the turnip truck.

"Is John there?"

"No, he's on nights this week, and they clocked him for two hours of OT."

I glance at the clock on the dashboard. It's a little before eight-thirty. "He normally gets off at seven, right?"

"Yeah. So, he should be home around nine-thirty or so. Why?"

Well, that's entirely too late. If I meet him at the factory, I could shave thirty minutes off this torture. "I need to talk to him."

"Oooookkkayyyy," she drawls. "About what?"

"About the fact that I'm madly in love with your daughter and can't live another minute of my life without her."

She clicks her tongue, and the noise thrums through the Bluetooth speakers of my truck. "Alrighty then. I'm working from home today. So I can start some breakfast and have it re—"

"I can't wait that long. I'll just wait for him in the parking lot."

"Wait for him in the parking lot?!"

"Yes, ma'am."

"Do you think that's a good idea?"

"It might be the best idea I've ever had."

We end the call and twenty minutes later I'm flashing my ID badge to the security guard, trying to gain access to the employee parking lot. Fortunately, I've been out here before on fire alarm calls, and he remembers my face. I guess that alone marks me low on the threat totem pole. Which is good because I'm not really sure he believes my cockamamie story about checking faulty terminals in John's truck, lest he have a battery fire.

I drive through the rows, quickly spotting his blue Tundra, and I park smack dab in front of it. It's twenty-one minutes and nineteen seconds before I see him emerge at the other end of the parking lot. He's dressed in his work coveralls, hauling a large cooler-lunchbox over one shoulder. Pushing off from my leaned position, I jog the distance, meeting him before he can even walk more than ten paces.

As soon as I'm within hearing distance, he asks the biggest necessity. "She's okay?"

"Yes, sir. She's perfect."

I guess he can read something in my tone, or see the shit-eating grin on my face, because he gives me a little smirk and eye roll. I fall in step beside him and flip a hand toward his lunchbox. "Need me to get that, sir?"

He snorts. "Damn. It must be more serious than I thought if you're offering to carry my empty water bottle and Ann's nasty left-over baked beans that I didn't eat."

Well, I reckon there's no sense in beating around the bush. "John, I'm madly in love with your daughter. Last night was...it was..."

He swings an arm between the two of us. "Whoa, whoa! I like you, Ridge. And it's obvious to everyone this side of the Mason-Dixon that you're deliriously happy, but keep in mind that I'm her father. And there's some things that a dad just don't need to hear."

I tuck my scalded tail between my legs. "Yes, sir."

We're quiet until we reach the vehicles. With one hand, he lowers his tailgate and motions for me to sit down. Once he's settled next to me, he gives me permission to continue. "Alright, now, what's going on?"

"I love your daughter. I've been in love with her ever since that night. I can't fathom the idea of spending another second without her by my side. I wanna ask for your permission."

"My permission for what?"

"For her to move in with me. And when she's ready, for me to ask for her hand in marriage. For her to walk down the aisle to me. For her to make me a husband, a father."

"So, you wanna marry her?"

"Yes. With my entire heart, yes."

"Correct me if I'm wrong, but wasn't your ring on another woman's finger less than forty-eight hours ago?"

Considering Kimber didn't give the ring back to me, it could very well still be on her finger, for as far as I know. Of course, I don't really think now's the appropriate time to voice that concern. "Yes, sir. And it was the biggest mistake of my life."

He tosses me a look. "Heard she cheated on you."

"She did. But in the end, that doesn't really matter because I was already going to break up with her. I was planning to end things, that very night."

"Why?"

"Because it's Orah. It's always *been* Orah. And it'll always *be* Orah. She's my *every*thing. She's my *only* thing."

His deep and laborious sigh only adds to the tension running through my body. Even my blood is thick and weighted. The strum of my heartbeat against my temple feels like a sledgehammer.

"John? I promise to treat her right. Through my dying day and into the afterlife. I'll love her. I'll respect her. I'll keep her safe." I rub my palms up and down my jeans, wiping my sweat on my thighs. "I'll count her numbers. I'll tie her hair back. I'll buy her flat shoes. I'll do anything and everything she needs. And one day, when she's ready, I'll show her that she was never broken. I'll show her that we can dress our daughter in white clothes. And take her to the movies. And dance in the waves at the ocean. I'll shatter the hold that those men have on her. And I'll give her all back to us."

He doesn't say anything.

For a very, very long time.

Eventually, he breaks into a wide smile and gifts me with the same words he gave his son. "What took you so long?"

A relieved and hearty laugh bursts from me. He joins in, shaking my hand and slapping my shoulder.

"Well," he starts, "I sure am glad you finally got your act together." He works his head back and forth. "I thought for sure you guys would run into one another within the first month. When January rolled around, I was this close," he holds his thumb and forefinger together, "to dropping her off in front of the firehouse with a basket of muffins."

"Huh?"

"I know this isn't a one-horse, one-red light kind of town, but it's not a big city either. I thought for sure you would at least see each other at the grocery store. Or even an event that your dad and brother catered. But then, Margo had to go and assign that one party to Anniah instead of Orah."

"John, what in the world are you talking about?" I can feel the line of wrinkles working my brow. My brain swishes back and forth with conspiracy theories, sloshing up the edges of my scalp like water in a mop bucket. "Did you know I was here? That I lived here? That this was my hometown?"

He shrugs. "Not until we saw the news."

"The news?"

"Christmas before last. When your friend had his legal trouble."

That's a mild way of putting it. "Holt's arrest..."

"Yeah, it was all over the national news for a couple of months. We saw you. You gave some interviews. We even saw your brother on there. Of course, we didn't know he was your brother until we started looking into things. That's when we finally put two and two together." He scratches his own beard. The morning sunlight plays off his white hairs. "That you weren't from White Sky, but here. And that the person you called 'C', which Orah thought was *'sea'*, was actually the Cullen guy she previously worked a few jobs with."

"I...I..." I stutter. Where the hell do I even start?

"And then your friend was all over the news again just two months ago. You were even in the background on one of the pictures that was on the front of the paper." He shakes his head back and forth. "I left that damn newspaper on the kitchen table so long that the ink made a stain. Still, she didn't even glance at it."

I state the obvious. "She avoids the news."

"Like the plague."

"So, she really didn't wanna move back here? Just like she said, y'all pushed her? You and Ann? Y'all gave up your lives in South Carolina to come here?"

"We knew if we told her we wanted to move here with her that she would do it. If she thought it's what we wanted, she wouldn't turn us down."

"You did all of that for us? Just so we might have the opportunity to see each other again?"

He bursts out laughing and once again slaps me on the shoulder. "Don't look so surprised, Ridge. Sometimes, that motherfucker named *destiny* needs a push."

Chapter 34

Orah

I tuck the blow dryer back in the cabinet underneath the bathroom sink.

Yes, it does skeeve me out a little bit knowing that I'm most likely using Kimber's hair appliance. But you know what? Screw it.

I pull my hair into a ponytail and slide on the fresh T-shirt that I pilfered from Ridge's closet. The dark navy-blue shirt clashes with his black boxer briefs that I'm wearing as shorts, but that's okay. It's not like I'm reporting for job duty anywhere.

I hear the telltale ping of the washing machine alerting me to an ended cycle. Flipping off the bathroom light, I march through the bedroom and head into the open-space living room, dining room, and kitchen. The stackable washer and dryer combo is hidden in a small closet next to the kitchen pantry. I flip the sheets from the bottom washer to the top dryer. I hope he doesn't mind my intrusiveness, but the bedding needed to be laundered.

Needless to say, the sheets resembled a science experiment gone incredibly wrong.

Or incredibly right, depending on how you look at it.

And trust me, I'm looking at it from all the right angles.

Last night—well, technically this morning—was nothing short of love personified. Mere words will never do it justice. Never. Ever.

Ridge was absolutely right.

Not only did he fit, but we were made for each other.

He slaughtered my demons, slayed my monsters, and killed my insecurities. There was not one single time that I wanted to stop. Not one single time did I have a meltdown. There were no tears, other than the ones that were meant to be shed. The tender sobs of lovers so overcome with happiness, that their joy could be bottled and sold to the world. Solving all sadness, hunger, poverty, and anger.

I make my way to the couch and check my phone for the umpteenth time. There's no new text message from him except for the last one sent forty-five minutes ago, where he told me he had one last errand before coming home.

I guess I could call Tabby again, considering she said she wants to hear all the details twenty more times before she gives it a rest. Glancing at the clock on the wall and knowing that it's an hour later in South Carolina, I would be calling her right at daycare pickup. Eden only does a half-day on Wednesdays, so it'll be madness getting her home and fed.

My body hums with the most delicious aches and pains. I stretch my body over of the arm of the couch, and the motion immediately triggers a yawn. I guess I could curl up and take a nap. Considering I've only had a couple of hours of sleep, that wouldn't be the worst thing. But there's no way I'll be able to calm my brain enough for that. Even the sleep I did have was perfectly haunted with remnants of Ridge. His touch. His taste. His power. Considering I woke up this morning mid-orgasm from a wet dream, there's a good possibility that a nap would just lead to further restlessness.

I'm about to flip on the TV and see what cooking and baking shows are playing when I hear a key rustling in the lock. I'm crawling off the couch when one of the apartment complex's lobby shopping carts comes barreling through the threshold hallway and into the room. It bounces off the corner of the kitchen island.

"What the heck?"

And then, Ridge pops from the shadows. His arms are loaded with bags, and he even has a small package of marshmallows dangling from his teeth. I rush over to him, trying to finagle my way around the buggy. He spits the slobbery marshmallows on the countertop and then flops the other sacks down. He must have a piece of plastic stuck in his mouth because he makes a funny face and then pops his tongue through his lips, making a puh-puh sound.

"What in the world is all of this?" I ask, laughing.

He turns to look at me, and the resulting smile that engulfs his entire face melts me. Turns me into nothing but a pile of mush. His eyes crinkle with happiness, and his shoulders relax, like seeing me has all of the tension racing from his body. He chucks the baseball cap from his head and pulls me into a tight hug.

His arms dip into the small of my back, molding my body to his. He inhales, chuckling when he realizes that I smell like him and not me. "No coconut?"

I nuzzle my nose into the collar of his shirt and kiss my favorite shoulder. "Maybe I like your scents better."

One hand slides down the roundness of my ass, and with perfect ease, he picks me up and sets me down on the countertop, right between the garden of grocery bags. He slides between my thighs, and I scoot closer to the edge, begging my body to be closer to his. His calloused palm cradles my jaw. Bending, he kisses me.

And considering he never wiped the wide smile from his handsome face, his lips are already parted, giving me a taste of his tongue. In sync, we both moan, filled with relief that we're back in each other's presence.

He drops his forehead against mine. "Hi, Little Bird."

"Hi, Hero."

"I missed you."

"Gone for ten years, now you can't handle ten minutes," I tease.

"You got that fucking right." He peppers a string of closed-mouth kisses from my chin down to the hollow of my throat, where he gives a playful bite to the skin where my necklace should be. Giving a content sigh, he eventually stands upright. Refusing to remove his hands from my body, his fingers chart a course, up and down my thighs, moving in and out of the wide legs of his boxer briefs. After he satisfies himself with staring at my face, his Tiger Eyes dart down to his hands. "My underwear?"

"Well, I could've gone home where my shampoo *and* my clothes are, but someone I know asked me not to leave."

"That's right." He licks his lips. "Don't leave."

"I didn't."

"I mean ever."

Oh...

One. Two. Three. Four. Five.

My heart flutters in my chest, sending a pure and innocent love coursing through my blood. The eternal emotion overshadows the lust that was flooding through me just one simple second ago. "Ridge, what are you saying?"

"I'm telling you that I love you, Zipporah. My home is with you. And your home is with me." He looks around the penthouse apartment. "At least until my lease is up. And then, we'll find a place that starts as ours and ends as ours."

"You want me to move in with you?"

"I want so much more than that. And you know it." One of his wandering hands slides underneath my T-shirt and settles on my waist. "But we can take it as slow as you want." He cocks an eyebrow. "Or as fast as you want."

I guess that's the million-dollar question, isn't it?

How fast do I wanna go?

I suppose for most new couples the important questions would be...*Is this gonna last? How serious is our relationship? Are we sure we can make it? Is this the real deal?*

Are you the one?

But I already know the answer to those questions. We both do. So, for us, the question is do we wanna cross the finish line at sixty miles an hour or six-hundred miles an hour.

I reckon we should split the difference. After all, he was just looking at wedding venues with another woman five days ago.

"Of course, I'll move in with you." He squeezes my waist and bounces on his tiptoes like an excited child. "But I need to talk to my parents first. I mean, they bought that house because it has amenities for me. The bigger kitchen, a huge guest bedroom. I don't want them to be upset. They've already given so much to me."

"They're perfectly fine with it."

"I'm sure they will be, but I just—"

"They're all good. They already know."

Surprised, I jerk back a little bit. My Hero doesn't like that and instead tugs me even closer. "What are you talking about? How do they already know?"

"Because that was one of my errands. I went and talked to your dad."

"My dad?" I bluster, with a point at my own chest.

He cocks his head to the side. A thick brown wave falls down on his forehead. "No, Tabby's dad."

I playfully push against his chest, making sure I touch the left side where my mark is engraved. "Haha."

"Of course, your dad. I went to the factory and talked to John as soon as he got off work."

"And you told him we were moving in together?"

He dramatically floats his eyes around the room. "Well, I didn't exactly 'tell' him. That wouldn't win me any future son-in-law points. I asked him. I asked for his permission."

"His permission? His permission to what?"

The amusing taunt fades from his features, fogging the air once again with the actual seriousness of the topic of our conversation. "To love all of you." His hand skirts around my waist, and his fingertips find their place on the small of my back. "To live with you. To share a life with you. To—when you're ready—make you my wife." He presses his free palm into the softness of my stomach, right over my navel. "To put a baby in your belly."

My god, how my life has changed in less than twenty-four hours.

My hands snake around his shoulders, and my fingers tangle in the hair at the nape of his neck. "And I'm assuming permission was granted?"

He rubs noses with me. "Mmm-hmmm."

"And what would you have done if he said no?" I tease.

He tilts to the side and nips my earlobe. His whisper sends a shiver down my jaw. "I would've gladly forfeited all my future son-in-law points and *told* him exactly what the hell we were doing. And then I would've locked you in my bedroom and thrown away the key."

My head falls back in laughter. "Well, I'm glad it didn't happen that way then."

He waggles his eyebrows. "Yeah, me too."

I give his hair another yank. "But I have to warn you. I can't pay much rent." I scrunch my nose like I'm about to share a secret. "I kinda lost my job yesterday."

His spine straightens, and he snaps his fingers. "Oh! That reminds me. We need to have dinner with my parents and C tomorrow night."

"We do?"

"Yeah."

Well, that's random. "Okay. You're not working, right? Your half-shift will end at your normal time tomorrow morning?"

"Yeah."

"And your dad is cooking?"

He looks at me like I've lost my mind. "Of course." He pulls his hands away from the curve above my ass and slaps them back on my thighs, searching for the skin underneath the hem of the boxer briefs. "Why? You want something in particular?"

I shake my head. "No, I was just gonna say that I could make dessert." I shrug. "I'll have free time on my hands. After I move my stuff from my parents' house, that is."

He spreads his hands wide in the air. "And you've got plenty of ingredients to choose from." He bobs his head left and right, nodding at the bags of groceries. His gaze lands on the packages still piled in the shopping cart. "Oh shit, the milk." He grabs the gallon of milk and sticks it in the fridge, along with some sticks of butter and a container of yogurt.

I twist to the side and start sifting through everything, pulling items from the sacks and stacking them around me like a fence. "Oh my gosh! What all did you buy?"

"I'm pretty sure it was one of everything in the aisle."

He's not kidding.

Flour, sugar, cake mixes, brownie mixes, chocolate chips, melting wafers, condensed milk, vanilla extract, and the list goes on and on.

"How much did you spend?"

He grabs my ankle, lifts my left leg in the air, and kisses the top of my bare foot. "That doesn't matter." He moves a little higher and kisses again. "I'm making this place a home."

"Until the lease is up," I joke, repeating his phrase from earlier.

Higher. "Yep."

Higher.

His breath skirts across my knee.

Higher.

"So, tell me, Little Bird, are you ready for the rest of my promise?"

Higher.

My throat constricts. Fiery tingles flare in my groin, making the tender flesh ache in the most delicious of ways. "Ready? You mean to put the groceries away?" I ask, feigning innocence.

Higher.

Giving a growl, he bites my thigh and then stands back up. "The groceries can save. They're non-perishable. But me?" He pushes closer. His massive erection rubs against me. "I'll fade away without your touch." Before I can even blink, he's hauling my hips forward.

My hands fly around his shoulders, searching for stability. He props me at just the right angle, with my low back balanced against the edge of the counter and my butt dangling in the air.

I struggle for oxygen, fighting my excitement over what is to come. "Remind me, what was the second part of your promise?"

He gifts me a wicked smile. "To fuck you."

I grind against the bulge in his jeans. The thick seam of his fly pushes the thin fabric of the boxer briefs between my slit. My core is already soaked, and if this underwear wasn't black, I'm sure a giant wet spot would be visible.

"I'm gonna fuck you every way imaginable." He pauses. With a furrow on his brow, he tosses a look behind him to the clock on the microwave. "Between now and six p.m, I mean. Then, I gotta shower and go to work."

I pump my crotch against him again, making him moan. "Of course, the Hero has to report to duty."

My T-shirt—aka *his* T-shirt—has slid down my body, exposing my left shoulder. Mimicking my frequent action, he dips his head and kisses it. "So, tell me, Zipporah Smith. How do you want me to start? With my fingers? With my tongue? With my cock?"

Knowing he would never let me fall, I lower my hands. I trail my fingers down the front of his jeans and make quick work of his button. His stomach muscles quiver under my touch. I don't actually unzip him, though. He's so massive I'm afraid the zipper will hurt his erection. So, instead, I shift the attention to myself. I grab the wide leg of the underwear and tug it to the side, fully exposing my pussy to his eager and wanting eyes. "I feel like we've had a decade of foreplay. Let's start with the best, shall we?"

His pupils widen, dilating in appreciation. "My Brave Girl, with you, everything is the best."

Chapter 35

Orah

"**Y**ou want me to what?"

Jeff pats my hand. "To be our dessert maker and baker."

"And part-time event planner once the venue opens," Cullen adds.

I sit, trying to absorb the mass of information being thrown my way. It's like my mind is working triple time but only absorbing a small fraction of the details. Ridge wraps an arm around my back and leans closer, fanning his sweet-as-cotton-candy whisper across the apple of my cheek. "Orah…"

Picking my jaw up from the table, I bounce my head back and forth, willing myself to focus. "I'm sorry. Can I see it again?"

Cullen slides the design renderings back in front of me. After the renovations, the old farmer's market will be one of the most eye-catching buildings in town. Brick and stone façade. Tons of flowers and greenery. Huge balconies overlooking the river below. An outdoor fountain with a waterfall that runs from the top—and private patio—down to the lower one. Massive stage and dance floor. Retractable glass panels that can be raised when the weather is good. And most importantly, an on-site and freakin' amazing commercial kitchen with more storage than I've ever seen. In my entire life.

"This…" I break off and eagerly cast my gaze from Dana to Jeff to Cullen. "There are no words for how gorgeous this is."

"Of course, we won't limit our catering options to just people booking the venue," he explains, "but they will get first priority." He taps the colorful design. "I've been dreaming about a kitchen like this ever since I first boiled a potato." He smiles brightly and gives Cullen's neck a loving squeeze. "I'm just glad I finally listened to my son. He's smarter than anyone gives him credit for."

Ridge snorts. "Debatable," he jokes.

Cullen shoots his brother a bird. "Jackass."

"C!" Dana yelps. "We have company." She non-discreetly bobs her head in my direction.

Ridge props his free forearm on the table and reaches for my hand. Without hesitation, my fingers intertwine with his. "She's not *company*, Mom. She's *family*."

I dip my head, trying to hide the flushed redness of my face.

But Ridge?

He doesn't hide at all.

He's open and free.

Back when we were younger, his true feelings were chained in a prison of shame and contrition. His love for me was a captive of the dark. A prisoner of dishonor.

But now?

His shackles have disappeared. They've vanished into thin air.

He's unencumbered. Liberated. Uncaged.

And more importantly, he's happy.

"Well, brother, if you'd stop groping the newest member of our family for two seconds, she might be able to give us an answer."

I cover my mouth, trying to stifle my giggle.

And once again, Ridge revels in his freedom. He tosses his head back and laughs, deeply and wholeheartedly.

Jeff tries to wrangle his sons back into a civilized conversation. "Alright, alright. That's enough." He folds his arms across the table and looks me in the eyes. "What do you say? Will you join us? Become a part of *The Elegant Taste*?" He points behind him to the kitchen island. "I happen to know that the Dixon Family would love—capital

L-O-V-E, love—to have that red velvet cake at their anniversary party next Friday night. It's got a country-chic theme."

"You're absolutely sure about this?" I fondle my necklace, rubbing my fingertips across the jewels. "You know it will make Margo mad. She'll be furious. It could really affect your working relationship with her."

Cullen shrugs. "Who cares what Margo thinks."

I turn and stare into the Tiger Eyes of the man next to me. The man who promises to always give me love and happiness, a home and a life.

And now, here he is, giving me a career too. Giving me the opportunity to do what I love.

And with a smile, I volley my good-humored banter. "I think I'm gonna need more eggs before Friday."

"Okay, so let me get this straight," Tabby mocks through the speaker of my cell phone. "In exactly two weeks' time, he pretended he was getting married to you on the balcony of some swanky mountain compound. He pranced around half naked, flashing his chesticles, with *your* brand and *your* tattoo all over his nipple kingdom. He confessed that he wanted to be with you back then—even though he thought it was wrong—but he couldn't, all because his bosses were gonna fire him and do everything they could to keep him from being a firefighter. During the process of breaking up with his fiancée, he caught her cheating, with a random guy and a dude old enough to be Methuselah's father. He confessed his undying love for you. Basically proposed to you. Impaled you with his Godzilla dick. Asked Mr. John for your hand in, well, in everything. Bought you cake products. Moved you into his apartment. Got you a job with his dad and sexy-as-hell brother. Took you to the fancy family farm where your first catering gig will be and walked you all through it, showing you all the exits and smoke alarms and hiding places. Saved some old couple from a burning house during his last shift. Sexed you up, like five hundred more times. Aaaannnndddd…you've not had one single nightmare the whole time you've been sleeping beside him." She pops something in her mouth and starts chomping. "Is that an accurate detail of events, Ms. Smith?"

I slide my extra phone charger into my purse. "I think you're being too generous with your descriptions."

"Too generous?!" She sighs, a little too over dramatically. "It's like I'm watching a soap opera. So much more exciting than what's going on here. Last night, your brother dressed as Little Bo Peep and served peanut butter crackers and orange juice at a tea party."

I lean against the kitchen island, picturing my brother with his black-haired, gray-eyed little girl. *My niece.* "And you loved every minute of it," I jest.

She sighs, her voice high, frilly, and dreamy. And most likely a compliment to Boaz's costume last night. "Hell, yeah, I did. That man is the best father ever." She grabs another piece of whatever and starts chewing again. "It's such a turn on." She smacks her lips. "I asked him to wear the bloomers to bed."

Eww. Gross.

I do my best to change the topic. "What are you eating? It sounds like a garbage disposal in my ears."

"Granola. I was gonna throw it in some yogurt, but it expired two weeks ago."

I'm about to remind Tabby that if she cleaned the fridge out once a week and kept a running grocery list those problems would solve themselves, when the bedroom door opens, and Ridge emerges. Wearing nothing but green boxer briefs, his muscular and taut body is fully on display. Drops of water slide down every curve and line. He stalks across the room.

Masculine. Real. And oh, so mine.

But what's even better than all that is the look on his face. He's giddy with boyish charm, and doing his best to hide it underneath a predatory glower. He points a finger in my direction, and then barks, "You."

I quirk an eyebrow and stab my unseen cleavage with a finger. "Who? Me?"

"You who? What'd you say?" Tabby prattles in my ear, confused by my retort to her breakfast debacle.

He skids to a halt, mere inches from my face. So close I can smell his minty toothpaste and his evergreen soap. "Yes, you," he growls.

"What about me?" I ask, feigning naïveté.

He plucks the phone from my hand and then checks to see who the caller is. He talks into the microphone, without even bringing it up to his ear. "Tab, she's gonna have to call you back." Ending the call, he tosses my cell in my open purse.

The man is utterly gorgeous. Unable to stop myself, I cup my palm across his jaw and rake my fingers through his damp beard. Small rivulets of water rush down and fall off my wrist.

I love this beard.

When the light strikes it in just the right way, the browns disappear, and it fires in colors of dusty red and burnt orange.

It's the beard that he had when he saved me.

It's the beard that scrubbed across my chin the very first time we kissed.

It's the beard that he grew back out just for me.

And it's the beard that warms my thighs when his face is buried deep between my legs.

He snatches my wrist and pulls my hand away from his face. I haven't put my watch on yet, so *our* Tiger's Eye tattoo is on full display. Lowering his head, he snakes his tongue along the black letters and numbers. My back arches, responding to the shiver that races down my spine and pools low in my belly.

He guides my arm over his shoulder and around the column of his strong neck. Obviously, I have no choice but to follow suit with my other hand.

"You showered without me. You purposely wore me out last night, just so I would sleep late, and then you showered without me." He attempts to harden his eyes, but the gleam in them can't be mistaken.

He's right. I did shower without him.

But I didn't wear him out on purpose last night. That was all on him. I think the man is singlehandedly trying to live ten years of fantasies in the span of ten days.

And because of that, I had no choice but to shower without him. Because our wet and naked time ends up getting us dirtier instead of cleaner. And I don't have time for that this morning; I've got work to do.

"My Hero had to scrub his back all by himself. Such a poor boy."

He pops a playful eyebrow in the air and jiggles my hips back and forth. "It's not my back that needed scrubbin'."

I burst out laughing and give his hair a little tug. "And that's why I showered by myself. I've got red velvet cake and chocolate fudge cake pops to finish." I lick my lips. "This baker and dessert maker has her first event with the ever-popular, growing-in-fame, catering extraordinaire, *The Elegant Taste*. And I need to leave for work." I give him a fake frown. "Your dad already called and asked if I could spare some of the cream cheese in the fridge. He said he needs some for his jalapeño popper dip."

He pouts, pretending he's not happy with my explanation.

I push my body against his, relishing in the fact that his erection responds to me. In one second flat, he's hard. A low and rumbling breath heaves from the depths of his lungs. His hand flies to my back, where he locks me against him, forcing me to grind into him even more. He's searching for the smallest amount of relief, the smallest amount of friction.

"My turn," I chirp.

He smiles and then snuggles himself against me, mapping tender kisses down the sensitive skin of my jaw. All the while his cock rubs against me with a bruising, demanding force. His actions are a glorious contradiction. Hard and soft. Commanding and obedient. Erotic and modest. He mumbles, spreading his hot words against my flesh. "Your turn, huh?"

"Mmm-hmmm."

"Okay, Little Bird. What's your question?"

"Will you forgive me? For leaving you all alone in that big, ol' shower? All by yourself?" I rub my breasts against him. "It must've been so very scary."

Now, it's his turn to laugh, unable to keep a straight face. "I'll forgive you. If you bring me some of the popper dip. And maybe a slice of cake."

I push away from him and grab my purse and smartwatch from the counter. With a daring sashay to my hips, I toss my quip over my shoulder on the way out the door. "Food? Kinky. I like it."

Chapter 36

Orah

The mid-March sun hits a little different today.

I push the sleeves up on my black shirt, letting the late afternoon sunlight warm my skin as I walk to my car. I just dropped a variety pack of four-dozen baked goods at a local church for their Spring Blossom Festival. Everyone fawned all over the decorated cookies and treats; which, of course, made me feel amazing.

With the ongoing kudos from Jeff and Cullen—and some quick word of mouth from our clients who attended the taste testing for the new *Granny's Kitchen at The Elegant Taste*—my self-confidence in my baking abilities has soared off the charts.

I'm a sugar warrior.

Wielding my sword of buttercream with a stealthy and lethal hand.

And every single day, I ride off into the sunset on my horse made of pink sprinkles.

But, my ability to bake a mean apple fritter isn't the only thing that has me in a good mood.

Jeff and Cullen closed on the purchase of the commercial building today. As of tomorrow morning, the old farmer's market will no longer be an abandoned and forgotten building down by the river. Renovations start at daybreak. And considering the renovation loan is being funded by the one and only Holt Hill, the contractors will be doing anything and everything to finish on time, if not early. Nobody, and I mean nobody, wants to disappoint the famous Holt Hill. He might have Super Bowl rings stacked in a glass case at his mansion, but he's also a state-winning high school football coach. Which, in Alabama, makes him more important than even the town mayor.

As of right now, the timeline has the renovations being completed by the beginning of October. As a collective, Jeff, Cullen, and I decided that it's best not to pre-schedule any large events or weddings at the venue until after the New Year. If for some reason the reno does fall behind schedule, we don't want the stress of worrying about ruining people's big days. So, once the building is fully operational, we'll book some smaller holiday events and Christmas parties.

Out of all of us, Cullen is the most excited. Not only is this his brainchild, but the whole top floor of the building is going to be remodeled into a massive apartment for him. He'll be right in the middle of all the action, for both the building and the bar. He can literally walk to both of his jobs. And unlike his brother, a modern penthouse condo is just what he wants.

I slide behind the wheel, set my purse on the passenger seat, and send a text to Ridge, letting him know I'm on the way. He's at the bar celebrating the expansion of the catering business with some of the other guys. Much to my surprise, I've come to enjoy spending time at *The Last Call.*

Yes, it's typically very crowded.

Yes, it's typically very loud.

Yes, it's typically a little overwhelming.

But I'm always surrounded by support. With those I love not only encouraging me to have a good time—to live and experience life in the way a young woman in her twenties should—but with those same kind people watching over me, keeping a vigilant eye out for danger. If something were to go wrong, I know Ridge would stop at nothing to protect me. And the same goes for all of his extended family.

And I reckon I'd be lying if I were to say that Cullen's plethora of non-alcoholic cocktails were anything less than addictive. He might not know how to fry an egg in the kitchen, but he sure can mix a mean mocktail. And that includes the newest addition to the menu, which happens to be my favorite. A pineapple and tamarind blend he named Brother's Sweet Bird.

I'm about to turn the ignition when a black SUV with tinted windows parks right in front of me, front hood to front hood. But instead of fully parking and walking into the church, they just sit there. I'm sure it's nothing more than a parent busy with packing supplies or whatever may be needed for the church festival that starts in two hours. Or maybe a teenager preoccupied on their cell phone. But for some reason, the slight angle of the tires and the blinding headlights that are flashing in my face—despite the sun still being out—make me nervous.

And of course, there's also the fact that the majority of the parking lot is open. Completely free. With spots even closer to the activity center door.

So, why on earth would this car park right in front of me?

I lower my visor, seeing if that will stave the glare of the headlights enough so I can see inside of the front windshield. But it doesn't work.

Nerves dance in my stomach, twisting and turning like little ballerinas on the stage. I reach for the comfort of my necklace. I attempt to slow my rapid breathing, trying to force my numbers in sync with my inhales and exhales.

One. Two. Three. Four. Five.

I pray I have enough strength to someday realize that not every unusual situation is a dangerous situation.

But, obviously, today is not that day.

I hit the button to lock my doors, tapping it three or four times for good measure.

I need to get out of here.

If I drive away, I can leave the threat of whatever or whoever looms in that SUV far behind me.

But...does that mean that I'm leaving everyone else inside of the church in peril? What if someone were to go inside and do something they shouldn't? With weapons meant to harm, meant to hurt, meant to destroy?

Could I live with myself if that were to happen?

No. Most definitely not.

I glance from left to right, my eyes quickly landing on the gas station across the highway. In the span of two seconds—which also feels like two-hundred lifetimes—I decide to split the difference between *not freaking out* and *playing it safe.* I'll move my sentry to the gas station. From there, I'll still be able to keep an eye on both the SUV and the front of the church.

Plus, the distance will shield me from my embarrassment.

Because when the 'perfectly normal' person finally emerges with their 'perfectly normal' basket of decorations for the 'perfectly normal' festival and takes 'perfectly normal' steps to enter the 'perfectly normal' activity center where all their 'perfectly normal' friends are...I'll be able to metaphorically tuck my tail between my 'not-so-perfect' legs and drive away.

I'll be able to shed my tears in the concealed cocoon of my car, wondering when I'll finally be able to break free from the terror of that night. Because, apparently, ten years hasn't been long enough.

With a shaky hand, I start the ignition; and with an even shakier foot, I maneuver through the parking lot and take a right turn onto the road. I immediately swap to the center lane and bank a left into the gas station. I ease my car between the air pump and a large sign advertising two-for-one fountain drinks. Looking down, I fiddle with the dashboard controls, making sure Ridge's contact information is on the touchscreen so I can quickly tap it in the event something goes wrong. Sometimes, when I'm flustered, the Bluetooth voice-activation doesn't understand me. And now is not the time to fight the battle between computer technology and southern accents.

When I glance back up, my heart stalls. I frantically spin in my seat, searching down both sides of the main highway. And then, my eyes catch in the rearview mirror. Bile catapults from the pit of my stomach and into my mouth, coating my tongue and cheeks with acid.

It's behind me.

It's positioned in front of one of the gas pumps. But nobody is pumping gas. Instead, the lumbering black vehicle just sits there.

Taunting me.

Haunting me.

Suffocating me.

When I blink, my eyes lock closed. My eyelashes glue together, refusing to grant me vision. It's like my brain knows that only bad things are waiting for me, so it refuses to allow my reflexes to do their jobs. Swirls of black and purple dots creep across my eyelids. I take a deep breath, and even though it's impossible, I swear my car is filled with the noxious fumes from the SUV's exhaust.

I grab my bird charm and dig my fingers into the Tiger's Eye stone.

Open. Open. Open. Open. Open.

My body listens. And then instantly regrets it.

It's. Still. There.

I fling my car into reverse and jerk out of my makeshift parking spot. Blood pounds against my eardrums, drowning out the sound of the passing traffic, as I hit the main road. My eyes flicker back and forth to my rearview mirror, and when the SUV follows me, my panic soars to new levels. With every turn of my wheels, my anxiety climbs.

Higher. Higher. Higher.

My vision blurs around the edges, making it hard to focus. Beads of sweat drip down my breastbone and pool into the crevice of my bra, soaking the scarred skin of my torso. My chest constricts, choking me of the ability to breathe. Reminding me of what it felt like in that brief moment, during that small splice of time after I called his name, after I reached for him. When blinding pain tore through my body and the world sucked all the oxygen from my injured lung, suffocating me in blood and bullet fragments.

I weave in and out of traffic, dying a tortuous death every single time I get caught by a red light. And at each one, the SUV lumbers behind me. It doesn't veer off course. Despite my silent pleas, it doesn't turn in the opposite direction or swing into the drive-thru at a fast-food place.

Fear and dread slither around me in a tight grip, splintering my bones with every block. The fact that I can even keep my car on the road, without careening into buildings or injuring pedestrians, is a miracle of epic proportions.

The seven miles between the church and the bar feel like seven-thousand miles. Adrenaline drugs me, morphing time and space into a conundrum of lagging seconds and galloping minutes.

Slow and fast.

Slow and fast.

Once I can see the bar's street corner in the far distance—and it's more than apparent that I'm not overreacting and that this vehicle is, in fact, following me—I tap the highlighted name on my dashboard.

He promptly answers, and his textured greeting floods the inside of my car, along with the background noise of music and clinking beer bottles. "Hey! How'd it go? Are you on your way here? Damn, I can't wait to see you."

"I...I think someone is following me." My theory is whispered. Because if I say it out loud, that makes it true.

And I really don't want this to be true.

Whatever *this* is...

There's a static-filled clamor, like he's shifting positions as he talks. "I'm sorry, Bird; I didn't hear you. What did you say?"

"Someone is following me."

There's a pause. Brief, but intense. "Did you say someone is following you?" His tone is clipped and precise.

"Yes."

"What do you mean someone is following you? Where are you? Are you walking?"

"I'm not walking. I'm driving. In my car."

"Where?"

The clatter on his side of the phone dies down, like he's walked outside or something.

The next dangling stoplight clicks from yellow to red, and the traffic in front of me inches forward, getting into a stopping position. "I'm at the red light before turning in front of the bar."

"On which street? Elm or Twenty-first?"

"Ummm..." My brain can't even process the things I know about my town. I know these streets. I swear, I do. "The one that runs past the courthouse and sheriff's department."

The telltale sound of his boots slapping against the pavement reverberates in my ears. He's running. And he's running fast. "I'm coming to you. I'm on my way."

I sit forward in the driver's seat, craning my neck, trying to find him.

Wait...

How am I sitting forward?

I look down and fan my hands over my sternum, gliding them down to my waist. Oh my gosh, I never even put my seatbelt on. As if to point out my ignorance, the dashboard flashes with the safety restraint image. I don't even remember the dinger going off. And it chimes for four minutes straight before stopping. I've been lost in my own head; I didn't even hear it.

I peek in the side mirror. The SUV inches forward, getting uncomfortably close to my bumper.

The turbulent energy flowing through my body, firing down every nerve-ending, stimulating every cell, suddenly stops.

It calms.

It ceases.

And with one pump of my heart, a tranquility engulfs me.

There he is.

He rounds the corner building. Full speed. Sprinting.

Instead of keeping to the sidewalk, he strays, taking the path of more resistance, simply because it's the route closest to the line of cars. The small set of businesses facing this side of the road has a grass courtyard. He jumps over the waist-high, decorative fence separating the doctor's office grass from the insurance agent's grass. "I'm coming," he repeats. "Where are you?! Which lane?"

I open my mouth, but he beats me to the punch. "I see you!"

Tears stream down my face at just the sight of him.

There's a flutter of activity that draws my attention back to the side mirror. Oh my god, someone's opening the passenger door to the SUV.

Boom. Boom. Boom.

My tranquility explodes. It evaporates right before my eyes. My fingers and toes grow numb, and my limbs fill with lead.

Through my flooding tears and all-consuming panic, I see Ridge on the other side of the window.

Boom. Boom. Boom.

He's banging on the glass.

"Open up!"

My foot slips off the brake, and my car jerks forward. I yelp and set the gear into park.

I fumble for the lock, cursing a scream because I keep hitting it at the same time he's trying to pull the handle. We're fighting against ourselves. Eventually, our timing works, and he yanks the driver-side door open. "Move! Scoot over!"

Even though my weighted body refuses to fully cooperate, I somehow tumble over the console, basically landing ass over tea kettle in the passenger seat. My left shoe flies off my foot and bounces off the backseat onto the floorboard.

The Bluetooth screeches a wild cacophony through the confines of the car, struggling against the frequency of the phone call and our in-person activity. Ridge taps the button on the dash to end the call, tosses his phone in the cupholder, and slams the door.

A few horns honk, nonverbally telling us that it's not right for people to be climbing in and out of cars while sitting in the middle of the road.

"Behind you?!" He's loud and commanding, yelling the questions in a deliberate and confident manner. "They've been following you?!"

I nod frantically and spin, trying to see out the back. The person still hasn't fully climbed out. But their door is open and they have a hand curled over the frame. And of course, their bright headlights are still blinding me. When combined with the glare from the sun and my flooded eyes, I can't make out anything but shadows.

The red light turns green, and everyone starts slowly moving forward. The body in the SUV sits back in the seat and slams the door.

Right then, another person comes racing down the sidewalk from the opposite direction.

Is that...

Yep. It's Crutch.

Dressed in jeans and a black polo with the sheriff's department emblem on it. He's decked in all of his police gear, which happens to include his utility belt. With his gun. And he's running with the same speed and agility that Ridge did.

Ridge lowers the window as he edges the car forward. "Behind us! The black SUV! Behind us!"

Crutch stops at the front of the SUV, angling his body toward it, with his hand on his waist. He starts screaming at them. But I can't make out what he's hollering.

Traffic finally clears, and Ridge takes off, taking the turn onto the side street as soon as he's able.

Unfortunately, Crutch's verbal assault doesn't stop whoever is following us. They cut around the corner, tailing us. Crutch takes off in a mad dash, rushing to catch up.

Considering the time of day, not all of the parking spots in front of the bar are filled.

Well, I should say they aren't filled with cars.

They are, however, filled with some of the men of the Conway and Hill families—Cullen, Jeff, Holt, and Will.

Ridge haphazardly parks in between two slanted parking spaces. I open my door, eager to get inside the sanctuary of the bar. If I can just get inside of four walls, then maybe, just maybe, all of this drama will magically stop.

But I don't think I'm that lucky.

Because all holy hell breaks out.

Cullen rushes to my side and basically puts his body between me and the outside world. Ridge flings open his door and races around to us. The SUV squeals to a stop. Losing control, its back end skids into the oncoming lane of traffic. A white truck slams on its brakes and jumps two tires on the sidewalk to avoid getting sideswiped, narrowly missing a woman walking with her dog.

Fortunately, those people seem to be okay. With the bar being on a side street, we're only dealing with two lanes of traffic. Not four lanes with two turn lanes, like the main road. So, I guess it could've been worse.

Holt, Jeff, and Will flood around the vehicle, waving their hands in the air and screaming.

Three people climb out of the SUV.

Two men and a woman.

A woman dressed in a bright red business suit. With impeccable hair and makeup.

Is...is that a camera? Does the guy from the backseat have a TV camera on his shoulder?

Ridge plucks me from the passenger seat and scoops me into his arms. I bury my face against his shoulder as he rushes me across the sidewalk and through the bank of outdoor tables.

Voices clash against one another, vying for top position. Daring a glimpse, I watch as Crutch bursts into the middle of the melee. His head is on a swivel, sizing up the entire area, carefully taking in the situation. His hand still hovers over his weapon. Just like us, he has no idea if these people are trying to injure me. Hurt me. Kill me.

He barks orders. "Get back! Turn around and place your hands on the hood of the car! Fucking now!"

The driver of the SUV points at him. "It's a free country, man! We have a right to be here! This is a public street!"

Crutch's thundering howl comes from the depths of the black abyss. "I. Said. Hands. On. The. Hood."

Above the hectic buzz of the men trying to protect me, the strangers trying to get to me, the gossip of onlookers, and one barking dog…the fancy woman shrieks her accusations. "Amy Smith! Is your real name Zipporah Smith?!"

The horror of my whisper shades the world in gray clouds and black night. "She knows my name…"

And as Ridge swings open the bar door, her piercing questions follow me inside. "Zipporah Smith! The ten-year anniversary is one month from today. Tell us what happened in that movie theater! Is it true you were having a sexual tryst? Who were you involved with? Was it the shooters? The Congressman?"

My soul flames in a deathly and violent fire.

It leaves me shaking and trembling.

The light inside of me dims.

A dark, contaminated soot rains down from the heavens.

Silly me.

I only thought my catastrophes were over. I only thought I was ready to dance on the ashes of my past.

Turns out, you can't survive in something that's still burning.

Chapter 37

Ridge

I tuck her favorite blanket around her body.

Turns out, she still has it. Her eighteenth birthday present that she didn't count as her eighteenth birthday present.

Yes, the colors have faded.

Yes, a majority of the faux fur is matted down.

Yes, it's covered in fuzz balls.

But she loves it. Just like she loves me.

She snuggles into the couch, finally happy to be back in our shared home, even though it's the penthouse apartment we both hate.

As a family, we decided it was best to spend the next several days at Holt's house. It only made sense, considering he has the most security out of any of us, with his property gates and security cameras.

The first three days were a blur, with everyone playing their equal roles in investigating what the hell happened. Crutch and Ella jumped into action, reaching out to all of their business contacts and affiliates. And even Marcum, who retired from the force when Holt was arrested, fell into the trenches, reaching far and wide to gain information.

We were all terrified that reporters were going to attack the rest of the family in the exact same way they did Orah—John and Ann, but more importantly Boaz, Tabby, and little Eden. So, while Ann stayed with us in the Children's Wing at Holt and Merit's house, John took a few days off and went back home to South Carolina. He kept a diligent eye on his daughter-in-law and granddaughter while Boaz worked. Tabby's job has more flexibility, allowing her to work from home, so at least their livelihoods weren't impacted too badly.

By the fourth day, Orah was ready to return to work at the storefront for *The Elegant Taste*; she had orders to fill. She had already used Holt and Merit's kitchen to bake three different cakes for someone's office party, and she felt bad for occupying their space, even though they told her it was no big deal. So, when I wasn't on duty, I became a de facto dessert apprentice, keeping her company at the shop. And when I had a shift, we made sure that Cullen was there, with Will picking up any slack from his disappearance at the bar.

True, Dad was at the shop too, but if shit was gonna go down, I wanted to make sure that someone who had lifted weights at least once in the past two decades was present. My father may be in pretty good shape, but he's not exactly been bulking up for self-defense training.

As the days passed, we gained more insight into what was going on. The reporter and camera crew were from ADNN—America's Daily News Network. Crutch was able to ticket them for some public nuisance charges and reckless driving, but that was about it. I guess that gave them enough pause, at least for right now, to stop their wild heathen interview tactics.

Fortunately, they're the only ones who have reached out to Zipporah. In the days since, I've had a few phone calls and emails from other news outlets, asking for comments or requesting meetings. None of them mentioned Zipporah—or Amy—by name. It seems most are just wanting some soundbite material for small reports they're running about the anniversary.

And not one single person has requested anything from Tabby. For right now, it appears that she's hovering below the limelight.

Which is the way it should be.

She has a child to protect.

Crutch and Ella were able to pull and review the recent Freedom of Information Act requests, and ADNN was the heaviest hitter in the past couple of months, with them trying to request documents and content that weren't readily available from the past several years. As you can imagine, FOIA requests started within days of the attack. And yes, they've slowed down significantly, but they've never truly stopped.

Ella doesn't have a reputable contact with ADNN, as it's not one of the networks she works with in the television production side of her forensics business. Believe it or not, she's had the opportunity to work with them in the past, but turned them down because she heard that some of their investigative methods were not exactly of the high ground.

Imagine that.

But she did have contacts with some of the others, and after speaking with them, she gleaned enough to know that a hard-nose sleuth might be able to put two-and-two together, but for the most part, Orah's major identifying information and certain events from that night were still redacted.

The *Witness 127* façade is still intact.

Well, as intact as it can be.

Because people still recall the social media celebrity who fell from grace. The scantily clad internet starlet who was shoved off the top of the 'red heart' pedestal by vicious rumors and snark. The scrollers and trollers remember how their worlds stopped turning when they could no longer see the younger version of My Brave Girl dressed in a panty-hugging miniskirt.

No more posts of her high school parties.

No more stories of her pumping gas.

No more reels of her seductively nibbling on the end of an ink pen as she pretended to do her math homework in bed.

But ten years have passed. The web has produced a thousand-and-one new stars, and the web has chewed up and spit out a thousand and two. Scandals have come and gone.

She may be remembered, but is she remembered more than the guy from two years ago whose lifestyle brand was demolished when they found out he was having sex with a dog.

So, the average reporter may realize that Orah Smith was a victim in the movie theater attack, but it would take a lot of dots to connect Orah Smith with Witness 127, and then connect Witness 127 with Amy Smith.

She gives a little moan, drawing me from my thoughts, and I can't help but wonder what she's dreaming. The beds in the Children's Wing are gloriously comfortable, but it was still hard for her to sleep. And for the first few nights, she had nightmares. I finally got to experience firsthand the torment of seeing her thrash and hearing her call out for me. Each time she woke, I held her in my arms for hours, grateful that I could finally give her what she's been reaching for all of these years—my undivided attention, love, and commitment. So, clearly, she's more than earned the right to take a nap now that we're back in the apartment after eleven days away.

My cell phone buzzes, vibrating in my pants pocket. I ease off the couch, careful not to disturb her, and make my way to the bedroom. Sitting on the edge of the bed, I field the call from my old nemesis-turned-somewhat-friend.

"Hey, Chloe."

"Hey, Ridge. It's good to hear your voice."

Back in the day, Chloe was the celebrity paparazzi assigned to Holt. She'd make frequent trips over from Atlanta, snap a few pictures of him, and sell them to the highest bidder. When he was arrested, she really stepped up to the plate, trying to warn Merit about what to say and do in front of the media. And of course, when Merit ignored her advice, she did everything she could to try to highlight the parts of the story that no one really wanted to hear. You know, aka the truth. In the end, Ella was able to connect her with a very respected and well-known crime journalist. Chloe works for her now.

"You too. Ella said she reached out to you. Said you were checking on some things for her?"

"Yeah."

"I really appreciate your help with this, Chloe. I...I've got to make sure I protect Orah. She's my number one priority."

For a moment, she's quiet. "I'm really happy for you. I'm glad you found your person."

I'd be remiss not to admit that Chloe's had a small, little crush on me over the years. Nothing ever happened between us, though. In my efforts to protect my best friend from scrutiny, I sometimes disguised my endeavors to safeguard and shield, with flirting jabs and teasing gestures. Chloe knew what was up; she's smart. But I guess it still stings.

She clears her throat. "So, I just got off the phone with Ella. I know she'll tell you everything, but I felt like you deserved a one-on-one."

My hands break out in a sweat. I wipe them back and forth across the comforter. "What'd you find out?"

"Some people I used to work with are over at ADNN. After a whole lotta talking and some very expensive drinks, I got a little bit of information. I promised not to give their names, and if anything ever comes of it, they will deny ever talking to me."

"Okay. I understand."

"So, apparently, over the years, the FOIA requests from the local authorities in White Sky, all of the responding Florida agencies, the FBI, DEA..." Her voice dissipates, indicating the unspoken masses. "Well, most of those were on the up and up. A lot of the information was redacted. I mean, there might've been one or two small slips. I think one report mentioned Orah and her friend's hometown. And I think Orah's dad's name might've been buried somewhere in another one. But all mentions of sexual assault, rape, or sexual intercourse were removed."

"Okay."

"But the kicker was the transcripts for the congressional inquiry. Apparently, ADNN has several high-rung House and Senate staffers on payroll." She clicks her tongue. "I don't mean they actually work for ADNN; I'm talking about—"

My heart starts drumming faster. "I know what you mean, Chloe."

"Yeah." Her breath roars like static against my ear. "So, most of the transcripts from that inquiry are public record, made available through the Government Publishing Office. With the offenders dying, there was less need for privacy around certain things. The closed-door portions of the transcripts are housed in the National Archives. They've just been sitting there. This whole time. Safe and sound. But certain staffers can withdraw the records on a temporary basis. Apparently, whoever reviewed the closed transcripts disclosed certain parts of them to ADNN."

A vise squeezes around my body. My bones feel like they're crushing, and my muscles cramp. "Meaning they know about what happened in that room? They know about the rape? And they know about what the shooters asked of her?"

"I'm not actually sure what all information they have. My contacts refused to go into specifics. They just kept saying it was so much bigger than all of us." Chloe sighs. "But Ella told me what happened to Orah. And she told me what the reporters asked when they were trying to get to her." She stills, allowing her sincerity to carry across the distance. "I'm so damn sorry."

I try to swallow, but I can't.

It's true.

Orah and I had no choice but to tell the family what happened to her. If we learned anything from Holt's situation, it's that people will try to go through anyone to get to their real target. And that includes family and friends.

"Ridge, you understand where this is coming from, right? This is all politics. It's a power play. The people who turned this stuff over to ADNN only have one thing on their mind. They're reading the writing on the wall, and they want to flip the tables of power." She shuffles on the other end. "You know he's on the list. And from what I hear, it's a very, very short list."

I can't even think about that right now.

Because if I do, I'll break my fucking knuckles punching the walls of my apartment until they come crumbling down around us. Like the concrete, steel, and wood are nothing more than gingerbread walls. Fake and false. Pretty but insubstantial.

I dive into another question, avoiding Chloe's previous comments. "How'd they find her? How'd they know she was here?"

"They traced her move to Alaska. Found the name change she recorded in the North Slope Borough. It was easy enough to follow her from there." She staggers a breath, and it sounds like she's about to choke. "But...they already knew she was in Alabama before they even pulled the Alaska records."

"What? What are you talking about?"

"Oh, Ridge," she whimpers. "You aren't gonna like it."

"I don't like any-fucking-of-it, Chloe. Just tell me."

"ADNN wasn't even planning on doing anything to memorialize the anniversary. I mean, just like everyone else, they were gonna run a small segment. You know, the same standard regurgitation they do every year. With no real feeling or emotion behind it. Until a couple of months ago, they weren't planning anything special."

"Okay. So, what changed?"

"They got a tip. That Zipporah Smith, the famous social media victim, was living in an unassuming college town in Alabama. Under a new name. That drew a little attention. And then, when they started digging, they realized that no one really knew what happened to her because her testimony was sealed because of her age. All they had were random witness numbers for the non-deceased victims who were minors. That led to the pay out to get the closed-door transcripts. And, obviously, that led to the massive shit pile that you're dealing with today."

"A tip? Who the hell could've tipped them off?"

She stalls. Not saying anything.

Her silence speaks volumes.

Anger flutters through me like a thousand vultures. They're flapping their massive wings and pecking through the remnants of my blood and marrow. "Say it, Chloe."

"The president of the network owns a vacation home in Siesta Key, Florida. And he has a penchant for pricey cars." Her insinuation hangs in the air, floating like a mist. "It's like an hour away from Tampa. Didn't Kimber-Shay's family…"

"Buy a luxury car dealership in Tampa? Yeah. They did."

"Ridge…" She doesn't get far in her attempt to soothe me. Because she quickly realizes there's nothing she could ever say that could ease the fury and disappointment coursing through me right at this minute.

"It doesn't make any sense. I only ended things with Kimber a month before those reporters showed up. You're telling me those reporters had time to follow-up on the tip, bribe D.C. bureaucrats, decipher stolen congressional papers, and send an interview team down here…all in the span of a few weeks? We're talking about politicians. The same people who take months to give me a tax refund. Hell, Chloe, I can't even get an appointment with my dentist that quick."

She blows a bubble through her lips, and the phone speaker hums against my ear. "The tip came in on January 21st. They've been hitting it nonstop for almost two months."

January 21st.

The day after our first wedding planner appointment.

The day after Zipporah Smith came back into my life.

The day after Kimber swore that she wouldn't tell anyone about Orah.

She swore. She promised.

And she lied.

I race my hand down my face and tap my chin.

One. Two.

The calming habit doesn't help.

"Oh, I'm gonna fuck—"

"You're not gonna do anything."

Chapter 38

Ridge

"You're not gonna do anything."

To say I'm caught by surprise—by both her sudden appearance and her firm declaration—would be an understatement.

Orah's standing in the doorway to the bedroom. Her black hair is pulled into a low ponytail, and she's dressed in an oversized black sweatshirt and black leggings that fall to just below her knees. Little fuzz balls from the shedding blanket decorate her whole ensemble.

"Bird." I drop my cell phone from my face, just enough to look at it. For some reason, it looks foreign and unfamiliar. "Uhhh, I'm just talking to..."

"I know." She pads across the floor and stands in front of me. "I just got off the phone with Ella."

"What?" My spine stiffens. "She called you? I didn't hear your phone ring. I didn't hear you talking."

"I know," she repeats.

"Ridge? What's going on?" Chloe muffles through the receiver.

Orah holds out her hand. "Give me."

Well...okay.

I gently lay the cell in my girl's outstretched hand.

Taking a deep breath and lifting her chin, she puts the phone next to her ear. "Chloe? This is Orah."

From my perched position, I can just make out Chloe's muted chirp. "Oh, hi."

"I just got off the phone with Ella, and she filled me in on all of the details." She licks her sleep-swollen lips. "I just want to thank you. You put yourself and your career on the line to find out what you could. To help me. To help my family." Her eyes lock with mine. "To help *our* family. You went above and beyond for us. Seriously, thank you, from the bottom of my heart."

I can't really make out anything that Chloe's saying now. She's talking too low and too fast.

After a beat, Orah gives a little smile. "I do."

Chloe chatters again.

And then, all I get from Orah is a simple, "I will."

Chloe goes at it again.

I'm about to tell her to put the phone on speaker when she ends the conversation. "I'm not sure I'll ever be able to repay you for what you've done, but I'll do my best. And hopefully, we'll meet in person one day."

She hangs up and holds the phone in front of my nose. I grab it and chuck it behind us on the bed somewhere. "What the hell was that about? And when did you talk to Ella? You were asleep on the couch."

"I *was* asleep on the couch. But then, my cell buzzed and woke me up." She reaches for her necklace and gives a little grunt when she remembers that she took it off when we got home. "And you didn't hear me because I hid in the laundry room closet."

"You hid in the closet?"

"Yeah."

"Why?"

Her lips turn in a half-smile. "So, you wouldn't know I was talking with Ella."

I finally grow a brain and comprehend what she's saying. "She was supposed to call *me* the second she knew something. Me. Not you. She wasn't supposed to bother you."

She slides between my legs. My hands eagerly reach for her, pulling her closer to me. "Bother me? Ridge, this is my life we're talking about."

I look up at the magnificent woman I get to call my own. It's a privilege I'll never take for granted. "I know. I just wanted to protect you." My head drops to her stomach. "I'll do anything to keep you safe. I love you, Zipporah."

Her hands tangle in the collar of my shirt. And when her fingertips dance across my scars, I shudder.

"I want you to protect me, Ridge. You make me feel safe and sheltered. Warded from every bad thing and bad person. You're My Hero. Always and forever. But I also want to fight my own battles. I'm so tired of going around in circles. It's like I'm on a never-ending merry-go-round. I have these little moments of bravery, and the next thing you know, I completely fall to pieces. But I'm so tired of that. It's like I heal one broken part of me, just to have another one fracture. I wanna be as strong for you as you are for me. After all, isn't that one of the reasons you left me in the first place? Was for me to save myself?"

She reaches her left hand between us. Cupping my chin, she raises my head, forcing me to disappear into her storm-cloud eyes. "If I never learn to save myself, how can I save *you* when the time comes."

"I told you, you've already saved me." I fold my arms around the small of her back and splay my hands across her ass. "A million different times you've given me fresh life."

"But what if time 'one million and one' is the one that really matters?"

I tilt my head back down and nuzzle my face across the soft dip of her stomach, that sweet indention right under her breastbone, wishing I could feel her skin, wishing this damn sweatshirt wasn't separating us.

"So," she spouts, "Ridge Conway, the firefighting paramedic hero will do nothing." She slips her right hand away from her favorite shoulder and gives me a comforting pat on the back, like she's trying to lessen the sting of her scolding. "He won't call his ex-fiancée. He won't stop by her house. He won't go to her dealership. And if he passes her on the street, he'll tip his chin like a gentleman."

My body snatches backward, but she keeps a firm hold on me, refusing to let me stray too far. "You've gotta be kidding me, Bird." I begrudgingly tug a hand away from her butt and flop it toward the window, indicating the great outdoors. "That woman still has the ring I gave her. The ring, might I add, that I'm still making payments on."

"And you'll keep making payments."

I slap my hand back in its rightful place. Maybe a little too hard.

But hell, if I don't think she likes it.

She bounces forward a bit and squeaks out a little moan. "Like I said, you'll keep making payments on it. Because the Ridge I know signed a contract to pay for it. The Ridge I know won't want to mess up his credit. And most importantly, the Ridge I know will keep making payments, hoping and praying that she comes to her senses and does the right thing. Because despite it all, he wants to give her the benefit of the doubt."

I cock an eyebrow. "He does, huh?" I grumble with a heavy dose of sarcasm.

"Yes, he does." Her fingers tangle in my hair and massage my scalp. "That's the kind of man I love. The kind of man I've *always* loved. And the kind of man I plan on spending the rest of my life with." She shrugs and sways her hips back and forth, playing coy, twisting her body against my firm grip. "Besides, what would you do with that big ol' ring anyway? Surely, you aren't gonna slide that same diamond on my finger."

"Hell no. My Little Bird is too good. I would never let something of hers taint you."

And it's true.

Plus, Orah wouldn't want a ring as big as the one I got Kimber. She cares more about the significance of the stone than the size of it.

And that's why Holt's jeweler is currently working a custom design for me.

When Pop passed, he left me Vivian's engagement ring and wedding band. Vivian—his first wife. The woman he loved who was taken from him too soon. And he left Gran's engagement ring and wedding band to C. And because my brother is one of a kind and loves with his whole heart and soul, he gifted Gran's rings to me.

On the night Orah agreed to join him and my father as one-third of *The Elegant Taste*...

On the night she engrained herself into our family forever...

On the night I told him that I was gonna have Vivian's rings melted down and re-worked for Orah...

On that night, he called me into his childhood bedroom and put our grandmother's rings into my hand, telling me that *my* happiness is *his* happiness.

So, just like the jeweler from almost ten years ago, this one is perplexed. He understands why I want to add a few black diamonds to the order. With Vivian and Gran's rings being older, their stones are small. When I mingle their regular diamonds with the black diamonds in the new setting, it'll look great.

So, that he gets.

What he doesn't get is why I want our wedding bands, both mine and hers, to be inlaid with Tiger's Eye stones.

"Then, what does it matter? We'll be the bigger person. We won't stoop to her level. After all, she did what she did because she's hurting."

"You can't say that..." I do my best to temper my rage, but even thinking about it makes me beyond furious. "She called in the tip the day after meeting you, Orah. That's not a byproduct of being hurt. That's just pure vindictiveness."

She thinks for a moment. "That doesn't mean she wasn't hurt. I think our future together was written in the Heavens. And she was astute enough to see that. We can't blame her for beating us to the punch."

"And what if they don't stop? The reporters, the journalists, the photographers? What if they keep coming for us? All because of her?"

"Then, we'll fight them. Together. Just like that night, and just like every night since. We'll fight the world. We'll pull each other from the fire. Long before we burn."

I hold her, marinating on her thoughts, realizing once again that her compassion knows no bounds.

It doesn't take long for the air between us to thicken with our love.

Our passion never wavers. Day after day, it only grows stronger. It's a braided rope, and every new hug, every new kiss, every new touch weaves another layer into the strands. It's a never-ending work of art.

Its beauty is intricate; its power is stout.

We're ornate and elaborate.

Permanent and perpetual.

My hands snake to the front of her waist. I lift her sweatshirt and draw on her heated skin with my lips. Across the flatness of her stomach. The curve of her hips. The raised skin of her major surgery scar. Her hands wind around my neck, and with every pass of my tongue, she shoves me closer, begging me to give more.

To do more.

To be more.

I wrench from her embrace. With a steadying hand on her waist, I direct her to take a step backward.

Her mouth falls open, catching on a sad and bewildered gasp. "Don't you want to—"

"Take off your clothes, Orah. Give me your body."

Her eyes flare. In the glow of the early-evening moonlight and bedside lamp, I watch as her pupils dilate.

She nods her consent.

So. Fucking. Slowly.

Starting with her pants, she hooks her fingers in her waistband and drops both her panties and her leggings to the floor at the same time. She steps out of the crumpled fabric. Her sweatshirt is baggy and long, covering the part of her that I'm feral for. The part of her that I can't wait to feel clenching around me.

The part of her I can already smell. With every rustle of her thighs.

Like a ripe and juicy fruit. Harvested just for me.

She hauls the sweatshirt from her body. The way her torso moves and elongates is almost too much.

Too good. Too glorious. Too appealing.

Drops of pre-cum ease from my cock, lubricating my hard-as-fuck dick.

She tosses her shirt away and bends her arms behind her, making quick work of her bra. She stands in front of me. Fully naked. And wholly exposed.

Shallow breaths race from her lips, leaving her antsy and restless.

Her brown nipples are peaked and hard.

Her heavy breasts are swollen and sumptuous. They're perfect teardrops, falling against the lines of her body, decorating her like the incomparable masterpiece that she is.

She's my magnum opus.

Her bare pussy is flushed and pink. And completely mine.

I stand up, rid myself of my own clothes, and sit back down. She watches me. The entire time. Visually devouring me. I grab ahold of my erection, pumping my sleek and throbbing flesh in a languid and controlled rhythm.

Up. Down.

Up. Down.

Needing pressure, her palm skirts across her pelvis. With a firm press, she kneads the skin above her pubic bone.

"Dip your hand lower, Zipporah," I order. "Pull your pussy lips apart. Show me what belongs to me."

She follows my instructions, cradling her crotch in both hands. And then, with her dainty, slender fingers, she spreads herself wide open.

Oh. Fuck. Me.

I squeeze my dick past the point of comfort.

My body breaks out in a sweat.

Well, obviously, I need a better look.

"Turn around."

Her hands drop, and she furrows a brow. But without question, trusting me in the most basic of ways, she spins, gifting me with the epic perfection of the round globes of her ass.

"Spread your legs and bend over. Keep your knees locked. Hands on the floor."

My Brave Girl complies with my demand.

With her palms splayed across the floor, she parades her pussy in front of me for my viewing pleasure.

My balls constrict, screaming for release.

"Now, lift your right hand. Put it between your legs and open yourself. Just like before. I need to see every single inch of you. From that puffy little clit to that sopping wet hole that you want me to fill."

She widens her stance, giving herself a little more stability. Her trembling hand flutters between her thighs, chasing the satisfaction of exciting me.

Holy. Hell.

Her satin folds are blushed in color, and the tunnel of her cunt glitters with her arousal.

My own legs start shaking, bouncing up and down uncontrollably.

"Clench your muscles. Tighten your core."

I don't have to tell her exactly which muscles I'm talking about. She already knows. And when she bears down, clutching her insides against themselves, a large drop of her own desire slips out of her.

Making. My. Mouth. Water.

She sways to the side, looking at me from her topsy-turvy position, all the while keeping herself on display. Her breasts dangle and jiggle, adhering to the rules of gravity as they swing away from the tight, rippled skin of her bullet wound.

"Stand up," I growl. I'm so damn hot and horny, it actually sounds like I'm angry.

But she knows I'm not.

She rights herself, taking a second to allow the blood to rush back into its proper place before turning to face me.

"My turn," I groan.

"Oh, yeah?"

"Yeah." I lick my lips, trying to gain the composure to speak. "Tell me what this is doing to you. How do you feel?"

Her voice is blocky and cumbersome, dominated by the power of our connection, even though we're not physically connected. Yet. "I feel hollow. Without you, I feel empty."

My love for her is so powerful, it rips my heart in two, tearing it right down the middle. "Come here."

She steps in my direction. Two tiny steps. And then she's within arm's reach. I snatch her, tumbling her into my embrace. She holds onto my shoulders and climbs on top of me. Straddling me, her knees dig into the mattress.

With one hand I hold my dick, preparing our bodies for what's about to come. I hold her with my other arm, fitting my forearm into the bow of her back. Into the curvature molded for me. And me alone. Her butt jumps up and down, impatient to sit.

But I force her to still.

I drag my lips down her jaw, feeding her soul with the nourishment of my vow. "You'll never be empty. Never. Because all of me belongs to all of you."

Her fingers drift down my chest and settle on *our* brand, on *our* tattoo. On the little bird and the promise of her being my wife.

She lowers. Her chest slips down mine, plumping her breasts against my sticky skin. As soon as the pulsing head of my cock slides through her slit, I let go, knowing that our bodies can handle the rest.

And they do.

Inch by delicious inch, her pussy swallows me.

Once she's fully seated, her head lobs back, and she moans. Loudly. Deeply. The noise reverberates through my erection.

Her tight and perfect walls strangle me.

And trust me, suffocation has never felt so good.

I slide my hands under her armpits and loop them around her shoulders. I press down, pushing her onto me as I thrust into her, forcing myself to hit the parts of her that no man has ever explored.

And no man beside me ever will.

She cries out, filling our sex-scented bedroom with the eroticism of her screams.

Her face falls forward, fogging her hot breath into my open mouth.

Our strokes are intense and deliberate, driven by a love that's steady and pure. Unequivocal and unconditional.

She glides against me, drenching my pelvis and thighs with her impending orgasm. I skitter my right hand down the beads of her spine and dip between her cheeks. Soaking my fingers in her moisture, I draw the wetness back to the tight circle of her asshole. I swirl my thumb around the sensitive skin, pressing hard but stopping short of fully penetrating her barrier.

"Oh, yes. Yes! Yes! Yes!" Her exuberance is timed with the gyration of her pussy on my shaft.

I lean back. Just a smidge. Just enough so that her greedy clit can graze against the firm edges of my pubic bone and the coarse texture of my hair. My stomach muscles quiver. I could support myself with my hands on the bed, but then I wouldn't be able to push down on her shoulder or play with her virgin, little ass. And that would just be a tragedy, wouldn't it?

The new position has my cock hitting her in just the right way.

The way she likes.

The way she loves.

And when her bliss hits her, it's with my name on her lips and my love in her heart.

Later that night, when she's fully spent from her multiple orgasms and covered in my cum and sweat, I hold her in my arms, petting her and cherishing her. Her frequent yawns slow, and her inhales and exhales turn heavy, stacking on top of one another, like snow on a flat roof.

And I ask her the question that's been plaguing me for weeks. "What would you have named her?"

She wiggles her forefinger, barely tapping it against my side. She had been tracing the rungs of my ribcage. Up and down. Up and down. But now, she's too tired to even do that. "Hmmm?"

"If Eden had been ours. What would you have named her?"

"Adira." The name tumbles from her without any hesitation, without any delay.

And when I ask her what it means, the only response I receive is her sleep-filled breathing. Once I know she's fully out and not just dozing, I sneak into the kitchen, open the fridge, and grab a beer. I set the bottle on the counter and set to work on my phone, typing with quick fingers the name that's been torched into my soul with a soldering iron.

Adira.

And of course, it doesn't surprise me when I read the meaning— *Strong One. Mighty and Majestic.*

Like mother, like daughter.

Like aunt, like niece.

Grabbing the beer, I down half of it in one swallow, letting the cold liquid drown the burning in my gut. The sizzle that's been there since my phone call with Chloe. Because try as I might, I can't fully extinguish the smoldering embers that are pulsing. They flame bright with every hit of oxygen that fills my lungs.

It's that nagging feeling that tells me something is coming.

That persistent fear that yet another catastrophe is just around the corner. Waiting for us. Biding its time. Twisting its fingers in a cat's cradle of delight. Because it knows...it's gonna hit us when we're down.

And this time, we might not come back from the explosion.

Chapter 39

Orah

April.

The block of days on the calendar that's my double-edged sword.

It's filled with happiness and sadness. Sun and rain. The joy of the future and the regret of the past.

And this April marks the official ten-year anniversary.

It always feels weird using the term 'anniversary'. Typically, it's reserved for the good things in life. Wedding anniversaries. Work anniversaries. Sobriety anniversaries.

But how do you commemorate something that's the best *and* the worst. Two completely different parts, all wrapped into one jumbled, messy ball.

I could do my research and find out exactly how many of us are still alive. I suppose that's something to celebrate. But even that number doesn't alter the fact that twenty people died.

So, today may mark the day that Ridge came into my life. But he came into my life because people were killed.

And yes, I survived, but it took nearly *dying* for me *to live*.

So, we're not really counting this get-together as a ten-year anniversary party. No. Instead, we're counting it as a belated birthday party for Ridge and an early birthday party for me. With Ridge's birthday being nine days *before* the attack and mine being exactly seven days *after* the attack, neither of our families said anything when we decided to postpone the gathering for his thirty-second birthday to today.

I reckon there's at least one other thing we can celebrate too. And that's the fact that there's been no further drama with the news crew. There's been no sign of them since that day. After learning what we did from Chloe, we were prepared for the worst. But slowly, those fears and worries melded into the normalcy of our routines. In fact, according to our family, there's been no coverage at all on ADNN today regarding the theater attack.

I lean against the railing of the wraparound front porch and stare out at the beautiful pond. I've been to Crutch and Ella's place once before, and to say it's breathtaking is an understatement. The front of the large house—with its white siding, green shutters, and stone veneer—faces a large pond. There's a small wooden dock, decorated with two Adirondack chairs. And between here and the water, there's a concrete patio filled with furniture and dotted in the middle with a firepit.

Crutch has cut a large yard area, but most of the surrounding land is woods. Over to my right is a huge, detached outbuilding/garage combo where he houses his yard equipment and even an old truck that Ella said belonged to his grandfather.

When the front door opens, a wild and rambunctious symphony of sounds disrupts the peace of the late afternoon. Most everyone is still eating, so I was taking advantage of the situation, soaking in some alone time before the kids rush out of the house, determined to play on the tire swing or cast a line in the pond.

I don't have to turn around to know it's him.

I can smell him. Taste him. Feel him.

He slides up next to me, one hand bracing against the rail, while the other snakes across my backside, possessively holding my ass and hip. "Well," he starts, "I happen to know for a fact that you haven't eaten yet."

"And how do you know that?"

"Because there's no way you finished that quick. It's prime rib. Even though it's tender as melted butter, it's still gonna take you forever." He gives a one-shoulder shrug. "It's fine, though. I asked Ella to make up the guest bed. By the time my alarm goes off tomorrow morning, you should be gnawing on the homemade French fries."

I bump him with my hip. "Haha. I do not eat that slowly."

"Little Bird, dog shit grows into a mushroom quicker than you eat."

I snort on a giggle and roll my eyes. "Such a poet, you are." I fight against my smile. "You really know how to sweep a lady off her feet."

He turns and faces me, rubbing the length of his body into my side. "Oh, I can *sweep* you. There's no need to worry about that. I can do it. Right here, right now. Just say the word, and I'll make it happen."

"And, what's the 'word', Hero?" I ask, knowing exactly what my tease will incite.

His whisper rumbles against my earlobe, filling my body with thunder and lightning. "If I remember correctly from last night, I believe it was 'Fuucckk me, Ridge." He moans through the syllables, imitating my hot and passionate pleas.

Yep. Those were the words.

Of course, could one expect any less from me?

I mean, his expert tongue was doing what it does best. Along with his fingers.

But don't get me wrong, it's about so much more than the mind-blowing orgasms. For years, I resigned myself to the idea that physical affection may never be in the cards for me. But here he is, showing me that our love can be mirrored in every kiss, every touch. We can take something indescribable and let our bodies tell the tale.

Each time we have sex.

Each time we make love.

Each time we fuck.

A new paragraph is written in our story.

The things that I was afraid would define me are only one small aspect of my character. They aren't my beginning or my end. They aren't my plot or my climax. They're just one teeny, tiny part of the saga. He alone has the power to erase and delete. With one simple click, he can remove my anxiety and fill me with pleasure.

I feel what he feels.

And because of that, my courage is building. He's making me stronger than I ever imagined I could be.

I thought sex was this intangible thing. This abstract notion just floating out in the middle of the ocean. Bobbing and weaving, sliding under the surface, never allowing me to swim close enough to grab it.

But nothing about being with Ridge is abstract.

It's substantial. Meaningful. And oh, so real.

The feel of his body pressing into mine, transforming the two of us into one…it's my opportunity to gift him a part of my soul.

And it's a gift I wanna give forever.

I twist, relishing in the little gasp that catches in his throat when my breasts brush against his chest. "Those might've been my words, but I don't necessarily know if you want me saying them right now." I flick my eyes toward the house, "Considering my brother is on the other side of that wall."

He frowns, squinting his eyes as if he can see through the door. "I could take him." He sighs, "But I suppose kicking his ass would put a damper on the festivities." He cocks a smile. "And I really don't want anything getting in the way of me eating my birthday cake. Did you know it's from *Granny's Kitchen at The Elegant Taste*?" He runs his tongue over his luscious lips. "I hear her goods are tasty."

His innuendo is layered with prime middle-school humor, making me laugh.

He pushes away from the railing and holds out his hand. "Feel like a walk?"

"I promised Eden I would play dolls with her. Laura is letting her borrow her babydoll, Felicia Stinkbottoms."

"Eden's still eating. Apparently, she takes after her aunt," he cautiously jokes with a loving wink.

There's a heaviness to his innocuous statement. I suppose it'll always be there. The weight of knowing what I gave *and* what I gave up.

Yesterday was hard.

The first few hours are always harder.

I stood in the middle of my parents' driveway and watched as Boaz pulled Eden from her car seat. She toddled back and forth on uneven toes, adjusting to the world after being stuck in the vehicle for entirely too long. Her eyes lit up, and she raced toward me. "Aunt WahWah! Aunt WahWah!" Her black hair was tied in pigtails and whipped behind her like a curtain. And just like always, my heart broke a little when I swooped her into my arms and smothered her in hugs and kisses.

I'm sure it'll get easier. As she gets older, as she ages, as she comprehends the truth about how she grew in my tummy because her mommy's tummy didn't have room...it'll get easier.

Right?

I slip my hand in his and follow him off the front porch. He leads us past the detached building and down a cut path. The wide, dirt trail is framed on either side by a cedar log railing. Each of the wood posts is topped with a solar-powered lantern. The kind that flickers like little flames when it lights up at night.

For several minutes, we walk in silence. We leave the landscaped yard behind and meander deeper into the woods. "I didn't know it went back this far. Where are we going?"

"There's a place I wanna show you."

I give a simple nod, squeeze him tighter, and shift even closer. The setting sun sinks low behind the trees, dropping the temperature by several degrees. He loops his calloused thumb, swirling it around and around on the back of my hand, sending heat and friction through my skin.

Eventually, the noises surrounding us change, and there's a distant roar echoing in my ears. "What's that?" I ask. "Is that water?"

He smiles, shy and coy. "Just wait."

And despite the excitement rushing through me, I do.

Patiently.

Step after step. Even as my black tennis shoes get covered in dust and dirt. Even as the last of the disappearing winter's leaves crunch under our feet, crying out in despair because the Alabama woods are now adorned in bright green, with pollen and dandelion fuzz hanging in the wind. Suspended in the air, the particles waltz together, swishing through the pockets of light and shade.

There's a slight incline to the path, and as soon as we round the top, we emerge into a completely different world.

The huge meadow is covered in thousands of wildflowers. More than I've ever seen. In brilliant hues of yellow and orange, red and pink, blue and purple. And slicing through the unexpected garden, in a wavy curve, is a creek. Water rushes, flowing over small rocks and large boulders, creating a lullaby of calm and tranquility. It doesn't appear to be too treacherous. Maybe knee-deep, if I had to guess.

Against the edge of the meadow is a landscaped clearing, filled with wood chips and small rocks. There's a wooden glider, some rocking chairs, and even a hammock slung between two trees. And there's some kind of big boulder wedged in the ground. Carried by a prior flood and deposited away from the water's edge, I suppose.

My hand flies to my necklace, rubbing the charm, even though the need to count eludes me.

I don't need peace.

This place is already giving that to me.

"Oh, Ridge..." My voice evaporates in astonished awe, and I turn to look at him, quickly losing myself in the man standing before me. Streaks of sunlight play across his face, gifting me the prism of colors that I love to see dance across his beard. "This is gorgeous. This belongs to Crutch and Ella?"

He nods, pulling me deeper into the oasis. "All of this land belonged to his grandfather. It's close to sixty-five acres." He points with his fingers. "His property line runs up to those far trees on the other side." He tugs me closer and pushes a hand into the back pocket of my black capri pants, palming my ass through the material. "But the guy on the other side is selling. He's got a hundred acres, and a small branch of the Black Warrior—it's what feeds this creek—runs through it. The guy even does float tours during the summer months. Well, Crutch and Ella are in the process of buying it."

I frown in thought. "They wanna run a tubing business?"

Chuckling, he jiggles my butt. "No, they just want the land." He lifts an eyebrow and then shrugs. "Well, I guess at some point, they could run the tubes, but that's not why they're buying the property."

From the corner of my eye, I catch a flutter. I watch as a butterfly dips down, losing itself among some violet blooms. "Then, why are they buying it? Isn't sixty-five acres enough?"

Leaning forward, he brushes a kiss across my temple. The smell of his soap mixes with the aroma of flowers and grass, moss and cool water, spring and happiness. "They want enough land so that all of their kids and grandkids can live near them. Growing up the way they both did, there's nothing more important to them than family."

Over the past couple of months, Ridge has shared with me some of their struggles. The addiction that plagued Crutch's childhood, and the narcissistic ambivalence that plagued Ella's. And the disasters that befell them when they were apart. And why Laura spends so much time with them. In addition, it turns out that the missing girl, the alumni of North and Camden school whom Celeste told me about, is Ella's sister. One of Ridge's closest childhood friends. A girl they spent over thirteen years looking for. A young woman, who unfortunately was abandoned and discarded. Along with the baby in her tummy.

"C'mon." Removing his hand from its nestled place, he wraps his fingers around mine again and pulls me behind him.

We walk toward the sitting area, and I can feel his nervous energy. It travels with every beat of his heart. Down his arm, through his fingertips, and into my own body. It overpowers me, dominating the cadence of my own natural rhythms.

Pound. Pound. Pound. Pound. Pound.

Why is he nervous?

We maneuver through the field, taking care to weave around the patches of really tall wildflowers. The closer we get to the gliders and chairs, the tighter he squeezes my hand. Our shoes leave the fluff of the grass and growth, and land on the wood chips and small, pebbled river rock. I glance around, surprised when I see what looks like fake stones and pavers.

"What's that?" I ask.

With jerky movements, he follows my line of sight. "Solar lights. The stone pavers light up green and blue and white at night."

I shift my gaze to the line of horizon that I can see between the tree line. It shouldn't be too much longer before the blanket of evening covers us.

I'm not scared, though.

When I'm with Ridge, darkness can never find me.

Plus, our cell phones have built-in flashlights.

He abruptly stops walking, and I slam into the hardness of his back. With a giggle, I sneak my arms around his shoulder. Hugging him from behind, I kiss his neck, swishing my lips back and forth across the hair that's grown since his last haircut. "Does My Hero need help with something?"

He grabs me and swings me around.

And then, he nods. At the large boulder.

Time stops. It completely stands still. The earth doesn't spin.

Everything hangs. Suspended in frozen perfection.

The boulder isn't just any normal rock, misplaced by time and currents and erosion. Oh, no. Because the face of this stone is polished smooth, and etched into it are a series of names.

Reality

Carrie

Evie

The child borne of Crutch and Ella's love.

The sister lost to addiction and disaster.

The baby who never knew life.

And all of those names are sacred and special. Forever protected and eternal.

But what really gets me is the last name.

The inscription is fresh, the letters clean and clear, not yet marred by time and weather, wind and rain.

Adira

Chapter 40

Orah

dira

A My body moves all on its own, with no commands from my brain whatsoever. I fall to my knees, drawn to the engraving like there's a magnet pulsing from the epicenter. I couldn't pull away, even if I wanted to.

My fingers trace the delicate letters, marking each one to memory. "Wh–what is this?"

"It's to honor those we've lost too soon. It's to acknowledge the parts of our hearts that are missing. To recognize the love that's been carved away, leaving an empty space in our souls. It's...to humble ourselves to the fact that love can't prevent loss." He kneels beside me and brushes his hands across my face, drying the tears that are flowing in thick, hot streams down my cheeks. "Your daughter might still be walking on this Earth, Zipporah. But that doesn't mean you didn't lose her."

I collapse into him, clawing at his shoulders, begging him to hold me closer. And when he does, immediately and without pause, I give in. Totally and completely. Violent and uncontrollable sobs devastate my body. Sharp pains shoot down my breastbone. My stomach knots, twisting in anguish and agony. My scars throb with a blinding heat. Like molten lava is pouring from my long-healed wounds.

All of them.

Every. Single. One.

From the decompression needle.

From the diaphragm repair and bullet retrieval.

From the drainage port.

From the C-section.

My battle wounds. They flay open wide, and my heartache floods out.

And he holds me. The entire time. Until my wails subside, my tears dry, and my hyperventilated breathing morphs into hiccups. Together on our knees, he sways us back and forth, gently rocking us. With a low and steady cadence, he fills me with adoration and love, doing his best to take from his *own* spirit all so he can replenish *mine*. "I love you, Orah. I love you."

Eventually, I lower my head. Just enough so I can nudge my snot-covered chin under the collar of his old, worn Belly's T-shirt. My salt-chapped lips edge across his muscles and bone. And I pepper his own tangled scar with my tender kisses.

He clings to me, pressing his fingertips into my sides with such force, I'll most likely have bruises tomorrow. "Is this okay, Little Bird? That I did this for you? For us?"

I straighten my back. Raising my head to look at him, I take a second to clean the mess that's now drying and making me itch. I must fail because he quirks a dreamy smile, lifts the bottom of his shirt, and wipes the crud from my face. When he drops it back down, I can't help but notice that smudges of mascara now decorate the well-loved fabric.

"Is it okay that I did this for us?" he repeats. His Tiger Eyes tentatively search mine, reading my emotions, gauging my thoughts.

"For us?" I parrot back, snorting on a sniffle.

He swallows. The motion bobs his Adam's apple. "Do you like it here? I mean this place? With the flowers? And the creek? And the woods? Is there peace for you here?"

I force my gaze to leave his. Taking a staggered breath, I soak in the surroundings. The flowers, the trees, the grass. The sun has almost set, and the pavers around us have awoken. They cocoon us in a comforting, ethereal glow. I close my eyes and listen to the ripple of the water as it flows, racing and churning with the never-stopping current. I blink open and turn back to the memorial, giving myself time to read the treasure of names.

Reality, Carrie, Evie, Adira.

Swiveling back to him, I sigh, content with the tranquility now floating through me. I chart my fingers down his nose. Landing in the soft tuft of hair, I tap his chin. One. Two. "Yes. I like it here." I study him. The hard line of his square jaw. The crow's feet lining the corner of his eyes. The wave of thick, brown hair that's hanging down across his forehead. He's utterly gorgeous. And what's even more attractive is that the beauty on his outside pales to the beauty on his inside. "But I like it the most because you're here. My most favorite place will always be with you. By your side."

He tilts his head, to the general direction of the land that he said Crutch and Ella were buying. "About three-quarters of a mile through those woods, is a five-acre tract of land. It adjoins the high-way. Crutch has already had it surveyed."

My heart skips, fluttering back to life in a wild pace.

"Once they close on the purchase of the big parcel, he's gonna sell that five-acre plot to me. To *us*. We can build something that's our own." He smiles, wide and bright, flashing his teeth. "Something with a massive kitchen and what-did-you-say? A big barn for fire-man drills?"

The inside of me is screaming yes, but all I can do is nod.

"And we'll cut a path up here to this place, just like they did." He looks around. "For the longest time, this place was their secret. None of us knew about it. But they said love should be anything but a se-cret." He cradles my face. "And they're ready to share that. With us."

Visions of the future play through my head, gifting me with an optimistic hope, that maybe—just maybe—all of our catastrophes are done. Finally.

With each flicker of my eyelids, a new scene unfolds.

Picnics by the creek.

Christmas stockings hung by a fireplace.

Midnight scrambles to find a dollar in our wallets so the Tooth Fairy can visit.

Our children running through backyard trails and paths, eager to meet with Laura and Hardy for a game of hide-and-seek.

And one day, a daughter, with the same black hair as me and Eden, but with the last name Conway, kissing a boy under the stars and in a bed of wildflowers.

"Yes." The word, wrapped in so much meaning, tumbles from my lips, eager to accept his offer for all of our tomorrows.

"Remember that word, Little Bird."

And with that, he contorts his body, pulling something from the pocket of his jeans.

It's a ring box.

Holy. Shit.

I start bouncing up and down, fidgeting from my head to my toes. I make a move, eager to stand. Simply because I'm unable to stay still.

But he stops me. Hooking his hand around my waist, he forces me back to my knees. He slowly shakes his head and merely reminds me, "The beach."

He's right.

We were both on our knees that evening, desperate to hold onto the feelings we were forbidden to feel. When we kissed for the very first time. When we said goodbye and he let me walk away.

I suppose it's only fitting now that we're both on our knees again.

"Zipporah, I—"

I hold up my hand. "Stop."

His brow furrows, and for a split second, panic washes over his handsome features.

"I forgot to say I love you. And I forgot to say thank you." Unable to keep my hands off him, I dip my fingers into his belt loops. "Thank you for *this*. For giving me a life I never even thought possible. Thank you for giving me the courage to fight my demons. And thank you for loving me enough to slay the ones I'm too weak to battle." I lick my lips, fighting back a whole new round of tears. "I love you, Ridge."

Despite the early moonlight, I can still see the pink flush as it rushes across his cheeks. "My turn."

I giggle. "Your turn, huh?"

"Yep." Palming the ring box, he reaches for my left hand. With nimble fingers, he undoes my smartwatch and pockets it. Taking a deep breath, he turns my arm, and drags his thumb back and forth across the sensitive skin on the inside of my wrist. Back and forth across the tattoo. The mark declaring him as mine. And no one else's. "Zipporah, I fell in love with you the moment I heard your voice. It crossed the depths of that room and saved me from a nightmare. I am so fucking sorry for what I put us through, for what I did to us." He bends and kisses my pulse point. "You are my one true destiny. My love, my luck, my tenacity. Wherever you go, I will follow. Whatever you need, I will provide. Whenever you call, I will answer. I am yours. I always have been, and I always will be." He moves my hand under his T-shirt and up to *our* brand. "My Little Bird. My Brave Girl, built by the flames and sculpted by the ashes. When the world fades to black, and the stars flicker to darkness, my love for you will still burn. Bright and everlasting." One single tear falls from his eye. "Let. Me. Be. Yours."

I fling my right hand away from his waistline. It lands on my necklace. And this time, I count. Not because I'm worried or scared or perplexed or anxious.

I count because I'm happy.

One. Two. Three. Four. Five.

At the end of the five seconds, he flicks the lid open.

Rose gold. White diamonds. And black diamonds.

Breathtaking.

Just like him.

My fingers scurry down, cutting a path across his nipple and down the contours of his abdomen. He hisses through a jolted inhale.

I bite my lip, joyously allowing myself to give in to the teasing. "Where's my Tiger's Eye," I fake pout.

He tosses his head back, bellowing on a deep laugh. "Don't worry, Bird," he taunts with a wink. "I think the wedding bands will make my wife happy."

"Oh, you do?"

"Absolutely."

"Well, last I checked, you have to actually ask the question to get an answer."

He inches closer to me, rubbing his torso against my breasts. "Will you marry me?"

My lip twitches with excitement. "Yes."

His mouth crashes onto mine. We tangle together, marking what's ours with the passion of our tongues and our hands. Our bodies and our words.

And when he slides the engagement ring onto my finger, I whisper into his ear. "But I have to do something first."

He lifts a questioning brow. "What?"

My reply is staunch and steady, unfaltering and unwavering. Because the solution to the dilemma has been in front of me. The whole entire time.

"Save myself." I smile. "I'm changing my name. Because it's not Amy you're marrying. It's Zipporah."

Chapter 41

Ridge

Wanna know what happens when there's a kitchen fire *and* an HVAC electrical fire...

In the college stadium.

During the spring scrimmage game.

With approximately sixty-two-thousand people in attendance.

And ten fire alarms going off.

I'll tell you what happens...a whole heap of chaos wrapped in a double shift with barely no sleep.

Yes, the fires were small. Yes, we contained them quickly. Yes, the stadium has more fail-safes than a nuclear power plant.

But people still panicked.

Which led to injuries. Which led to people getting separated from family members. Which led to more panic. Which led to chaos. Which led to fist fights.

And on top of everything, I was stressed the fuck out because a hodgepodge of my family was there. Slap dab in the middle of the havoc.

Holt was the celebrity guest coach for the "away" team. So, obviously, Merit was there with Daire. And Ray and Teresa. And since the scrimmage is a free event, allowing families the chance to experience a ball game without the hefty price tag, tons of kids were there, including Laura, Anna, Ty, and Nate. But all of our crew was sitting on the sidelines, down on the field, so they were able to escape quickly and without too much drama through the locker rooms.

The kitchen fire originated from human error and was contained to two flash fryers. Of course, our local code requires a fire suppression system for commercial kitchen equipment, and that pretty much had everything under control by the time we got there. And the HVAC fire, which started almost simultaneously, was of no relation to the kitchen shenanigans, and fortunately happened in an empty sky box.

I wasn't on paramedic duty today—well, yesterday, today...you know what I mean—but that shifted after the first several hours. Luckily, the most serious injuries were minor concussions and a few 'clean' leg breaks. And after all of the medical calls were completed, I had to bounce back to firefighter duty because we had to complete a grid-by-grid, room-by-room search and inspection of the entire stadium.

On a positive note, everyone said the team was looking damn fine before shit went crazy. On a sour note, I'm fucking exhausted. All I wanna do is tumble into bed, with my girl bound in my arms, and sleep until my brain is free of clutter and 'figure-eight compression wrap' is no longer in my vocabulary.

But I can't do that.

Okay, I can do *some* of those things. I can sleep. I can rid my brain of blood pressure numbers and O2 stats. And I can finally shower and wash the hot dog vomit off my forearms.

But I can't hold my girl.

Why? Because my father and brother have kidnapped her. The top-rate trio of *The Elegant Taste* left before my double ended, driving down to Mobile for a closeout sale that a restaurant supply company is hosting.

At least My Little Bird didn't leave me totally high and dry. She dropped by the station before heading out of town. She left dozens and dozens of muffins, scones, and turnovers. We were in debrief, but I was able to sneak away for a quick hug and kiss. She never sleeps good on the nights I work, so I can only assume she was up all night baking.

I park in the lot and drag my weary body from the truck. It even hurts to toss the duffle over my shoulder. I snort, thinking back on the times when a double with no rest was no big deal. Unfortunately, that's no longer the case. And I think that can only mean one thing…I'm getting damn old.

My feet are about to hit the sidewalk when a familiar, yet irritating, sound stops me in my tracks. "You're marrying her? It's only been a few weeks, and you've already proposed to her?"

I close my eyes and sigh. What I wouldn't give for this to be a complete figment of my imagination.

Please, oh please, oh please.

Holding my breath, I turn.

Nope. Not a figment. Just an elitist.

"Kimber, what are you doing here? It's eight in the morning."

"How dare you get engaged!" She clicks her heels across the pavement, swooshing her leather-clad ass from side to side. She lifts her hand and flips it, waggling her fingers in my face. "*Your* ring is still on *my* finger. Do you even know what you've done to me? My entire social circle is treating me like a piranha. That girl," she spits in disgust, "did a cake and cookies for Harper's baby shower. She was there, just flaunting that ring all over the place. And when someone asked her who she was marrying, she had the gall to speak your name! To my friends! Who didn't even know that we broke up! You have no right to do what you've done!"

My jaw tenses, clenching into my teeth with such force, a stabbing pain shoots straight across my face and pierces my eardrum. "No right?! Are you kidding me?! You're one to talk!" I shuffle in my boots, fighting the urge to be an epic asshole and crowd all up in her face. Kimber may bring out the worst in me, but even that's a line I won't cross. Despite what she's done, I'm still determined to treat her with a tiny modicum of respect. Not only because it's the right thing in the end, but because it's what Orah wants. "Did you honestly think we wouldn't find out about what you did? About your tip to ADNN?"

Her face blanches white. She opens her mouth but nothing comes out.

I shake my head and scrub my hand down my chin. "Kimber, they chased her through the middle of town. They were reckless and wild. Someone could've been killed, for fuck's sake."

She worms an arm around her stomach, cinching her waist, and for just a second, she actually appears remorseful. "I...I had no idea that was gonna happen. That's all on them. Not me. They didn't even tell me when they were coming into town."

A cynical chuckle flies out of me. "That's your takeaway from this? That you shouldn't be blamed because they didn't send you a Google Calendar invite?" I crack my neck, praying for the strength to keep my cool. "You went to them the day after you met her. The day after you swore to me that her true identity was safe with you. You violated my trust, Kimber."

"And what about you, Ridge?! I'm not alone in this. You violated my trust too. You were involved with her. You were the one having a *real* affair."

"Well, call me old-fashioned, but there's a cum-stained rug in the middle of the city dump that says your affair was pretty damn *real* too. And by the way, I finally found Gandalf's dental partial inside of the Kleenex box in the living room." I hold up a hand. "I don't wanna know how the hell it ended up in there, or even think about how many times I blew my nose on a snot rag covered in his spit, but you'll be happy to know that some rodent in the back alley can now chew his food scraps and rotted meat like a world champion."

"This? Again?" She rolls her eyes. "I told you they meant nothing to me. It was just business. It's you I love. I only want you, Ridge. Just apologize, and I'll take you back. I'll forgive you."

"Forgive me?" My voice pitches high, like a middle school boy who just got punched in the junk.

She widens her eyes and scoffs. "Yeah, for cheating on me."

Oh, sweet shit. "We've already been through this. I told you I never slept with her when we were together. I never even kissed her." Despite the truth of my rebuttal, disappointment still finds me. Once again, making me realize, that I am most definitely one of the bad guys in our two-bad-guy situation. The fault doesn't lay with just Kimber. I'm stained with the darkness of poor decisions too. It's the soot from the fire that refuses to wash off, no matter how many times I shower.

I take a play from My Brave Girl and count her numbers before continuing.

One. Two. Thre—

"Dude! I can tell you wanna say something. Stop being a pussy. Just man up and say it."

And...that's the woman I was gonna spend the rest of my life with.

What the hell was I thinking?

"It's like I told you that night. I didn't kiss her or sleep with her or anything like that." I exhale trying to push the bitterness from my body. "But you're absolutely correct; I did things I shouldn't have done. I loved her. And then...I fell *in love* with her even more."

She looks down at the ground and kicks away a pebble with her stiletto.

"I should've ended things with you. Even before Orah came into the picture. We aren't right for one another, Kimber. We never were."

When she finally glances up, her eyes glisten with unshed tears. And for a split second, I'm reminded of the handful of good times we had. But then, her true colors flash in bright and vivid Technicolor. Just like one of those old movies that Merit loves to watch. "Well, I've got a ring that tells me otherwise," she snarks. She flashes her diamond and then tucks it against her breastbone, trying to draw my attention to her cleavage, just daring me to come and get it.

And as much as it pains me, as much as it hurts to see the little dollar signs I've worked so hard for roll past my eyes like a ticker tape, I end the conversation. "That sounds like a *'you'* problem, Kim."

But, because it's her, she refuses to have anything but the last word. "Really? Because from where I'm standing it sounds like an *'us'* problem, Ridge Conway."

Refusing to take the bait, I leave her fuming in the middle of the parking lot. Part of me wants to stay behind. Talk more about her tip to the news channel. Grill her on who else she told, find out if there's anything I should be watching out for—reporters in the bushes, podcasters in the elevator. But the other part of me is holding onto the false hope that maybe, just maybe, Kimber will prove Orah right. That Kimber will do something honorable. That she'll keep her mouth closed about Zipporah's past. And one day, recognize that I did us both a favor by ending things, by severing our toxic and feigned relationship.

Once I'm in the apartment, I collapse into bed, too mentally drained to even shower and wash the frankfurter giblets out of my arm hair. I knew I should've taken time to shower back at the station.

But fuck it.

If I can deal with Kimber-Shay Willis before I've even had my morning coffee, I can certainly deal with a little kid's throw up.

Chapter 42

Ridge

As soon as I hear her key in the lock, I turn damn giddy. There's a very good chance I'm more excited now than I was the Christmas that our parents bought me and Holt paintball guns. Which, of course, we then dared C that he couldn't withstand a shot to the brown bear and two cubs.

Best thirty dollars spent of my entire ninth-grade year.

Needles to say, I can't wait to see her.

I slept until after seven tonight, took a thirty-minute shower, and put fresh sheets on the bed. I'm even in the process of cooking a late dinner for us. They did stop for a bite on the way home, but she said all she got was an order of French fries and a soda. My Little Bird needs energy for what I plan on doing to her tonight. I lay the knife down on the cutting board, wipe my hands on a towel, and rush to meet her in the hallway. She barely even has time to greet me before I sweep her into a crushing hug and slam my mouth onto hers. And when her tongue darts out to taste me, I moan.

Literally.

Giggling, she pulls away from my lips and instead brushes her nose back and forth across the sensitive skin where my neck and shoulder meet. She moves to my scar and inhales, breathing in the scent of my soap. "Oh, it's so good to see you. I know you said the stadium thing was no big deal and that everything was under control, but I was so worried about you. Tabby said they kept playing clips of it all over the national news."

My hands creep down to her ass. "I told you everything was gonna be fine. There's no need to worry about me."

She looks up at me and sighs, softly and contently. "That's like telling the sun not to shine."

I furrow my brow in thought. "Is that why you don't sleep well when I'm gone. Because you worry about me? I thought it was…"

"My nightmares?" she murmurs, finishing my thought.

I nod.

Her fingers loop in circles around the back of my neck, dipping low to include my shoulder blades, drawing a pattern that lulls me into a trance. "Sometimes, it is. But most of the time, I just miss you. I miss hearing your breathing. I miss feeling the heat from your body. I miss the energy that floats in the air between us. And that loneliness feeds my worry." She shrugs, like what she's saying is of no major consequence, even though sadness is etched across her beautiful face. "Ridge, if something were to happen to you, I'd never recover. Your love is the catalyst for my heartbeat. Without you, it stops. For almost nine-and-a-half years, I lived on CPR. I was one missed compression away from ceasing to exist. And now," she grabs my arm, shifting my hand from her backside to her chest. My thumb presses against her sternum, and my pinky finger slides across the edge of her bra cup. "I'm beating. Strong and firm. Ready to live my every moment with you."

I lean forward, dropping my forehead to hers. "Nothing's gonna happen to me. To you. To us. Destiny is finally on our side, Zipporah." I shift, readying myself to pick her up, to kiss her, to touch her.

But the flittering Little Bird wiggles away from my grasp. "I thought someone was cooking me supper?" she asks with a playful tease.

Grunting, I make quick work of adjusting the painful erection straining against the seam of my gym shorts.

"Nothing fancy. I grilled some chicken. I was just chopping some veggies so we could have a salad."

"Perfect." She takes off, walking right past me. "I'll be back. I'm just gonna change."

I immediately follow her. "Need some help?"

She laughs. "Nope. I'm good." And then, she actually shuts the bedroom door right in my face.

Right. In. My. Face.

Fuck. That.

I wanna see her.

I open the door, but she chastises me. "Ridge, you march that good-looking butt back into that kitchen and get to work." She gives me some sort of weak imitation of a lighthearted chuckle. But I can tell something's wrong. Her fingers are working double time over her necklace, pacing over the diamonds and bird's eye in a fast and furious pattern. And that energy she talked about? Yeah, it's there. Except this time, it's vibrating with a foreboding heaviness.

I cross the distance, folding one hand around her hip and setting the other on her chin, forcing her to stare into my eyes. "Zipporah, what's wrong? Did something happen?"

She takes a staggered breath. "Nothing's wrong."

"Something has you nervous."

She gifts me with a genuine smile. A smile that breaks my heart and puts it all back together again, in the span of one single second. "And so, My Hero *does* feel what I feel."

"You're nervous?" I ask again, even more concerned now that she's confirmed my suspicion. "Why? What's going on, Bird?" I let go of her chin and snake my palm down the curve of her waist.

"I have a surprise."

"A surprise?" I parrot back. "For me?"

She shakes her head. "It's for me."

"If it's for you, then you already know what it is. How can that be a surprise?"

"It just is."

I click my tongue between my teeth. "I may not be the sharpest knife in the drawer, but aren't surprises supposed to be fun? Not frightening."

"I'm not frightened. I'm...cautious."

My eyes dart around the room, trying to see if anything looks weird or out of place. I didn't notice anything before, but maybe I missed something. "What do you have to be careful about? Is there something in here that could hurt you?"

"The things that have always hurt me the most are the things that are inside of here," she whispers, touching her temple with two black-painted fingernails.

I'm not exactly sure what she's trying to say, but it feels like my evening has suddenly taken a turn for the worse.

If she's in pain or hurting, afraid or panicked, I need to know. Because her burdens are my burdens. And I'll be damned if I ever let her walk a dangerous journey alone. When the road gets too treacherous, it's my job to pick her up and carry her.

"Tell me what's going on. Let me be here for you. Let me help," I beg.

"You wanna help?"

"More than anything. Always and forever."

"Then, give me some time." She rushes to clarify. "I just need a few minutes to gather my thoughts. And when I come out, we'll talk about everything. I'll *show* you everything. I promise."

What can I do?

My Brave Girl needs me to step away.

She needs me to turn and walk out the bedroom door.

And just like her, I have to be brave. I have to do it even though I don't want to. Even though I don't want to drop this conversation, end our discussion.

But really, I have no choice. Because the woman holds my undying trust in the palm of her hand. And I'm trusting that she'll follow through on her promise.

And so, after planting a gentle kiss on her lips, I begrudgingly put one foot in front of the other, pull the door shut behind me, and return to my post in the kitchen, where I lean against the countertop and try to push the door open through sheer willpower and mind tricks.

Five minutes pass. Then ten minutes. And finally, fifteen.

Grunting in frustration, I pick up a cucumber and start slicing it.

If she doesn't come out in the next five minutes, I'm going in. No *ifs*, *ands*, or *buts* about it.

The second I complete my internal handshake regarding my defiant pledge, she emerges.

And life as I know it completely ceases to exist.

This.

This is the pinnacle of a rebirth.

Of *her* rebirth.

The reinvention of a brand new woman.

She's been Orah, the social media star garnering attention and jealousy.

Zipporah, the mortally wounded teenager fighting for her existence.

Witness 127, the frightened victim giving testimony.

Amy, the shy beauty recovering from disaster.

Sister, the guilt-filled relative substituting her body.

And now? Now, she's Zipporah Conway. A remarkable amalgamation of the past, present, and future.

She's no longer regretting her former self. No longer doing her damnedest to forget all the monsters of her past. Fuck, no. She's embracing them. Holding her arms wide open and using the suffering and damage to reveal the power of her soul.

The strength of who she is.

She claimed she was on CPR, barely living all of the years without me by her side. But now, I know she *would've* survived. There's no doubt in my mind about that. She's not only saved herself, but she's revived herself into a warrior.

And I'm the luckiest bastard to ever live. Because I get the privilege of walking through this life beside her.

This woman doesn't need me carrying her over treacherous roads. She can bulldoze them. All on her own.

And hot damn, if I don't get to call her mine.

Her hair's down. No longer confined by the bun she had it in when she came home, the waves gather around her shoulders. She's dressed in a white negligee.

Snow white.

And almost see-through.

In fact, I not only can make out the pebble of her nipples, but the mouth-watering circles of her areola too.

The top part cups her large breasts, much as her bra normally does. But the front of it is wispy and flowy, reminding me of the sheer curtains Gran had in her kitchen. When she'd open the kitchen window, they would fly and flutter, dancing in the streams of sunlight.

The nightie, which grazes the tops of her thighs, is open down the middle, giving me a glimpse of the very edge of her surgery scar. The scar that brought us together and also tore us apart.

And through that split, I can see her white lace panties. Covering the pussy that was made just for me. Because no man could appreciate it the way I do...the color of her flesh, the scent of her arousal, the taste of her cum, the clench of her muscles.

My eyes land on her feet.

Well, there's no white here.

Nope. Definitely not.

Because My Brave Girl is wearing cherry-red stilettos.

I can't even think straight. All of the blood is trapped in my throbbing cock.

And that can be the only reason for why I don't pay attention to what I'm doing.

A sharp pain sizzles across the knuckle of my left middle finger. "Oh, shit!" The knife clatters against the cutting board, and blood drips onto the vegetables.

"Ridge!" She hurries to my side.

I cup my right hand over my finger trying to stave the bleeding so she doesn't see it. I slide over to the kitchen sink and pop the faucet lever with my elbow. "Back up, Orah. I'm fine. It's just a small cut."

There's no way the average person could understand how much struggle she's gone through to get to this point, to get to tonight. To wear white, to dress in high heels. For the first time. In over a decade.

There's no way I'm gonna ruin that.

I can't do that to her.

The last thing I would ever want is to derail her progress. I'd rather bleed out than turn her triumph into tragedy.

She reaches for me. "But you're hurt."

I shuffle, trying to grab a paper towel. Her searching hands collide with mine. On instinct, I gently brush her away, thinking if I do it quick enough, she won't be scathed.

I'm wrong.

My fingertips graze across the top of her bosom. Instantly, the white fabric stains with streaks of crimson.

Blood.

She's covered in someone else's blood.

One of her worst fears. And I'm the manufacturer of it.

She freezes. In slow motion, she glances down, trying to comprehend what's happened.

Blood and water trickle from the small wound and drop on the floor, decorating the area between our feet. Cursing, I rip off a paper towel, wind it around my finger, and then turn the sink off.

"Oh, Bird, I'm so damn so—"

She holds up her palm. "Stop."

I clamp my mouth closed. I issue a thousand prayers, begging her to stay strong, begging her to be the warrior she just showed me she could be.

"Stay here."

Her directive is solemn, giving no real clue as to what she's thinking or feeling. With her back pulled straight and her head held high, she disappears back into the bedroom. From my stunned and stationary position, I see the light flicker on in the bathroom. And after a scuffle of clinking and clanging, she comes back into the kitchen with the small first-aid box in hand.

Her steps are confident and deliberate, with her shoes clicking through the quiet like a metronome. I watch, slack-jawed and astonished, as she opens the small container and rummages through, pulling out an antiseptic wipe, ointment, and a Band-Aid. She licks her plump and rosy lips and nods to my paper-towel-covered injury. "Take it off. Let me see."

"I can do it. You don't have to."

She bores into my Tiger Eyes, pinning me in place with her firmness and composure. "I want to do this. I *need* to." She opens the antiseptic packet, setting it to the side. She follows with the salve and the bandage, until all of her tools are arranged in front of her. "We want children, Ridge. What would you have me do every time our little boy skins his knee? Turn him away from his mother's touch?"

I shake my head, unable to speak because my throat is clogged with emotion, thick and suffocating.

"Tonight's about me. And *this*," she says with another poignant head bob, "is part of tonight. Don't coddle me; let me fight."

I unwrap my finger and hold it as an offering in front of her.

The cut is small, but as with any injury to the fingers, it produces a lot of blood in comparison to the size of the wound. The cut sits just below the folded skin of my knuckle. With careful purpose, she wipes the area, smudging away the blood that's already dried into the wrinkled skin. When she drags the small cloth over the slice, the swollen edges flutter open and a dollop of fresh blood pools.

She swallows.

Meticulously, she opens the Band-Aid, taking care not to let the edges fold in or stick to her own fingers. She squeezes a teeny-tiny bit of the salve on the cotton pad of the bandage and then expertly wraps it around my finger.

Once my finger is dressed, she tosses away the trash—including the bloody cucumber pieces—wets a fresh paper towel, and cleans the countertop. Then, she stoops down and wipes the mess from the floor, scrubbing until there's no evidence. When finished, she adds that rag to the garbage can too.

With a deep sigh, she returns to her position in front of me. Leaning forward, she splays my hands, turning them over and checking for any rust-colored remnants. There's a faint stain on my right palm.

She stares at it.

The air between us crackles and hums, snapping and popping. It's real and authentic. It's an audible noise that reverberates through my bones and into my marrow.

We're the dead short.

The direct electrical connection with no resistance.

We're the excessive surge in danger of burning everything around us.

To the ground.

She lifts my palm to her open mouth, and the flat of her tongue licks me. Over. And over. And over. Until she's satisfied that she's purified me.

Passion fires in the pit of my stomach.

My fingertips dance across her breast, tracking across the smears, and her nipple peaks, long before I even reach the sensitive bud. "I'm sorry. I ruined your nightgown."

"It doesn't look ruined to me." She takes a small step back, removing herself from my stroking caress. "I guess blood will always be a part of our story." She pushes a lock of her raven hair behind her shoulder. "It started with blood, and it could very well end with blood. One day." Her storm-cloud eyes glisten, shining bright with her unshed tears. "But I refuse to think about the end of our story.

Because we have so much life to live. So much *love* to give. I refuse to cower in fear when there's so many words that need to be written."

A low and hungry growl rumbles from my chest.

I need her.

Fucking. Now.

I charge in her direction, but she scurries back. And for the second time tonight, she asserts the one little decree that she knows I'll always obey. Always.

"Stop!"

My bare feet freeze in position, with my toes digging into the floor. I reach for the countertop, gripping it tightly, tethering myself to it so I don't move and accidentally frighten her.

"Orah?"

Grinning just enough to let me know that she's okay, she walks backward. She seduces me with her body. Her movements are an aphrodisiac. Sensual and graceful, the epitome of a woman in full embrace of her sexuality. She folds her arms behind her back, bracing herself as she nears the wall. And when she finally hits it, she straightens her spine, standing to her full height. The slit in her negligee blows open, making me weak in the knees with the glory of her scars and her soft stomach.

My knees shake.

My mouth waters.

And my cock aches.

Her eyes widen with the promise of pleasure. Her voice is the sweet nectar of a honeysuckle. "I'm the one writing the words to our story tonight. *Me.* I'm the author of this chapter. I'm the one in control."

"Then control me, Little Bird. I'll be a good boy...I'll listen."

Chapter 43

Orah

Oh, he'll be a good boy, all right.

Is he ever anything less?

Dressed in nothing but some low-slung gym shorts, he's an Adonis of perfection. My eyes devour him, visually picking the flesh from his bones like a hungry and ravenous vulture. From his broad shoulders to *our* brand and tattoo. From his peaked nipples to his rippled abdomen. From the dusting of hair above his waistline to the monstrous bulge between his legs. From his twitching thigh muscles to his wide calves.

I'm so enthralled with my perusal of him, it's like he's already touching me.

Even though, he's ten feet away.

I lift my chin, emboldened by my confidence, fortified by the assertion I spoke out loud to him earlier. I meant what I said. Tonight, I don't want to be coddled; I wanna fight. I wanna brawl. I wanna kick the ever-living-shit out of the memories and fears that consume ninety-nine percent of my life one hundred percent of the days.

And what better way to do that than with sky-high heels and white lingerie covered in streaks of blood.

Trust me, I'm not obtuse enough to believe that my mental health journey will magically turn into some forward-facing, straight line. It's never been that. Never. I have no reason to believe it should start now. It's always been three steps forward, two steps back, with a hop, skip, and a jump to the left. I flourish those seconds, minutes, hours, days when I'm feisty and outgoing. Friendly and carefree. But it never lasts. Because my mind flashes with visions of that night. Of what happened in that movie theater, of what happened in that room, what happened in that hallway.

But you know, it's okay to have setbacks. I need to embrace those just as much as I do my successes.

Because I'm one of the lucky ones.

So many women have no one by their side.

But me? I've got a remarkable group of family and friends.

And an even more remarkable partner, soulmate, and lover.

None of them will ever let me fight alone.

When I get too tired or weak, they'll pick up my sword and slay the enemy. They'll lift me up and carry me across the war-torn and conflict-filled battlefield, never letting me fall, stumble, or stop. They'll shield me with themselves, protecting me at all costs.

But once I've recovered, once my body has reinvigorated itself, they'll gently set me back on my own two feet, hand me my weapon, and let me march. They'll step back and let me command my own fate.

A long and excited breath whooshes from my lungs. "Take off your shorts, Hero. Show me what you're gonna give me."

Ridge obliges. Making quick work of his shorts and underwear, he forcefully kicks them out of the way. They slide halfway under the refrigerator.

His massive cock bobs against his stomach. His velvet skin is pulled tight. Glistening with red and purple hues. Lined with pulsing veins. Wide and thick. Long and hard.

And all for me.

He makes a move to fist himself.

I tsk him. "Uh-uh-uh. I didn't say you could do that."

He groans. He works his fingers, opening and closing his palm, squeezing air instead of his dick.

I slip my right hand into the cut of my nightie, skim it down the planes of my stomach, and dip down into my panties. As per usual, just the sight of his naked body has me moist, steeped in my own want and need. So, when my palm hooks around my heated mound and my two fingers push inside of my core, I'm not met with much resistance.

Disappointment, yes.

Resistance, no.

But I'm discontent because it's not *my* fingers I crave. Right now, my own fingers feel like nothing. Zero. Zilch. They give me absolutely no satisfaction. No relief. No pleasure. It's like trying to scratch an itch I can't find.

Because I need *him.*

But I suppose it wouldn't be much of a momentous occasion if I didn't make him earn it.

I bend one knee and turn my leg outward, giving myself better access. I pump into myself, making sure to coat my fingers in wetness. Well, as much as I can, I mean.

This time he moans, low and loud.

I tug my hand from my crotch, allowing my panties to snap back into place. Turning my left wrist, I smear my clear juices all over *our* tattoo. I can't help but wish that I were more turned on by my own touch. I wish I could show him white streaks of desire covering the black letters and numbers.

But...he'll just have to use his imagination.

I hold my wrist up. "I got my tattoo dirty," I playfully pout.

The last syllable barely has time to reach his ears before he's lobbing a response back to me. "I can clean it for you."

"Really? You wanna do that for me?"

"Fuck, yeah, I do."

I give him a shy smile and an indifferent shrug.

He's so damn fast. Lightning fast. He's already taken two leaping paces in my direction before I have a chance to yell, "Stop!"

He freezes.

"Uh-uh-uh." My eyes flicker down. "Crawl to me."

I. Can't. Believe. I. Just. Said. That.

Without any hesitation whatsoever, Ridge drops to his knees. Bending forward, he fans his hands on the kitchen floor and crawls to me.

Eyes on mine.

And with his erection grinding into his six-pack.

Hand. Knee.

Hand. Knee.

Hand. Knee.

I rub my thighs together, seeking friction.

He stops mere inches from me. He kisses up the length of my body.

Foot. Ankle. Calf. Knee cap. Lower thigh. Upper thigh.

He scooches between my legs. He draws his face across my covered pussy, and through the delicate lace, I can feel the tiny pokes from the hair of his beard. His hot, steaming breath dampens the fabric even more. He plants a kiss right at the apex where my swollen clit sits, just begging for attention.

He straightens his back a little more. His thumb hooks in my waistband, and he drags my panties down, just a smidge, bunching them around the base of my pubic bone. With my C-section scar exposed, he kisses it.

Holding open the gossamer sides of my nightie, he continues.

Belly button.

Drainage port scar.

Surgery scar.

Base of my sternum.

Cleavage.

Tops of my breasts.

And when he's at his full height—on his knees—and his pinkish, brown lips can reach no farther, he grabs ahold of my left forearm. He nuzzles against my wrist, inhaling the intimate scent trapped on my flesh.

"For years, my favorite smell was your coconut shampoo. And then, I finally got the honor of smelling your pussy. Tell me, Little Bird, what makes you so damn sweet?"

He kisses the markings for silica. "Is it all the sugar you use?"

Iron oxide hydroxide. "The frosting?"

Aluminum. Magnesium. Sodium. "The chocolate?"

He bites me, and then soothes the sting by licking me. "Mmmm. So. Damn. Sweet." He flips my hand over and sucks my ring finger into his mouth. All the way up to my engagement ring. The ring forged just for me. From his family heirlooms. "When can I make you mine? When will you walk down the aisle to me? Into my arms?"

"It's only been ten days."

He looks up at me. His thick black eyelashes blink heavy with lust and love. "Uh-uh-uh," he mimics. "Not ten days, Brave Girl. It's been ten years *and* ten days. Don't you think I've waited long enough?"

I purse my lips and bobble my head from side to side. "We're about to enter our busy season. *The Elegant Taste* is completely booked. Three weeks from now, I won't have a single weekend free until October." I arch my back, fluffing my breasts against his cheek. "It's wedding season," I taunt.

"It needs to be *our* season."

"I suppose I can check my calendar, but for right now, you have other tasks to worry about."

He guides my palm to his face, scraping my hand along the scruff of his facial hair and gifts me a smile filled with equal parts of adoration and wickedness. "Oh, yeah? What's that?"

"You're gonna feed on me." His pupils dilate. "Take my panties off and show me just how much you wanna marry me."

He wastes no time in shoving my underwear to the floor, and then he tosses them over to his right, somewhere into the darkness of the living room. Which draws my attention to the windows that run nearly the whole length of the open space.

They're wide open.

He hasn't drawn them closed for the night.

He's one split second from connecting his tongue with my screaming clit when I slide my hand between us and cover myself. His nose bounces off my knuckles.

"Orah," he whines in frustration.

"The blinds are open. Go close them."

He turns his head and studies the night lights of our mid-size town. "What the hell?!" Standing up, he stalks across the room, naked as the day he was born, massive cock still standing proud. "You're mine. And mine alone. I'll be damned if some Peeping Tom gets a glimpse of you."

A laugh bellows from deep within me. "Says the man who's currently waving *my dick* high above the city streets for every Voyeur Vickie with a pair of binoculars to see."

He works the cord of the last blind, shielding us from any unwanted eyes. Spinning around, he places his hands on his hips and gives a little thrust, jokingly humping the air.

I laugh even harder.

If someone had told me at the beginning of the year that I would be having regular sex, and laughing during the middle of it, all before Momma's Knock Out Roses bloom, I would have called that person the biggest liar to ever walk the face of the earth.

But here I am.

Enraptured in yearning and silliness.

And loving every minute of it.

"So, what you're telling me, Bird, is that you like this?" He grabs himself and glides his hand up his shaft. When his thumb works his slit, spreading his own wet eagerness across the mushroomed head of his dick, he shudders.

I lift my hand, unhiding my pussy. "I'll like it even better when it's filling me full."

He erases the distance between us and once again, sinks to his knees, falling back onto his haunches so his mouth better aligns with me. His calloused thumb rakes across my swollen clit. My body bucks forward. I wish my hands could reach my favorite shoulder, but they can't. So, instead, I tangle my fingertips in the thick brown hair at the crown of his head.

That same thumb trails down my slit and slides deep inside my vagina. He circles it around and around, pausing with each rotation and pressing firmly against my back wall, packing me with a pressure that I can feel all the way in my asshole. Pulling out, he wets my clit and the surrounding skin. He works his fingers back into my folds, teasing the entrance of my tunnel, and then he pinches the base of my clit between his thumb and forefinger.

Hard.

Forcing the already engorged nub to blossom forward. He takes me into his mouth, suckling the bundle of nerves with extreme force. With expert precision, he repeats the same motions. Over and over and over, each time freeing my clit with a satisfying little popping sound.

Pinch. Suck. Pop.

Pinch. Suck. Pop.

Pinch. Suck. Pop.

Pinch. Suck. Pop.

Pinch. Suck. Pop.

I suppose a part of me will always be connected to the number five.

Always.

Because by the fifth suck—and to be honest, it could be the third or the eighth, I'm not really in the right frame of mind to count—I lose control and come all over his chin.

And it just so happens to be the way he likes.

Wet and messy.

"Oh, hell, yeah," he mumbles against my flesh.

My legs weaken, and I start to fall forward, but he shackles his arms around my thighs and slams me back against the wall, giving some stability to my wobbly frame. Spreading me wide, he lavishes me, licking me and tongue-fucking me until I'm dizzy and blind, and on the verge of another orgasm. My whimpers and mewls come quicker and quicker, timing themselves with the contraction of my core, drowning out the sloppy and fevered noises coming from where his mouth is joined with me.

He knows I'm close, so he moves his mouth back to my tender and sex-sensitive clit. His left hand leaves its nestled location—that plump little curve where my ass cheek meets the top of my leg—and with one swift and seamless motion, he drives two fingers into me. And he pounds me.

Relentlessly.

Until, in perfect harmony, he takes what he wants...all the while I freely give it to him.

When my second climax eases, he pushes off his haunches, raises back to his knees, and buries his soaked face into my cleavage, nipping and nibbling at the parts of my breasts not covered by the nightie. His hands clutch my waist. I grab ahold of his shoulders, instantly noting how his body is both slick with sweat and pebbled in chill bumps.

"Tell me, Ridge Conway, are you hard?"

He bites my erect nipple and yanks at the gauzy fabric of the negligee, trying to tear a hole into it with his teeth. I wouldn't be surprised if he were successful. This nightgown wasn't built to withstand much. "I'm about to fucking come all over your legs and feet, Zipporah."

"We can't have that, can we?"

He looks up at me, awaiting my instruction.

Cheeks flushed.

Beard glistening and drenched in spots of white.

Tiger Eyes ravenous.

"I love you, Ridge. Take me. Break Me. And then put me back together again."

He flies up from his kneeled position, and slams his mouth onto mine, kissing me with a wild and feral appreciation. I claw at him, desperate to have him closer, desperate to taste myself on his tongue. He jerks back, dips his hands into the little twist of cloth under my breasts and tries to rip the lingerie in two.

And when it doesn't happen, he frowns at the offending garment.

I snicker.

He cocks a brow, not amused and completely unwilling to be bested by a textile.

He moves a little to the left, pulls the thin fabric even thinner, and leans forward, ferociously gnawing on it, slobbering all over my tit in the process. He pokes a hole in the cloth with his incisors and gives me an award-winning smirk. Hooking his fingers in the hole, he easily tears the nightie, shearing the breast piece from my body. With a shimmy to my shoulders, it rumples to the ground.

His eyes flicker down my naked body, and when his gaze lands on my heels, he frowns again. "Aren't your feet hurting you by now?" he asks.

My cheek twitches as I fight against a smile. "I'm miserable," I admit.

Squatting in front of me, he lifts each foot and gently removes the stiletto. Standing, his sticky skin snakes across mine, setting me ablaze with even more desire. More want. More need. More every-fucking-thing.

"You trust me, Little Bird? Not to let you fall? To love you forever?"

"I trust you. My Hero. My Husband. My Always."

Bending low, he swoops his arms between my legs and hauls me into his embrace. Caught by surprise, I inhale, sucking oxygen into my lungs. He nimbly wrangles me into the position he wants.

My shoulder blades flush against the wall.

The underside of my knees hooked over his forearms.

His hands splayed across the back of my hips, with his thumbs digging into my waist, marking me with his power.

He widens his stance. Thereby, widening *me*.

With a controlled measure, he lets me drop, just enough so that the backs of my knees slide into the crooks of his elbows.

And so that my open and weeping core aligns perfectly with his thick, mammoth erection.

His breathing is heavy and frenzied. He lowers his forehead to mine. A drop of his sweat slides down my chin.

And he enters me. One slow and perfect and miraculous inch at a time.

Until he's buried.

Until all parts of me are stretched and filled and wholly complete.

He pulls out and waits for my protesting cry. And then he pacifies my barren emptiness by slamming into me, ramming my body up and against the wall.

His whisper sails between us, tumbling from his dry and cracked lips to my own. "I don't have to put you back together, Bird. Because you could never break."

Chapter 44

Ridge

I shut the door, lock it, and race into the bedroom. Tossing my duffle bag next to the chair in the corner of the room, I strip from my clothes, flinging them left and right.

She knows that I was on the way home; I always call or text her. But of course, even though she knows it's me, that doesn't mean that her body doesn't react to fright. After the first time, when I opened the shower door on her and she nearly slipped and busted her head wide open on the tile bench, we decided to play it safe with a little overhead light flicker. We've also tried the whistle method. Which is something my whole family does. If one of us is looking for the other, we whistle. It started with Dad, but both me and C picked it up.

But Orah says I whistle louder than a fire alarm, and it makes her pee a little.

So the light trick seems to work the best.

The steam hits me, the second I walk into the bathroom. The glass door is fogged, giving me a hazy view of her round ass and the curve of her spine. She's shampooing her hair and humming. I give the light switch a couple of hits.

"Ridge?"

I grab a fresh towel and hang it on the hook next hers. "It's me, Bird." I open the shower door and step inside, making sure that I don't steal any of the heated spray away from her. From underneath a pile of bubbles, she squints open an eye, scrunching her face. "Hi."

"Hi," I chuckle.

I let her rinse in peace, and when she steps out of the blast, I wrap her in my arms, giving a deep inhale to her shampoo. "Missed you."

Her head folds against my shoulder, and she kisses the healing fingernail scratches from her most recent handiwork. "I missed you too. I'm glad your shift was..." She pulls back and exaggeratedly looks left to right, like she's making sure no one is eavesdropping on our conversation. She leans on her tiptoes and whispers into my ear. "Boring."

I give her a shrug. "Eh." She knows all about my love-hate relationship with uneventful shifts. But considering I'm still recovering from the all-hands-on-deck stadium double, I didn't actually mind.

We do our normal shower routine, waltzing around one another and talking. I shampoo while she conditions. I condition while she shaves. I wash my body while she washes her face. With three different products.

Why three?

Hell if I know.

And then, there's the best part.

The part where I get to help her clean her body. And trust me, I leave no piece of her real estate unattended. Just call me Ridge 'Suds' Conway.

I put her body wash on her loofah and sit on the bench. Bending, I start at her heels and work my way up.

"So, no orders today?"

"No, nothing today. I'm gonna go with your dad and pick up some paint samples, though. Cullen's been so busy with the bar lately, he asked if I could pick up some of his slack with the design."

There's no missing the excitement and pride pumping through her, all the way from the top of her soaking wet raven hair to her sudsy little toes.

"And I've already lined up meetings with three new couples. They're all looking at using the new venue for their weddings next spring and summer."

"That's amazing. I'm so proud of you." I pause for a second at her hips and waist, admiring the pale blue bruises of my fingertips. Just thinking about our wall session from the night before last makes me hard. I slip my hand through her butt crack, causing her to giggle. I soap up her back and around her shoulders. She knows she needs to spin around, but she always waits for me to say it. "Turn."

She rotates, and I'm rewarded with boobs.

Right at eye level.

Hot damn.

How can any dude not wanna shower with his girl? This right here? It's the highlight of my day.

I bend again, soaping all the way up her legs. "The guys wanna know when you're gonna make more of those yellow things. You know, you had the regular ones and then the pink ones and the blue ones."

And just like with her backside, I hug the loofah to my chest and clean her pussy with my hand. Slipping my fingers between her folds, I make a purring sound effect.

You know, like the sophisticated, thirty-two-year-old man that I am. I mean, a clean kitty is a happy kitty.

C'mon. What do you expect? How else will she know that her toot-toot maintenance has been performed.

And yes, unfortunately, our relationship has made me privy to all sorts of things about Tabby that I wish I didn't know.

My thumb hovers over her clit, barely grazing it. She looks down at me, and with a soft smile, shakes her head. "Not this morning, Hero."

I furrow my brow and pretend I don't know what she's talking about. "I don't need the desserts this morning. Just by the next shift." I press into her pink and ripe nub even harder.

She immediately responds, arching her back and moaning.

My dick jumps to life. Even more than it already was.

But then, she scolds me. Laughing, she grabs my hand and pushes it away. She points to the loofah. "Scrub me, Ridge Conway. I've got a busy day."

I squeeze the head of my dick, nonverbally telling him to calm the hell down. I soap her stomach and her scars. I skip over her breasts and clean her shoulders and her arms.

She bops my nose and rushes her fingers down to my chin. Tap. Tap. "And yes, I can make the chess bars for your next shift. Regular ones. Strawberry ones. *And* blueberry ones," she offers.

I harrumph, pretending to be barely satisfied with my consolation prize. "Okay."

She just rolls her eyes, indulging my role play.

I squeeze an extra dollop of her body wash into my palms, creating fresh suds. And then just as I always do, I slide my bare hands up her stomach and over her breasts, rubbing her immaculate tits in languid, leisurely circles. Orah has large breasts. But I have large hands. That's what you call an absolute perfect match. I massage her clean, taking *way* longer than necessary to wash her chest. And for the last swipes, I meander to her sides, crawling up her round curves and under her armpits.

What?

It happens in a nanosecond.

But a nanosecond is all that it takes to change a life.

I've borne witness to that.

One. Single. Second.

Can create a lifetime of happiness or an eternity of misery.

My hands whip back down, searching for *something*. Praying that it's *nothing*.

And when I push against her skin, trying to retrace my route, I nearly collapse in relief when I don't feel anything.

I sigh. So deeply it sends a piercing pain slicing through my shoulder blades.

Oh, thank goodne—

My pleasant train of thought is suddenly derailed. In fact, this locomotive flies off the tracks and careens into a vat of plutonium.

My heart thunders, pounding so fast that my princeps pollicis artery echoes the beat of my own pulse like a drum. It's rapid and furious in the pad of my thumb. It's so distracting I can't even feel her properly.

I switch the position of my hands, setting my thumbs toward the center of her sternum. My fingertips trace up and down her ballooned flesh, navigating her breast tissue with intense professionalism. I move with precision, exacting the same meticulous motion on both the left and the right, just hoping that I'll feel the same thing.

Because having the same thing on both sides would be better, right?

That would make it normal, wouldn't it?

I wish upon every star in the galaxy that it's just a typical body anomaly. Something unique for Orah compared to perhaps other women, yet totally unusual for the human race as a whole.

But my wishes fade and disappear. Like a heavy rain washing away the spring pollen, my optimism drips to the tiled shower floor and swirls down the drain, right alongside her coconut and vanilla-scented soap.

"Ridge?" Her utterance is shaky and quiet, smothered by the reverberating patter of the water against the tile.

I glance up at her, wide-eyed and dazed.

"What's wrong?" she asks.

I squeeze her tighter in my arms.

Hot water streams down her hair, decorating her back in a curtain the color of the midnight sky. Rivulets circle around her neck and race down her front, finding all of the intricate, gorgeous, and one-of-a-kind pathways that make her body *hers.*

She's so beautiful.

An Angel sent to save me.

When I don't answer, her chin starts to quiver and her lips shake. "Something's wrong." Tears spill from her storm-cloud eyes, mixing with the spray of the shower. "I...I feel what you feel."

And what I feel is a lump.

Chapter 45

Ridge

Fuck. This.

Being called into the doctor's actual office is never good.

I'm not talking about the exam room. With its table, crinkly paper, and stirrups.

I'm talking about the doctor's *actual* office. You know, the one with the ornate desk, expensive framed diplomas, dying houseplant, and overstuffed leather couch.

It reminds me a lot of Dr. Evans's office from back in the day.

I scratch my hand down my scruff and tap my chin.

I could definitely use a little therapy right now. I should've kept up with it. Like Orah.

I wonder if Dr. Evans is still in business. I should give her a call. I'm sure she'd shit a golden brick to know that my ring sits on Orah's finger, and that I'm literally counting down the seconds until she has my last name.

Orah reaches across and grips my knee. Her black fingernail polish is chipped. "Stop shaking your leg. You're vibrating the entire floor."

I give her a nervous smile, pick up her hand, and kiss her knuckles. "I love you."

She nods, eagerly accepting my declaration. A black strand falls from her bun and feathers across her cheek. "I love you. So much. Always and forever."

The door opens, and Dr. Skinner walks through, files and clipboard in hand. "I'm so sorry to keep you waiting. I thought doing this on a Sunday afternoon would be the best thing, but I had a set of twins who thought differently," he jests with a chuckle.

I stand, turning to shake his hand as he passes, noticing he's dressed in hospital scrubs with a dab of sweat on his brow. His office is next door to the hospital, so I can only imagine he jogged from one building to the next. "Thank you so much for seeing us so quickly, for re-working your schedule, for coming in on your day off." I wave behind me at the office door. "Your staff too. We really appreciate it." I only saw one nurse working, but still... I can't imagine he normally sees office patients on a weekend, so knowing that he even brought a member of his staff in to help us is above and beyond the call. I'll be forever thankful.

He sits behind his desk and motions for me to return to the seat in one of the two chairs opposite of him. "Anything to keep our first responders happy." He leans forward and smiles warmly at Orah, trying to calm her very visible nerves. "Especially this one," he says, hooking a thumb in my direction. "He's told you that he's delivered babies before, right?" He winks at her. "He may be one heck of a firefighter, but I think he missed his calling with med school."

She attempts a lighthearted giggle, but it comes out more like a whimper. "No, he didn't tell me that. But it doesn't surprise me." Her eyes lock with mine. "There's nothing he can't do. He's My Hero."

He chuckles, thinking she's using the common turn of phrase as a tongue-in-cheek quip.

He doesn't know what those words mean to her.

He doesn't know that her faith in me gives me the power to be a better man.

I sit back in the chair, spread my legs in front of me, and drag a palm down my face, hiding my eyes from hers, trying to give myself a moment to regain my composure.

Because she makes me anything but composed.

It's been a whirlwind five days. The gynecologist that Orah used to see when she lived here before retired, so I called in a favor to the go-to OB/GYN for the women in my family. Dr. Skinner's delivered Anna, Ty, Hardy, and Daire. Not only that, but we've had interactions together, through both work and personal settings. I was able to get her in for an appointment that afternoon, the afternoon after our shower together. The next day, she went for a mammogram. The day after that, an ultrasound. Then, we had a fourth tortuous day waiting for today's appointment.

Dr. Skinner clears his throat and opens all the folders. They fan around him like the tail feathers of a peacock. "Well, I suppose y'all would prefer to skip the small talk and jump right in."

Orah nods. "Yes, please."

"Well, as discussed during your examination, there's no denying there's an abnormality in your breast tissue." He pauses for a moment, before reading the room and realizing that we want layman's terms. "You have a lump."

I reach over and take her hand in mine. Our fingers lace together.

He further explains. "We divide the breast into four quadrants—upper outer, upper inner, lower outer, and lower inner. Plus, we have the nipple. Your lump is in the upper outer quadrant of the right breast. I know that when you feel the area, it seems like the lump is very close to your armpit. And it is, but it's important to note that I didn't visualize any swelling in that area and your lymph nodes were not palpable by touch.

"I've reviewed the results of both your mammogram and your ultrasonography with the radiologist and an internalist." He pushes some of the papers across the desk and starts pointing to them. They're black and white, and somewhat fuzzy, images of Orah's breast. "You see this white spot here," he taps at the printed mammogram picture. And then he switches to the sonogram, circling his finger around a rough-edged shadow. "And this darker spot here with this shadow behind it?"

Orah lifts her free hand, working her fingers across her necklace. She's in the middle of counting. So, instead, I speak for her. "Mmm-hmmm."

"This is the area of concern. See these little spikes around the edges? This is what we call a spiculated mass. Orah, you've got a 14-millimeter spiculated mass of unknown origin."

Once again, she nods. The motion sends a single tear cascading down her rosy cheek. She wipes it and quickly returns her hand back to her necklace, clutching the bird charm so tightly I worry she may cut herself.

I tap the offending piece of paper. "But it could be nothing, right?"

Dr. Skinner nods. "It could be. You're absolutely correct."

"A cyst?"

His lips thin, and he inhales.

My Brave Girl squeaks, unable to fully find her voice. She forces her fidgeting fingers to leave the comfort of the base of her throat. She lifts her thigh and sits on her hand, demanding silence from her numbers. Choking through a cough, she locates her hidden vocabulary. "Please, Dr. Skinner, be honest with us. Obviously, we realize there are a lot of things at this point that you simply don't know, a bunch of unanswered questions. But please be forthright with us regarding what you typically see."

He adjusts in his seat, rocking a little in his fancy chair. "I would be surprised if it were a cyst. Typically—not always—but typically, a cyst will have smooth, well-defined edges. More often than not, it'll appear as a low-density mass on the mammogram, but this," his eyes flicker to the snow-white, spiky, oblong shape, "is high density. And the ultrasound usually shows a slightly brighter area behind the cyst, not a shadow." He looks to Orah. "And just to reconfirm, you've had no pain? No tenderness?"

"No, nothing like that," she verifies.

"What about a fatty tumor?" I break in. "Or a fibroadenoma?"

Dr. Skinner pulls his bottom lip between his teeth. "Again, anything is possible."

"But?"

"A fibroadenoma would present different in the clinical. It would feel firm, yet rubbery, to the physical touch, and based on its depth in the breast tissue, the mass would be movable." He swallows. "This one isn't. It's fixed."

I blow out a frustrated exhale. "Same thing with the fatty tumor, right?"

"Yes, a lipoma would usually feel soft and pliable. And would most likely image differently on the mammogram and sonogram."

Orah squeezes my hand. When I turn to look at her, my fragile heart breaks. The whites of her eyes are bloodshot, stressed and irritated from holding in her sobs. She moves her hand from underneath her thigh and shakes the sleep from her fingers. I can only assume they are buzzing and tingling. "So, what does all of this mean, Dr. Skinner?" she questions.

"Well, you've been rated as having a BI-RADS score of 4C. You'll need to have a biopsy."

"A biopsy? With a needle?"

"Well, your surgeon will discuss the options with you; and together, you'll make the final call, but I would suggest an excisional biopsy."

Her brow furrows in thought.

"A lumpectomy," I say, trying to clear her confusion. "Take out the whole lump, make sure there are clear margins."

She frowns.

I scoot my chair closer to hers. Hell, if it wouldn't freak the doctor out, I'd pull her over onto my lap and pepper her face with never-ending kisses. Instead, I settle for tugging our clasped hands over onto my thigh.

"What's the likelihood that we're dealing with c–cancer?" she stutters.

"I don't want to get into any specifics like that. As we've discussed, there are too many variables, Orah. We could be dealing with anything. Or nothing. Every single person and every single body is different. There are no two people alike." Dr. Skinner readjusts his glasses. "Now, your surgical oncologist may discuss things more in depth or go into different details, but I'll leave that to him or her."

Her fingernails cut into the top of my hand. "My granny had TNBC. It was metaplastic breast cancer, and it metastasized to her lungs, spine, and brain."

He grabs his ink pen and makes a note in her chart. "Triple Negative Metaplastic. That's quite rare." He thumbs through some of her paperwork. "For some reason, I was thinking it was something else," he mumbles to himself.

"She had a different type of cancer when she was younger. She had one of her adrenal glands removed when she was in her forties. It was...adrenocort..." Orah slows trying to remember the correct pronunciation.

"Adrenocortical carcinoma?"

"Yes, sir. The whole time I was growing up she had to take medicine because of it. Hormones and such."

"And this was your paternal grandmother?"

"Yes."

He cocks his head, staring at her. "She had both an adrenocortical carcinoma and metaplastic breast cancer?" His syllables are a little longer than necessary, drawn out just enough to announce there's something hiding behind his scrupulously crafted jargon. This question is definitely more than just a simple follow-up.

Orah loosens her vicious grip on my hand and steals a look in my direction. Her pupils widen in fear.

I lean forward, bracing my forearm on the desk. "Why are you asking it like that? What's wrong? Lots of people experience different cancers during the course of their lives."

Dr. Skinner just holds his pen in the air, begging for a moment. "What about your father? You didn't mark anything for him on the family history questionnaire."

"His types of cancer didn't have a box on the form. Breast and adrenal had boxes. Not thyroid and melanoma."

"He had thyroid cancer?"

"Back in high school. He had his thyroid removed. Just like Granny, he's taken medicine all of these years because of it."

"And the melanoma?"

"A couple of small spots over the years. Two on his back and one on his stomach." Her body shakes, like the temperature in the room has suddenly plummeted. "But...but...the dermatologist got all of it. Each time. And he goes every six months for a checkup."

Dr. Skinner scribbles in the chart, frantically filling the pages with illegible cursive.

I wrangle my fingers out of her grasp and wrap my hand around the back of her neck. Her skin is cool to the touch, but wet with sweat. I press against her and nearly come unglued when I feel the erratic and frenzied rhythm of her heartbeat. Its strumming against the pads of my fingertips, vibrating through my body like one long, continuous roll of thunder.

So, I do the only thing my fucking pitiful and fried brain can do...I count for her.

My thumb taps the comforting pattern against the delicate column of her neck, right underneath her earlobe.

One. Two. Three. Four. Five.

One. Two. Three. Four. Five.

"How many siblings do you have?" Dr. Skinner's query is a shadow. A ghost. A hallucination. And it's being swallowed by the reality of my thumped tempo.

One. Two. Three. Four. Five.

"Just one. An older brother."

"Does he have a history of any cancers or other significant illnesses?"

One. Two. Three. Four. Five.

"No. He's always been completely healthy."

"And you have just one child?"

Stop.

My numbers completely stop. Because now, even *I'm* too worried to tap.

"I…I…explained the situation to your nurse." Orah lowers her head. She pretends to be scratching her nose, but really, she's wiping her tears.

I massage her neck, trying to ease the tension, trying to convey my love with just my touch. "Orah was a surrogate for her brother and sister-in-law. So, yes, she physically gave birth to a child. But she isn't currently a…"

What the hell am I supposed to say?

She sniffles and lifts her chin high. "I'm an aunt, not a mother."

Dr. Skinner looks between the two of us, his face filled with compassion, despite his no-nonsense topic of conversation. He gives her a small smile. "Surrogacy is a very selfless act. I'm sure words can't express their gratitude for the gift you've given them." He relaxes a smidge, determined to convey his sincerity. "The way I asked that question was very insensitive. Please forgive me."

Orah bobs her head up and down.

"You were the egg donor for the surrogacy as well? Biologically, your niece has your parental DNA?"

"She does. Yes."

He flips to something in the chart. "Your niece is about to turn two?"

"In a couple of weeks, yeah."

"And she's never had any health problems?"

Orah turns to me. Her beautiful face is filled with concern.

"Okay, Darren," I bark, using Dr. Skinner's first name, "what's this about? Just spit it out."

"Have either of you ever heard of Li-Fraumeni Syndrome?"

Chapter 46

Orah

I'm a ticking timebomb.

And someone just hit the fast-forward button on my detonation.

"An inherited predisposition for cancer? What the hell does that mean? Like *every* cancer?" Ridge's hand left my neck a while ago, and now he's holding my thigh in a fierce and tense grip. Like if he squeezes me hard enough, I won't disappear. Right in front of his very eyes.

If he holds me, this catastrophe won't be able to steal me away.

"So, LFS is a genetic condition in which there is a variant in the TP53 gene."

"Variant?"

"A mutation," he clarifies. "Which gives those affected a substantially higher risk of developing, well, any cancer really. But there are, what we refer to as 'core cancers', which are most often associated with Li-Fraumeni. And those include breast cancers and adrenocortical carcinoma. LFS is inherited from a biological parent in an autosomal dominant pattern, meaning if a parent has it, there's a fifty percent chance that their child will have it."

I lower my head, trying to focus my bleary, pressure-filled, and bloodshot eyes on something. On anything. I wiggle my toes, watching in a fog as my black Mary Janes scrape against the thick Berber carpet.

Ridge heaves an exasperated sigh. "So, you're thinking there's a possibility that her grandmother had this, passed it to her father, and her father pa—"

My speech is as detached as my thousand-yard stare. "He's saying there's a good chance I have breast cancer, and that even if I beat it, there's an even better chance that another cancer will pop up. And worst of all, there's a fifty percent chance I just sentenced Eden to the exact same horrific fate." There's a muffled noise at the window. In the distance, a maintenance worker mows the grass.

"Zipporah…" Ridge shuffles in his seat. He hooks his fingers under my jaw, forcing my face to turn to his, not giving me room to wiggle away. Not that I would do that, of course.

Because what if my embraces with him are limited? On time that I didn't even know was borrowed?

Not caring about our current audience, he presses his lips to mine, kissing me.

Softly. Sweetly. Lovingly.

Dr. Skinner gently clears his throat. "No, Orah. That's not what I'm saying. And I'm not even using the terminology 'good chance'. I just think having a genetic test to rule out LFS as a possibility is a prudent course of action, given your family history."

Ridge slides an arm around my shoulder. If I weren't so drained and tired, I would play with my necklace.

But I don't even have the energy to do that.

"Your primary care physician never discussed any genetic testing with you?" He picks up his discarded ink pen and circles some sentences in one of the open files. "Dr. Peck? I'm not familiar with that name."

My tongue is numb in my mouth. "He's in South Carolina. Despite moving, I've kept him as my general doctor. He knows everything about what I went through. About what my body went through after the…" My surgery scar burns, knowing that I'm talking about it.

There's no point in finishing my sentence. Dr. Skinner saw my scars when examining me, and for once, I was completely forthright with a new doctor and told him my injuries were from the attack. "Plus, he and my therapist have worked together over the years to monitor and update my medications. I have sensitivities to some medicines. And I'm adamant about not taking something if I don't have to. I don't wanna suffocate every single thought, I just wanna be able to breathe through them." I shrug. "Anyway, if there's an emergency, and he's not available for a telehealth consult, I just go to a walk-in clinic."

Over the years, I've tried to switch physicians. But it never worked out. There was the one who just wanted to ply me full of sleeping pills, even though I told her that I would never use another sleeping pill. And let's not forget the one guy who actually found out I was 'Orah' instead of 'Amy' and that my wounds and scars from a 'random act of gun violence' were actually from the movie theater attack. During our second appointment, he acted like he won the damn lottery. All I wanted was an antibiotic for strep throat. All he wanted was to show me the old social media posts, pictures, and screenshots he found of me online.

Yeah, no, thank you.

I'll stick with Dr. Peck.

And Dr. Crandall. Fortunately, none of my anxiety medication has ever fallen into the controlled substance category, so I've been able to fill her prescriptions in both Alaska and Alabama, as well as South Carolina.

Dr. Skinner nods. "That's totally understandable. And you meet with your therapist via web calls and videos, as well?"

I close my eyes, wishing I could make all of this go away.

"She does," Ridge affirms. "They do a two-hour session once a month. Unless, of course, she's in a crisis and needs more."

But I haven't needed more.

Not since Ridge kissed me. Not since he gave me his love, his soul, and his body. I think, sometimes, the world discounts how healing physical touch can be, when it comes from your one true love.

"That's excellent. I'm glad you have that trusted relationship."

I'm reading between the lines. I'm pretty sure that's fancy-talk for *keep her on speed dial.*

Ridge points at the paperwork in front of Dr. Skinner. "So, what's the next steps? A biopsy and genetic testing, right?"

"Correct. Do you have a specific surgical oncologist in mind?"

"Who do you recommend?" he asks.

Dr. Skinner scrunches his face, "Ah, well, we have some really excellent surgeons in town and the surround—"

"No, we don't want excellent. We want the best. If this were Sabrina? If this were Tatum? Your wife or your daughter? I want *that* person." Ridge adjusts his hold on me, sliding his hand back up from my shoulder to my neck. His finger dips underneath the rose gold chain of my necklace. "No one touches my wife unless they're the very best."

Dr. Skinner bends his thumb against his palm and spins his wedding band. For a moment, it appears that he may not answer. "Dr. Robicheau. She's at Vanderbilt. I went to med school with her."

"Perfect. That's who we want."

With a sigh, he leans back in his executive chair and rocks. "I'll have my office call and line up the consultation. It'll probably take a few weeks. In the meantime, we can start the gen—"

"The hell it will!" Ridge roars, making me jump. He jerks his head toward the side of Dr. Skinner's desk, where his black cell phone is sitting. "We're not waiting weeks for an appointment and then weeks for a surgery. You call her. Now. Tell her it's an emergency."

"Ridge..." I whisper.

"No, Zipporah, we're talking about your life. I'll fucking drive there and hold the woman hostage if I have to. We're getting this thing out of you. Fucking asap."

"Ridge!" My hushed tone morphs into a surprised shriek. "You can't say stuff like that!" I admonish him.

Dr. Skinner rises from his chair and tempers his arms in the air, trying to calm the sudden discomfort. "It's fine." Sighing, he gives me a reassuring grin. "It's fine." Grabbing his cell phone, he pushes his glasses on his nose and walks out from behind his desk. "Let me see what I can do."

As soon as he shuts his office door, I light into Ridge. "How dare you speak to him like that?!"

Completely ignoring me, he pops his tennis shoe against the leg of my chair, pushing me sideways. And before I can even form another sentence, he pushes his own chair away from the desk, grabs my arm, and yanks me out of my seat. I tumble onto his lap. He doesn't even take the time to readjust my body into something more appropriate for our surroundings—like a side-saddle position. Nope. He hauls me into his arms via the path of least resistance. My knees bend, and I straddle him. The armrests of the office chair cut into my hips and legs.

My heart picks up speed, rapidly defrosting from its numb and frozen state. He wipes his calloused thumbs across my cheeks, trying to clean my chapped and sticky skin. His Tiger Eyes bore a hole into me. Like he alone is trying to dig the anomaly from my breast.

And trying to patch the hole with his love.

"What have I done, Ridge? What if I've passed this on to Eden?" A horrid thought enters my mind, making me physically sick. If I'm the reason something bad happens to Eden, does that make me a murderer?

Does that make me the very monster I tried to run from?

My stomach lurches, and my diaphragm paralyzes in a cramp.

"No, nothing's gonna happen to her. You heard him. This test is just a precaution."

"They'll never forgive me—Boaz, Tabby, my parents." Bile races into my throat. "I'll never forgive myself."

"Oh, Bird..."

His tenderness and desperation break me.

He always says that I'm too strong to be broken.

But if that's true, why do I feel so...disintegrated?

I collapse against him, falling into the safety of our love and filling the quiet of the room with screaming sobs, ragged breaths, and defeated tears. His arms hook around my waist, pinning my body to him. I claw at his back and shoulders, wishing I could curl up in the shadows of his soul and take a nap.

He tucks his lips against my ear, doing his best to comfort my spirit with his worship and affection. "I love you. I love you, Orah. We'll get through this. It's all gonna be okay. You'll see, Little Bird. It's all gonna be okay."

It seems like hours pass, but eventually I'm exhausted. My eyes are scratchy, my throat is raw, and my chest is sore. As soon as I straighten my back, lifting my head from his soaked and snotty T-shirt, he cradles my face, giving me all of his attention. "We're gonna be okay. *You're* gonna be okay."

He says we're gonna be fine, but his eyes tell a different story. They are marred. Little red blood vessels streak across his sclera, their ominous tendrils working hard to swallow the beauty of his irises. His dark black eyelashes are wet, drenched with his sorrow. His beard flames with flashes of orange and burnt sienna, twinkling in the sunlight streaming in from the window.

Normally, I would find those colors sexy. But now, they remind me of falling leaves. And how he said he would take me to the cabin this autumn. How he'd take me hiking and show me the changing colors of the trees. How we'd sit on the deck, cuddled in my favorite blanket, and drink hot chocolate. How we'd make love and spend all night talking about the plans for our future house.

What if the autumnal equinox comes and goes.

And I'm not even here on this Earth to enjoy it.

Sighing, he shakes his head. His hand wanders down to my left wrist, where he makes quick work of my watch. Since I'm sitting on his pocket, he can't hide it away. Instead, he just sets it down on the carpet. He kisses *our* tattoo and then lays my wrist against his chest. His fingers press into my bones, trapping me against his torso. And even though *our* brand is covered by his pale, yellow T-shirt, I can still feel the heat and intensity of his flesh as it absorbs into my body. His warmth seeps into my veins, mingling with my own blood. And together, they travel to my heart, filling me with his never-ending love and steadfast determination.

"Can't you feel it, Zipporah? Can't you feel that nothing will ever rip us apart?"

I run my tongue across my lips, trying to part them so I can talk. "Do you remember the night we first made love? When I asked you if catastrophes were attracted to us?"

His lips thin, and his chin quivers. "Orah, no."

"Catastrophes aren't attracted to *us*. I think I *am* the catastrophe."

He doesn't have time to react before the door opens.

Dr. Skinner freezes, halting his progression into his own office when he sees that we're entangled in the same small chair. "Uhhh…"

Ridge helps me stand, and then he immediately follows. He takes my hand in his. My engagement ring turns sideways, basically locking his finger in place next to mine.

"Well?" Ridge asks. There's an uneasiness in him. He's unsure if he should be filled with apprehension or appreciation.

He waves his cell phone in the air. "Well, you've volunteered to teach a weeklong first-aid class to a group of eighth-grade enrichment students who are doing a summer camp at Vanderbilt in July."

Ridge nods, eagerly. "Yeah, okay. No problem."

Dr. Skinner cocks his head to the side and blows a raspberry. "Pack a bag. You should leave tonight."

Chapter 47

Orah

Surgery.

Something I hate.

Even my C-section was terrifying.

Yes, I'm grateful that Dr. Skinner pulled strings to get me in with a specialist so soon, but the gratitude comes in waves. It ebbs and flows, never staying the way I wish it would. Because the sad truth is, I wouldn't have this thankfulness if I didn't have a lump in my breast.

So, each surge of relief—that things are happening in days versus weeks or months—quickly recedes, and is swallowed whole by debilitating fear.

Fear for myself.

Fear for Eden.

Fear for my dad.

Fear for Boaz and Tabby and Mom.

Fear for Ridge. Fear of not having the destiny we deserve. Of leaving him too soon. Of having my name etched in stone next to my daughter who never was.

Ridge's grip on the steering wheel is tight and unforgiving. Just like me, he's lost in thought. His knuckles are white, and his jaw is tense.

Tomorrow's day will start at six a.m., with an in-person consultation and a clinical exam before Dr. Robicheau's day is technically scheduled to start. She usually doesn't accept appointments before eight. Dr. Skinner already forwarded my mammogram and ultrasound, so I don't have to repeat those tests. But I will have pre-admin lab work in the afternoon, followed by genetic counseling and separate lab work for that.

The day after tomorrow will be my surgery.

Assuming there are no complications, it'll be an out-patient procedure.

There's so much to do, so much so think about. I barely know where to start. And on top of everything, Dr. Skinner said I should pause the process of switching my name from Amy to Orah. I had already received notice of my court date for that, but he said everything would be easier if I wait until after all of the insurance claims have been processed, especially since I'm working under a COBRA policy right now because of my firing. And the majority of the large claims will be out-of-state.

He flicks the blinker and makes a left turn. It's the opposite way from the apartment. "Where are you going? We've gotta head home and pack."

He shifts in his seat, trying to loosen the tension coursing through his every muscle. He holds the wheel with his left hand and drapes his right forearm over the console. "I'm heading to your parents." He utters it with such innocence, like it should be completely and totally obvious. "We're telling them in person, right? Not over the phone..."

"No. Turn around. We're not telling them anything."

His head whips in my direction with such fervor, he accidentally swerves over the line. His tire rubs against the curb, making a loud, horrid sound. "Shit!" With a yelping curse, he maneuvers back into the lane. He checks his side and rearview mirrors, making sure his carelessness didn't affect any drivers around him. Satisfied, he side-glances at me. "What are you talking about?"

"I'm not telling them. Not until we know something. I've already hurt my family too many times. I'm not making them worry more than they have to. Not Momma or Dad. Not Boaz or Tabby."

"You can't be serious, Orah."

I reach for my necklace. "Not your parents. Not Cullen. Nobody." I bite my lip. "We can't tell anyone."

His mouth drops open. Unable to gape at me the way he truly wants, he growls under his breath and pulls into the first parking lot he comes to. Which just so happens to be the strip mall with Merit's stores.

Run and Jump and Twirl and *The Letterhead.*

Craning my neck, I see Holt's truck parked in one of the front spots. Merit's stores are closed on Sundays, but if she has work to catch up on, Holt and Daire usually go with her to keep her company. Fortunately, Ridge parks at the far end of the lot, with his front windshield facing the street. So hopefully, they won't see us.

Although, in all honesty, nothing would make me happier right this very second than to take baby Daire in my arms, inhale his sweet scent, and plant kisses all over his cute little nose. My hand falls from my necklace, and I stick a fingertip right on the window. I tap the glass, whispering in my own head, *'Hi Daire'.*

Ridge turns off the ignition, pops his seatbelt, and leans back against the driver-side door. "What do you mean we can't tell anyone? You're having surgery, Orah. They're gonna find out."

"They won't find out unless we tell them, and I'm not gonna tell them until I can give them certainties and not assumptions. I don't want them to worry."

"Of course, they're gonna worry; they love you. It comes with the territory. Those two emotions are not mutually exclusive, they're…" He scoffs when he can't think of something poetic to say. "They're fucking peanut butter and jelly."

"It'll be hard enough to tell them once we have the answer we already know is there. At least, let me give them these couple of weeks. Until the genetic testing comes in. I owe them that."

"The answer?" He leans across the console and slides a hand around my thigh, squeezing my leg through the thin fabric of my black, dress capris.

Everything about his body is perfection. His long, thick fingers. The three freckles that form an odd-shaped triangle on his wrist. The veins that run the length of his forearm.

His body is flawless.

With his only imperfections being related to me.

The jagged scar from the twenty-five stitches. The half-moon marks from my fingernails. Even the healed and barely visible cut on his finger has to do with me. If he hadn't looked up from the cutting board, he wouldn't have injured himself.

Here I am, always injuring the man I love more than life itself.

Never saving him, yet always hurting him.

And now, I'm about to do the same thing to the rest of my family. I'm about to take a daughter away from her parents. A granddaughter away from her grandparents. My goal was to never take another thing away from Tabby. Away from my best friend. Away from my sister. Ten years ago, I stole her most precious gift. And here I am, about to do it all over again.

"Hey!" He bends his head, forcing me to look at him. "We don't *have* an answer. You're acting like they've already diagnosed you with..." He fades, unable to even speak the vile word.

"With cancer." I take a deep breath, hating the way I'm super aware of every single part of myself now. It's like I can feel the small lump sinking into my chest every time I inhale. I imagine it bouncing off my lungs like a rolling marble and landing with a thud on the diaphragm long ago shredded and repaired.

With cow parts.

I exhale, and shoot the lump back into my breast, back into the place where it's been hiding in plain sight for who knows how long. "I. Have. Cancer."

He sits back, solemn and shocked. Like I've physically slapped him. He vibrates with anger. His syllables wobble like a tin roof in a thunderstorm. "You. Don't. Know. That."

I scoff on a cynical chuckle. "And neither do you."

He blinks, and a tear rolls down his sun-kissed cheek. It catches in his beard, slowly getting lost in the hairs I love. "You think I don't know that?" His swallow is achingly audible. "My hands are on you every single day, Zipporah. For over two months, I've had the gift of mapping every inch of you. In some shape, form, or fashion, I've touched you." Another tear. "Every. Single. Day."

Another swallow. Except this time, it catches in his throat. "I've kissed your flesh. Made love to you with my hands. Lavished you with my tongue. I know everything there is to know about your body. About your breasts. I know there's four brown freckles around the areola on your left side. They're shaped like a diamond. There's a whitish-pink stretch mark at the top of your right side. I know how far out your nipples peak when you're turned on, when you're excited and ready for my touch."

Another tear. "We've showered together. Dozens and dozens of times."

Another pained swallow. "And each time, I've cleaned you in the exact same way, massaged you in the exact same way."

Another tear. Followed by another.

"And I missed it," he croaks.

A sob roars from deep within his own personal Hell. "I fucking missed it! I'm so fucking sorry, Bird!"

I fly across the seat, screaming in frustration when I get trapped by my still-attached seatbelt. I fumble with it, popping the button and wrangling out of it as quickly as I can. I catapult myself into his arms. The console digs into my stomach, keeping me from crawling onto his lap like I did at the doctor's office.

But that doesn't matter.

It doesn't stop me from holding him closer than I ever have before.

His arms loop around my back, squeezing me near the point of suffocation. And for once, he's the one with his face buried against my shoulder. His violent tears rain down my neck, ease underneath my bird charm, and slip into the collar of my shirt. Wetness pools into the fabric of my bra.

My fingers curl into his hair. I gently massage his scalp. I lower my lips to his ears and shush him in a calm and comforting voice. "It's okay. Shhh. It'll all be okay."

I return the favor.

I hold My Hero while he mourns the unfathomable idea that our future might not be *ours*.

And just like with me, eventually, his massive sobs slow into sniffles and his rapid tears dim into drops. He pulls away, but he doesn't go far. One hand slides up the side of my face, tangling in my hair, tugging pieces loose from my bun. His other hand pins to the front of my neck. But the chokehold position doesn't choke me, of course, because his touch is featherlight. His caress is filled with snow-white compassion and blood-red passion. I open my lips and invite his kiss. He knocks my necklace out of the way, presses his thumb into the hollow of my throat, and taps a rhythm that coincides with the swirls of his tongue against mine.

We kiss, each determined to stake a claim to our fate with nips of our teeth. With heated moans. And with traded breaths.

Sighing, he lays his forehead against mine. "I'm so damn sorry," he repeats.

"It's not your fault."

"And it's not yours, either."

We soak in each other's love for another minute before I finally ease back down, fully sitting my ass in my seat. "Ridge, I know you want me to be optimistic, but you heard what all the doctor said."

"He said nothing is for certain. No two bodies are alike."

I fold my hand around my right breast. It's heavy and full. Something I've always loved. Because the teardrop is big enough, weighty enough to cover a major portion of my scar. "I feel like there's a parasite in me. Like it's feeding off of me, sucking the marrow from my bones and the beats from my heart."

I let go, and my breast falls back into the nestled structure of my bra. A part of me wishes I could express my legitimate concern about what a lumpectomy will do to my body. How will it make me look? Yes, I'll be adding another scar to my already heavy-hitting arsenal, but will it look...weird? Will my breast be dented and uneven? Lopsided and unattractive? Will I have to wear a pad of some sort in my bra cup? What if I need a mastectomy?

But then, another part—a louder and more obnoxious part—tries to tell me that those concerns are stupid. That I *shouldn't* worry about uneven boobs. That I *should* worry about my life.

That I shouldn't worry about having my tits removed because Tabby had her whole uterus removed. I would be rude and thoughtless if I were to compare the two.

That demanding and commanding tyrant tells me to be quiet. Because what would people say if I talked about my fears of my physical appearance? They would tell me to shut up and just focus on fighting for my life.

But why is that?

Tell me.

Why the fuck is that?

Why is one fear supposed to be greater than the other? Aren't they all part of the same devil? Can't I be terrified of losing my life, while also scared to death of deforming a part of me that has brought me comfort?

And just how does my boob comfort me, you ask?

Because making love with my soulmate fills me with solace and happiness, pleasure and euphoria. Making love to Ridge gives me strength. It renews my energy. It replenishes my soul.

And when we make love, he sucks on my nipple. He bites my plump flesh. He pushes my breasts together and licks me from side to side. Slowly and passionately.

Am I not allowed to fret about changes to our intimate relationship?

I drop my head into my hands and massage my temples. I'm over-whelmed with all of these emotions, all of these feelings that are vying for top position. And what's even more oppressing is the fact that now I know, Granny navigated these same emotions all on her own.

Because she sure didn't share them with me.

Yes, I cared for her, but now that I look back at it, she kept the caregiving portion of her battle all about the disease itself. Doctors' appointments. Surgery. Recovery. Chemo. Surgery. Recovery. Radi-ation. Medicine.

She never once sat me down and said, 'Orah, I'm scared'.

With my grandfather having passed away so very long ago, she didn't have a partner to share her feelings with. And I guess, despite our closeness during those years, she still felt the need to protect me. To protect all of us.

Because now I know, that although I was sleeping in the bed-room next to her, she fought this battle all by herself.

"Orah? What are you thinking about? Tell me what you need. What you want. I'll do anything for you. Anything."

I lift my head and drop my hands into my lap. My engagement ring hits the glare of the sinking sun, flashing a brilliant prism of light against the top of the truck. I slide my palm across the console. He immediately locks his fingers around mine.

"I meant what I said. I don't wanna tell them until we know what we're dealing with. I want us to do this. Just me and you."

Accepting my decision, he just nods. His eyes flicker back and forth in thought. "Well, we can't come back here after your surgery, then. Even if we tell everyone you've got a contagious flu, they'll still stop by to check on you and bring you things. And you've got to have some peace and quiet to recover. Dr. Skinner said you don't even need to lift your arms above your head for five to seven days."

"So, what? We'll get a hotel room? For how long? What about your shifts?"

"The cabin's three-and-a-half hours away from Nashville. That's even closer than from here to Nashville. We can go there. We'll tell everyone that I decided to surprise you with a week-long trip before the busy wedding season starts.”

“But what happens if my follow-up appointment isn’t in a week? What happens if I have a drain? I’ll need at least a two-week recovery. *You* can’t miss that much work. *I* can’t miss that much work.” I frown, unsuccessfully trying to shove my guilt deep in my stomach. “I’ve already lied to your dad and brother. I don’t want them to regret hiring me. I don’t want to disappoint them.”

“Hey,” he brushes loose strands of hair away from my face, “they’ll never be disappointed in you. Never.” He pecks my lips. “What have you lied about? Tell me. I’ll take care of it.”

“Well, today, for example. Jeff was working on the Martingale casseroles for tomorrow. I left the kitchen a little after one for our appointment. I told Jeff I was meeting some possible clients for coffee.” Shame courses through me. “And I turned down a couple of jobs—just cookies and cakes—because I didn’t know what was gonna happen.”

“Orah, that’s no big deal. I promise, they’ll understand.”

“But what will they think about me just randomly leaving them high and dry and going on vacation?”

He chuckles and gives me a warm smile. “They’ll think that their son and brother can’t get enough of his future wife and wants to whisk her away for some private time.” His grin twitches, lost with the hope of that statement. “When’s your next job? For desserts?”

“A week from Tuesday. But I’ll need the full day for it. It’s got a five p.m. delivery.”

“That’s only seven days after your surgery.” He pushes his free hand down his face and taps his chin. Sighing deeply, he leans forward and kisses me again. This time a little deeper. This time a little heavier. He tugs his hand from mine and nods to my seatbelt, nonverbally telling me to put it on. Straightening in his seat, he buckles in, turns the ignition, and backs out of the parking lot. “You know what? It doesn’t matter. We’re just gonna have to figure out the rest as we go. We’ll go home and pack. I’ll call the Chief; I’ve got some guys who owe me back for doubles. I'll call my parents, your parents, and C. I'll book a hotel room for Nashville for tonight and tomorrow night. We'll do your appointment, do your surgery, and spend some quality time at the cabin."

I giggle. The innocuous and lighthearted act feels foreign and unusual, especially after so much darkness, so much despair. "And then, we'll what? Cross the other bridges as we come to them?"

He steals a glance at me and cocks a playful eyebrow. "Brave Girl, for you, I'll build all new bridges."

Chapter 48

Ridge

"So, I'll be starting on her in about thirty minutes. Surgery typically takes sixty to ninety minutes, but it could be longer because I work in conjunction with the radiologist and pathologist during the procedure doing an intraoperative consultation. So, don't let the time frighten you. Our goal, of course, is to obtain clear margins. But, with her being the first of the day, things shouldn't run too far behind." She nods to my wristband and then points to the row of big-screen monitors mounted on the wall. "The nurse showed you how to track her surgical progress using that assigned patient number?"

"Yes, ma'am."

Dr. Robicheau smiles and pats my arm. "You never mentioned yesterday, when's the wedding?"

"She wants to legally change her name first. From Amy back to Zipporah."

"Well, congratulations." She glances at the clock on the wall. "I better get back there."

She's walking through the open door when I finally come to my senses. "Dr. Robicheau?" She spins, and her non-slip clogs make a squishy, rubbery sound on the floor. "The wedding was ten years ago. I was just too young and stupid to realize it."

She chuckles and fiddles with her scrub cap, scratching at the hair that's trapped underneath the hat—blue with pink breast cancer awareness ribbons all over it. "Mr. Conway," she quips with a soft-spoken tease, "I think we were all young and stupid ten years ago. Let's make sure Zipporah gives you the opportunity to make up for that." And with a wink, she disappears around the corner.

It's barely seven in the morning, and the surgical waiting room is already filled with people. Some are sitting by themselves. Some are sitting in a small cluster with others. Some are quietly talking. Others are playing on their phone or reading. Some are drinking coffee. Others water or sodas. The front desk staff bustles with activity. Nurses and doctors pop in and out. Each corner has a television playing either the local or national morning news. Or a game show rerun. The morning sun slashes through the windows, highlighting a sprinkling of dust motes. The tiny particles float in a wavy line from the windowsill into the vastness of the room.

A room that's filled with hope and heartache. Dreams and nightmares. Faith and doubt.

I find an empty seat, facing both the doors and the status monitors. Sitting, I lower my head, and I pray. I give thanks for her life. For the fact that she survived not only the attack itself, but the rape that came before it and all of the traumas that came after it. I pray for her safety. For Dr. Robicheau and the entire surgical team. For her healing. I pray that she doesn't have cancer. And then, I pray that *if* she does have it, that we can fight it. That we can beat it. That we can kick its pathetic, life-altering, life-destroying, nasty punk ass. I pray that she doesn't have LFS. That her father doesn't have it. That her brother doesn't have it. That her niece doesn't have it. I pray for our life together. For strength to be the man she deserves. A husband she can be proud of.

And as the minutes tick away, I pray for those around me. For those who will receive good news today. And for those who will receive bad news. For those who will laugh in happiness and for those who will cry in despair.

Twenty minutes.

Forty minutes.

Sixty minutes.

Eighty minutes.

One-hundred-twenty minutes.

One-hundred-forty minutes.

My stomach grows queasy, and I start sweating. My T-shirt clings to my chest. The fabric grates against *our* brand, like a knife piercing my skin. Like the healed scar is filleting open, allowing all of my doubts and all of my worries to seep into my blood. The corrosive thoughts devour the small modicum of calm that I was forcing myself to cling to.

And without that, I'm lost and utterly frantic.

I look up every time someone enters or exits the room. I pace back and forth. I wear a bald spot on my chin from tapping. I take off my baseball cap, readjust it, and settle it back on my head. I keep stuffing my hand in the pocket of my cargo shorts, obsessively making sure her necklace and engagement ring are still there. She didn't wanna leave her jewelry in the bag with her black clothes.

She wanted me to hold it.

And I just wanna hold her.

Please. Please. Please.

I steal a glance at the status monitor for the ten-thousandth time. Except this time, it doesn't say 'Surgery Concluded', it says 'Front Desk'. In fucking blood-red lettering.

What the hell does that mean?

Why is it in red?

I race to the desk, blubbering over Orah's name, forgetting to call her Amy. Finally, I just have to yank my wrist in the woman's face so she can scan my bracelet.

"Okay, family of Amy Smith, correct?"

I nod so fast I give myself a headache.

"Okay. Dr. Robicheau wants to speak with you. I'll take you to one of the family rooms."

A family room?

Why the fuck does she wanna talk to me in a family room?

Bad stuff happens there. Doesn't it?

The woman cuts around the side of the desk, and numbly I follow her. We take a left turn outside of the waiting room. She opens a door with a sign next to it, labeling it as 'Family Conference 1'. As soon as I cross the threshold, she leaves. "Dr. Robicheau will be in shortly."

The room is small, with just a round table, surrounded by four chairs. There's a box of Kleenex sitting in the middle.

Why the fuck are there tissues in here?

Does that mean I'm gonna cry?

I wildly glance around. One wall has a framed poster of a seascape. Another has a framed poster detailing how to rate the hospital on service.

Rate the hospital?

Holy crap. Do they have to put that in here? Legally? Like if something went wrong with the surgery, are they required to tell me in *this* room, with *this* poster, all so I know I have a legal right to complain?

There's one small wooden side table in the corner of the room with a fake peace lily plant on it. And laying in front of that is a book.

I take a step in that direction.

Oh. My. God.

It's a Gideon Bible.

Dr. Robicheau thinks I need a Gideon's Bible for this conversation?!

I'm already reaching for the door handle, ready to fly down the hospital corridors screaming my girl's name when Dr. Robicheau walks in, forcing me to jump backward.

The self-closing door doesn't even close before I'm pelting her with a barrage of questions. "Well? Is she okay? What happened? Is it...?"

And then...

Dr. Robicheau smiles brightly.

And that's all I need to see.

I stumble backward, physically overcome with relief. It's so powerful, it literally knocks the breath from me. I splay a hand across the small, round table, balancing myself and gulping huge swallows of stinky, antiseptic hospital air into my lungs. "It's…it's not…"

She gives a gentle shake of her head. "It doesn't *appear* to be cancer, no." She does cover herself, though—for the endless amounts of medical possibilities or complications that can occur—and emphasizes the word 'appear'. But I'm reading between the lines.

And *between the lines* has never sounded so good.

She bounces her hands in the space between us, trying to get me to calm down. "It still has to be sent for official pathology, but I had them run two initials and both came back as the same thing. Fat necrosis and scar tissue."

Is she serious?

"Tissue death?" I ask.

"It's safe to assume it's a complication from her gunshot wound and subsequent surgery. At some point, the adipose tissue lost its blood flow. The cells died, basically clumped together, calcified, and created scar tissue." She gives me a second to absorb the news. "So many people think that surviving a gunshot wound is all there is to it. Complications can arise years, even decades later."

I bite my lip, fighting the urge to lift Dr. Robicheau into my arms and twirl her through the air. One, not only is that inappropriate; but two, the room's so small I'd knock the tissues and the Gideon's to the floor.

"I didn't have to place a drain; I think she'll be fine without that. But I did mark the area with a surgical clip. As you probably know, it's biocompatible, so it shouldn't cause any complications."

I sigh, trying to wrap my brain around all the ideas, thoughts, and questions swirling from one side of my noggin to the other. "Okay, yeah. For future mammograms?"

"Precisely. If she does test positive for Li-Fraumeni's, she'll need to be monitored closely for the rest of her life. Regular mammograms, ultrasounds, full-body MRIs, dermatology exams. Most tests would be annual, but some would be more frequent, depending on the treatment plan designed by her specialist. The surgical clip can help establish a baseline of where the original abnormality was."

"And we still won't know about that for a couple of weeks?"

"Correct." She lifts her hand and works a muscle on her neck. "But today has given us very good news. I think there's every reason to be optimistic. But, even if she is a carrier for the mutation, she can be proactive in her health journey. She doesn't smoke or drink. She maintains a healthy diet." Her lips quirk to the side. "And she has someone in her life who will help her. Call me a psychic, but I don't foresee you ever letting her miss an appointment, clinical, or scan."

I shake my head. "Oh, hell, no."

She lowers her hand and rolls her shoulders, obviously trying to loosen up for the rest of her very long day. "And as a reminder, if she tests negative for the TP53 mutation, she'll still need to be diligent with her healthcare. After all, she does have a family history of cancer, which in general, presents a risk. Technically, from a medical perspective, one can still be classified as identifying with LFS, while not carrying an actual TP53 mutation. And if she's negative, I still recommend that her father and brother speak to their doctors. Considering I've never examined them, I stop short of recommending genetic testing, but it's something they need to discuss with their medical teams. Especially considering the grandmother's history and the father's battle with two forms of cancer."

"Yes, absolutely."

"Alright. The nurse will come get you soon so you can sit with her in recovery. Once she's had a little more time to wake up, I'll come in and discuss everything with her." She turns to head out the door.

"Dr. Robicheau?"

"Yes?"

"She'll wanna know when her follow-up appointment is? She

has a big brookie whoopie pie order seven days from now."

Her brows furrow. "Brookie whoopie pie? What's that?"

"A half-brownie, half-cookie sandwich with whipped frosting in the middle."

Her eyes widen. "Oh, my." She jokes, "Well, we wouldn't want to derail a masterpiece like that. Since everything appears benign, I'll be fine doing a follow-up at just six days post-op. Someone from my office will come by the recovery room with all of the after-care instructions, and they'll schedule a post-op with my physician assistant, Michelle."

"Thank you."

"Absolutely." The phone in her pocket pings, and she checks it.

"Dr. Robicheau," I repeat.

"Yes?"

"How many surgeries like this are you doing today? Lumpecto-mies, biopsies?"

She tucks her phone back in place, a solemn look on her face. "Seven surgeries are on the calendar for today."

"Seven," I whisper in horror.

"And how many families out there," I nod my head at the side wall, indicating the waiting room that's on the other side, "won't get the same good news we received?"

"Statistically, two. But I have a mastectomy on the schedule. So, you might as well say three."

I feel like throwing up.

Three families who will have to go through the unimaginable.

"And you do this how many times a week?"

"Two. Today's Tuesday. I'll do it all again on Thursday."

Fucking damn.

These past days have been pure hell for me. And yes, I know we may have a different kind of hell looming just around the corner, but at least we've been given a reprieve. A rest. A beacon of light in a dark and grave tunnel.

But these three families?

They're about to be tossed directly into the flames of hellfire.

And I only wish there was something I could do. But this is one inferno a firefighter can't put out. I'm not the one who can save them, no matter how much I wish I could.

"How do you do it? How can you survive this much hurt?"

She gifts me with a soft and genuine smile. "I fight for *them* because someone fought for *me*."

I'm taken aback. "You? You had…"

"When I started med school, I wanted to enter orthopedics. But then, everything changed during Christmas break of MS1. My body had been changing, but I brushed it off as stress and the winter conditions. After all, this Southern California girl wasn't meant for the harsh winters of New York. I was young and busy and thought I knew it all. There were skin changes to my left breast. Dry patches, redness, thickening. Even my nipple was flaky. I didn't think my intimate partner had noticed; after all, he was just as busy as I was. But sure enough, that boyfriend showed up on my parents' doorstep the day after Christmas, all the way in small-town Solvang, California, and refused to leave until I had a mammogram. Turns out, I had IDC. Invasive ductal carcinoma."

"Holy shit."

"Fortunately, it was caught early so I was very lucky. But I refused to take time away from school. As you can imagine, it was hard for my parents to fly from California to New York regularly. I mean, we didn't have a lot of money. I was in med school on a grant, a thousand different student loans, and a prayer." She laughs, the lines around her eyes crinkling with fond memories. "My boyfriend stayed by my side through it all. He was there for all of my treatments. Without him, I have no idea what may have happened."

"Sounds like a good guy."

"Most of y'all good ol' Alabama boys are," she drawls with a thickened accent, ribbing my vernacular in a lighthearted, good-humored joshing. "Perhaps, you know him. His name is Dr. Darren Skinner."

And with a wink, she walks out the door.

Chapter 49

Orah

It's rained.

For three days straight.

But I don't mind. Nothing could dampen my mood right now.

Despite being in the throes of recovery, my pain has been minimal and manageable with just over-the-counter pain relievers. I'm having to wear a special post-surgery bra that's wireless with an adjustable Velcro front and shoulder closures.

And it's pink.

Not black.

Today was the first day I could shower. I was able to shave my legs, pubic area, and left armpit. My right armpit, however, is starting to get a little shaggy. And because I'm not allowed to lift my arms above my shoulders until I get clearance after the post-op appointment, Ridge took it upon himself to perform extra duties in our couples' shower this morning. He shampooed my hair, conditioned it, and blew it dry.

I asked him if he remembered blow drying my hair ten years ago, back when I was in the hospital.

He does.

He's My Hero. Of course, he remembers.

After two days of sponge baths, it felt wonderful to be fully clean. And how did we celebrate? Well, the master of ceremonies thought it would be completely appropriate to play a rousing game of 'lie perfectly still on this bed while I eat you out and don't move a muscle lest you rip a stitch and tear a hole in your healing wound'.

I liked that game.

I won.

And considering I couldn't return the favor because we knew it would put too much strain and burden on my healing chest, I got to watch in eager fascination while he masturbated. He stood between my legs and came all over my belly and pelvis. And when he scooped the milky white remnants of his desire onto his fingers and pushed it deep inside of my aching pussy, I nearly lost all control.

Of course, that might not have been the wisest move for us considering I'm on an antibiotic and the paperwork says that we need to use a backup birth control method because my continuous-use birth control pills may be rendered less effective by the antibiotic. Not only that, but Dr. Robicheau told us that if I do test positive for LFS, I may have to stop taking birth control pills altogether because the pill can sometimes increase the risk of breast cancer. She said that's something we would have to discuss with a specialist, if and when the time comes.

Obviously, Ridge and I are praying the time *doesn't* come. We're praying the genetic testing will be negative.

"I need some water. Do you need anything?" He draws me from my inner thoughts, shrouding me in his considerate and attentive ways. He's sitting on the couch next to me, holding my feet.

I snuggle my favorite blanket closer. "No, I'm good."

He snorts on a chuckle. "I have no idea why you packed that scraggle muffin of a blanket. I can buy you a new one, you know." He scoots out from underneath me and gently sets my feet on the cushions.

"No, sir, you most certainly cannot. You gave it to me for my birthday."

"You know I didn't *know* it was your birthday when I threw that blanket in my Jeep and drove it to the hospital."

"Ridge Conway, don't you dare ruin my eighteenth birthday present that wasn't my eighteenth birthday present," I fuss with a mischievous grin, reminding him of what I called it back then.

"Yes, Little Bird," he mocks.

He rummages around in the kitchen, and my eyes venture away from the baking show on the TV to the wall of windows. We've been unable to sit out on the deck because of the nonstop rain, but that hasn't stopped us from admiring the beauty of the bright green trees, the foggy mountaintops, and the roaring river in the near distance.

"What do you think of having big windows like this in our house?"

He walks back, glass in hand, planting a kiss on my temple as he rounds the couch. "I think it's a great idea." Right as he's about to sit down, he stubs a toe on the old recliner that's facing toward the front door/kitchen area. A dollop of water splashes over the side of his cup and lands on my sock. He harrumphs through the pain, "Ow! Motherfucker!" Scowling, he set his drink on the coffee table, flops on the far side of the couch, and yanks his toe up to his face, investigating the damage.

I lean forward, trying to edge into his business. "Oh no. Let me see."

He quickly puts his foot down. "It's fine. Don't worry about it." He gently pushes on my left shoulder. "And don't lean forward too much."

I roll my eyes. "You're scared about me leaning forward? After what we did up there?" I point above our heads to where the master bedroom is.

"Hey, the name of the game was 'lie-still', I can't help it if you wiggled like your butt was on fire."

"Says the man who had his tongue shoved inside of me." My tease is more seductive than I intend for it to be, wafting through the living room on a heady mewl.

He licks his lips, adjusting his position. And the growing erection in his gym shorts.

A heated blush rises to my cheeks. Being a good little patient is difficult around him. Damn near impossible, if I'm telling the truth. But what do you expect? He's been sauntering around this chalet, shirtless, for days on end.

Trying to be good—all the while my newfound lease on life makes me wanna be totally bad—I point to the recliner. "Why do you never sit in the recliner? You could angle it a little differently so it has a better view of the windows."

"That was Pop's chair. That poor thing has been broken more times than I can count. And if I wasn't home to fix it, he just used whatever was laying around. It's basically held together by bent nails and superglue."

I've never seen someone look so affectionately at a piece of furniture before. In all honesty, it brings a new level of love to our relationship. "And you don't wanna get rid of it because it reminds you of him?"

He leans a little closer to me and props my feet back in his lap. "Well yeah," he raves with a point, "look, you can still see his ass grooves in it."

My eyes flicker around the room, trying to picture the patriarch sitting in his favorite spot. "Why didn't he wanna look out the windows?"

Overwhelmed with a snicker, his head lobs against the back of the couch cushion.

I poke his belly with my toes. "What?! Tell me."

"Well, he loved sitting out on the deck. And going for walks and hikes on the trails. He did that most days. But if he had to sit inside, he wanted to sit with his back to the windows because he liked the feel of the sun on his bald spot."

A laugh bursts out of me, sending a small pain into my breast. He watches me with a peaceful look of contentment on his face, just basking in the pleasure of my cheerfulness. He slides his palms up from my ankles to my shins.

I fiddle my fingers, wanting him to hold my hand. He immediately takes me in his grasp. His thumb edges down and traces back and forth across *our* tattoo. As always, there's a thick callous on the pad of his finger, and his caress sends both a sharp tingle and a comforting warmth crawling up my skin. "Why don't you fix it? You said there's a bunch of tools in the garage. You could pull it apart and fix it while we're here."

He studies the once-plush leather lounger, giving it some serious thought. "Yeah, I think I migh—"

The blare of my cell phone cuts him off. We both look down at the coffee table, trying to read the type scrolling across the top of the lighted screen. We're met with the general *Healthcare* subtitle and a Nashville area code. He picks it up for me and points to the slide bar, nonverbally asking if he can answer and place it on speaker. I nod, barely moving my head. He manipulates the phone and places it on the blanket.

"Hello?" I reach for my necklace but come up empty. I didn't have Ridge put it on me after our shower. It's still on the dresser upstairs. I settle instead for twirling my engagement ring.

"Ms. Smith?"

"Yes, ma'am, this is she." My voice wavers, shaky and low, like the intermittent rolls of thunder that have been echoing through the mountain valleys.

"This is Michelle from Dr. Robicheau's office. I just wanted to let you know that the official pathology report is complete and has confirmed the benign nature of your breast mass. As per the initial intraoperative consultation, it was fat necrosis and scar tissue."

My eyes blur, not only from the confirmation of the good news that we were already hanging our hats on, but because of the smile plastered across Ridge's face. He's smiling so wide that his lips are nearly lost in his beard.

I love it.

"Ms. Smith?"

"Ye—yes. I'm here. That's wonderful news."

"Yes, absolutely." She ruffles some papers. "And how is your recovery going? Have you removed the initial bandages? Showered?

Any unusual redness or discharge? Fever or chills? Anything of concern?"

Ridge reaches over and swipes at my cheeks, making me realize that my unshed tears are no longer unshed. They're falling from my eyes in over-plumped, overjoyed drops. "No, ma'am. Everything appears to be normal. We removed the initial bandages. I used a waterproof one while showering this morning. And then we put fresh dressing and gauze on. My pain's been minimal."

"And you're remembering to keep your hands and arms below your head?"

"Yes."

"Perfect. Well, we've got you on the calendar for Monday at eleven a.m. for your follow-up. Is that time still good?"

"Yes."

"Okay. If you have any questions, please feel free to call our office. We are about to close for the evening, but in the event of an emergency, our call service will reach out to us. Have a good weekend, and I'll see you on Monday."

As soon as we end the call, Ridge tosses my cell back on the table, ducks one of my legs behind his head, and scoots between my thighs. Of course, he gets hung up in the blanket. Scoffing and pouting, and eventually cursing under his breath, he yanks it off me and tosses it over on the armrest of Pop's chair.

"Hey!" I giggle, but that makes my nose run so I start sniffling instead.

Unencumbered, he shifts closer, until his hip is flush with my crotch. Taking care not to press down on my chest, he leans forward, bracing one arm on the back of the couch and one arm down by my waist. "I love you, Zipporah."

"I love you, Hero. Always and forever."

Words we've each said to the other. And words we both seem to love.

His lips find mine. We kiss tenderly, in an unhurried fashion, relishing in the fact that our time no longer seems borrowed. Despite what obstacles may come our way with Li-Fraumeni, in this cabin, in this moment, in this second, it seems like our time is infinite. His tongue pushes against mine, swirling and drawing me into a lover's dance.

He meanders away from my lips, pampering me with his love. Licking my cheeks. Wiping my face with his beard, ridding me of the salt and stains. And when I lift my chin, moaning for him to return to my needy mouth, he does.

And we kiss.

For every possibility and every future.

Every destiny.

And when my hand trails down from his tattered shoulder to the long and hard erection pressing against my inner thigh, he hisses and bites my bottom lip. Hard.

I buck against him, ignoring the pinch of my stitched skin against the side of my specialized bra.

And then...

The lights flicker, and we hear the telltale click of all the appliances shutting off. He lifts his head, and we both take stock of our surroundings.

No lights. No TV. No hum of the refrigerator.

The overhead ceiling fan winds down. Like a Jack-in-the-box, slowing and slowing. Except it never pops back to life. It just sits there.

"Huh. Well, that's a mood killer." He scrubs a hand down his kiss-swollen lips and rubs his jaw. "Let me check the breaker box. See if the neighbors lost power too."

By neighbors, he means the houses through the woods.

Seeing as how my hand is still in, well, quite a nice place, I give his cock a little squeeze before he slides away from me.

He gifts me with a wicked grin. "Don't be acting so brave, Brave Girl. You haven't got your clearance from the doctor."

I tilt my head, watching him stand up. Now that the lamp isn't on, the house is covered in dark shadows and shade. There are no streaks of late-afternoon sun filtering through the dense clouds and spattering rain. He looks dark and dangerous. "You realize that she's most likely not gonna give clearance for sex on Monday? That she'll probably say we need to wait until the two-week mark?" I snort. "I can't lift anything over ten pounds for two weeks." I bite the inside of my cheek, trying to stave my smile as I nod my head to his giant erection.

He laughs. "Way to make a guy feel like a real man, Little Bird."

He plucks his own phone from the top of the fireplace mantel, slips his feet in his tennis shoes, and pecks the top of my head. "I'll be back."

After a few minutes, he returns. With rainwater dripping from his hair and down the hard lines of his chest and stomach. "Looks like the neighbors to the left and to the right are both without power. Doesn't seem to be anything wrong with the breaker box, so it must be a system-wide issue. But on a bright note, it's only sprinkling now." He sits down at the kitchen bar and pecks on his phone.

"What are you doing?"

"Reporting the outage to the power company." After a second, he plops the phone down. Looking around, he frowns. "Well, under different circumstances, I know exactly what we would do to pass the time."

Once again, I giggle. Damn, I love him. "Yeah, I can only imagine."

He sighs dramatically, "But I guess you're stuck just talking to me."

We spend the next hour talking and laughing and telling stories. Sharing loving kisses and intimate touches. And when it grows even darker, he fishes some candles out from the closet and lights them around the living room and kitchen.

"Well, we have no idea when this power is coming back on. Why don't I run into town and get us some supper. When I get back, if the power's still out, I'll light the fire. I know it's May, but we can open the windows if it starts to get too hot. It'll definitely give us more light. Sound like a plan?"

"Yeah, sure."

He runs upstairs, using the flashlight on his phone, and grabs a T-shirt before leaving.

He's only gone for a couple of minutes when I have to pee. Grabbing my own phone, I use the half-bath and wash my hands. When I'm walking back into the family room, there's a knock at the door. It catches me by such surprise, I trip over the rug decorating the hardwood floor and nearly tumble face first into the massive brick hearth.

Shit. That wouldn't have been good.

I turn around, wondering if Ridge forgot something. The front door, which is nestled between the actual, functioning part of the kitchen and the dining room table, has a large oval in the middle with a thick, frosted glass. I can't really make anything out from here, except that the person on the other side is most definitely not Ridge.

It looks like a woman.

It must be one of the neighbors.

I scurry closer, eager to see if she knows anything about the power outage. But as my hand reaches for the knob, a sickening wave of anxiety floods my stomach. Bile shoots up into my mouth, coating my tongue in acid.

Is that…

My hand trembles as I open the door. "Kimber-Shay?" A gust of rain-cooled wind hits me in the face, splattering small raindrops across my eyelashes. I blink, trying to clear my vision. "What in the world are you doing here?"

And then a hand pushes her aside.

A man in a white dress shirt steps in front of me.

He rocks back on his heels and shoves his fists into the pockets of his black slacks.

My hand flies to my mouth, literally trying to hold my vomit inside of my body. Through clenched teeth, I gasp.

"Levi."

"Please, call me Congressman."

Chapter 50

Orah

He walks over the threshold, without any hesitation, without any fear. I stumble backward, doing my best to avoid him. I scatter across the hardwood on my socked feet.

"Wh—what are you doing here?" My wild eyes dart from him to Kimber. And now to the other man bringing up the rear. The stranger, dressed all in black, is tall and bulky. Not as tall as Ridge. And nowhere near as muscular, but still intimidating. "What's happening?"

Levi smiles. "What's the matter, Orah? Or should I say *Amy*? No welcome hug for your one-time lover? It's a reunion."

Gripping the edge of the kitchen island for stability, I shake my head back and forth. It feels like my brain is sticking to the sides of my skull. Thick and viscous like a sludgy, wet oatmeal. "No. No. No. We were never lovers."

Levi lazily saunters into the kitchen. He picks up a green and white dishtowel, looking at the leaf pattern as if he's never seen anything more interesting. He drops it back on the counter and pokes at a bag of pretzels. "That's not what I remember. I remember you wanting every single thing I gave you."

I claw at my neck, wishing more than anything that my necklace was tucked right where it should be. But it's not. Taking a play from Ridge, I press into the hollow of my throat, mashing the area as I count. My thumb crushes against my windpipe, cutting off my air supply.

One. Two. Three. Four. Five.

"You…" I have to cough to find my voice. "You raped me. You know you did. I was only seventeen. You were twenty-four. You know what you did was wrong."

He works his clean-shaven jaw back and forth. "You never called it 'rape', Orah. It was only after those attorneys got in your head that you started thinking that way. You said *yes*. You wanted it." His snide chuckle irritates my eardrums. With his mouth gaped open, he looks like a demon feasting on the shadows from the flickering candlelight.

"Consent is more than just a word." I parrot back the same counsel Ridge shared with me. All of those years ago.

He snorts, "Just another woman who thinks all men should be mind readers."

My gaze bounces to Kimber. Despite the darkness slowly swallowing the house, I can see she's nervous. And that's not something I've ever seen her be. She's huddled on the far side of the dining room table, shielding herself behind the placemats and pottery bowl filled with fake apples and lemons. Her bright pink blouse is spotted with rainwater, and she's nibbling on a hangnail.

With the engagement ring still prominently displayed on her finger.

The stranger is standing sentry by the closed front door. With his hands scooped inside of his black blazer, I can see a double gun holster wrapped around his shoulders.

And dangling on each side of his ribcage is a gun.

My heart is beating so fast I wouldn't be surprised if I have a heart attack. With each blink of my eye, I imagine the organ atrophying in my chest and dropping down into the web of my diaphragm. Like a baseball landing in a glove. At a hundred miles an hour. Pow!

"Why don't you take a seat?" Levi shoos his hands in the air, telling me to move back into the living room.

I walk backward, afraid to take my eyes off him. My calves bump into the coffee table. I skirt around it and sit in Pop's recliner. My fingers instantly connect with my favorite blanket, and I clutch the once-fluffy material in my fist. "What are you doing here?" I nod to the woman who was going to marry my man. "How do you know Kimber-Shay?"

"What am I doing here?" He sighs in exasperation like I'm a total moron. He walks around and takes a seat on the couch, facing me. Leaning back on the sofa like he's the master of the manor, with one arm draped over the back cushion, he props his left foot on his right knee and folds a hand around his ankle. My sight is adjusting to the darkened room, minute by minute, as night descends around us. And through it all, I can see the twinkle of the diamonds on the massive face of his watch and the little yellow polka-dots on his fancy socks. Socks that probably cost more than Ridge's penthouse rent.

He turns his head, just barely, and speaks to the stranger still hovering in the kitchen by the door. "Sam, can you go ahead and get started?"

He lumbers across the room; but instead of heading for me, he stops in front of the massive fireplace, yanks the mesh fire screen to the side, and starts stacking logs in the firebox. He makes quick work of the wood from the log rack, making sure to add what I can only assume is the appropriate amount of kindling from the metal bucket sitting next to it.

Pretending my fear doesn't exist, I shoot up from the chair. "I think you should leave. Ridge will be back any second, and he won't be happy to see you. If...if you need something, you can just call me."

He cackles like a hyena.

Well, that backfired. Even I'm underwhelmed by my pathetic performance.

Lifting his arm from the back of the couch, he spears his fingers through his gelled hair. It's more coiffed now than it was back then, with a little pouf to the front. "Oh, sit down, Orah."

I don't. I stand.

My freshly stitched wound throbs, pulsing with pain from the frenzied expansion of my chest as I inhale and exhale like a hyperventilating maniac.

He rolls his eyes and balances a hand in the air, clearly awaiting a handout. "Sam?"

With a frustrated groan, Sam stands, playing into the dynamic of his role as the subordinate underling. He reaches into his jacket, emerges with a gun, and places it in Levi's palm.

Without any hesitation whatsoever, Levi points the weapon.

Straight. In. My. Face.

"Sit the fuck down." He drags his creepy gaze over my body, all the way from my head to my toes, drenching me in his sickening oppression. "I really don't want to mess with that gorgeous face." His lips thin. "Despite the end result I have planned for you."

My knees give out, flopping me into the chair...regardless of my desire to pounce across the coffee table and poke his eyes out with my fingernails. Clawing so deep I leave chips of black nail polish in his brain matter.

Sam returns to his position and the task at hand.

From her hidden corner, Kimber sniffles.

Levi shifts on the couch and waves her over. "Stop your sniveling and come over here."

She tiptoes across the hardwood, clacking her high heels in a sparse pattern, like a windshield wiper on the lowest setting. It's so far apart, you almost forget that you turned it on. And then, swish, it slides across, scaring the crap out of you.

Once she's hovering by the couch, Levi shifts, balancing his forearms on his knees. "So, what am I doing here?" He mimics me with a high-pitched tone. "Well, that's complicated. It has many moving parts." He cocks an eyebrow. "Do you know how much I had to pay ADNN to kill the story about you? About us?"

The reporters...

That's why he's here?

"Let's just say, it cost more money than you could ever imagine. More money than you could ever dream of making." He quirks a grin. "And once that money was in the right hands, they were very eager to disclose their source." He sucks his bottom lip between his teeth. And when it releases with a popping sound, he takes the opportunity to smack Kimber on the ass. She squeaks out a half-sob, half-gasp.

"That's what this is about? You were worried about the reporters? About what the news would say?" I wobble my head up and down, back and forth, surprising myself when the motion makes a tear fall. "I wasn't going to tell them anything, I swear."

"That's a chance I wasn't willing to take. Not to mention, I don't need anyone digging into that night. Asking questions about what happened in that room. Not now. There's too much on the line."

"On the line?"

I side-glance at Sam, watching as he lights the fire.

"You are so dense. You still avoid the news?" He tilts back and tugs his slacks away from his crotch, making me want to gag. "That's no way to live. That's a completely ignorant stance."

How does he know that? How does he know I don't watch the news?

Sam stokes the flames, pushing the wood into what he deems is the proper place. Light dances across the ceiling, flooding all of us in shades of orange and yellow and black. Rising from his haunches, he spins toward us. Deciding he needs to be prepared, he lifts the other gun from its nestled house and holds it down by his side. I'm not sure if he's a bodyguard or a henchman or a lapdog, but I already know I hate him.

"The Vice President's medical retirement commences in two weeks. And at that time, the President will nominate me to the position. *Me*," he enunciates, pointing at himself with the tip of his gun.

What an idiot.

For that split second, I send a thousand prayers for an accidental discharge.

"I don't need anything—or anyone—fucking with the congressional confirmation." He stands up, pushes past Kimber, and paces back and forth in front of Sam and the blazing fireplace. "I mean, it should be a lock. I've spent the past six months making deal after deal. And well," he shrugs with a scoff and does a little side shuffle, "you know what happens to the motherfuckers who don't like to take deals." He slaps Sam's shoulder. "How do you think those affair and meth head pictures of Senator Poulter got leaked?" He howls in laughter. "Dumb bastard."

He stops wandering, looks down at his chest, and messes with the buttons of his shirt, making sure I have an optimal view of his mangy chest hair. "But there's still those who want to see me fail. They've been searching for dirt, and they dug up what they could with those sealed inquiry transcripts." He points a thin, wiry finger in my direction. "The things that happened that night have been dead for nearly a decade. I don't need anyone resurrecting them. Not someone on the opposite side of the aisle. Not some reporter with dreams of an Emmy. And definitely not some hack social media cunt who decides to exact a vendetta because she couldn't keep her legs closed."

I'm too shocked to even gasp.

So, Kimber does it for me.

Sweat rolls down my back, flowing down the beads of my spine like a waterfall. Like a rapid whitewater. Like the hard-flowing, rain-fueled Little Pigeon River roaring just below the back deck.

"Anyway, in a few short months, I'll be Vice President, and considering the President only has two years left on his second term, in just a couple of years, I'll be the Presidential nominee. And a fucking shoo-in."

My hands tremble.

My stomach cramps.

My old scars feel like they're slicing open, carving my body in gaping scalpel gashes and rounded bullet wounds.

"So, you're doing what? Threatening me? All so you can protect your career?"

He cocks one hand on a hip and wiggles the gun at the floor. "Oh, Orah. I'm not here to threaten you. I'm here to make sure you don't survive."

Chapter 51

Orah

Blank.

I have no feelings. No thoughts. No heartbeat.

"Survive?"

"Carbon monoxide, my dear." He edges closer to me. "It's such a sad outcome for the young couple who just got engaged. The star-crossed lovers who are just beginning their lives together." He sniffles and scratches his nose. "But what do you expect. When the power goes out for such an extended time, you need light. Not to mention, even though it's May, that rain has sent a chill through the air." He crosses his arms at mid-waist and pretends to shiver. "Brrr."

"You said you wouldn't hurt her? You said you were gonna pay her off. Convince her to leave town. Convince her to leave him." Kimber's objection is weak and weary. Tears flow down her face, marring her with streaks of mascara.

He shoves her out of the way. She stumbles into Sam, who gives her the same kind of treatment. "You stupid bitch, just look at her!" He jerks an arm in my direction. "You think she'd take money over him?! You think she'd ever leave him?!"

Huffing in anger, Levi sits back down on the couch, sets the gun beside him, and stretches his right leg out straight. He pilfers through his pocket and emerges with a small plastic bag.

Like really small.

Like what a jeweler would put an earring in.

Except this doesn't have an earring, it has a white powder.

He thumps the bottom of the baggie and looks around the coffee table, searching for something. What? I don't know. "Don't play dumb, Kimber. You knew what would happen." He spots a magazine on the corner of the table and snaps his fingers in excitement. "After all, you're the one who went to ADNN with her true identity and all that 'inside' information," he balks, with a one-handed finger quote. "You wanted this to happen. You were begging for it. You were just too spineless to do anything about it."

He carefully opens the bag and spreads some of the powder on the magazine, before closing it and shoving it back in his pocket. He pats his other leg. "Sam, give me a card. I don't have my wallet."

With a frown on his face, Sam reaches in his back pocket, picks through his wallet for a credit card, and hands it to Levi before returning to his post. Levi karate chops the white stuff with the piece of plastic and then molds it into two lines. Bending, he sucks one of the lines up and into his nose. He squinches his eyes and pinches his nostrils closed. He waits until his face turns bright red before releasing his hold and whistling through his teeth. "And to answer your question, Orah. It's not just about my career. I have a wife and kids. My family has a reputation to uphold."

"And k–ki—" I can't say *'killing'*. It won't even form on my tongue. If I don't say it, maybe it won't happen. "Giving me carbon monoxide will protect your reputation?"

"Of course, it will. Because the introverted, shy, and hidden-in-plain sight Amy Smith will no longer be around to hide. And of course, that's why *he* has to go too."

He?

Who's he?

A fear like I've never known before slithers from the pit of my stomach and into my heart, filling my body with a poisonous venom. The organ I was worried would atrophy turns black. It rots and withers away. And in its place, exploding in my chest cavity like a Big Bang is pure, unfiltered, undiluted panic.

Ridge. Ridge. Ridge. Ridge. Ridge.

"With you gone," he continues, "there will be no one to rein him in. He may get a wild hair to start talking, yapping about something he knows absolutely nothing about." He coughs, getting strangled on his own spit. "I told that shithead I was gonna have so much fun fucking up his life." He leans forward and does another line. His hands waft through the air. "And the fun is just beginning."

Ridge. Ridge. Ridge. Ridge. Ridge.

I repeat his name over and over and over.

My numbers have never been less important.

Him. He's the only thing that's important.

"You can't. Please. I'll do anything, Levi. Please don't hurt him." I scoot to the edge of the recliner. "I'll leave. I'll leave and never contact him again. Just please don't hurt him."

"Levi," Kimber reaches for his shoulder, "don't do this. There has to be another way. You said he would be mine after this."

Levi backhands her. Right across the cheekbone. The sound of his knuckles connecting with her skin is sickening. The grimace plastered across his face, downright terrifying. But what alarms me even more is that Sam is stoic. Completely unaffected. Hell, the dude almost seems bored. So that tells me that this kind of behavior is nothing new for Levi.

And that horrid thought feeds my panic. Growing it bigger and bigger. Enlarging it to the point where it doesn't even fit inside of my body anymore.

Kimber clutches her cheek and cries. Unable to stand, she gingerly sits on the arm of the couch, trying not to invade Levi's space.

He licks his forefinger, mops it all over the magazine, and then pops it in his mouth, sucking whatever residue may be there. "Really, y'all have made this so much easier than I ever thought it could be." He laughs so hard he starts coughing again. "I mean, literally. It's like y'all wanna get knocked off." He stands and stretches his back. "I spent all this time worrying about how to get to you. Down there in your hometown. Surrounded by the five-thousand people that y'all can't go one single day without seeing. Moms and dads and brothers and cousins and cousins of cousins. You're adults, for fuck's sake, grow a set of balls and move away from Mommy."

Sam leans around and tosses two more logs on the fire.

"But then, y'all gave me this gift. A secluded mountain vacation. I hit the fucking jackpot." Standing, he yanks on Kimber's hair, snapping her neck back. Her hands fall into her lap, and he shoves his mouth on top of hers, kissing her with such force I can hear the smack of his tongue against her teeth.

When he pulls away, her face reddens, flushing the bruise that's already forming. She peeks at me, shamed by embarrassment, dismay, and alarm. It's clear to see that things aren't going according to *her* plan. But what did she expect? Getting involved with someone like Levi...

All to what?

Hatch some scheme to win Ridge back? To get me out of the picture?

When Levi shuffles over to the kitchen and opens the fridge, I take the opportunity to lock onto her. With a subtle eye roll, I draw an invisible line to the discarded gun on the couch, nonverbally begging her to get it, to do something. She moves her head, just a millimeter, effectively shutting me down.

"So many things can go wrong in a place like this. I went through the whole gamut." He slams the fridge, obviously not pleased. "Where the hell is the beer?" he bellows, getting sidetracked from his soliloquy.

He's right. Ridge drank his last beer last night with the pasta and garlic bread he made.

Unhappy, he starts opening up all of the cabinets, giving a little yelp when he reaches the liquor cabinet, high above the sink. He fishes out half-filled bottles of vodka, gin, whiskey, and tequila.

Who knows how long they've been up there.

Despite his history at Belly's and his own brother's astute prowess behind the bar and his foray into Drunkville after catching Kimber cheating, Ridge prefers beer. If I had to guess, those bottles haven't been touched since the last time Cullen came to the cabin.

He opens the fullest bottle—some kind of tequila—sniffs it, and then takes a hearty swig. He sets it down with a violent slam. The clear liquid splashes out of the rounded top and drenches his right forearm. "Ugh. Peasant's piss," he mumbles. He shakes his arm in the air. A little tequila droplet sprinkles onto one of the candles, making it shoot up in a vibrant, yet somewhat controlled flame. Levi snorts on a stupefied chuckle, "Oh, shit. Better be careful."

He sighs and blinks rapidly, trying to restart his brain. "Where was I? Oh, yes, so many things. Fall down the stairs. Drown in the bathtub. Drive off a cliff. But each of those present their own problems. A fall down the steps only takes care of one of you. Same thing with a bath. And obviously, that would look suspicious since you aren't supposed to be soaking in a tub after your surgery." He stares down at the rolled sleeve of his shirt and decides it needs adjusting after getting halfway soaked. "Congratulations, by the way." He gives me his version of a gracious nod. "On the negative biopsy. What a relief to know cancer isn't gonna get ya." He exaggerates an accent, gives me a wink, and bursts out laughing at his own perverted joke. "And driving off a cliff? Yeah, no, thank you. It's too risky. No way to control the outcome. One of you could survive. And I don't have the time to fly in some computer expert to override the electronics on that bastard's truck." He finishes with his shirt and shrugs. "Cutting a brake line is too old school."

When he walks over to the fire, Sam shifts to the side making room for his boss. I attempt to get Kimber's attention again. And for one small moment, I think I may have won. She scoots from the arm of the couch and gently eases her bottom onto the couch cushion. But instead of reaching for the gun, she cowers in the corner, huddling as far away from it as possible.

I try to calculate my risks. Which is hard to do with a pounding headache and adrenaline fogging every little move. Even swirling my finger around on my blanket wipes me out, zapping me of all my energy and strength. I don't see how I can leap across the coffee table, gallantly grab ahold of the one weapon that nearly caused my destruction ten years ago, and learn how to use said weapon...all before Sam decides to, well, do what I can only assume Sam does.

"And that's when the idea hit me. Carbon monoxide. It'll be investigated, sure. But when the fire department report aligns with the medical examiner's findings, nobody will think twice about it. It's the perfect crime. Power went out, you needed extra light, and the drunk dummy," he waves a hand at the liquor-decorated kitchen counter, "forgot to check the damper. The firefighter getting killed by fire. Ironic, huh?"

I try to swallow, but my body revolts over even the simplest of actions. "But...but..." I'm not even sure where to start. And does it even matter? Will I even be able to change his mind? "But the power could come back on any second. That alone would raise suspicion. Sure, the rain cooled it off outside, but it's nowhere near cold enough for a fire."

He flashes his white teeth. "Power's out for the top third of this mountain, and it will be until after ten tomorrow morning."

"How do you know that?"

"When will you learn that I have connections, Orah? Power goes out all the time; no one will raise an eyebrow at a faulty transformer."

"But people are gonna know that you were here."

"How?" he mocks.

I toss my hand to the closed front door. "There's a doorbell camera right there. Everybody has security cameras nowadays."

With arrogance, he puffs his chest out and then fiddles with the large watch on his wrist. "You think we didn't do our due diligence? That I didn't have Sam learning everything there was to know about this area? Checking it out?" He smiles with pride down at the diamond and platinum timepiece. "The cameras here don't have battery backups. They need electricity. Same with the neighbor right below here. Now, the neighbor above does have battery-operated cameras, but with each of these lots being three-and-a-half acres, they can't see jack shit through all the woods."

"But what about all of the other houses? Down the mountain? The camera at the security gate? The red light cameras in town?"

"Oh, you mean, the cameras that caught us driving here today?" The rain has picked back up, and I can hear it pattering against the wall of windows and sliding door, behind me. "Well, those cameras picked up the driver. The driver who happens to know the security gate code and punched it in." He smirks at Kimber. "The side and back windows in that SUV are tinted so dark, you couldn't see two clowns with neon hair fucking." He pats Sam on the shoulder. "That's why me and Sam sat in the backseat. As far as the world is concerned, Ms. Kathryn Kimber-Shay Willis was the only one in that vehicle. Not to mention, it's registered to Willis Luxury Automotive."

Kimber's jaw drops. She winces, giving an indication of how much her cheek is still hurting. "You set me up?"

"Don't look so hurt. Just call it my insurance policy. After all, your internet order history shows the paint stripper too."

What paint stripper?

"Now, I'm not a complete monster." He walks in my direction. I immediately slide backward, trying to push my body as far away from his as possible. It's a moot point, though, because he sits on the coffee table.

Right. In. Front. Of. Me.

My knees fly apart, widening my legs like open butterfly wings, all so I don't have to touch any part of him.

Dropping his elbows to his thighs, he steeples his fingers underneath his chin. One of his legs bounces in nervous, hyped-up energy. The movement hammers his fingernails into his chin. "I brought something to help you relax. I know how anxious you can get. It's just a little something to make you forget the fate that's waiting for you at the end of the night. After all, it's not like we can stay in here once we close the damper. There will be smoke and noxious fumes. And we have to make sure you're nice and cozy for your little slumber."

From my periphery, there's a blur as Sam adds even more wood to the fire. But I can't tear my eyes away from the demon in front of me. There are two dangling light fixtures in the kitchen. And from where Levi's sitting, it looks like they are connected to his head. Like devil horns.

The firelight flickers across his face, highlighting the redness in his eyes.

Like blood.

He reaches into the front pocket of his dress shirt and pulls out a vial. There's some kind of clear liquid inside. "If regular sleeping pills can knock you out like that, what do you think GHB will do?"

"How do you know about that?" My whisper rakes against the inside of my raw and sore throat, making it feel like I'm covered in a million tiny papercuts.

His fingers collapse together into a fist, with the little vial hidden somewhere inside. "You think I can't get ahold of some measly ol' medical records. How did you think I knew about this..." He leans into me and harshly takes hold of my right breast. Squeezing. Hard. A sharp and debilitating pain sizzles through every nerve-ending in my body. A curtain of black blinds me for a moment. Even after he releases me, it takes several blinks for my vision to return.

Fresh beads of sweat pool into the bottom band of my surgical bra.

My stomach lurches, sending the remains of our afternoon snack of cheese and crackers into my mouth. I swallow it back down.

He grabs Ridge's half-full water cup from the far corner of the coffee table. Setting it beside him, he screws off the top of the container and pours the substance into the water. The two liquids instantly combine. I can't tell one from the other. I expected it to do something. To look different. To slowly dissipate and fog, like when Cullen pours pretty and colorful liquids into the fancy cocktails he makes.

He puts the empty tube back in his pocket. "Assuming you react the same to this as you do the sleeping pills, this should be more than enough. Your boyfriend, however, has a much bigger dose."

He's not my boyfriend.

He's my everything.

He dangles the glass in front of my face. "Drink up, *Amy*. And let's see what fun we can have before you pass out."

Kimber's blocked from view, but still, I hear her.

Down to the jingle of her stacked gold bracelets and the shuffle of her stilettos as the heels scrape against the living room rug.

"And if I don't?"

"Did you think I forgot my gun is right back there?" His eyeballs roll back into his head, indicating the area of the couch behind him.

So, he hasn't forgotten about it.

He knows.

It's within arm's reach of Kimber. And he knows, without a doubt, that she won't do a damn thing about it.

I try to let go of my blanket, but my fingers won't work. The synapse doesn't fire from my brain. Try as I might, the fabric is still clenched between my white knuckles. So instead, I lift my leg, where my left hand has been trapped underneath my thigh, and with a noticeable tremor, I grab the glass. Closing my eyes, I tip it back to my mouth and drink.

Every last drop.

"Such a good little girl." His chuckle is filled with the malignancy that I was fortunate enough to avoid with my body. "You listen so well. You know, I've always had a thing for a teacher's pet." He places the empty glass back on the table. "It'll probably hit you in twenty or thirty minutes, and I need you to drink the other before you go night-night. What on earth do you think we can do in less than twenty minutes?"

Drink what other?

He leans forward and wraps his disgusting palms around my knees. He inches them up.

Up. Up. Up. Up. Up.

It feels like thousands of wasps are stinging my skin, feasting on my flesh, turning me into a swollen and disfigured shell of myself.

His thumbs drift under the hem of my shorts.

This time my neurons discharge with exact precision. My fingers move just the way I need them to. I pop the heels of my hands into his, stopping his prowl. Refusing to grab my throat, refusing to count, refusing to sob, I hold my chin high, ignoring the steady stream of salty tears as they cascade down my face. Snot drips onto my upper lip. I refuse to wipe it.

"You win, Levi. Just take me away from here. Let's leave. Right now. You can do whatever you want with me. Kill me. Lock me away in a dungeon. Make me your trophy wife. I don't fucking care. I'll do anything and everything you want. Let's just leave before he comes back." Levi's demented pupils widen even farther. "Leave Ridge alone, and I'll be yours."

The kitchen door slams open with such brutality, for a moment, I think the house is caving in. It bashes back against the wall, cracking against the waist-high chair rail so violently, a hinge actually breaks off the frame and sails through the air. It hits one of the still-burning candles on the kitchen island and fractures the decorative Mason jar. The candle collapses into three sections, quickly extinguishing under the weight of its own wax.

The night sky serves as his backdrop. The heavy-falling rain pelts his broad shoulders.

"Get your filthy fucking hands off MY WIFE."

Chapter 52

Ridge

My ass bounces on the cushiony vinyl seat. Leaning my head back against the wall, I can't help the smile that threatens to overtake my face. She's gonna flip out over these cheese fries. I guess, in a way, the power going out was a nice little surprise. If it hadn't, we would've been cooking.

In fact, the container of flour is still out on the counter. It's one of the many ingredients I used in last night's pan fried-chicken pasta. I must say, it turned out better than I thought it would. So good, I sent Dad a smiling photo of me and Orah stuffing our faces. Orah said for me to leave the flour out because she was gonna teach me how to make homemade snickerdoodle biscuits tonight, and we could have that and eggs and bacon for supper.

You know, everybody loves a little breakfast for dinner.

But I'm not gonna lie.

That idea was daunting. I mean, c'mon, there has to be a reason my dad doesn't like to bake. Biscuits can't exactly be easy, can they?

Alas, our stove is electric and not gas. So that idea was squashed the second the power went out. But now? Now, I get to ply my girl with her favorite—French fries. Of course, I ordered an extra-large helping. So, there's a good chance the cheese will curdle before she can even finish, considering her sloth-like eating speed.

Unless she's stuffing her mouth with my cock, My Bird likes to go slow.

I'm about to laugh at my own runaway thoughts when a debilitating pain pierces through my chest. It's like a serrated blade has sliced into my heart. The hurt is so tangible, so real and visceral, that I press my knuckles into my sternum, trying to transfer the ache from the inside of my body to the outside of my body.

My stomach seizes, clenching in a cramp so intense that I can't even draw breath into my lungs.

I blink. Starbursts shoot in front of my eyes.

Fear and panic and anxiety push every rational thought from my brain.

My blood thickens, oozing through my veins and arteries with a viscosity that feels heavier than motor oil. I feel toxic. Unhealthy. Poisonous.

Drugged.

I feel what you feel.

I feel what you feel.

Something's not right.

I shoot up from my position in the waiting area of the restaurant and race toward the door. My senses are overwhelmed by the sounds that resonate behind me as I open the outside door.

Clanking bar glasses.

Chatting patrons.

Rattling plates.

From my periphery, someone in a black apron walks into the lobby with two overflowing plastic bags.

"Sir!" The girl behind the hostess counter screams for me. "Your food?!"

A woosh of wind swallows my reply. "I'll be back!"

Sprinkles hit me in the face as I sprint to the truck. I jog through puddles, splashing dirty water and pebbles of asphalt all over my shins. I don't even take time with my seatbelt. I just crank the ignition and slap the vehicle into drive. I'm already propelling forward by the time I shut the driver-side door.

The trip through town and back up to the cabin is a blur. I'm not even gonna lie, there might have been a few horns honked. And I keep telling myself that I'm gonna feel like a major asshole when I get back home and everything is perfectly fine.

But you know what?

This won't be the first time I've turned myself into an ass for Orah, and it sure as hell won't be the last.

When I get to the security gate at the base of our mountain neighborhood, I punch in the code, cursing and fumbling when it takes me three times to get it right. The rain starts falling harder, but I don't even take the time to raise my window back up. As I drive up the mountain, the on and off downpour of the past few days reactivates. Water drenches my body, soaking into the leather trim of my doorframe. Stinging drops pound into my face. Like ice picks with a personal vendetta against me. I force a hand over my beard, wringing my hair out like a wet towel.

My headlights bounce off the trees and dance off the log cabin chalets. Unoccupied vacation homes and vacant rentals are barely lit, surviving with just one or two outside security lights. And once I cross the invisible threshold of where the power outage takes effect, I'm cast into even more darkness. Everything is eerie and still.

Except in my own body.

My heartbeat drums so loud in my ears, it reverberates through my bones, rattling me like I'm nothing more than a skeleton. My panted breaths resonate through the hollow of my chest, low and soggy, like the rainwater is literally melting my insides, leaving me empty.

I round the last bend, and our driveway comes into view.

I can't even describe what feelings assault me when I see a black and tinted SUV parked in front of our cabin.

Well, in all honesty, I'm sure I could describe my feelings if I wanted to. But I don't really want to.

I slam the truck into park, flip the ignition, and run to the front door, not even caring that the truck door doesn't latch all the way. I take the front porch steps two at a time, nearly busting my ass when my sneaker slips on the wet wood.

The closer I get to the front door, the more I can *feel her.*

Her terror gales through the air just the same way her coconut shampoo does. I can smell it. Taste it.

Live it.

And without any hesitation, I fling open the front door and come face to face with my worst fucking nightmare.

I size up the scene in less time than it takes the douche in front of the fireplace to swivel and point the gun in my direction.

There's a man.

Rephrase: There's a man, with his hands on *My Brave Girl.*

Rephrase: There's a *dead* man, with his hands on My Brave Girl.

Rephrase: There's a dead man, with his hands on...*My. Wife.*

"Get your filthy fucking hands off MY WIFE."

The asshole is sitting on the coffee table, and his legs are pushed between hers, with his knees extremely close to her crotch. His fingers are splayed underneath the fabric of her black shorts.

The orange firelight creeps through the room. Her storm-cloud eyes are wild and frantic. The contours of her face glisten with tears and snot. One strap of her black tank top sits askew, giving everyone a glimpse of the thick, pink band of her medical bra. Strands of her raven hair fall from her ponytail and cling to her brow and neck.

Despite the heat from the fire, she's shaking.

Trembling.

And with each shiver, my flayed heart rips open a little more.

My fists close, firm and tight, readying my body for what's to come.

He doesn't have to turn around for me to know it's him.

And just like ten years ago, I'm gonna enjoy every single second of pounding his face. Of slicing my knuckles on his teeth. Of making blood pour out of his nose.

But there's one big difference between then and now. Back then, I wanted to be the good guy. I wanted to keep the moral high ground.

Well, guess what?

Now?

Here. In our house. In our living room. With his hands. On my woman…

Yeah, there is no moral high ground.

Turns out, there's no fucking ground at all.

We've already descended into the pits of Hell.

And I'm gonna chain this devil to the flames.

I propel myself forward, and in no time at all, I cross from the kitchen area and into the living room. The guy with the gun shuffles in front of me. "I'd think twice about that if I were you." He nods at the weapon pointed directly at my chest. "Safety's already off."

There's an unusual noise coming from the couch. A sort of combination moan and sniffle. My head whips in that direction.

Holy shit.

What the hell is Kimber doing here?

I was so laser focused on Orah and what was happening to her that I didn't even pay attention to the fact that my ex-fiancée is huddled up on the sofa. Leaned against the exact same side that Orah was when we received the good news phone call from the doctor's office, just a few short hours ago.

Why the hell would he kidnap Kimber and bring her to the cabin?

Levi pulls his fingers from Orah's shorts and slaps his hands on her thighs. Hard. Her spine stiffens, but she doesn't make a sound. Sighing dramatically, he stands and turns around. Cocking his head—in that ultra-condescending way that weaselly motherfuckers tend to do—he balloons his lips into a pucker. "Ridge, you really do have impeccable timing, don't you? I was just about to scratch an itch," he spews, hurling his sexual innuendo at me.

"The fuck you were," I growl.

He bounces on his toes. "Back away, Sam. You're in the way," he whines.

The dude in front of me eases away, taking sentry in front of the blazing fireplace; although, he never lowers his weapon from its target.

Me.

Levi maneuvers to Orah's side. Standing next to her, he strokes the top of her head. Like a master placating his pet.

A fresh tear rolls down the apple of her cheek. Her skin is splotchy and chapped.

"As I was saying, I wanted to have my fun while she still had a bit of spunk left in her. It seems the older I get, the more my dick likes a feisty girl. Oh, I can still get hard when she's passed out too, but the fight adds a little bit of excitement to it all, don't you think?"

"Passed out?" The words catch in the back of my throat, but I force them out anyway.

"Yeah." He crosses one ankle over the other and leans on the back of Pop's recliner. It sinks just a bit and makes a creaking noise. Not satisfied that the chair can hold him, he straightens. "The GHB should be kicking in soon."

Red hot rage floods through my body. "You gave her Liquid E!? A date rape drug!?"

"Oh, calm the hell down, Ridge."

I turn to Kimber. Her own cheek looks swollen and red, like someone hit her. "You drugged Kimber too?"

His stupefied gaze darts from me to Kimber to the guy he called Sam. And then, he bursts out laughing. "Why the hell would I drug her? I'm already fucking her."

What?

She jumps up from the couch and attempts to reach for me. In reflex, I sidestep, avoiding her grabby hands. Of all things, her engagement ring is still on her finger. "Ridge, it's not like that. I—"

"Oh, shut up and sit down," Levi orders.

She casts a sheepish look at Orah and then follows Levi's instructions.

"You don't have to look so upset about it, Ridge. It's not like I actually have feelings for her. Screwing is just a perk of our business arrangement."

"Your business arrangement?"

"When I killed the ADNN story, I reached out to her." He grins at her, the action a cynical component of his malcontent. "Kimber's been quite the assistant. More than eager to help with the demise of your relationship with Amy Smith, the wedding planner." He pinches the end of his nose and sniffles. "Interestingly enough, she's still carrying quite the torch for you." He scratches his jaw. "Believe it or not, the buxom bimbo actually thought she could win you back after this. But since you'll be six feet under, she'll just have to find some other worthless hack to push down the aisle."

"Six feet under?" I scoff. "You're fucking delusional."

"No!" He points a finger at me. "If you think for one second I'm going to let the two of you ruin my life, my future, you're the one who's delusional. My past needs to stay in the past. I don't need idiots like you talking about shit that happened ten damn years ago!"

I rake my palm down my face and tap my chin. One. Two. "That's what this is about? Politics. You want the Vice-Presidency."

He rolls his head in a circle and snorts. "Of course, I want it. Everyone wants it." His lips thin, and his jaw tics. "But I'm the one who deserves it."

Oh, I beg to differ.

"So what?" I counter. "You kill us? We're not the only ones who know what you did. There's plenty of people who know what you did to Orah. You raped her, you worthless piece of shit."

His eyes narrow into small slits. And he issues an edict for my demise, merely by uttering a name. "Sam."

The guy launches at me. I'm taller than him so I'm able to put my hands up and pivot to the side before he lands the blow.

But he still gets me.

And it still hurts.

Like a son of a bitch.

The handle of the gun connects with my temple and scrapes down the side of my face. At least, the angle of my body somewhat protects me. If he hit my temple the way he intended to, I'd already be sprawled on the floor. Maybe even dead. A flurry of little white starbursts explode behind my eyes. Pain sears down my jaw and into my neck. My shoulder tenses, pumping my scar with a muscle spasm so intense it feels like my rotator cuff is about to pop out of socket. Blood leaks from my scalp. It races down my face and catches in my beard. Like a bad game of Plinko, it zigzags through my facial hair and plops onto my T-shirt.

Kimber screams.

Orah, My Brave Girl, sits there. Refusing to weaken herself for Levi, she holds her chin high. Her shoulders are square; her back is straight.

But I can see it.

Through my hazy and now nauseous stare, I see it.

A small section of her favorite blanket is snatched between her thumb and forefinger. And she's rubbing the faux fur in a slow, methodical pattern.

One. Two. Three. Four. Five.

One. Two. Three. Four. Five.

"Great. Just look what you made me do. Now, we have to clean this up. Carbon monoxide isn't supposed to be bloody."

Carbon monoxide? At that precise moment, the fireplace crackles with a loud pop. A piece of burning wood falls, sending a small snowstorm of black ash through the firebox. "The fire?"

Levi cocks his hands on his hips and looks around the room. "Sam, once he's out, we'll just position him by the hearth. Make it look like he fell and hit his head when he got too disoriented. Be sure to actually knock his head on there. Get some blood on the brick and little pieces of dirt and stuff in his hair and cut."

Sam nods. Pilfering the wood rack, he tosses another log on the already overbuilt burning pile.

"Exactly what the hell are you planning?" I ask. My mind works hard to put the pieces together, despite the throbbing headache thrumming against my skull. "Drug me and then what? Close the damper?"

"Exactly."

"That's fucking stupid."

Levi's face turns an epic shade of red. "Excuse me?"

"The house will fill with smoke. The fire alarms and the carbon monoxide alarms will go off. There's a good chance the neighbors, or someone driving by, will hear it. They'll call for help."

"What does that matter? You'll already be dead."

I shake my head, egging him on, trying to buy enough time to come up with some kind of plan. "There's a chance the fire will die before enough carbon monoxide builds up. If you close the damper, you're cutting off the oxygen supply."

He secures a hand around the back of Orah's neck. A hatred unlike any I've ever known courses through me. Orah gives a little moan and shakes her head. Her tears have stopped falling. Her eyelids are heavy. Her salt-covered eyelashes are acting like a glue, making every blink a nanosecond longer than the one before it.

"Well, holy shit," he deadpans. "I guess I didn't think of that." He clicks his tongue against the roof of his mouth. "Sam, Kimber, gather your things. We best leave."

Kimber actually perks up from her shrunk position on the couch. "Huh?"

Is that a gun next to her?

Levi ignores her. Thankfully, he lets go of Orah and stabs a hand through his gelled hair. "You must take me for a fool."

"The thought has crossed my mind."

"I'm smarter than you'll ever be." He pops out his chest and licks his lips. "That's what the methylene chloride is for."

Oh no.

"Aha!" He chuckles. "I can tell by your face you know exactly what that does."

Of course, I know what it does. I'm a firefighter and paramedic. It used to be an ingredient in things like paint strippers, adhesives, degreasers, and nail polish removers. Before they realized just how toxic it is. Inhalation can prove deadly in low ventilation circumstances. When the body metabolizes it, the liver converts it into, yeah, that's right, carbon monoxide.

"You know, I sat on an FDA commission where we investigated some nail salons for using gel polish removers with methylene chloride in them. Learned more about dichloromethane than I ever wanted to." He waggles an eyebrow, proud of himself for remembering its other name. "Who knew it would come in handy one day. And believe it or not, there's still unregulated websites where you can order paint strippers with almost one hundred percent of the measured chemical."

"Just how many working parts does this plan of yours have? You drug us with GHB to make us more compliant, make us breathe paint stripper, and then leave us for dead? In a house with a burning fire and a closed damper?"

"Ding Ding."

His random sound effect makes Orah laugh. Her eyes are glassy and her body is starting to sag like a wet noodle. Her giggle is loud and boisterous. Frowning at herself, not quite comprehending why she found that funny, she wiggles in the recliner.

"Uh-oh, someone's starting to reap the benefits," Levi gloats. He leans over and sniffs her hair before affirming my theories. "Your assumptions are surprisingly accurate. And just to be completely candid, I think I'll have you inhale the paint stripper *and* drink it. Better to be safe than sorry." And in an effort to further antagonize me, he pecks a kiss on the top of her head.

Hate for him seeps from my pores. My sweat is thick and soupy, muddled with my putrid disgust.

Orah's eyes close, and her head bobs forward, snapping her neck. She jerks it back and coughs. She takes a few hyperventilating breaths, suddenly terrified of falling asleep.

Terrified of never waking up.

"The GHB will metabolize quickly in your system. Even if it's not all the way gone, a standard Tennessee autopsy won't test for it. And they won't test for methylene chloride specifically. Especially when everything points to regular old carbon monoxide poisoning from a drunk idiot who forgot to fix the damper."

"Drunk?"

He tosses a hand in the direction of the kitchen. I look to my right, seeing for the first time that the liquor cabinet has been raided.

"Now, I would say that it's about time to get this show on the road, wouldn't you? After all, this'll probably take a couple of hours, and I have a private flight to catch out of Knoxville at two a.m." He squats next to her. "What do you think, Orah? Are you feeling good?"

She struggles to shake her head. "Fu–fuck you," she mumbles.

He tsks her. "Oh, come now, that's not very nice." His hand slides up her arm, making her shiver and convulse more than she already is. He pauses his ascent, hovering on her bicep. "What's this? Why's your shirt wet?" And then, like the cowardly pervert that he is, he manhandles her healing right breast, squeezing her so hard her plump bosom flattens like it's in a mammography machine.

Her mouth falls open and she just stares, knowing that she should feel pain, but perplexed as to why she's not.

I launch forward, but I'm quickly thrown off balance by Sam. I'm able to push past him. Size and anger are on my side. But then he brings the butt of the gun down on my left shoulder, right across the waxy skin that's been battered and shattered over and over and over again throughout the past decade. Pain races through my spine, briefly paralyzing me and making me fall to my knees. Something sharp must've gotten me because I can feel the rip of my flesh. Blood seeps through the collar of my T-shirt, filling my nostrils with iron.

Iron. Smoke. Fire. Ash.

I watch in horror as Levi removes his hand from Orah and displays his palm in front of him. With a maniacal and unhinged gleam plastered across his psychotic face, he waves his hand in the air, showing me that it's covered in Orah's blood.

Her sutures are torn. Her body is in the throes of what must be debilitating pain, yet she can't even feel it because he's muzzled her senses with drugs.

For a moment, I can't help but think, how even in agony, Orah and I are two halves of the same whole. It's always her right side and always my left side. Injury after injury, we're split right down the middle.

"Uh-oh," he sing-songs. "I think someone popped a stitch. I can take her shirt off and check it out, if you want?"

"You motherfucker, I'm gonna—"

"You ain't gonna do shit!" He stands and wipes his hand all over his white dress shirt. "Now, go pick your poison, Ridge. It's time to start." He rocks back on his heels. "And I'd avoid the tequila. I've had homemade hooch better than that piss."

"Ridge," Orah strains. Her eyes lag from one corner of the room to the other, unfocused and weary. "I...I can save you."

Chapter 53

Ridge

I'm overcome with emotion, strangled with my love for this woman. My Little Bird. My Brave Girl. My one and only.

And no matter the cost, I will not let tonight be her last night on this Earth.

"Orah, look at me. I need you to stay with me. Stay awake. Stay with me, Bird."

I grip the armrest of the couch, scrambling and turning to push myself off the floor. Kimber folds her arms around me. Her long fingernails press into my maimed shoulder. Her forehead bangs against my bruised and aching temple. I hiss in pain.

"Oh, Ridge, I'm so sorry. I had no idea he was gonna do this. I love you. I just wanted you to be with me. Not her. None of this would be happening if it weren't for her."

I tip against her ear. "Kimber, get the gun. Hand me the gun."

Levi yells at me to hurry. Sam stokes the fire, sending flames rushing high.

Kimber slowly lifts her head. Her face is colored with black mascara, smeared lipstick, and glittery eyeshadow. She stares at me.

"Kimber, did you hear me? Reach beside you and hand me the gun."

"I'll save you," Orah repeats. Her speech is slurred and sloppy.

My head automatically whips in her direction.

Because it always will.

I'll always be there for her.

I'll listen. I'll answer. I'll come.

Just like I told her in that hospital courtyard...I'll help her fight. I'll help her heal. I'll aways come running.

"Bird, stay with me."

Levi yells again.

I turn back to Kimber. My nose brushes against hers. "Kimber. Get the gun."

Her eyes dart from me to Orah and back again. And with a barely imperceptible nod, she shakes her head no.

Tired of waiting, Sam grabs me by the collar of the shirt and lifts me, giving me a shove into the kitchen. I stagger over to the kitchen counter, running through one-thousand plans in the span of one solitary second.

I suppose I have *no* choice.

Simply because I'm not left with *many* choices.

I pick up the bottle of vodka. I test the heaviness of it in my hand, playing the scene over and over in my mind.

"Sir," Sam interrupts my internal movie. He tips his chin between the bottle and the fireplace, trying to tell Levi a story without using his words. Of course, Levi's a moronic dipshit and can't interpret the situation. "He may try something with the liquor and the fire? Remember the candle?"

What candle?

Are they talking about the candle that broke when the door hinge flew off?

Levi screeches like a giddy schoolchild and rushes into the kitchen. Sam levels the gun at my head as soon as Levi gets within my arm's reach.

"Oh, Ridge! You aren't planning on growing a set of balls, are you?" He yanks the vodka from my hand, setting it back down. And then, for good measure and to prove he has the upper hand, he picks up a whiskey bottle and chucks it across the kitchen, crashing it into the sink. He's at an angle, somewhat shielded by the fridge. I'm not. I whirl away, protecting my face and eyes from the flying shards of glass. Something hits the back of my neck, stinging my skin like a papercut.

Laughing, he does the exact same thing with the other bottles.

The clattering noise jars my brain. It's deafening and obnoxious. Just like Levi.

A shard lands against the collar of my T-shirt. I pull the fabric away from my back, shaking it out. The house fills with the stout stench of alcohol. The mixture burns my eyes, nose, and throat. It turns my stomach. It makes me think back to a couple of years ago, when Ella—a non-drinker, like Orah—got drunk on Long Island Iced Teas.

There's a dense thud, indicating a bottle that didn't break. He tosses the next one with extra vigor to make up for it. Another sharp sliver hits my ear. And then, he misses the sink altogether. A bottle filled with gin slams into the cabinet underneath the sink and bounces off the floor. It slides back in front of him. Bending, he picks it up, twists off the top, and attempts to chug it.

Considering gin isn't really a chuggable party liquor, he ends up choking and spilling half of it down the front of his shirt. It mixes with Orah's smeared blood, causing his shirt to cling to him.

He walks over to the dining table and sets the near-empty bottle on it, keeping it far away from the candles that are still lit. Wobbling, he pulls a mini test tube-looking thing from the wet front pocket of his button-down and then dangles the tube in my face, so close I have to cross my eyes to look at it.

It has to be the GHB.

"Time to party." He carefully lays the vial in front of the bottle of vodka I selected. "Shoot the Liquid E and then chase it with this," he demands, tapping the liquor label.

Alcohol fumes float through the house, stealing all of the breathable oxygen. I swear, if the power was on, we'd see wavy little lines in the air, mimicking the heat shimmer that bounces off the asphalt on a hot, summer day.

"Nooo. Levi." Orah tries to stand up, but he yells at her.

"Sit the fuck down, bitch!"

I shove against him. Hard. His back slams into the countertop. His exhale whooshes in my face, making me sick. My fingers clutch his collar, and I toss him back again. With all my force. So hard, he moans and attempts to fold over. I contort him into just the right position, flinging him left and right like a limp ragdoll. Lifting him to his toes, I make sure his left kidney is lined up perfectly with the unforgiving corner of the cold, hard granite. And I slam him. The impact is so hard, I can actually feel the vibrations from his twitching body. They cascade from my wrists, down my forearms, and into my biceps. He cries out. A mammoth, ear-piercing shout of pain rings through him. Like his body is an empty cavern, filled with no substance. No soul. No essence.

Holding him with one hand, I haul back, readying myself for the punch of a lifetime.

I want him to pay a bodily penance for every single girl he's ever hurt.

I wanna feel him crumple underneath my knuckles.

One bone for one girl.

Fingers. Toes. Ribs. Vertebrae. Humerus. Ulna.

Neck.

Oh, this is gonna be fun.

And then... a gun is placed against my bleeding temple.

"One more move, and I'll drop you. Right here. Right now. And dump your body in the river." Sam pushes the barrel of the gun into my sore-as-shit scalp. Like he's hoping there's an unseen crack to my skull, and he can slip right into my brain matter.

"Ridge!" Kimber screams. "Oh, Ridge, just stop. Listen to him. Do what he says."

Of course, *she* would say that.

But what does My Brave Girl say?

Her tongue is thick, her vocals sluggish. "Levi, ta–take me. I told you, let him go. I'll be yours. I'll…" She licks her lips and swallows. "Anything. I'll say anything. I'll do anything. I'll give you anything."

What. The. Hell.

She offered herself to him? In exchange for me?

She's prepared to sacrifice herself? For me?

Once again, she's prepared to *save* me.

Levi finally recovers. He gets right in my face and hurls a string of unintelligible profanity. His eyes are bloodshot. His brow is sweaty. And somewhere along the line, he got a fat lip. He picks up the small container and removes the top. "Drink. It."

And with a gun pointed at my head, I dose myself with what I can only imagine is enough date rape drug to sedate a horse.

It tastes a bit salty, but other than that, there's no distinguishable flavor. No wonder women have to be so careful when they're at bars or parties. They're fighting monsters with smiling, handsome faces who wield weapons that can't even be seen.

Or tasted.

He pockets the empty vial and nods to the vodka. "Now. Drink."

Sam moves the gun away, just a smidge, giving me room to work the large bottle.

I've never been much of a liquor drinker. Beer's more my game.

The liquid scalds every part of me. My mouth. My throat. My belly. I try to gulp it without even breathing. It's the only way I'll be able to follow through on his instruction. Heat pools all the way in my toes, making my feet numb. When I drop the bottle, a combination of vodka and bile not only shoot back into my mouth, but it squirts out of my nose.

I cough. I blow snot on the floor. I holler in disgust and wipe my mouth on my arm.

Levi rolls his eyes. "Don't be such a pussy about it." Sighing, he grabs the vodka bottle and heads off into the living room. "That's a good start. We'll do more in a minute." He hits Sam's shoulder. "Build the fire more. It needs to be higher, hotter. And then clean up the mess I made in the kitchen. We'll take the trash with us when we go."

The effects of the alcohol are already wreaking havoc on my brain and body. I feel like I'm moving in quicksand.

Fucking think, Ridge.

Think!

And then, a small iota of an idea happens.

Of course, it's bat-shit crazy and probably has a negative ten percent chance of working. But I meant what I said, I will do anything to make sure this is not Zipporah's last night on this Earth.

With Levi's back turned and Sam preoccupied with the fire, I quickly grab the large plastic Tupperware filled to the brim with pre-sifted flour. I pop the lid and hide the huge bin down by my side.

"Bird."

Hearing the need in my voice, her eyes find mine. Shadows and flames waltz together, enhancing her beauty in the danger I spend half of my life erasing with water.

"My turn," I say.

Her perfect lips part. Even that small action leaves her exhausted.

"You trust me, Little Bird? Not to let you fall? To love you forever?" I recite the words I said to her the night she fought her demons and wore white for me.

I can't hear her whisper with my ears, but I hear it with my heart. "Always and forever."

Not giving myself time to second guess, time to back down, time to change my mind, I sprint from the kitchen and into the living room. I push past Levi, making him grumble in protest.

And then, right before I'm out of range of the fireplace and the roaring fire within, I heave the bin forward, tossing all of the flour into the air.

Right in the direction of the fire.

Of course, a big portion of the white powder immediately clumps to the floor. But it's not that clump I'm worried about.

Or hopeful for.

It's the massive plume of flour dust that floats, suspended in the room like the dust motes I watched in the surgical waiting room. But the tiny particles don't stay in one place for long.

Oh no.

Because fire is a hungry, greedy beast.

And sometimes, it likes to feed on the most innocent of things.

Knowing I've got less than a second—literally—I catapult myself in the air. My body flings against Orah. As she sits in Pop's recliner. Through the adrenaline, I hear the wood frame splinter and crack. I feel the give of the superglue and brads.

And then, the propulsion of the primary explosion sends us toppling the rest of the way.

I tangle around her body like a spider monkey. And when we hit the ground, I roll us off the tattered chair. Over and over. Until we are, I hope, out of the blast radius. We come to a stop next to the sliding door and floor-to-ceiling windows.

Uh-oh.

I lie directly on top of her body, covering her from head to toe. I cock one knee sideway, propping myself so I don't suffocate her, and then I shield the top of her head with my hands, doing everything and anything to protect her before the second—

BOOM!

The secondary explosion hits with a ferocity of two colliding freight trains.

The windows and door blow out. The majority of the glass propels onto the deck and out into the mountain trees. But shards and pebbles still pelt us. Like small balls of hail. Filled with switch blades.

Rain blows in the open frames, hammering our battered and broken bodies.

My ears ring. My eyeballs bulge forward, wanting to pop out of their sockets because of the massive pressure building in my sinus cavity.

My head swims. I think my brain is drowned in vodka.

Leaning on an elbow, I turn away from her and vomit on the porch.

I struggle to breathe through the ozone and the smoke. As soon as I clear my airway of puke, I look down at her. She's covered in blood.

"Orah! Orah!"

There's ash in her hair. Soot on her face. Blood pouring out of her nose. And a thousand little cuts and shrapnel pockmarks all over her arms.

"Zippporah!"

Even though her eyes are closed, I can see her trying to blink. After what feels like an eternity, she peeks at me, gifting me with storm clouds and love.

Albeit drugged love.

I press my lips to hers, unable to even function for another drunk second without knowing that she's real. That she's here. That at least, she's alive.

I roll off her and clamber to my knees.

Holy. Fuck.

I was right. The Dust Explosion Pentagon. The five factors were present.

Fuel—the flour dust.

Oxygen—yep.

Ignition—the fire.

Dispersion—me tossing the flour and creating the dust plume.

Confinement—inside the cabin.

And let's just say that Levi's 190-proof sink concoction provided more than a little help too.

A crippling pain paralyzes my body. Everything hurts. My head, my shoulder, my chest, my stomach, my arms, my legs. I press my palms against my head, hissing when that only creates more pain. And of course, the chirping and beeping fire alarms don't help. They're fucking going wild, excited that they finally have something to do.

The living room is basically eviscerated. There's a huge fire burning through the kitchen cabinets. Flames shoot up to the ceiling, trying to eat their way to the upstairs. The living room couch, rug, and curtains are blazing.

Heat pounds me from the front.

Rain and wind beat me from the back. With every breezy gust giving new energy to the flames.

Sprawled in front of the blackened fireplace is a charred and burning body.

Sam.

I look around for Levi and Kimber, but I don't immediately spot them.

Of course, my line of sight is no bigger than the head of a needle. And what I can see is blurry.

I'll have to worry about them later. Orah is my only concern right now. I have to get her out of here. Before the whole damn cabin explodes or collapses.

I crawl back over to her. Red water pours off of me. I'm not exactly sure how much of it is blood, how much of it is rainwater, and how much of it is sweat. I try to inhale, but the smoke doesn't want to free me. I cough and spit, hacking a black pile of nastiness from my lungs. The spit doesn't travel far, instead getting caught in my beard and dripping down onto my shirt.

She's dazed, trying to sit up, but she can't really make her limbs work the way they should, the way she wants them to. I suppose I should do a Fireman's Carry or a Ranger Roll, but I just want to get her to complete safety as quickly as possible. So, I scoop her into my arms.

Like I'm about to carry her into the bedroom.

Carry her over the threshold of our new home.

Carry her into our future.

Her hands involuntarily swish through the air, before plummeting to my shoulders, slapping against me like heavy paperweights. She shifts, clamping them around my neck. She yelps, screeching through whatever agony her own body is suffering. I'm about to escape the confines of our smoke and flame-filled family cabin when something slices across my right shoulder.

Literally.

It feels like my skin and muscles are being flayed from the bone.

From my periphery, I see the glint of a blade as it flashes among the flames. Flames that are creeping up the walls, eager to reach their end destination.

Motherfucker has a knife.

Are you serious!?

Like he hasn't put us through enough. Now, he's coming after us with a steak knife from the expensive-ass set that C and I bought Gran for her seventieth birthday. He's wanting to kill me with my own damn kitchen knife?!

Not happening.

I lean out the section where the sliding glass door should be. I set her on her feet. Her raven hair falls into her face. I give her a little push, making her already-feeble body stumble even more. "Fucking run, Zipporah!"

I turn around and push the burned and disfigured Levi farther back into the house, disappearing into the flames.

Chapter 54

Orah

"**R**idge!"

Did that scream even come from me?

It sure doesn't sound like me.

My foot edges forward. My socks are soaked and hard pieces of stuff keep poking through the fabric and stabbing me.

I...I can't think of the words.

My brain doesn't work.

What are the names of the pieces of things?

My knees weaken, and I nearly trip. My hand darts out, catching on the wood logs that gave this family home such charm.

All I want to do is lie down and go to sleep. If I just go to sleep things will be better. When I wake up, everything will be back to normal.

No cancer.

No LFS.

No drugs.

No carbon monoxide.

No death.

No pain.

No suffering.

No. Catastrophes.

If I can just go to sleep, I'll wake up fresh and new. I'll no longer be the catastrophe.

Ridge will want me because I won't be the magnet anymore. The magnet attracting disaster after disaster.

My hand drops down.

I should go to sleep.

But then something tells me I can't do that.

The roaring fire is loud. Too loud. It sounds like a thousand jet airplanes are flying through my ear canal. And on top of that, wood is popping and snapping. And pieces of glass are shattering.

Wait...

Ridge went back in there.

He's inside of there.

I...I can't go to sleep. Ridge is still in there.

I reach for my necklace. But come up empty.

I try to count anyway. It doesn't work.

Fucking wake up, Zipporah.

Go get Ridge. Go get Ridge.

I step into the house. I'm instantly assaulted by the smoke and the heat. My body lurches forward. Bending at the waist, I throw up, projectile vomiting across the ashen and soot-covered floor. Too tired and dizzy to maneuver around anything, I just walk through the mess I made, further soaking my socks.

"Ridge! Ridge!" I try to holler, but I'm not even sure I'm successful.

A funny sound has me looking above. Flames dance across the ceiling, creeping and crawling like the waves of an ocean's tide.

Well, that can't be good.

I take a few more steps and then I see him.

I have no idea *how* I see him, but I see him.

I collapse by his side. Tears stream down my face, but they evaporate before they even hit my chin. The floor is so hot that it's scalding my knees.

My Hero.

His body looks shattered. Burned and bloodied.

His eyes closed. His pink-brown lips barely parted. His facial features relaxed.

The world around us is burning to the ground, and he is passed out.

I shake his shoulder. My hands sink into a puddle of thick, sticky blood. "Ridge! Ridge, wake up! We have to get out of here!"

Nothing. No response.

My vision is blurry, and thick black spots keep bouncing across my eyes, temporarily blinding me. The smoke is so bad, I know—somewhere deep, deep down inside of me—that my eyes should be hurting worse than they are.

Maybe my eyeballs are on fire, and I don't even know it.

I scoot back and flop his hands above his head. I grab ahold of his wrists and try to yank him in the direction of the deck. He doesn't even move a millimeter. He's a mountain of a man. Tall and made of nothing but hard muscle and soft love.

How the hell am I supposed to carry him?

Wait...

Shouldn't my breast be hurting?

I'm not supposed to be doing any heavy lifting or repetitive mo-tions. Because I'm healing. I'm healing from surgery.

Wait...

What was I doing?

Oh, yeah, Ridge!

I scramble to my feet, falling back to my knees more than once. Finally, when I think I have a stable stance, I grab his wrists once again and try to pull him.

I end up falling backward onto my butt.

Something cuts my ass.

I ignore it. Which isn't hard to do because the pain isn't regis-tering.

I'm wiggling, trying to get back beside him, when someone walks right up to us. I lift my head. I have to slide my hand across my brow to see anything past the midnight shadows and blinding flames.

"Kimber!"

Oh my gosh. It's Kimber.

She's missing her shoes. I claw at her bare foot. "Kimber, help me! We...we have to get him out of here. We..." I lose my train of thought. There's a very real possibility that I doze off for a split second. I beat my hand against her shin and then clutch Ridge's now-destroyed Belly's T-shirt. "Help me, Kimber! Grab his legs!"

I shimmy across the hot floor and back up to his head. I clamp my fingers around his elbows.

She doesn't move. At all.

I lift my head again, swallowing down another bout of bile in the process.

And there she is. Standing over us.

With *My Husband's* engagement ring on her finger.

And my rapist's gun in her hand.

And the gun is pointed right at my chest.

A totally inappropriate and uncharacteristic laugh rips out of me. I laugh so hard it feels like my tongue is hanging out of my mouth. Pictures of panting dogs race through my mind. Which makes me think of Laura. And the future Pet Peeve.

Wait. What?

I swirl my head back up at Kimber.

Bitch has a gun.

Are you serious!?

I begged her to pick up that gun. To turn it on Levi. To save us.

And now, she has it trained on me.

"Kimber, help me! We...we have to...to...get out. He's hurt!"

It looks like she's burned. Long, black strips of skin curl off her face and neck.

She steps closer to me. Her eyes lock with mine. "I. Hate. You." Her scream doesn't reach me. The other noises are too loud.

But through the stuff pouring from my eyes, I watch as she mouths the words.

This is it.

It's not Levi who's gonna get me. Not the drugs. Not the carbon monoxide. Not the fire.

Not the cancer. Not the LFS.

Not the shame. Not the fear. Not the anxiety.

Not the sorrow of losing a child.

Not the boys in the movie theater.

Kimber.

Kimber's gonna get me.

I push away from his body, not wanting him to get hurt—well, more hurt—in the process of my death.

I lean toward her and grab the bottom of her skirt. The fabric tears off in my hand. "Hurry, Kimber. Do it. But once I'm dead, you have to pull him out. You have to save him. Promise me, you'll save him."

And then...she turns and disappears through the smoke and flames.

Another giggle erupts, and the act of opening my mouth has me throwing up again. I'm not even sure where it lands.

I flop back over next to Ridge and beg for him to wake. I shove his shoulders, I slap his face, I bang on his sternum.

Nothing.

I frantically search around me. The smoke's getting so bad, I have to basically lie on my stomach to see anything. My tank top rides up, and the wood burns my belly. But still, I don't feel anything.

It's like touching the burner of a stove.

For a quick second, before your mind comprehends the sear, you don't feel anything. My loopy brain is in that limbo, never quite catching up with the reality of what's happening.

The broken and severed top/back of the recliner is a few feet away from me. Not only is it on fire, but the wood floor beneath it is on fire. I swivel around on my stomach like a breakdancer. And there's the bottom of it. Tipped and lying on its side. And underneath it is my favorite blanket.

Wait. Would that work?

I move as fast as I can. Which could be fast or could be slow. Hell if I know.

I snatch the blanket and spread it out next to Ridge. Grabbing the sides of it, I shove it up and under his back, bunching a pile of it beneath him, from the curve of his low back to the tops of his thighs. I make my way to the other side, tuck my hands underneath him, and try to pull the blanket.

It's not perfect, but it'll work.

Well, I hope.

I do the exact same thing to his upper back and head, and then to his legs and feet. By the end, he's all cattywampus, stretched at an odd ankle.

Bending over him, I snag the end of the blanket, circling it around my fists. Like a prizefighter wrapping his hands for the fight of the century.

And then I pull.

I can't believe my eyes when the blanket—and his body—inches forward. Hope blossoms in my chest. I tug. Over and over and over. Slithering his body across the floor, one cumbersome hardwood slat at a time. When I get to the frame of the sliding glass door, I frown, disappointed that the bottom of it is still filled with jagged icicles of broken glass. I push the handle, laughing like a straight-up lunatic when the frame glides across the track like normal. I jump over his body. My socked feet land in a pile of rubble.

I continue with my laborious efforts. Rain whips against us. The night sky blazes with an orange horizon. Once I have him pushed against the far railing, I curse myself, realizing I should have gone to the left and down the stairs.

What if the deck collapses. We could roll all the way down the mountain.

Down from Tennessee to Alabama.

Tumble. Tumble. Tumble.

Somewhere in the distance, there's another large explosion, rumbling the sky like thunder.

A piece of fascia falls from the roof and lands only a foot away from us. Ash mixes with the rain. It drifts down, coating everything in shades of gray and black.

Uh-oh.

All of a sudden, everything fades.

My mind and body are calling it quits.

They are officially done with this shitty day.

I crawl on top of him, determined to protect him with my body.

Despite not being able to see, not being able to focus, my lips find the shell of his ear, and I whisper.

"I can help you. And then you can help me. We can save each other."

Chapter 55

Ridge

I check my reflection in the small bathroom mirror and adjust the collar of my white linen shirt.

My hand grazes across the smooth material of the jacket.

Not too shabby.

Of course, it just looks like a suit to me. I'm not exactly sure what delineates a jacket and pants from normal suit-status to tuxe-do-status, but apparently, this is a tuxedo.

Best of all, she's not asking any of us to wear a tie.

And, we can wear normal brown boots instead of fancy shoes that cut off our toe circulation.

Well, I take that back....

The best thing of all is that I finally get to marry her.

Today is the day that Zipporah Smith—yes, her name change happened—becomes Zipporah Conway.

And it's about fucking time.

My Little Bird did, in fact, make me wait until her busy wedding season was over. Talk about torture.

Of course, I suppose she had a good reason. Multiple good reasons, if I'm telling the truth. And all of them revolve around her bravery. Her strength. Her courage.

The night of the fire, she saved me.

After I fought off the liquor-burned motherfucker known as Levi, I collapsed. Overcome with the drugs and alcohol, the smoke and flames, the injuries and damage, my body just gave out.

And hers should have too. But it didn't.

Because she was determined to not live a single moment of her life without me.

She pulled me from the burning inferno of the cabin fire. All by herself. Our neighbors found us on the back deck, her body covering mine, keeping me sheltered from the literal Hell raging around us. A group of them carried us to safety before the fire department and ambulances arrived. Of course, safety was quite a distance away, because even the front driveway was engulfed.

With a car explosion.

Apparently, Orah heard it right before she passed out.

Levi and Kimber reconvened at the SUV and tried to make a getaway. But the chemicals were still in the cargo hold—the chemicals they planned to use on us. Turns out, Kimber wasn't too good at following Levi's instructions. Instead of ordering black-market, nearly one-hundred percent methylene chloride paint stripper—which metabolizes to carbon monoxide in the body, yet isn't very flammable— she ordered methylbenzene paint stripper. Which, as you guessed it, does *not* metabolize to carbon monoxide in the body. And *is* highly flammable and should always be kept away from excessive heat, sparks, and flame.

Well, we sure as shit had a lot of that around.

And we had the injuries to prove it.

We spent days in the hospital. Well, days for me and a week and a half for her. Besides being covered in bruises and cuts and scrapes, and despite being on the verge of a lethal overdose—for both of us— we were lucky. I had a concussion from being pistol whipped, a torn rotator cuff from the blow to the left shoulder, and my right shoulder is now decorated much like my left. Except it only took twelve stitches to close the knife wound; not nearly a match for the twenty-five stitches from the movie theater attack. Oh, and I had second degree burns on both of my calves from lying on the scorching hardwood floor. They healed nicely, and you can barely see the scars, thankfully.

And My Brave Girl...

Well...

I remember forcing my way out of the hospital bed after my rotator cuff surgery. I sat by her bedside for days on end. Her healing lumpectomy wound was completely demolished. She not only needed surgery to repair that, but one to fix the new hole in her diaphragm. The exertion of pulling me from the fire literally ripped her body in half. So now, for the second time in her life, she's healing around biologic bovine mesh. She's been using that as an excuse to eat less hamburgers and more French fries.

All of her cuts and bruises have healed without any lasting damage, except for a small little scar at the base of her throat. And if you look close enough at it, it almost looks like a baby bird. She said that's her consolation prize considering her necklace was never found in the charred rubble of the cabin.

But what she doesn't know is that I've had another one made. And tonight, after I spend hours making love to her, to MY WIFE, I'll crawl across the floor and give it to her.

Unless I break down and give it to her the second she meets me at the makeshift altar.

Because she deserves it all.

Everything I'll ever have to give.

Everything I am.

And everything I'll always be.

Because she's the strongest and bravest person I know.

Even after we left the hospital, she had so many storms to weather. And together, we've battled every single raindrop, every single thunderclap, every single lightning strike.

We had to come to terms with the knowledge that we contributed to the deaths of three individuals, including one I had planned to marry.

Let's just say my web-based sessions with Dr. Evans are going well.

And yes, she did have quite a bit of feedback and commentary regarding my and Orah's reunion. But all of it was positive. She said she always had a feeling that destiny would toss the two of us back together again. When we were older, when we were ready.

How right she was.

And we had to deal with law enforcement.

Once again, we were grilled by police, lawyers, FBI, DEA, ATF, DOJ.

Give me an acronym; I can assure you we talked to them.

And let's not forget about the fucking tornado of the healing, the typhoon of recovery—the press.

The reporters. The cameras. The news crews.

Ella brought Chloe in, as well as Chloe's boss, famed crime reporter Alaina Ontario. Much to our chagrin, the only way to quiet the noise was to do an in-depth interview. But, true to her word, Alaina treated Orah with respect and compassion. And I suppose, that's the most we could ask for, given the situation.

There's still a criminal investigation underway, but we don't have much hope of anyone getting prosecuted. And that includes the people from ADNN, the congressional staffers who leaked the sealed transcripts, and even the power employee who took a payout to keep the electricity off.

We were advised that we could file a civil suit against Levi's estate. But we didn't want to drag his wife and four kids through even more trauma. Same with Chip. We could've filed a lawsuit against Willis Luxury Automotive. But Chip and Kimber's mom are having to navigate a life without their daughter. And despite everything that happened, Orah refuses to drag Kimber's name through the mud in a public venue.

But good things happened too.

Our love grew. It's more powerful and vibrant. More potent and triumphant.

We not only grew closer to one another, but to the rest of our family as well.

And two weeks after the fire, we received confirmation that Orah tested negative for Li-Fraumeni's. Following her lead, both John and Boaz were tested. And both were negative.

Collectively, it feels like we've all been given a new lease on life.

An opportunity to carve a new path and live every day to the fullest.

Taking a deep breath, I open the bathroom door. We've been using the small apartment in the back of Crutch's detached garage as the groomsmen headquarters. The girls are all inside the house getting ready.

And in one short hour, as dusk falls, our small group of family and friends will walk side-by-side down to the creek, where I'll wed the love of my life. In a field of wildflowers. Next to the stone memorial commemorating those who left our family too soon. And the one little girl who's still here, but not technically ours.

I step into the large bedroom/rec room area and immediately stop in my tracks. There, standing in a row, are half the men in my life—Cullen, Holt, Crutch, Will, and Boaz.

Excuse me, I mean, half the jackasses in my life.

Because these dumbasses are standing there in white T-shirts instead of their assigned white button-downs. And the shirt reads, *'Snickerdoodle Biscuits Saved My Life'*.

Holt cocks a brow. "What? Too soon?"

As soon as I crack a smile, everyone bursts out laughing.

"You better take those off. That's not what my girl told you to wear."

Boaz shakes his head. "I already showed her. She thinks it's hilarious."

I prop my hands on my hips. "Seriously? She said you could wear those to her one and only wedding?"

C slaps my healed shoulder. "Best sister-in-law ever."

"She's gonna be your *only* sister-in-law, C."

"Damn straight. Because I need those all-spice cake bars in my life like I need air to breathe."

And I need her.

My Little Bird.

My Brave Girl.

Chapter 56

Orah

He shifts me in his arms, lifting me a little higher so he can enter the keyless entry code to the security system.

He opens the door and carries me across the threshold of the Children's Wing.

After we were discharged from the hospital in Tennessee, neither of us wanted to return to the penthouse apartment that he picked because of Kimber. Because of her wants, her desires. Her need to have a secondary fuck pad for the 'wine and dine' interactions outside of her father's mansion.

After everything we had been through, the landlord allowed Ridge to break his lease. So, we moved into the Children's Wing at Holt and Merit's place. It's true that we stayed here for the short-term after my car chase with the reporters, but it hit differently this time. Knowing that we would be here for months on end while we purchase the land from Crutch and Ella and build our home. Knowing that this would be the first place we sleep as husband and wife.

He kicks the door closed and spins around in a circle before setting me on my feet. "So, are you telling me the truth, Mrs. Conway? Are you really fine forgoing a honeymoon?"

I toe off my sparkly white and rose-gold sneakers and stretch my back. "We *had* a honeymoon. It included way too many days off work and way too much green Jell-O. We have the medical insurance claims to prove it," I deadpan.

He chuckles and wraps his hands around my waist. "Yeah, we do, don't we?"

I reach up and race my hand down his face, from his nose to his chin, where I give him a tap. One. Two. His facial hair is sharper today, having just been trimmed. "I love you."

His smile fades, taking with it his lighthearted humor. "I love you, Zipporah. Always and forever." He licks his lips, studying my face with a sensual and sexual intensity, so powerful it has me rubbing my thighs together beneath the cover of my floor-length gown. He grabs my left wrist, turns it over, and works his tongue across *our* tattoo. Righting my hand, he laps a trail down my skin. He pauses at my ring finger, forcing to memory the look of my wedding band. The perfect match to my engagement ring. And the perfect companion piece to commemorate the necklace that used to adorn my neck, during nearly every single waking hour.

"So. Damn. Sexy." He growls.

"Uh-uh-uh," I tsk. With my right hand, I tug his left hand from my waist. I kiss his knuckles, lavishing love on all of his little white scars. The mementos he's received throughout the years. His souvenirs. From saving me. From saving others. From doing his duty. "This," I wiggle his rose gold band inlaid with Tiger's Eye stones, "is so damn sexy. On your finger. Declaring to the world, to all of those women who chase after you, that you are mine...that's what's sexy."

His eyes flare, glistening bright. "Why, Bird, are you jealous?"

"Always and forever," I smirk.

He tosses his head back and laughs, happy and carefree.

I take the opportunity to slide away from his hold.

He doesn't like that. He comes for me.

But I hold up my hand, palm facing toward him. "Stop." Like the good boy he is, he listens.

Dragging a deep breath into my lungs, rejoicing in the fact that my chest can inhale and exhale without any soreness, I rake my gaze from the top of his head to the bottom of his boots. His thick brown hair is rumpled and wavy. Because of the mild weather, a summer sunburn still colors his cheeks. His untucked white linen shirt is unbuttoned to the middle of his chest, his sleeves rolled up to his elbows. His light brown tuxedo slacks hang low on his hips. Which reminds me, his jacket and belt are in the backseat of his truck. His boots, with their scuffed toes, bring the ensemble all together.

And what's the name of this classic, timeless look?

Fucking. Mine.

That's the name of it.

"I like it when you look at me like that." His voice is low and gravelly.

"Like what?"

"Like I'm yours."

I nibble on my lip. "Because you are."

He returns the favor, devouring me with his stare, making me burn with a heated ache. One corner of his mouth tilts upward, giving me a small taste of the fun that's yet to come.

Today's been another day where I've been the author of our story.

Where I've had all the control.

A day where he's worshipped me. A day where he's given me everything I could ever want.

I shake my head, enjoying the feel of my loose curls as they dance across my shoulder blades. I've given myself to him in a snow-white wedding dress. Strapless, with a fit-and-flare silhouette, and a lace overlay. And much to his excitement, a slit in the side that goes all the way up to my mid-thigh. After all, I needed a way to show off my special tennis shoes. The plain white slip-on sneakers have been decorated with hand-drawn, rose-gold metallic designs and a hodgepodge of stick-on sequins.

The artists?

Eden, Laura, Anna, Ty, Hardy, and Daire. And I even saw Laura standing over Nate, giving him pointers on how to draw a heart with a cupid's arrow running through it. I'm sure that was her idea; I can't imagine a sixteen-year-old wanting to jump on the shoe decorating train with a bunch of kids and toddlers. But he did a good job; it's on the back of my left heel. And obviously, Daire is too young to do anything much. But he was able to fist a wide acrylic paint marker and bounce up and down, making a series of dots. Under the guided hand of his parents, of course. Holt and Merit laughed and took pictures like he just scored a winning touchdown in the Super Bowl.

It was utter perfection.

Even my nails are white, painted just for him. With a little golden bird on each of my ring fingernails. And my curled hair is styled half-up, half-down and is held in place by the gift presented to me by both my parents and Jeff and Dana. Two hair combs, decorated with Tiger's Eye stones.

The ceremony was short, simplistic, and meaningful. Exactly what we wanted. And when the preacher announced, *'You may kiss the bride'*, everyone kissed.

And I do mean everyone.

As per my request. Like I said, *I* was in control of the day.

Dad and Momma.

Emmett and Laurie.

Jeff and Dana.

Ray and Teresa.

Marcum and Nancy.

Boaz and Tabby.

Will and Raylee.

Holt and Merit.

Crutch and a very pregnant Ella. Their son, Mason Elijah Crutchfield is scheduled to join the family in December.

Even Chloe and her new boyfriend. And Dylan and his girlfriend. And Merit's store co-owner and best friend, Kyra and her husband Toby.

And I suppose I would be remiss not to mention that Laura forced Nate to kiss her hand.

After Ridge swept me off my feet, with a kiss that was definitely more than what our family should've seen, my wandering gaze fell on Cullen. Behind his wide and pleasant smile was a pain I haven't seen before. Not on him.

But it's a pain I know.

Because I lived with it. For almost nine-and-a-half years. I felt it from the moment I left Ridge kneeling on the sandy beach until he crossed the penthouse apartment and declared me as his.

I have no idea what all Cullen has been through, but I have faith in my new brother. And I have faith in destiny. I suppose, we just have to trust the process. Give that love, luck, and tenacity time to sync.

"Do you know just how fucking sexy you look?" Ridge stirs me from my reverie.

"No. How about you tell me?"

"How about I show you. Take off your dress. Now."

I cock my head. "I thought I was the one in control today?"

"You were. But I'm the one in control tonight."

Desire courses through me. My body readies itself for him. My nipples peak. My core tightens. My pussy lips throb.

I slowly turn around and gather my hair over one shoulder, nonverbally telling him that if he wants it, he has to come and get it. I can't exactly unzip myself.

He slides behind me, rubbing his hard cock against my ass. I arch into him. Wanting more. More pressure. More contact. More him.

But instead of working my dress, his quick and nimble fingers flutter around my neck. Something hits my collarbone. In a flurry of activity, I try to glance behind me, but I freeze in place when I see my necklace—*our* necklace—tucked neatly where it belongs. I gasp. My own fingers fly to the bird charm. In habit, I flitter my touch across the black diamonds and Tiger's Eye stone. Instantly, a calm and hypnotic peace rushes over me. It's like walking outside and feeling the sunshine on your face after a harsh and cold winter.

One. Two. Three. Four. Five.

One. Two. Three. Four. Five.

He folds his arms around me from behind, circling around my stomach with a firm grip. He kisses my shoulder. "Happy Wedding Day, Little Bird."

"H—how?" I stutter.

"I had the jeweler make another one. Those bastards already stole too much from you. I refuse to let them steal this too."

Tears well in my eyes. My complex emotions overwhelm me, oppressing me with love and gratitude. Fear and anxiety. Scorching flames and powdery ash.

My chest rises and falls.

Quicker and quicker.

Mimicking the frantic and erratic thought patterns and memories of our past.

I want nothing more than for him to fix me, to make things better. To solve all of my problems with his kiss. I struggle to spin in his arms.

His hold on my abdomen tightens, his arm muscles locking like steel.

He slides his massive right hand up the planes of my stomach, over the mound of my cleavage, and splays his palm around my neck. His thumb slides underneath my necklace, settling on the hollow of my throat. And because he feels what I feel, even more so now than he did back then, he gives me just what I didn't even know I needed.

"No, Brave Girl. It's not my kiss you need to wipe away those bad memories. Those vicious images, those vile thoughts. Everything you need is right inside of you. Living in your heart, in your soul, in your spirit. Because you're not broken, Zipporah. You're totally and completely whole."

He takes his time, lazily pressing the pattern of my numbers against the sensitive and tender skin of my neck. Right where the small scar from the fire lives.

And he's right, after a few moments, I relax.

He's always right.

My Hero. My Husband. My Forever.

I melt into his embrace, wanting to fill this night with nothing but happiness, so every time I touch this new talisman, I'll remember the way it feels to have his body against mine. The way it feels to be the owner of his heart. The way it feels to be his everything.

He gave me the first necklace on the night we celebrated my belated eighteenth birthday. When he already knew that our paths would diverge. That he would say goodbye. That he would leave me. That he would sever our destiny. Before it even began.

But now, he's giving me this new necklace on the night that he's declared himself as mine. For all eternity. With his ring on my finger, and *our* brand on his chest.

I lift my arms behind me, looping myself around him, forcing him to nuzzle against me. He inhales my scent. "Mmmm..." He moans. He adjusts his position. His fingers splay wide and move past my belly button, down to my pelvis. He pushes me backward, grinding me against his erection. "I've been waiting all day for this."

He lifts his head. My arms fall to my sides, and I grunt in frustration. "Don't be impatient, Mrs. Conway. Because this boy wants to be so, so good to his wife. And good things take time."

With measured control, he lowers my zipper, and then he pushes the fabric down my hips. The wedding dress pools into a puffy hula-hoop around my bare feet. I dig my toes into the plush living room rug. He chuckles, the intoxicating sound a blend of gruffness and sweetness. "What the hell is this?"

I know exactly what he's talking about. I wiggle my butt back and forth, garnering his attention. He draws a line down the beads of my spine, murmuring in satisfaction because he doesn't have a bra to contend with. He dips into the waistline of my panties. The minor action hits a nerve, and I buck forward. He scoops the sides of my underwear onto his index fingers, like he's picking a wedgie for me, and holds the fabric out for a better view.

My black bikini-cut panties are custom-made. And right on the ass is a picture of a tiger's face. And across both cheeks, in hot pink script, it says *'The Eye of the Tiger'*.

"Tabby had them made."

"So, I guess that means it was really her behind the T-shirts and not Boaz?"

"I think it was a team effort. I'm sure it's hard to be married to her and not pick up on some of her antics." I bounce on my toes. "Do you like them?"

"I absolutely like them. But I'd absolutely *love* you without them." With a sudden pull, my panties clear the swerve of my hips and tumble on top of the wedding dress pile. The cold air hits my overheated pussy, instantly breaking me out in chill bumps.

I hear his boots clunk as they hit the floor. I turn my head, wanting to look over my shoulder, wanting to see him. From my periphery, I watch as he removes his shirt and takes off his pants and boxer briefs. Of course, because I'm giving him the side eye, everything is slightly blurry.

Which I don't like.

Once he's naked, he picks me up by the waist, kicks my wedding gown and panties out of the way, and sets me back down again, still facing away from him. My sultry giggle tinkles through the dimly lit room. "Be careful with that, Hero. I'm gonna have it preserved. One day, your daughter may want to wear it."

His hand returns to my belly. His cock, free and unencumbered, glides from my ass and up to the small of my back. To the curve he insists was made just for him. "Trying to tell me something, Bird?"

I smile and lay my hand on top of his. "Not yet. Soon...but not yet."

He sucks my earlobe into his mouth and bites. "When our time comes, you're gonna make an excellent mother."

A tear falls down my cheek. Not one of sorrow, but one of hope.

Suddenly and without warning, he drops to his knees. He kneads the plump roundness of my ass and bites my left butt cheek. "Three fucking weeks." He meanders in a nonsensical path, licking and biting my flesh. "Three weeks of not sleeping in the same bed together. Three weeks of not sharing a shower. Three weeks with no foreplay," he pauses for a second before continuing, "postplay, or sex."

"I don't think postplay's a word."

"Well, it should be. Because I'm rarely done with you after I fuck you."

An involuntary moan escapes from my mouth.

"Tell me, Little Bird, why would you put me through such torture?"

"I think your mind is playing tricks on you. Because it was you, dear husband, who imposed the pre-wedding celibacy rule."

Another bite. "Oh, really? And why would I do such a thing? That doesn't sound like me."

"Because you said you wanted me so worked up that I would be drenched, just from looking at you."

Another bite. "And are you? Drenched?"

I spin, turning to confront him. My fingers tuck under his chin, lifting his face. I stare down at him, nearly coming unglued from the unwavering and unfailing devotion etched into him. The infinite loyalty carved into every laugh line, every freckle, every eyelash. "I don't know," I tease. "Why don't you check?"

With eyes pinned to mine, he pushes two fingers deep into my core. My eyes drift closed, and I lift to my tiptoes. My head lobs back, and a passionate whimper rushes to fill the quiet.

Squatting back on his haunches, he takes my clit in his mouth, working the sensitive bud with his expert mouth. My fingers tangle in his hair, tugging with an unspoken plea. I push him into me, refusing to give him a break, refusing to even let him breathe.

Because I need him. I need this.

So. Damn. Badly.

Taking his cue from my actions, he changes his momentum, morphing from languid and unhurried to frenzied and feverish. His mouth opens, and his tongue flicks back and forth over my nub, flicking with a tight and firm precision. He pulls his digits out of me, swirls them around my puckered asshole, and then rushes back to my pussy, fingering me with short and powerful thrusts. He jackhammers into my depths with a maniacal speed, with the tips of his fingers brushing, ever so lightly, against that spot so damn deep inside of me that it literally makes my stomach convulse.

I cry out. "Yes! Yes! Yes! Yes! Yes!"

And then I lose it.

I come so hard I literally collapse.

But of course, Ridge doesn't let me fall.

He moves his mouth away from my clit and leans to the side so he can tuck my favorite shoulder underneath my abdomen. He supports my body, stabilizing my wobbly knees with his torso. With his fingers still inside of me, he chases my orgasm to the very end, stroking me with affection and care, draining me of every last drop.

"That's what I wanted. That's what I needed," he purrs. "For My Brave Girl to bathe me in her love."

I force my way to the floor and basically tackle him. I knock him off balance and waste no time in straddling him. He bumps his head on the side of the loveseat and starts laughing. Lifting his ass in the air, he maneuvers us to the right so we're out of the danger zone of the furniture.

His beard and lips glisten with my cum. My crotch easily glides across his stomach and thighs and cock, wet and slippery, like I'm careening down a waterslide. My fingers land on *our* brand, instantly attracted to the part of him that was mine, long before I even knew it was. I bend forward. My black waves fall against his chest. My necklace dangles between us, swinging back and forth, back and forth.

His breath catches in the back of his throat. His hands clutch my waist, locking me in place with a punishing dominion. "Oh god, I love you, Zipporah."

His massive erection bobs against me. The velvet skin is pulled tight. Rosy and red and begging for release.

"Can you feel me?" I whisper. "Can you feel what I feel?"

He nods, struggling to speak. He lifts my hips, guiding my open and wanting pussy onto the head of his dick. And then he lowers me, just an inch or two. Just enough so I can feel the delicious burn of him stretching my body, stretching my core.

His cock swells, begging for my cunt to swallow it whole.

"I'll always feel you. Always and forever." His oath—his promise—finds me. And when I blink, I can see him standing at the door of the movie theater supply room. He bolts it closed, protecting me from the ugliness of the world around us. "Yes, Bird. It's time to save each other."

He slams into me, joining us as one.

One body. One soul. One eternity.

One destiny.

Always and forever.

Nearly Three Decades Later...

Epilogue

Ridge

I slide up behind her and trap her in my arms.

She fits just as well now as she did back then.

Her back arches, falling into position against my crotch.

"Your daughter's getting married today. Did you ever think the day would come?" Her tongue-in-cheek comment is happy and content, filled with a naughty friskiness.

I snort. "I knew those kids would get their shit together sometime. I had no idea it would take them this long, though."

She laughs and lazily draws a loop over the top of my hand. "I guess it runs in the family, huh? The Conways, the Crutchfields, the Hills, the Marcums. It takes us a while to get it right."

"But once we *get* it, we hold onto it. Forever." I kiss her temple, watching as the sun sinks lower in the horizon.

It won't be long now...

Soon, we'll start our walk, down the cut path and into the field of wildflowers, down by the creek. There, we'll meet up with the rest of the family from the other side of the woods, and Thea will marry the love of her life. In the exact same beautiful spot that we did. All those years ago. The scenery is much the same. Flowers of all variety and colors bloom. The roaring water bubbles and swirls, cutting over the same rocks and stones that it did centuries ago.

One thing has changed, though. Unfortunately, more names have been added to our memorial. Life has given to our extended family, but it's also taken away. And I guess that's one of the many reasons that we hold onto one another so tightly. In a world where everyone comes and goes, rushed and frenzied, in a hurry to get from one adventure to the next, knowing that our loved ones have a bond that can't be broken is irreplaceable.

We are blessed beyond measure, that's for sure.

True, we weren't able to fill our house with all the children we wanted. But we were able to fill it with one little girl, whose larger-than-life personality made it feel like we were dealing with ten kids instead of one. We knew it might not be an easy road, and we were prepared for that. After her second diaphragm surgery, Dr. Skinner told us that pregnancy might be difficult for Orah. And it was. She always wanted to try for more babies, but I was unwilling to take that chance with My Little Bird. Her amazing and wonderful body had gifted our family with two little girls—a daughter and a niece. And I was at peace with that.

Bethea Carrie Conway has Orah's raven hair and storm-cloud eyes and my mischievous smile and potty mouth. Her name is a play on Bithiah, Pharaoh's daughter who saved Moses from the Nile River.

And every time my little girl—who's now a grown woman—smiles at me, I feel like she's saving me.

Just like her momma.

Feisty and full of spunk, Thea's peers often mistook her behavior for indifference or ignorance, when nothing could be further from the truth. Gifted with extreme intelligence and enough bravery to kill a wild boar with her bare hands, she just wanted her destiny to begin sooner rather than later. But as we all know, sometimes the harder you chase it, the more elusive it becomes.

The screen door opens, and Merit joins us on the front porch. She cocks her hands on her hips. "Can you please, for the love of all that's holy, go over to Crutch and Ella's house with all the other men? Apparently, the only person who can wrangle them into control is the Fire Department Chief. I just talked to Adam, and he said that Daire is still planting fresh Bermuda around the dance floor. It's less than an hour to the ceremony, and he hasn't even showered. And apparently, your best friend and brother thought playing tackle football with the little kids was an excellent way to pass the time, and now, someone has a sprained ankle. And there's something about Nate and Hardy and a water lantern and a snake."

I turn, spinning Orah with me just so I can plant my hand around her hip and snuggle my forearm into that sweet, delectable curve at the top of her ass. "And all of that surprises you?"

She opens her mouth and then closes it. "Well, I suppose not."

Then the screen door opens again, and this time, Ella joins us on the porch. "And Mace wants to talk to you." Her shoulders roll back, and that regal little nose points in the air. But, despite that, there's a wicked little smile on her face, telling me there's more to the story. "He wants to ask you something."

I snort and wave a dramatic hand over my tuxedo. "He already asked me something. Why else do you think I'm wearing this?" Once again, it's not black. And I'm not having to wear a bow tie. Don't get me wrong, that makes me happy, but I'm with Crutch...why couldn't we just wear cargo khakis?

Orah pushes away from me. "Go save the day, Hero. I've gotta double-check the cake anyway. I may wanna add a few extra flowers before they take it down there." Her navy-painted nails dance across her bird charm. Her matching navy dress dips low in the front, gifting me with a view of her plump cleavage.

And just because she knows it'll drive me crazy, she cocks a leg to the side, showing me the split that rises to her thigh.

Hot damn.

I can't wait to get her alone tonight.

Begrudgingly leaving my wife behind, I hop in the side-by-side all-terrain vehicle and trek the well-worn path between our house and Crutch and Ella's.

Sure enough, the reports from Holt and Merit's youngest son, Adam, were correct. Daire was covered in sweat and filth, which if I'm being honest, is the way my godson, owner of the Browning Sod Farm, likes it. But I did inform him that, despite his desire for the landscaping to look impeccable, my daughter couldn't give one tiny rat's ass about whether or not the grass around the temporary dance floor is crunchy brown and dying, or fluffy green and thriving.

And the sprained ankle belongs to one of the little kids, but it's nothing that some children's ibuprofen and some ice can't fix. But, of course, he wanted Uncle Ridge to wrap it up like a mummy's foot. Well, mission accomplished, he now looks like he crawled out of Tutankhamen's tomb.

And Nate and Hardy, in their infinite wisdom, thought the only way to take care of the non-venomous water snake that was attempting to hump the water lantern in the middle of the pond was to shoot at it with Hardy's non-service, off-duty weapon. From the videos they filmed, the little kids—who were all a safe distance away, with earplugs and eye goggles—thought it was hilarious. And that's how Felicia Stinkbottoms Number Twelve ended up at the bottom of the pond. Since the shot was just to scare the snake and not kill it, Dalton thought the snake needed a 'friend', and so he sacrificed yet another Felicia. Let's just say that he'll be buying his sister Felicia Number Thirteen with his allowance money.

With only fifteen minutes to spare, I find Mason up in his old bedroom. Technically, he could've gotten ready in his and Thea's big house across the pond, but he didn't wanna miss out on any family time. His childhood bedroom hasn't changed much. There's still old football trophies on the bookshelf, old newspaper clippings tacked to the cork bulletin board, and a pair of old cleats in the corner. And of course, the fireman's helmet that I gave him so many years ago is resting on the corner of his desk.

When he turns to me, his smile widens. "Hey, Chief."

The boy, whom I've loved like a son since the moment he was born, has transformed into the man in front of me. Authentic and genuine. Honorable and dependable. Strong and protective. And more importantly, fucking head over heels for my little girl.

"Mace, it's time to go. We need to head to the creek."

"Thank you, Ridge."

I pop an eyebrow. "For?"

"Raising such an amazing and resilient woman." He chuckles. "And for not beating my ass when I was wallowing in my own stupidity."

I scratch my hand down my beard and tap my chin. "Not gonna lie, I might've thought about it a time or two."

He nods. "And it would've been justified."

I shrug, playing if off. "Eh, I have faith in you."

"And *I* have faith in her."

"I know you do."

He heaves a light and satisfied breath. His eyes glaze over, his cheeks pink, and I swear, the dimple on the right side of his face twinkles. There's no denying...this boy has got it bad.

"I love her, sir. So fucking much, I can't even see straight. I'm gonna spend the rest of forever pouring my devotion into her."

I turn back to the door. "So, let's make it official." I draw out the syllables, teasing my last word. "Finally."

"But there's a question I need to ask you." He rocks on his heels and plasters a shit-eating grin on his face. "My turn." He mimics the phrase he's heard Orah and me banter back and forth to one another throughout his entire life.

"Yeah? Your turn, huh?"

He furrows his brow and pats his hands down the front of his jacket and dress shirt, searching for something. He snaps his fingers, suddenly remembering the lost item's location. Fishing in the front pocket of his button-down, he grabs what looks like a photograph. He holds it in front of him, and I immediately reach for it.

And his burning question flames against my ears before my eyes even have a chance to focus on the ultrasound.

"What's your thoughts on becoming a grandfather?"

What. The. Hell.
Destiny has never sounded so good.

Who's ready for Cullen and Langley's story?
Coming 2026
The Burden of Shadows: The Shadows Duet Book One
The Freedom of Sunshine: The Shadows Duet Book Two

After all, we now have to make
our way toward Mace and Thea, right?
Join me for the journey!

Ridge and Orah...

Phew. This one took it out of me. The dynamic of their relationship (in both books of The Flames Duet) was a fine line. Like walking a tight rope over a den of rattlesnakes. I pray I did them justice. And I pray that you love them just as much as I do.

Because despite my never-ending love for Crutch and Holt, I gotta say...Ridge is one hot damn of a man.

A super big thank you, with hugs and kisses to the Original Halcie Dawn Permanent ARC Team. My OG Gals! Thank you for your friendship ideas and input. You are invaluable to me... Heather S.S., Jenney M., Ashley R., Erica A., Ali S., Amber W., Jennifer S., Jessica V., Jessica A., and Kandi S.

And on top of that, this year gifted me with a Street Team! Yeah, that's right. I'm that cool. LOL. I've been able to meet and connect with some amazing friends via Halcie's Honeys. I'm so grateful that you're in my life and taking a chance on little ol' me and The Hill Family Universe. Thank you, thank you, thank you... Mudge, Payton, Brittany, Jennifer S., Ali, Ashley G., Jenn G., Amber W., Amber T., Jenney, Dara, Filippa, Madison, Melanie, and Nicole.

Thank you so very much to Mudge with Kindles and Coffee Author Services. I'm so happy we connected. You are so kind, hardworking, beautiful, friendly, and just all-around awesome. Thank you for putting together the Halcie's Honeys Team, and thank you for helping me navigate the trenches of social media.

And of course, I can't thank Mudge without thanking the other team member of Kindles and Coffee Author Services, Payton (aka smut.n.sowers).

Together, Mudge and Payton have eased my burden. But I think what's most important is that both of these women are not only pillars of strength in their personal lives, but in the book community. They love and support their authors wholeheartedly. They're my Lucy and Ethel. And I'm blessed to have them in my corner.

Thank you so very much to Erica Anderson with Get Lit Author Services. You have been so kind and supportive. Your content creation is gorgeous, and I will be forever grateful that we had the opportunity to work with one another.

And a special thank you to some of my other social media and book conference/signing friends I met. I love y'all! Thank you so much for your kindness and support. Y'all made my first signing events so much fun! I'm proud to call you my friends, and I'm so glad we met in person... Jenna C. (and sister Sarah), Hannah M., Kim B., Sandy, Sarah A., Jessica P., Carrigan, Kennedy, Tina O., and Chrissy P. I know I met more, and I promise to keep better notes next time. LOL!

Thank you to Stacey Blake with Champagne Book Design for designing the most gorgeous covers ever. Like ever. You have brought all of my visions to life. And you hang in there with me when I change my mind. Which seems to happen frequently. LOL. You have given life to The Hill Family, and I can never repay you for that. I fall more in love with each new cover we do. I can't wait to see what the future brings for us.

Oh, my Sweetie Elaine.... a huge thank you to my dear friend, Elaine York with Allusion Publishing. Well, I was a little late on getting *Dancing on the Ashes* to you. Hehe. Like I said, my mind writes way faster than my hands do. But you hung in there with me, and you just rolled with the flow. Thank you so much for all of your hard work. Thank you for your friendship. I love when we talk; it feels like I'm talking to a member of my family. We go together like Chick

Fil-A French fries and Coke. You always seem to know when I need an encouraging word or laugh. You make me a better writer. And I promise to one day know when to place a comma after 'so' or 'but'. Above all, I hope I make you proud.

And a huge thank you to my book conference "assistants", Dandy and Aunt Karla. And Cindy too. Man, we had some fun. And I can't wait for more!

To Dandy and Big, aka the most amazing parents ever... I love you. The level of your support never ceases to amaze me. From doing my grocery shopping so I don't have to take a break from writing to watching your grandpup to cooking for us. I'm blessed beyond measure because the Lord didn't gift *me* to *you*; He gifted *you* to me.

To my Boo Boo Bear, my college student... I am so damn proud of you. You are the bright light in my day. I am so excited for all of the amazing adventures that you're going to experience in your life. You're intelligent, kind, handsome, compassionate, and still...a king of one-liners. I love you, son.

To Kuntry, my husband and my best friend... I can't believe how much I love you. Every day, you shower me with love, generosity, compliments, and encouragement. I feel like something has shifted in us these past few years. As we got older, and as I was forced to take a step back (albeit, an unplanned one) from my "day job" career, I can't help but sense a change in our relationship. And it's one for the better. Our love has deepened, our connection has grown, our passion has flourished, and our need to rely on one another has strengthened. I know I'm about to head back to the work drawing board, but I promise you, those things will not change. You are my home. And as Ridge would say, you are my destiny. I'm so glad our love, luck, and tenacity were in sync. You are my world.

To the Lord my God, my Almighty Savior Jesus Christ... Thank you. Your blessings pour over me. I am loved and worthy by Your Grace. You sustain me and keep me whole. All glory be to You.

About the Author

HALCIE DAWN is a happy and blessed wife and mother. She attended the University of Alabama where she graduated with a bachelor's degree in Business Management. A lifelong avid reader, her love affair with books started with the original *The Babysitter's Club* series when she was in the third grade and morphed into a love of all things romantic. After years of thought and countless dreams about the sexy men and strong women of the fictional Hill Family, she penned her first contemporary romance. *The Reality Duet—Escaping Our Reality* (Book One) and *Finding Our Reality* (Book Two) released in November 2024. *The Skeptic's Duet—The Skeptic's Playbook* (Book One) and *The Believer's Game* (Book Two) released in April 2025. When not writing or reading by the swimming pool, she can be found watching true crime documentaries or *Psych* (for the millionth time). Halcie lives in Alabama with her amazingly wonderful, funny, kind, and handsome husband and son. And she lives next door to her parents, whose antics often have her laughing so hard she pees her pants. But without a doubt, the star of the home is the family morkiepoo, Princess Doodle Fluffybutt.

Connect with Halcie:
Linktree: https://linktr.ee/halciedawnromance
Website: https://www.halciedawn.com/
Instagram: https://www.instagram.com/halciedawnromance/
Facebook: https://www.facebook.com/halciedawn/
Facebook Reader Group:
https://www.facebook.com/groups/halciedawndaydreamers
TikTok (Reels): https://www.tiktok.com/@halciedawnromance
TikTok (Static Posts): https://www.tiktok.com/@authorhalciedawn
Threads: https://www.threads.com/@halciedawnromance

www.ingramcontent.com/pod-product-compliance
Lightning Source LLC
Chambersburg PA
CBHW070928100726
47908CB00001B/144